Extraordinary Praise for
Ed Ruggero's Bestselling

☆ 38 NORTH YANKEE ☆

"Capt. Ruggero . . . uses his fine writing talent and first-hand knowledge of life in the infantry to excellent advantage. *38 NORTH YANKEE* is an auspicious beginning to what may well prove a brilliant literary career. . . . Capt. Ruggero's novel shows he has the heart of a real soldier; it shines through every page."

— *Washington Times*

"I appreciate your sharing your work with me, and I'm pleased to have it for my future Presidential library."

—President George Bush

"Engrossing . . . Depictions of battle—and all the confusion and horror that battle usually entails— are as skillfully written throughout as they are compelling to read."

—ALA *Booklist*

"I could smell the cordite, hear the firefight and feel the battle. . . . *38 NORTH YANKEE* is a 1990s *From Here to Eternity.*"

—Colonel David H. Hackworth, USA, (Ret.), author of *About Face: The Odyssey of an American Warrior*

(more . . .)

"The universal fear and suffering of war is well presented by Capt. Ruggero. . . . Readers will find the story riveting, many of the characters engaging, the combat scenes paralyzing. . . . It is highly unlikely that this fine first novel will be Capt. Ruggero's last. It certainly should not be."

—*Pointer View*

"The action is swift and sure. . . ."

—*Dallas News*

"Compellingly readable . . . Ruggero weaves a masterful story which mixes psychological glimpses of characters, personal insights, an intimate knowledge of politics, and old-fashioned suspense to produce a cliff-hanger that is truly tough to put down. . . . A powerful, emotive, must-read book . . . a superb first for Ed Ruggero."

—*Assembly* (West Point)

"The insights in *38 NORTH YANKEE* are remarkable. . . . The description of infantry combat and soldier behavior [is] very authentic. . . . A fast-paced and intriguing story."

—General John A. Wickham, Jr., USA (Ret.),
former Commander-in-Chief, U.N., U.S.
and ROK forces in Korea, and former
Army Chief of Staff

38 NORTH YANKEE

ED RUGGERO

POCKET BOOKS

New York   London   Toronto   Sydney   Tokyo   Singapore

This book is a work of fiction. Names, characters, places and incidents are either the product of the author's imagination or are used fictitiously. Any resemblance to actual events or locales or persons, living or dead, is entirely coincidental.

Excerpt from the *Infantry Journal* used by permission of the *Infantry Journal*, now *Army Magazine*, published by the Association of the U.S. Army.

POCKET BOOKS, a division of Simon & Schuster Inc.
1230 Avenue of the Americas, New York, NY 10020

ACKNOWLEDGMENTS

I owe a great deal of thanks to the people who believed in this project, and in me, even when I didn't. To Renee, best friend and believer; to Annette Burke, coach and counselor; to Tom Clancy, who told a group of cadets, in my presence, that they shouldn't wait for their dreams to come to them. Tom helped me get my dream off the ground, and he believed all the while that it would fly. To Pat Hoy, who taught me that writing was hard—and worthwhile—work. Thanks to Robert Gottlieb, for his vision, and to Paul McCarthy, for sharing his imagination.

Thanks also to Joe, for his legwork; to Maryanne S-T; Terry B., friend and reader; Greg the aviator; Scott the computer man; Brock, Gimlet-2; and George, Apache Chief.

And to the men of the Second Brigade, 25th Infantry Division, 1981–1984, who taught me the most important lesson in soldiering—it's the men who count.

Men are the essence of fighting power . . . the tougher and harder and keener and abler the soldier, the better the Army.

INFANTRY JOURNAL, August 1941

For he was likely, had he been put on,
To have proved most royal; and for his passage
The soldiers' music and the rites of war
Speak loudly for him.
Take up the bodies. Such a sight as this
Becomes the field, but here shows much amiss.
Go, bid the soldiers shoot.

Shakespeare's *Hamlet*

NEWS ITEM: Seoul, South Korea. 12 March. (AP) The student protests that have become a daily part of life in this city took a dramatic turn for the worse today when South Korean troops fired on a crowd of demonstrators. The soldiers, who were called in to protect government offices, were pelted with rocks and bottles and at least a half-dozen firebombs before they opened fire.

South Korean officials put the number of casualties at two killed and five wounded. A British newsman at the scene estimates the number of dead at "more than forty, the wounded triple that."

MEMORANDUM FOR: COMMANDER, US FORCES KOREA

FROM: FAR EAST COMMAND (FECOM) INTELLIGENCE

21 MARCH

1. Reference report from this Headquarters, date-time group 251600 FEB. Human intelligence (HUMINT) sources in the 2d Division area indicate an increase in the number of North Korean agents operating in the villages and countryside south of American positions along the Demilitarized Zone.

2. Units in the 2d Division report an increase in petty thefts, destruction of U.S. property, and general harassment of American soldiers.

3. Republic of Korea forces in the area report that they are conducting increased patrolling and counterterrorism operations. 6th ROK Corps, which holds responsibility for the sector, has failed to provide timely information to our HQ as to what they are finding.

4. Request that you coordinate directly with the ROK Ground Forces Commander to secure information on ROK operations.

/signed/
McCARVEL
COL, MILITARY INTELLIGENCE

The International Institute for Strategic Studies estimates that the Democratic People's Republic of North Korea, which has a population of only eighteen million six hundred thousand, maintains a standing military organization of seven hundred and eighty-four thousand. North Korea has more people under arms than any country of its size, and has the largest per capita military force in the world.

from the *Welcome to Korea* brief
given all U.S. soldiers reporting
for duty in the Republic of Korea

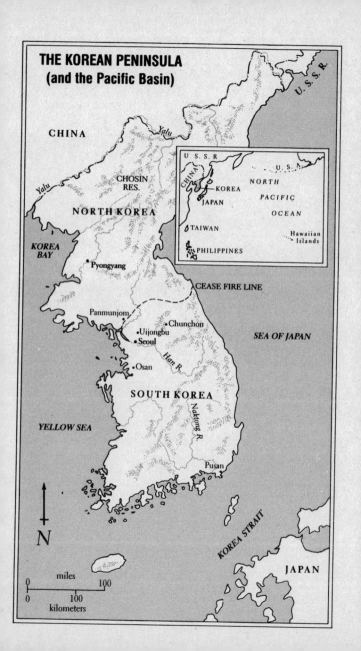

THE KOREAN PENINSULA
(and the Pacific Basin)

CHINA

Yalu

Yalu

CHOSIN RES.

NORTH KOREA

KOREA BAY

• Pyongyang

U.S.S.R.

U.S.S.R.

CHINA

KOREA

JAPAN

TAIWAN

PHILIPPINES

U.S.A

NORTH PACIFIC OCEAN

Hawaiian Islands

CEASE FIRE LINE

Panmunjom

• Chunchon

• Uijongbu

• Seoul

Han R.

• Osan

SEA OF JAPAN

SOUTH KOREA

YELLOW SEA

Naktong R.

Pusan

KOREA STRAIT

JAPAN

N

miles

0 — 100

0 — 100

kilometers

Prologue

1 April · Friday · 2300 hours (local)

The tunnel closed in on them over its last several hundred meters, narrowing as it made its way toward the surface of the earth. They moved in near darkness, so that their eyes would need no adjustment to the night waiting outside. Only the first and last man carried lights—small flashlights that barely enabled each man to pick out the shadow of the man to his front. The tunnel measured a mere four feet high by three and a half feet wide, so even these small-framed North Koreans were cramped, and the cumulative effects of the twisting shadows; putrid air; wet, collapsing walls; standing water; and sounds of scratching rats were starting to wear on them.

The leader, a wiry thirty-one-year-old lieutenant named Kang Min-Chul, moved more quickly as the passage became smaller. The ten men following him struggled to keep up, weighed down as they were with almost seventy pounds—half their body weight—of explosives each. Lieutenant Kang was eager to clear the tunnel that had encased them for over a mile, though his broad face was the impassive mask his men knew well. He was a master at hiding his concerns, but was still afraid his claustrophobic reaction would show. There was nothing to be gained, he believed, from showing weakness.

Kang and nine of the other men usually worked under quite different conditions. They were paratroopers in the Special Purpose Forces of the Korean People's Army, members of an elite fighting force of over one hundred thousand men, which prided itself on physical toughness, technical proficiency, and ideological purity. This night, they were far from their wide-open training spaces near Maengsan, north of the capital city of Pyongyang. They were a little more than a hundred feet below ground, somewhere, Kang's map indicated, below the sparsely populated area south of the Demilitarized Zone in South Korea. The tunnel they were in represented years of backbreaking work by the various engineer units that rotated through duty along the northern side of the DMZ. It was one of eighteen such tunnels, some large enough to put a fifteen-hundred-man regiment through to the enemy rear, that extended far enough into the Republic of Korea to be of some use to infiltrators. More important, it was one of only five that the intelligence section of the VII Special Purpose Corps, Kang's parent unit, believed to be as yet undetected by the watchful South Koreans and their American allies. Tonight, it was to be the launching pad for an important escalation in the continuing struggle between North and South Korea.

Kang paused and counted his men, squeezing by the figures in the cramped blackness. No one spoke as he used his hands to check equipment he couldn't see. He checked the loads of explosives by patting down each man, feeling for and counting the satchels of explosives, the plastic boxes of detonators, and the bandoliers of ammunition. When he touched the next to last man in line, he felt a decided stiffening. This man was not one of the soldiers he had trained for months for this mission, but one who had joined the squad only hours before the mission's start.

Pak Ki Ho was a political officer from the Central People's Committee, the civilian overseers of the North Korean military. Pak had been trained to be an intelligence analyst in the hierarchy of the Special Purpose Forces. Good family connections and unbridled ambition had prompted him to leave that rather dangerous service for a safer job in the civilian side of the government. The son of an influential party servant, Pak was tall, at five nine, for a Korean, and he fancied himself a physically attractive man. He was exceedingly vain about his thick, jet-black hair, which he wore longer than was the fashion among the very conservative ranks of the Communist party.

Kang had taken an almost immediate dislike to the civilian interloper. Pak was a bureaucrat, a privileged intellectual who had neither the training nor the experience to second-guess the lieutenant. Kang had met more than a few such dilettantes, most of whom he dismissed out of hand. There was something else about this man that unsettled Kang, something that triggered an alarm in the soldier's head.

Kang was an excellent soldier who had gathered an impressive array of military credentials since leaving his family farm years before. He could lead small units in combat operations, run parachute operations and small amphibious missions; he could move his men for miles in unfamiliar territory while subsisting off the land, all the while remaining undetected by pursuers.

The army had taught him a great deal, and had given him the opportunity to rise above his simple peasant roots to a position of responsibility. But he was painfully aware that while he had become a consummate man of action, he was not an intellectual. The peasant stock in him was still awed by the more sophisticated thinkers he saw around him. Though a man of great physical courage, he held better-educated men in awe. As long as he stayed in military circles and addressed only military affairs, he was fine. Outside that circle he felt exposed, as if he wore his untutored mind like an amulet. Consequently, he guarded his views like a terrible and secret sin.

Kang shied away from the political discussions he sometimes encountered among his fellow officers, joining in only to chant the party's dogma. He was uncomfortable with the give-and-take and gray areas of political intrigue. He did not appreciate nuance or suggestion or influence. Like military men throughout the world—in western as well

3

as Communist armies—he liked things to be clearly defined, he liked to get the word straight from one boss, from one commander, with no frills or room for interpretation.

Pak was not of Kang's world. Where Kang was a man of action, Pak was a man of words. He dealt in implication and inference. He did not seem like a man who could be pinned down, and Kang was sure that Pak could, by dint of words alone, slide out from under responsibility for just about anything—even if he was caught red-handed.

For the most part, Kang was happy to let his ignorance extend to government infighting, but he did know that there was a strong military faction in the North Korean government that was at odds with its civilian overseers. The militarists wanted to discredit the civilians, whose chief sin was suggesting that reunification with rich South Korea might be accomplished without a war.

Pak had looked disdainfully on Kang when the army lieutenant said that he had come from a farming community on the east coast. To Pak, that made him little more than a country bumpkin, and Pak wondered how Kang, old for a lieutenant, had ever made it into the very selective Special Purpose Forces.

Still, Pak had to admit the man was thorough and professional. Kang had lavished a great deal of attention on his men before their departure, checking each man's foot gear, each individual's meager supply of food, and the distribution of the load of explosives they would use in ambushes and sabotage over the coming days. Kang even carried an equal share of the load himself. Pak, who knew that all work must be shared in the People's Army, also believed that leaders must save their strength in order to be able to make the difficult decisions. Pak carried only his personal gear and weapon.

"We will surface soon, within fifty meters or so," Kang told his men when he finished the inspection, whispering even here under dozens of feet of rock and tons of earth. They were intensely aware of the possibility of discovery, and the next few minutes would be critical as they surfaced in the Republic of Korea. This would be their most vulnerable time: some men would be exposed on the surface while others were below, unable to bring their weapons to bear as they squeezed out of the well-hidden tunnel opening one by one. Their discovery would also uncover the tunnel itself, and negate the months of work by their dedicated comrades in the engineers.

"Check pull-fuses," Kang hissed.

He could hear a small rustling as the men pulled open their sweat-soaked shirts to check the Chinese-made fuses taped to their chests. With a quick pull on the ring hanging loose from the plastic cylinder, any member of the patrol could blow up himself and any captor unlucky enough to be within several meters. These men were determined not to be taken alive.

"Check," Kang said. With a silent ease born of countless hours of rehearsal, they passed a signal forward from the rear: a slight pat on the shoulder of the man in front that meant they were ready to proceed. The first and last men switched off their lights.

Kang, the leader, would go first.

The last few feet of the tunnel turned sharply upward, so that the soldiers behind Kang, had there been any light, would have seen only his feet as he pushed against the dirt and crumbling rock to open the passage. There was no lining to the tunnel's exit. The hole narrowed until, at last, Kang was digging his way out. The technique made exit difficult for the first members of any team, but left only a small hole that was easy to hide from South Korean patrols.

As the cool air of the early April evening rushed in on him, Kang felt a tremendous relief. He would not die in the tunnel. He believed he had at least a fifty percent chance of dying before he left South Korea, but he was not afraid of that. He had feared only dying, blind and helpless, in the cramped tunnel. As he breathed in the wonderful fresh air, he felt a renewed determination to complete his mission.

A few meters back, Pak fingered the ring on his chest as he waited his turn to leave the damp, dark passage. He had extended the tape meant to hold the detonator to his chest, so that it covered the pull ring itself. There would be no accidental discharge. He had no intention of pulling the ring, not because he was afraid of death, he told himself, but because he had important things to live for, important work to do for the party. He believed as fervently as did Kang, he rationalized, in the rightness of the struggle they were about to undertake, but he believed more fervently in his own destiny.

It was after midnight when the last man surfaced from the tunnel, a half mile south of the DMZ. Kang, who had heard countless stories of the amazing work done by the engineers on these infiltration tunnels, was impressed. A tremendous amount of work went into moving that much earth, yet the exit showed fine detailing. The mouth of the tunnel lay concealed in the rough terrain that characterized most of the Demilitarized Zone: sharp hills and thick undergrowth that favored the undetected movement of foot soldiers.

They planned to move only between dusk and dawn for the first two days in South Korea, holing up for the daylight hours before moving south toward the roads heavy with ROK Army traffic. They had a series of safe houses to contact on the trail, but Kang was determined to use them only in an emergency. They moved steadily at a pace that Pak, even without the load that the soldiers carried, found hard to maintain. He was sure that Kang was doing it to impress him, or to lose him.

They spent their first day in South Korea in a small valley twelve miles south of the DMZ, where they hid their patrol base in the woodline just above an untended field. After they slept for a few hours, Kang awoke to recheck his map and make sure his navigation was correct.

The timing of their mission was critical, and depended, to a large extent, on the accuracy of his plotting. Their first mission was to ambush a column of ROK Army vehicles that was supposed to include several groups of officers returning from meetings at a headquarters near the DMZ. Their mission was to gather documents, maps, identification, and other information from the victims. All of this data, delivered to agents in a series of dead drops, would go toward piecing together a portrait of South Korean readiness in the area. They were then to remain in South Korea, striking targets of opportunity and hiding out in the countryside. The nature of the attacks—he was to leave no survivors—was an escalation of what had come to be seen as "normal" North Korean agitation. Kang suspected that the intelligence was to be used for something that was not at all business as usual.

To avoid compromising the mission, they could not arrive in the target area more than a few hours ahead of schedule, and so the business of timing a foot movement over many miles and two days, with a small margin for error, became the first critical task of the mission.

Pak came up beside the lieutenant.

"How are we situated?" Pak asked.

"You are supposed to remain still during the daylight hours," Kang said without looking up from his map.

"The soldiers must remain still; we leaders must be free to move around and get our bearings, so that the patrol may move quickly when night falls again."

"I am the leader here, Comrade Pak. And my soldiers are forbidden to move—lest they give away our position— under penalty of death. You know that the Americans overfly this area frequently."

"Ah, yes, the American reliance on technology," Pak said reflectively.

He doesn't want to confront me, Kang thought, *or perhaps he is the one baiting me.*

"That is why they will never be able to keep us from crossing the Demilitarized Zone," Pak said. "The Americans never believe that hostilities are possible until someone shoots at them. It comes from living a life of ease, in a country unused to invasion. They do not have the fortitude or the stamina to patrol the Zone on foot, which is the only way to do it correctly."

Kang fixed Pak with a look the political observer thought might signal an intellectual interest.

Perhaps he is surprised that I know about the foot soldier's historical dominance of the battlefield, Pak thought.

"Did you know," Pak went on, "that in 1950, during the Fatherland Liberation war, the Chinese entered our country with half a million men, and yet remained unde-tected by the Americans, because the enemy relied solely on aerial reconnaissance?"

Kang looked at him blankly, his pencil poised above a small sheet of paper he had made notes upon. He didn't believe that Pak was engaging in idle chatter. There had to be a point to his story. The lieutenant had heard rumors in the officers' billets that the army was conducting a mobilization, under the guise of training maneuvers, in preparation for a lightning invasion of the south. He also knew that the civilian government was dead set against the idea and would do anything to upset the militarists' timetables.

I wonder how much he knows, Kang thought, *or how much he thinks I know about what is going on north of the DMZ?*

The political officer paused, waiting for Kang to say something, but the lieutenant just returned to his work.

As Pak turned to go back to where he had been sleeping, Kang spoke quietly. "Do not move again until dusk," he said.

Pak turned, ready to tell Kang that he was not under the lieutenant's or the army's control, thought better of it, and went back to his sleeping position.

After Pak left him, Lieutenant Kang planned the march for the night. He wanted to arrive at the ambush site between 0100 and 0200 on the third, which would give the men plenty of time to plant the explosives and even get some rest. He checked the three soldiers he had set out to secure the position. They were alert, quiet, and well-camouflaged. Satisfied with the security of the position, he crawled up under the low-hanging branches of an evergreen to get some rest.

After he saw Kang bed down, Pak moved quietly out of the patrol base to a prearranged rendezvous with an agent who was posing as a South Korean government official. He was back with the group in less than forty minutes. No one had missed him.

2 April · Saturday · 2100 hrs

Kang woke his men an hour before they were to start the last leg of their journey. He would allow them to move about the immediate area after dusk. They could prepare food, although there would be no fires for fear of detection by alert Republic of Korea forces. Kang's soldiers, used to privation, ate cold, sticky rice from paper wrapping. Each man also carried small packages of bean paste, and a tiny, precious bit of salted meat. The men knew from their intelligence training that even the combat rations of American soldiers had several courses, including desserts. Kang's men were envious but uncomplaining. North Korean soldiers had a much better fare than their civilian counterparts.

Kang tried to avoid Pak, but it was impossible in their small patrol base. When Pak sat down next to him, Kang was torn between a desire to remain quiet and obscure, and a giddy temptation to talk about things he had forbidden himself. For all of his adult life he had found safety in political dogmatism, in toeing the party line. Now he was tempted to engage this civilian—a man of dangerous power —in political dialogue.

"This mission will go a long way to further our efforts here in the south," Pak said to Kang's back as the lieutenant buried some of his papers.

"Yes, it will," Kang agreed.

Pak went on. "The thing to do is to keep the ROK Army on alert. Let them wear themselves out in useless patrolling."

He's talking about wearing them out before we strike, Kang thought. *The rumors about the mobilization must be true, the militarists are going to start a war here in the south. But where does he stand?*

"Why do you say that?" Kang asked.

"Come, Lieutenant, surely you can't be the one officer in the army who does not know of the militarist faction's desire for a war with the ROKs?"

Lieutenant Kang, who had trained all of his adult life for mortal combat, was unprepared for and uncomfortable with this verbal confrontation. Junior officers were not supposed to speculate on their superiors' motives and aims, much less discuss them openly with a civilian. Kang was privy to nothing about the militarist faction's plans. Worse, he was uncertain as to what he should admit to—what if this political officer went back to Kang's boss in the Special Purpose Forces? For all of the appeal of the intrigue, the lieutenant decided to keep quiet.

"I happen to agree with the generals who believe that our chances for defeating the ROKs diminish every day we allow their economy to flourish," Pak added.

Kang didn't go for the political officer's bait.

"You know, of course, why we are wearing civilian clothing and carrying these unmarked weapons?" Pak said, raising his voice in a question.

"So that if any of my men fall into enemy hands, our government can claim the work was done by South Koreans who want to overthrow their own government," Kang answered as he had been briefed.

"Precisely. It is very important that there be some confusion about who is carrying off these raids," Pak said, referring to a half dozen similar missions that the military had scheduled to be carried out over the next week.

"American and European journalists are inclined to believe our claims that these ambushes, and the general unrest throughout the south, are the work of South Koreans who want a reconciliation with their northern brothers. The world press must believe that the students who protest in Seoul, who throw rocks and firebombs at the police, are responsible for these attacks as well."

Quite suddenly Kang saw the whole struggle outlined clearly. For this man who would never have claimed to be a thinker, the clarity of his perception was exhilarating. The North Korean Army would be poised to strike in a week or two, and could, he believed, defeat the ROKs quickly. That would put the military faction on top in North Korea, and the civilians who wanted a peaceful reconciliation with the south would be silenced. But it all hinged on what the Americans would do. The reason for the secretive mobilization, for the civilian clothes on these missions, was to avoid giving the Americans any excuse whatsoever for reinforcing their units in South Korea.

"As long as we carry on this ruse and limit our targets to South Koreans, it is unlikely that the Americans will reinforce their units here," Kang said.

He was amazed at his new brashness, discussing volatile political topics with a civilian official. He had no doubt that Pak would report him as a political risk if it would advance his career one whit. But something about having and wielding this knowledge intoxicated Kang. He felt as if he had glimpsed a whole new realm of power, where gargantuan struggles were played out in the quiet halls of government.

Besides, Kang told himself, *I can always kill him and report him as a casualty before we return north.*

"Of course," Pak said, "there are people in the government who would like to see the Americans send heavy units here. They believe that will keep our army from attacking South Korea."

Kang looked hard at Pak's figure, dim in the failing light. *What are you thinking?*

The lieutenant plunged ahead. "The Americans can reinforce their worldwide forces now in a matter of hours. No one wants a war with the Americans."

"That is true, Comrade Lieutenant," Pak said.

The two men stood quietly in the darkness as the soldiers around them prepared to move. Kang felt as if he and Pak were locked in some dangerous dance. He could not be sure that Pak's assessment was correct, though it sounded convincing. Worse, he could not be sure that Pak truly supported the militarist position. Kang believed that the time was ripe for the inevitable war with the ROKs, and Pak had confirmed his suspicions that there was a large mobilization going on. Now his mission made more sense: he was here to gather intelligence just before the attack.

He felt a new sense of importance at the thought. The great army that stirred to the north was waiting, was depending on him and a handful of men like him. Perhaps it was that feeling of importance, but at that moment he decided he had nothing to fear from Pak. Even if the political officer was lying about his support of the army, there was nothing he could do to stop the rolling power of the military machine. History itself was on the move. What could one civilian—set down in the darkness of the South Korean countryside and dependent on Kang for everything, even the knowledge of where he was—how could Pak make a difference?

Kang decided he would kill him right after the first mission. He almost laughed at the discomfort he had felt in front of the weak bureaucrat, and felt better already thinking that Pak would be dead soon.

"Well, comrade," Kang said finally, "you can rest assured that my men are under tight control and will not make the fatal mistake of accidentally engaging American troops."

"I am not worried," Pak said. "My intelligence sources indicate that there are no American units in the area we will operate in."

"That is good to hear," Kang said. "I am glad to know that the Central Committee is looking out for those of us on the front lines."

They moved quietly, almost soundlessly, through the last few kilometers to the ambush site. Kang was very careful in approaching the target area, and he took his time looking at the site. He spent nearly forty-five minutes choosing the positions along the road for the flank security teams that would notify him, using a wire-telephone, when the target was in the kill zone.

Even in the pitch blackness it took the demolitions men only fifty minutes to set up the array of explosive devices they would use sometime near dawn. Pak made himself comfortable in the thick grass at the top of the hill that overlooked what would be the ambush kill zone, and dozed as the soldiers worked. When he woke, Kang was next to him, silent and motionless only a foot away. Pak couldn't even hear the man breathing, but was sure that the lieutenant was awake.

Kang checked his watch just after five. Sunrise at this time of year was about fifteen minutes past six, and it would be light enough thirty to forty minutes before that to see clearly. They did not expect the convoy before dawn. They had been briefed that the first target convoy would consist of three or four staff cars following a truck loaded with ROK military police. Kang would use a command-detonated mine to blow up the security force in the lead vehicle. He fully expected to kill everyone in the cars, but planned on removing every shred of material—maps, briefing papers, overlays, codebooks—that might provide intelligence.

Kang had briefed his men carefully, so that each knew exactly what to expect. He had picked his best men for the flank security teams, for they had to get a positive identification of the target. If something unexpected came along—a column of tanks, for instance—these men had to tell the patrol to let the target pass. He had done everything he could to prepare his men. Now Kang had to endure one of the commander's hardest tasks. He had to wait.

In the growing light of morning, Pak could see the features of Kang's stolid, unlovely face slowly appear as the darkness washed away. Kang had not lost his intense seriousness, and if the night had worn him out, he was showing no signs of fatigue.

When Kang turned his head, Pak slipped a small pair of wire cutters from his shirt pocket. He was only a few feet away from Kang, and so had to be careful not to pull on the telephone wire that connected the lieutenant's phone to the flank security positions as he slipped the cutters over it. If there was a slight change in the tension on the phone Kang held, the lieutenant didn't notice.

Pak reached inside his shirt and closed his other hand on the grip of his pistol. There was a round already in the chamber—Kang's head was only a couple of feet away. Satisfied that his complex plans were on course, Pak opened his mouth to speak. Kang silenced him with a sharp signal, bringing his hand up to his own mouth.

It was a good fifteen seconds before Pak heard the sound that had alerted Kang. Trucks. The convoy was right on time; Kang's land navigation had apparently been flawless.

Pak looked to his left, away from Kang and down the narrow road that stretched to a bend a quarter mile distant. Kang's men had placed an explosive charge under the roadway, just after a small rise in front of the ambushers. The driver of the lead truck, even if he saw the telltale loose dirt, would not have time to react before Kang triggered the explosive and halted the convoy.

The men had also placed a string of antipersonnel mines in the tall grass at the foot of the hillside. In an ironic twist that Pak appreciated, the mines were stolen American-made "claymore" mines. Their curved bodies held plastic explosives and seven hundred steel balls. The shot, stuck in the explosive putty as if to flypaper, would spray the area in front of the weapon with a deadly hail that could rip a man apart. Wired to a single circuit, these mines would go off simultaneously. Kang also held the detonator for these.

Pak squeezed the wirecutter, cutting Kang's communication with his left flank security team. Pak kept his head turned to the left, away from Kang and toward the sound of the truck. But he heard Kang fumble with the phone, squeezing the push-to-talk switch repeatedly. If the lieutenant were anything other than a disciplined soldier, Pak knew, he would be cursing out loud.

Kang had only seconds to make his decision. The vehicles entering the kill zone sounded like the American-made trucks the ROKs would use, and they were right on time, in the exact place they were supposed to be. But without the link to his security team, Kang could not be positive that he was hitting the right target. Still, he could not imagine scrubbing the mission after all they had invested, certainly not in front of Pak, the civilian. If he didn't trigger the explosives and assault the enemy, he would have to make up another story to explain Pak's death. It would be much easier to say he was killed in the assault.

The lead truck turned the corner and came into view, a gray-black shadow that lurched forward as the driver shifted gears coming around the turn. Kang felt as if he were being swept along, as if control had somehow been wrested from him. He wondered why the telephone wasn't working.

The lead truck was within a few meters of the mine.

The wire ran from Kang's phone to a stake where he had tied it off to prevent it from being pulled out of the phone, then under Pak's body.

The truck was over the mine.

The line was dead.

He looked at the road and saw the second vehicle was also a truck, and he saw a black soldier standing up in the cargo area.

These were Americans!

Kang dropped the firing devices and swung at Pak, who had drawn a pistol from his shirt. Both men were still flat on the ground, out of sight of the roadway. Kang managed to knock the civilian's hands away, and the pistol slipped to the ground between them, sliding down the slope. Kang bent to reach for the handgun, expecting Pak to fight him for it.

But Pak had gone for the firing device.

I have lost this round, Kang thought as he brought the pistol up.

Kang pulled the trigger just as Pak squeezed the detonator, and the sound of the mine drowned out the report of the gun.

1

Near Hongch'on, Republic of Korea

3 April · Sunday · 0555 hrs (local)

The first bomb went off exactly as planned, directly under the cargo bed of the American five-ton truck. The vehicle did a little hop, and from the hillside where the attackers crouched it looked like a child's toy that had been dropped and had bounced. The canvas top burst, spraying bright orange flame and the bodies of the fifteen soldiers who had been on board. The antipersonnel mines along the side of the road nearest the ambushers were not fired, thus saving the sixty-plus GIs who spilled from the other trucks in the convoy, just as the attackers had hoped they would.

The platoon leader had been in the lead vehicle, and the platoon sergeant was in the trail vehicle, policing up a broken-down truck about a mile back. By the time the ranking squad leader got the platoon off the road, the attackers had cleared off the hillside. In the circle of yellow light from the burning truck, the young sergeant tried to give comfort to a soldier he couldn't identify. The dying man's face was burned, his eyes blackened, his lips and most of his nose gone. He made no sound save a rattling, liquid breathing.

The platoon sergeant arrived within minutes after hearing the explosion. When he later climbed the hill beside the road to investigate, he found a Korean man dressed in civilian clothes—dead of a gunshot to the head—and the detonator for the unexploded claymores. Had the detonator worked, there would have been a bloodbath. Whoever set the ambush knew what he was doing.

The platoon sergeant slid back down the short, steep embankment on his butt, followed by a military policeman from the traffic control party that accompanied all convoys. The MP had a loaded .45-caliber pistol on his hip, making him the only armed man in the whole convoy. The soldiers crouching on the sides of the road below had their personal weapons, but U.S. soldiers do not, as a matter of course, carry ammunition in training exercises. These soldiers had been heading to the docks at Pusan to assist in the outloading of equipment. Though their presence was proof of American commitment to South Korean freedom, they made conspicuous and completely helpless targets.

The platoon sergeant was left with fourteen dead, one dying man, a burning truck, and sixty-two badly shaken GIs who, until that moment, had never been shot at and who were quite frankly surprised that anyone would want to shoot at them.

2

East Range, Oahu

5 April · Tuesday · 1535 hrs (local)

Captain Mark Isen never tired of the roadmarch out of Oahu's East Range training area. The red clay trail led to a straight hardtop, with pineapple fields to the left falling away in a gentle downslope toward Honolulu. Then under the highway bridge (an interstate they called it, even here) and onto the flat expanse of the Leilehua plain. A quarter mile farther, the platoons posted orange-vested roadguards and crossed the small, two-lane road to the east gate of Wheeler Air Force Base. The quickest route back to Schofield Barracks was through this former army airfield. Isen stood at the gate and watched his soldiers amble across the highway in a trot that wasn't any faster than the march pace, but which made them look as though they were hurrying. He faced to the east and the column's rear and greeted by name these men he had known for the year he had been in command of Company C. He was twenty-seven years old, a second-generation professional soldier whose looks lied about his identity. He had the kind of face that was hard to remember the first, maybe even the second time you met him. He was of average height and build, with unremarkable hair and features—except for his eyes, which were a flat gray and which always gave away his thoughts.

His troops called him "the Professor" because they didn't think he looked much like a soldier, certainly not like the chiseled warriors whose pictures decorated recruiting offices around the nation. Isen's noncommissioned officers, who had been around the block a few times and knew the difference between image and substance, called him "the Professor" because Isen *thought*.

He turned with his men and was struck again, each time as deeply as the first, by the beauty of the Waianae mountains that formed the rich, blue-green backdrop to this scene. Kolekole Pass cut a deep notch in the mountain curtain just to the west of Wheeler and Schofield Barracks. In 1941 the Japanese fighters coming down to Oahu from their carriers to the north had used this pass as a guidepost. They had pivoted in a sharp left above the mountains and in a moment were over Wheeler, bombing and strafing the Army Air Corps planes that were parked so obligingly wing tip to wing tip.

Whenever Isen walked on this field, he felt close to that day, to its drama and the brazen shock of surprise and the righteous anger that it spawned. The light here sharpened the edges of what he saw, and the rich flowery smell was the same as it had been then. He had no trouble conjuring up the images of the burning planes and the terrified, running groundcrews and the pilots cursing in frustration because they couldn't get the damn planes up in time to fight. Something, perhaps the intensity of those hours, perhaps the ghosts of the young men lost there, made it seem to Isen that the flat, sun-bright plain was alive with the lingering memory of that battle.

Isen had grown up around army posts. He had graduated from high school while his father, a career NCO, was stationed at Fort Benning in Georgia, so he called that home. He had lived in seven states in the twelve years before college, and he had the vaguely southern accent that people in the army affected regardless of their background.

He had grown up in places where it was normal for kids to stop the ball game and face the lowering flag as "To the Colors" was played at the end of the day. He had spent his boyhood watching soldiers, listening to his father and his father's friends as they sat on the front steps of the interchangeable quarters at Fort Benning or Fort Hood or Fort Stewart in the long summer twilights, talking about Vietnam or the next pay raise or what was right or wrong with the new commander.

He listened to their stories and fetched them beer, holding the bottle necks in his small hands and pressing the cool glass against his body as the summer heat spread out in the night.

They were quick to complain, these men, to bitch about an officer or a new directive, but they were the first to offer their limited free time when it came to coaching Little League or the post swim team or setting up for the school fair. Isen grew up around generous spirits and learned giving as a norm, and he learned from his father that people were the army's most valuable asset.

Joining the army had seemed the natural thing for Isen to do, not because he couldn't imagine himself doing anything else, but because he thought it was important work, and because he valued the company and respect of men such as his father. But for all the talking his dad did over the years, he confined his remarks on the day the younger man took his commissioning oath to the simple admonition, "Take care of your soldiers, son."

* * *

Isen's company was only five days back from Team Spirit, the annual exercise in Korea that involved elements of the U.S. and ROK armies, navies, and air forces, and Isen already had them back on the road. They had had a hectic, sometimes harrowing stay in Korea this year. The towns were full of demonstrators denouncing the American presence. In the field, rumors of terrorist gangs and bandits ambushing American units flew thick as fleas.

He let the platoons pass him as he waited for his XO to come up with the rear of the column. On paper the company was authorized one hundred and thirty men. The three rifle platoons, each with three nine-man squads and a headquarters section, were the mainstays of the company's fighting power. The company headquarters section had, in addition to the commander, an executive officer and first sergeant, a thirteen-man anti-armor section, and a six-man mortar section. In practice, Isen farmed the anti-armor weapons out to the platoons and kept the mortars under his control. Isen had taken ninety-five men to Korea on Team Spirit, and was now watching the last of the seventy-eight men that went with him on today's roadmarch.

First Lieutenant Dale Barrow was in the center of the road, between the two files of soldiers who walked along either side, talking animatedly with all the men within earshot. Barrow was a solid block of determination and energy. Years of weight lifting gave him the appearance of having been cut out of stone. He wore his pale blond hair cut painfully short, because that was the style currently affected by the army's elite troops, and because he subconsciously associated the beautiful corn color with his sister—whom he loved but did not want to resemble.

Barrow loved this stuff. Whenever he got a chance, Barrow would let the first sergeant take the lone company vehicle, usually used by the XO, to the rear so that he could get out and walk with the troops. He had a knack for knowing when it was most important to do so, as it was today, with their feet still sore from humping the hills in South Korea.

Barrow had been a business major in college for a while, drifting into the discipline only because it sounded practical. His only real passions in his college years were parties and ROTC. The other cadets in the program called him "Marvin Military"—but not to his face. His military instructors wished that they could take his enthusiasm for even the most mundane subjects and distribute it evenly among his peers.

Late in his sophomore year, Barrow changed his major to English when he finally accepted that he would not get through accounting. He had no great passion for literature, but had noticed that there seemed to be a lot of women in English, and very few of what Barrow would call men.

He did not dive into the deep intellectual waters his discipline offered, but was content to flail along on the surface. Characteristically, the only gem he remembered from all the richness of poetry and drama and fiction was the term *carpe diem,* seize the day. Mentioned only in passing by a professor who framed it with other, more insightful comments, it seemed to speak directly to Barrow. Though he was clever enough to keep this observation to himself, he wrote it on his notebooks, hoping that young women would notice and ask him what it meant; or, better yet, would know what it implied.

Not surprisingly, he loved college: the absolute sameness of routine, the nameless days strung together in an imitation of constancy. And if there was a nagging feeling that something was missing, he could conveniently assume that he was simply anxious to get into uniform.

Isen had complete confidence in Barrow's technical competence, his drive, and his concern for the men. But sometimes he had to wonder how much of his lieutenant was still eighteen years old.

Barrow ambled up to his commander. "Hey, sir, how's it going?"

"My dogs are barking here, Dale. Other than that, everything's great."

"Alpha and Bravo won't be back on the road 'til next week," Barrow reported. He tried to sound as if he were just presenting facts, but couldn't hide the hint of smugness in his voice.

Yeah, Charlie Company, the troops would say to their peers in other companies, *back on the road in a few days. The marchin' fools of Company C.* There was more to this litany than bragging. Though it would certainly seem strange to an outsider, even to soldiers who weren't infantrymen, the C Company men considered themselves fortunate. According to the hybrid value system of these eighteen- and nineteen-year-olds, C Company was better because they'd marched farther (though they'd had no real choice), because they always went the extra distance.

"They training back in the quad?" Isen asked.

Isen hated doing training, any kind of training, on the golf-course-green grass of the "quad," the square formed by the 1930s-style barracks at Schofield. His troops thought he didn't want them to get soft, and that was true. Their chatter was good-natured, but served a purpose, helping them to justify the work they did. In the absence of the ultimate test of combat, this was all they had, this and a sense of satisfaction at being soldiers. *Move out to the field, man, no mess hall, no Coke machines, no lunch at home with Mama and coffee breaks when you feel like it. Just the business at hand.* Isen's fellow company commanders thought him a bit eccentric. He was the only commander who carried a rifle, an infantryman's weapon, instead of the pistol he was authorized. And here he was five days back from a long field problem in winter conditions and he had his company out on the road again, shuffling along, humping weapons and rucks, sweating under the Hawaiian sun.

There were a few things that C Company men just did not do: train in the quad when they could go to the field, ride when they could walk, or transfer to other companies. Isen didn't enunciate these points—his soldiers did, anytime they got a chance. In the barracks they would complain, and certainly the newly assigned soldiers had no idea what was going on and it sure looked to *them* like they'd rather be in Bravo Company, cooling out back in the quad. But the peer pressure soon got to them, and before they knew it they were won over. *Hard-Chargin' Charlie.*

Off duty, Isen's young troops wore the same cheap rayon-blend T-shirts that soldiers in other companies did, the shirts from some shop just off Fort Benning, with logos like *Airborne: Death from Above;* or *Kill 'em all and let God sort 'em out;* or *Peace through Superior Firepower.* But the C Company soldiers walked with a gingerly step that was pure tough-guy. They rolled their shoulders forward as they walked, swiveled a bit at the hips, loose-limbed, grabbing some extra space. The walk was perfect articulation. It said, *My feet hurt, but it's from humpin', baby, humpin' the boonies. And if you ain't got blisters, well, you just ain't.*

Isen himself didn't subscribe to this showmanship. He was glad to see it in the youngest soldiers. It was an unsophisticated but genuine spirit. He did enjoy seeing them develop simple self-confidence and pride in their skills and what they could do.

Isen's lieutenants, for the most part, seemed capable of making the distinction between hype and reality. Surprisingly, it was Barrow, the most senior lieutenant in the company, who sometimes seemed to blur the lines.

Most officers and NCOs understood that in trying to get young soldiers to overcome natural apprehension about physical risk, a certain amount of grand-standing was useful. It was most apparent in places like Airborne School, where in order to get young people to jump from perfectly good airplanes, the system told them that they were special, a breed apart and somewhere above the non-paratrooper, the mere "leg" soldier.

Along with the paratroopers, infantrymen were most apt to develop this swagger. The grunts slept on the ground when other troops had tents, the grunts walked when others rode, the grunts humped and sweated and, in combat, would carry the heaviest burdens. In return, they got to strut a little bit. As long as you kept it in perspective and didn't let your ego run away with you—the philosophy was harmless enough. Isen wondered how much of Barrow's enthusiasm was showmanship, and how much he truly believed.

C Company turned into the quad and closed ranks in front of the company area. The "grab-ass" was louder here for the benefit of the soldiers in other companies who watched from the balconies (lanais here in Hawaii) that stretched the length of the upper floors of all the barracks.

"Hey, First Sergeant, we're all stretched out now. We can really get on with some *serious* walkin'."

"Talk to me, man. Yeah."

The mortar section soldiers bent over at the waist, supporting their upper bodies with their rifles so that the weight of the tubes strapped to their rucksacks would fall off their shoulders for a moment. But they were no less vocal from their hunchbacked stance.

"Yeah, mortars *do* it. You guys hump one of these babies for a while and tell me about walkin', man." Their chatter was a colorful barometer of morale, a background noise of contentment, and Isen liked to hear it.

Isen could see the battalion commander, Lieutenant Colonel Rand Tilden, and the operations officer, the S3, watching him from the lanai at battalion headquarters. Tilden was Isen's boss and the commander of the five-hundred-man battalion. Just as there were three platoons in a rifle company, there were three rifle companies—Alpha, Bravo, and Isen's Charlie—in the battalion. The fourth company, Headquarters Company, was made up of six platoons that provided limited medical, signal, reconnaissance, transportation, indirect fire (from four eighty-one millimeter mortars), and anti-armor fire support to the battalion.

Major Jan Bock, who was the S3, or operations officer, waved at Isen, but it looked more like a summons than a greeting. Bock was the battalion commander's main adviser when it came to plans, training, and combat operations. He was the third-ranking man in the unit, after Tilden and the battalion executive officer.

Sure enough, Isen had barely gotten out of his sweat-soaked battle-dress uniform blouse and LBE (load-bearing equipment) when a soldier from headquarters knocked at his office door.

"Sir, the colonel would like you to come up to battalion as soon as you can."

"Right."

Isen wrung his blouse out over the trashcan, then reached into his desk drawer and produced a dry T-shirt, which he put on. He rolled up the sleeves of his BDU shirt and slipped back into its dampness.

"First Sergeant, I'm headed up to battalion to see the old man. Get these guys cleared out as soon as you can, whenever you think they're ready. Tell the XO that he doesn't have to keep the platoon leaders around, 'cause I don't know how long I'm gonna be."

"Roger that, sir," the first sergeant called from the orderly room. "Your wife called a few minutes ago."

"Thanks. I'll call her when I get out. I think the old man's in a hurry. He had the three flagging me down from the lanai when I got into the quad."

Isen went over the next day's training in his head. "Let's get some good stretching at PT tomorrow, First Sergeant. My old legs are tight."

He knew this would get the first sergeant going. First Sergeant Savia Voavosa was, at thirty-eight, the oldest and the most physically fit first sergeant in the battalion. He was Samoan, a hugely muscled rock who created the impression of vastness, though he stood only five feet seven. The troops both adored and feared him. In one breath he would refer to them, unashamedly and without irony, as "my babies," and in the next he would threaten to snuff out their miserable lives with his bare hands if they didn't do his bidding—*what* he wanted and *when* he wanted it. He delighted in telling everybody how old he was, not because he felt sorry for himself, but because it embarrassed younger men into hanging tough longer than they thought they could.

"Your old legs? Hell, sir, my legs were old when yours didn't have hair on 'em. Talking about old legs . . . hunhh."

Isen grabbed a soda on his way up the stairs, popping the top and sucking the foam from around the edge. He was thus unceremoniously posed when he came face-to-face with the brigade commander, Colonel Hastings, his own boss's immediate superior and commander of the sixteen-hundred-man brigade.

"Hello, Colonel," he managed to get out without spilling any soda on his already-soaked blouse.

"Hello, Mark. How was the roadmarch today?"

"I told them I wanted to get them back out in the sunshine because their tans had faded. Paco wasn't buying it, sir."

This got a chuckle out of the brigade commander. Paco, Lieutenant Marist to his troops, was black, a deep and handsome mahogany black. He was the best platoon leader in the battalion, maybe the whole damn brigade, and well-known for his humor and brazen practical jokes. One of the reasons Isen liked him so much was that Paco complemented Isen's own dry sense of humor. Isen was quiet, and Paco was anything but. Isen enjoyed having him around.

Isen was surprised to find the outside door to the conference room locked. He couldn't enter from the lanai, but would have to go through the battalion headquarters hallway. He and the other captains who were gathering slipped into the room to stand behind their chairs and await the entrance of the two colonels. Isen was surprised to see that the brigade intelligence officer, a major named Rickoff, had accompanied the brigade commander and was also waiting in the conference room.

"Hello, sir." He didn't know Rickoff, but it never hurt to be pleasant with people who someday might be inclined to screw you over in an inspection. The S2 didn't respond, though he looked Isen right in the eye.

When all the company commanders were in the room, the battalion executive officer, a thirty-three-year-old major named Don Shelby, asked three of the staff officers who normally attended these meetings to leave. That left only the commanders and the key members of the staff—a sobered group. The Alpha and Bravo Company commanders, who had been talking between themselves, quieted. Isen straightened and opened his notebook on the long conference table that was decorated with the regimental crest, a blue and white shield that sported one word on its scroll: Duty.

The last time he had been in a meeting where the air was this heavy, one of the company commanders had been absent, and the colonel had announced that he had relieved the man. Rickoff's presence precluded that kind of meeting. Tilden would never air his problems in front of a brigade staff officer.

Everyone in the room rose as Tilden and Hastings entered. They sat at the head of the table.

"Siddown."

Isen wondered if Tilden had dispensed with his usual joviality because Colonel Hastings was present. One of the things Isen liked best about Tilden was his sense of proportion: he was serious when he needed to be, without overdoing it.

Tilden was the only man in the battalion who was a Vietnam veteran. He had celebrated his twentieth birthday by assuming command of a twenty-man rifle platoon—in the middle of a firefight—when his lieutenant and his platoon sergeant were wounded. After that night, he once confided to Isen, he had found very little in the peacetime army worth getting ruffled about.

As Isen tried to puzzle out the battalion commander's expression, he noticed a map tacked up behind Tilden that hadn't been there yesterday. On the wall, the Korean peninsula jutted out into the blue of the Sea of Japan like some obscene appendage.

"Gentlemen," the battalion XO began, "let me start out by saying that whatever is said in this room is to stay in this room. What you're going to hear is not yet for publication to anyone." He dropped his voice—melodramatically, Isen thought—on the *anyone.* Isen heard the Alpha Company commander swallow hard, saw the man's Adam's apple slide up and down. He looked up again, past Tilden, to the map.

Mark and Adrienne Isen had been married for five years, and they had known each other since high school. It did not surprise Isen when his wife, in the first few minutes he was home, sensed that something was terribly wrong.

"What's bothering you, Mark?"

"Nothing." He knew this wouldn't work.

"Don't give me that. You think I can't tell when something's bothering you? Is it the company?"

"Yeah, sort of. I really can't talk much about it." This was their signal, worked out over the twelve months he had commanded the company. Adrienne turned to face him, leaning back on the counter and placing a foot on the opposite calf. She had her hair pulled back in a simple ponytail and was wearing one of Mark's shirts. She arched a perfect eyebrow at him in what he called her Scarlett O'Hara look, but got no response. She knew that she would get no more out of him. They shared most of what went on in their respective careers, and more than a few times Mark had sought and used her advice—especially when he was dealing with the personal lives of his soldiers and their families. But this was not going to be one of those times.

Adrienne took another tack, approaching him and placing her forearms on his shoulders, locking her hands behind his neck. She stood nearly two inches taller than Mark when they were barefoot.

"Well, is this secret mess you've made of things going to be a permanent adjustment to our life here in paradise, Mr. Big Shot?"

"Not at all." Mark responded to her concern, to her touch. He told himself that there was no need to upset her . . . yet. There was still the possibility that the unit wouldn't be going back to Korea. Or that, if they did, it would only be as a show of force. He kissed her, consciously trying to hide his tension, then headed off to the shower, peeling his clothes off in the hallway as he went.

Adrienne was not without her sources. She resolved to call Bette Tilden, the battalion commander's wife, as soon as Mark, reliably predictable and quite exhausted, had fallen asleep on the living room floor at nine-thirty. She could hear him in the shower, and she waited for his off-key singing. It bothered her only when he did it early in the morning (in the army, an early day could well mean four o'clock), or when he crooned Elvis songs. Tonight there was just the rattle of water on the shower curtain.

Bette Tilden was surprised when Adrienne, who generally had little use for the wives of Mark's fellow officers, called. Bette wasn't able to tell her anything, but when Adrienne turned on the car radio as she drove to work in Honolulu on Wednesday, the following day, she heard the news of the ambush on the American soldiers.

So that's what Mark was so uptight about, she thought. *I can't believe he didn't tell me.*

She put her car in the parking garage and bought the morning paper at the bottom of the stairs. The story was page-one news, but was maddeningly short of details. Adrienne was specifically looking to see if the soldiers were from the 25th Division, which would mean that their families also lived on Schofield Barracks. But the army spokesman, true to form, would release no details as to the identity of the dead until after notification of next of kin. Some army family, somewhere, was probably even now finding out that their husband, brother, son, was dead or hurt badly. Adrienne felt a small stab of guilt at her relief. Her husband had spent the night safe at home in their bed.

While Adrienne was making her way toward Honolulu that Wednesday morning, Isen was sitting on the ground in his physical training gear: gray shorts and a gray cotton T-shirt with ARMY stenciled on the front. A soldier in BDUs came up to him behind the company formation, where Isen was stretching before the run.

"Captain Isen?"

"Yes." This was probably the message he didn't want to receive. Good news would have waited until after the company had finished PT.

"Sir, you're supposed to go to the brigade conference room right away. Can you point out where I could find the Alpha Company commander? He's the only one in your battalion I haven't found yet."

Isen sent the soldier trotting down the road between the chapel and the nearest quad after A Company, which had left the field for a run only seconds earlier. He waved at the first sergeant to continue as he moved away, then he pulled his XO off to the side.

"Dale, listen. All the company commanders and Colonel Tilden have got to go up to brigade for a briefing. I guess all three battalions will be there. I want you to get showered up after PT and stand by the phone in case I have to call you."

Barrow was clearly puzzled, but did not ask questions. He trusted Isen to tell him everything he could.

"Roger that, sir," he said and he trotted back to the formation of soldiers sitting on the ground, stretching their tired legs before the run.

Isen jogged off in the direction of brigade headquarters. At the edge of the field he took a quick look back at the company. Ninety-eight men. He was struck by how small the group looked from just a hundred meters away.

Major Rickoff, the brigade intelligence officer, and Major Hathorne, the brigade operations officer, were red-eyed and rumpled and had obviously been up all night. Hathorne was holding a Styrofoam cup of coffee and a cigarette in one hand. There were two NCOs handing out packets to the brigade's company commanders as Isen made his way to his seat. All three battalion commanders and twelve of the thirteen company commanders in the brigade were present. All but one of the officers were wearing PT gear, meaning they'd all been called in as Isen had—right from physical training.

Isen sat and started leafing through his packet. He suspected that his had been put together in a hurry because it was out of sequence. The top sheet was marked "Appendix A" and was the list of map sheets that the brigade had used during the Team Spirit exercise. The next page was a light and weather data table that showed sunrise and sunset times, moonrise and moonset times and percentage of illumination that the moon would provide; as well as the expected weather patterns—rainfall, temperature, fog—for Korea. The start date at the left-hand side of the page was today's date.

The brigade intelligence officer, the S2, began the briefing by rehashing what they already knew. "Two days ago a convoy from our division was ambushed near Hongch'on. Fifteen soldiers were killed. This attack is probably related to reports by Second Division intell sources of increasing hostile activity by North Korean agents in areas south of the Demilitarized Zone." He paused to let this sink in, his words dropping like stones in the soundless room.

"As far as the big picture goes, the G2 and the CINCPAC intell center are convinced that this attack, the reports of North Korean agents, and the so-called "student" protests in Seoul are related."

The G2 was the Division Intelligence Officer and his staff; the CINCPAC was the staff of the Commander in

Chief of the Pacific, who directed all U.S. forces on this side of the world.

"But by far the most important information comes from satellite photos taken over the last week."

For some reason, Isen expected a projector to click on at this cue, but Rickoff merely glanced at his notes.

"The North Koreans are mobilizing just north of the Demilitarized Zone—probably in preparation for an invasion of South Korea."

There. It was out in the open now. Isen felt strangely relieved that someone had finally mentioned what was really on everyone's mind.

Rickoff continued. "CINCPAC is telling us that the State Department believes that the North Korean government is divided on whether or not to go to war. There's been a power struggle over there in the last few years, ever since Kim Il Sung's son took control. He wasn't as strong as his old man and there's been a lot of infighting. It comes down to this: there's a civilian faction that wants to reduce the military and get the economy moving. The military is looking out for its own hide and is saying that they can own South Korea's industrial plant in a few weeks instead of waiting to develop their own. The people are unhappy, but there's nothing like a war to get people's minds off their everyday troubles—and there's the promise of all that loot in the South. This military faction thinks they can take the whole of South Korea before we can get there with heavy forces—it *is* a long boat ride. If they can do that, they don't think that Americans will go for a protracted war that will have to start with an amphibious invasion.

"Our State Department believes that the civilian moderates might even be encouraging the attacks on Americans, hoping that we'll reinforce our units there. If we start sending U.S. troops, this group of civilians figures that even the hawks will know that an attack won't work. But the hard-line military guys might just go for it all.

"The question is: will the military clique invade, even if we do begin reinforcing our field army? After all, it would take us a while—say six weeks—to get a lot of heavy stuff over there from the States. There's a lot of talk about the air force carrying tanks and heavy equipment over in C-5s, but even if we do that, we'd be doing only piecemeal reinforcement. They can carry the stuff, but not fast enough for the kind of buildup we need.

"If they think they can beat the ROKs in just a few weeks, they might very well try it and hope the American public will accept the loss of South Korea. Faced with the prospect of another war in Asia—especially one that has to start with an amphibious invasion—the public just might decide to say 'screw it, let 'em keep the country.'"

Tilden, who had been looking at the table while the S2 was briefing, spoke up. "For us, the question becomes: if they invade, can we stop them long enough to get our heavy forces over there? That's not what this division is designed to do. The LIDs, the new light divisions, can certainly get there, but I'm not willing to bet that merely showing the American flag is gonna be enough. It wasn't in 1950."

When he was first assigned to the unit, Isen had to learn the history of the regiment, the unit whose lineage and battle history the battalion shared. In 1950 the regiment had been part of the army of occupation in Japan: fat, understrength, and still believing that the memory of America's might in World War II would be enough to keep foolhardy enemies at bay. The first American unit committed in Korea, Task Force Smith, had been unceremoniously overrun. Those men had been sent in to fight North Korean tanks with vintage bazookas that simply bounced off the North Korean armor.

Just a few weeks earlier, during their deployment to Korea, Isen had participated in a simple wreath-laying ceremony commemorating that action. A bugler had blown taps, the notes lingering cold and blue out in the desolate countryside.

There was an awkward pause, then the S3 got up and announced that the division was beginning again the outload sequence that had taken them to Korea only—what was it?—five weeks before. This time there was no fixed schedule of training ahead of them. Instead, there was the at-hand familiarity of the alert procedures, then the frightening possibility of war in Korea.

* * *

Isen called the company from the headquarters, beating out three of the other commanders who were trying to use the same phone. He expected to hear the charge-of-quarters answer. He got his XO.

"Barrow."

"Dale, this is the CO." He had a sudden flash that perhaps he wasn't supposed to use the phone for what he was about to say, but he plunged in. "Get Top and tell him the QRF hour sequence commenced at 0700. The time is now 0720. I'll be in the company area in five minutes."

Barrow, if he was surprised, managed to conceal it. "I understand, sir."

I understand. Isen wondered how much any of them understood about what was about to happen. They were part of one of the army's new Light Infantry Divisions, a unit designed to move quickly to trouble spots around the globe. They could do that. Isen wasn't sure how the other company commanders felt, but he knew his company could march, patrol, fight, do all the things that would be required of them. Everything except fight tanks.

The slowdown of procurement in the late eighties had left the army, particularly the new light infantry divisions, in a tight spot with respect to tank-killing weapons. Isen had no confidence in the Dragon, the medium antitank wire-guided missile that his company would have to rely on. The LAW (light antitank weapon) was good against bunkers, sandbagged fighting positions and light-skinned armor vehicles. All it would do to a tank, Isen was sure, was piss off the crew.

Isen left the brigade headquarters, taking the stairs down to the street two at a time. He rolled the S3's packet in his hand and trotted off toward his quad, thinking about the alert sequence that had just been launched.

The QRF, or Quick Reaction Force, sequence was a very orderly plan that laid out exactly how the division was supposed to move its soldiers and equipment, weapons and ammunition, medical supplies, food and water, repair parts and vehicles, to the departure airfield. The N-hour sequence was a step-by-step, time-keyed plan for getting the QRF up in the air. The plan rested in a black binder on a shelf in Isen's office. It was typed, its pages laminated, its sections marked by colored tags. Each company commander kept his copy updated. It was the epitome of the army's penchant for plans. What Isen saw develop in the quad over the next few hours was the antithesis of "plan."

Most of the soldiers were still in PT gear. There were vehicles backed up to the company supply rooms; other trucks bringing supplies up from the Corps Support Command warehouses were parked on the grass in the middle of the quad. Great stacks of cardboard boxes and wooden crates were moving about on the barely-visible-under-the-piles legs of sweating soldiers. Isen noticed that there was concertina wire blocking the corners of the quad. There had been no time for a proper alert, so the quarantine that the plan called for wouldn't pan out. His soldiers were going to have to go home to get their equipment, their uniforms. And that meant that the word would get out. He hoped that the MPs at the gates would be able to keep the media people out for a while, at least so his soldiers could see their families in peace.

Within hours of the QRF alert, Schofield Barracks was awash in hurried soldiers moving about in vehicles and on foot. Though the plan dictated that the public telephones in the quads be disconnected—ostensibly to keep the alert a secret—there was no disguising the activity. Some of the quads were immediately adjacent to housing areas, and soon there were crowds of children and women standing on the thick lawns across the roads, watching the commotion and beginning to worry.

Connie Barrow, whose husband was the Charlie Company XO, lived only a few doors down from one of the quads. As the activity increased, she paced back and forth over the few front yards between her front door and the street, walking her baby and asking the other women on the corner what was going on. When she despaired of that, she tried to call Dale, but the lines were disconnected. She called Adrienne at work.

"Adrienne, something's going on at the quad." There was the edge of panic in her voice. It occurred to Adrienne that Connie wasn't the type to cry, but she just might scream. "I can't get through on the phone, and there have been trucks driving up and down the post here all morning.

Driving like crazy people. I tried to walk down there with the baby, but there was so much traffic, I couldn't get across the road by the PX." She paused, breathless, waiting, Adrienne supposed, for consolation or information.

"I haven't heard anything, Connie." Adrienne was surprised at how easily the lie came to her. "Why don't you try calling Bette Tilden?"

"I tried there, but no answer. I don't know what to do. Dale never tells me anything that's going on."

That didn't surprise Adrienne. She liked Dale well enough, but he was just a bit Neanderthal in the way he kept his wife in the dark. He never exactly told her not to worry her pretty little head, but Adrienne suspected it was on the tip of his tongue.

"Listen, Connie, I'm sure Dale will call you soon. When I get back up the hill I'll try to get hold of Mark and find out what's going on, okay?" Adrienne did a rough translation, in her own mind, of what she told this woman: *I don't know what's going on either, but when I panic, I'll let you know so we can lose it together.*

"Call me soon as you can. Promise?"

"I promise, Connie."

Adrienne picked up her newspaper, abandoned her open briefcase on top of her desk, and made her way down the hall. In the two years that she had worked for the county of Honolulu as a tax consultant, Adrienne had never taken a sick day. And though she had arrived at work looking healthy enough, her boss couldn't deny that she didn't look well at all as she got her things and headed back up the hill to Schofield Barracks.

Over the course of the next few days, the division was put on and off alert footing several times. They were ready to go on Thursday, the day after the initial call, but were put on hold late in the day. On Friday morning they were called out again and even moved to the airfield. But the buses were turned around. The constant turmoil was a tremendous emotional drain as the men prepared themselves psychologically, then were let down, then had to prepare themselves all over again.

In achieving a quick deployability with these forces, the

United States had added another wrinkle to the diplomatic situation. If the division went to Korea, it was an unmistakable escalation—but because the forces were pared down to be able to move quickly—in just over five hundred aircraft loads—if they faced an armored force the U.S. Army would be doing what boxers called "leading with the chin."

Adrienne tried hard to maintain her composure in spite of the emotional roller coaster she was riding on Wednesday and Thursday. On Friday morning she got into a shouting match with her boss, who told her that she shouldn't even be at work. She was as afraid of being home alone as she was of missing Mark when he did get away for a few hours.

On one level she felt that trying to maintain some sense of normalcy would help her. But as she worked around the house on Friday afternoon, doing things that she usually had to put off to the weekend, she found that she wasn't comforted at all. In fact, her anger built throughout the day as she listened to the radio and watched the news. She believed she detected a slant to the news, as if the media wanted to blame the *American* military for what was happening.

So she walked about, getting more and more frustrated with the media, and then frustrated at herself for siding with the army position. She knew that the role was odd for her; she had never been in a position to defend anything the army did. By way of consolation, she told herself that it was because her husband was going away; she wanted the world to feel as she did, as if the bottom had dropped out of her stomach.

But, by Friday evening, after the fight with her boss, she knew it was something else. Her anger had been building as the week dragged, because each day underscored how helpless she really was. No matter what she did, no matter if she continued to go to work or if she stayed home and waited for Mark to come back late in the night, nothing was going to change. Some stupid diplomatic failing a half a world away had reached over to her, out on this jewel of an island, to touch her with a diseased finger.

Adrienne knew that there was no way to affect Mark's leaving, but, as the sun set on Friday, she told herself that if he got home at all, she would do everything she could to make him forget the army.

He came home at eleven and found her waiting in the darkened kitchen when he opened the door.

"Hi, babe. You still up?"

"Of course I'm still up." Adrienne bit off the bitter retort she wanted to add. *What did you think I'd be doing, sleeping?* She reminded herself, for the ten-thousandth time, that it wasn't his fault.

He came to her, without turning the lights on, and took her in his arms. He smelled strongly of sweat, and she wondered if he had changed his clothes in the past few days. He kissed her deeply, his rough beard chafing her lips, his hands pressing against the small of her back. She started to unbutton his shirt, then pull at it when it wouldn't come, tearing the buttons off finally as her rage and her frustration mounted. She was pushing the shirt back off his arms, and when it stuck she pushed him harder, almost knocking him off balance. Mark felt her anger and passion mixed. He did not know where to draw the line himself, and he let the pent-up emotions of the days play themselves out as the two of them stripped him to the waist, then her. They stumbled against the doorjamb and sent some pictures crashing to the floor in the small hallway. They never made it farther than the living room. They lay on the floor there, sweating and panting and losing the rest of the world in the heat of the close night and the hot white of their struggle.

3

10 April · Sunday

As the predeployment phase stretched into the weekend, Isen spent more and more time in the quad. He spent Friday night with Adrienne, but slept on a cot in his office on Saturday. Hectic as it was, he was glad to have a competent first sergeant and XO. They did most of the nuts and bolts work of sorting out the company equipment and getting the men ready. Isen spent his time with Bock, the S3, and the other company commanders, working out possible contingency plans for their arrival in Korea. He also spent a great deal of time talking to the troops, trying to quiet their fears as they listened to the news reports for some word of what was going to happen in Korea.

By Sunday morning it looked as if the North Koreans had quieted down. There were no more attacks on American troops, and even the street riots faded, though that could have been due to the terrible weather on the peninsula this early April.

There were mountains of details to attend to, and Isen, the first sergeant, and Barrow threw themselves at the work with a fever born of knowing that they were getting their men ready for combat.

Soldiers had to be immunized, new men had to fire and battlesight zero their weapons, electronic equipment had to be tested and calibrated, batteries ordered, radios cleaned and checked, protective ("gas") masks cleaned and equipped with new filters for combat, communication wire rewound on spools, torn sleeping bags exchanged, broken personal gear replaced, weapons cleaned. They had to check wills and power-of-attorney papers. Men who lived in the barracks had to pack up all their personal property and move it to locked storage areas. There were refresher classes in radio procedures, encoding and decoding messages, calling for artillery fire, night firing, air assault procedures, procedures for air medevac, land navigation, chemical detection and decontamination, nuclear strike reporting, enemy vehicle identification, and load planning for aircraft and vehicles.

And for Isen, who carried the matchless burden of command, there were the men and their families to face every day. The wives came in singly, less often in twos or threes. Unable to approach the busy quad, they would wait under the dark green trees by the Post Exchange, where the division chaplain had set up tables and chairs, sensing that the families needed the kind of support that came from togetherness.

Isen had gone down there at least once a day since Thursday. He made an extra effort when he knew the soldiers would be locked in until long after dark. When they spotted him at a distance, some of the small children would run up, shouting "Daddy, Daddy!" and believing, in their pure hope, that the man in uniform was *their* man in uniform.

Isen was moved most by the youngest wives, so obviously terrified and so obviously told by their husbands that they must hold up, and by the children who were old enough to be told that their fathers were going away again.

One such was the seven-year-old daughter of C Company's communications sergeant, a beautiful dark-haired girl with doe eyes and flawless skin. Isen had seen her dozens of times before at family-day picnics, at functions on post, and, most recently, when she was waiting for her dad at the party the wives threw to welcome the men back from Team Spirit. Isen had been in the lead vehicle, and so had seen the little girl standing on the curb in front of the company, scanning the big trucks for some glimpse of the familiar face. She had been holding a flowered lei in her hand, and even from his perch in the front of the truck Isen could see that she was biting her bottom lip in nervousness and anticipation.

Then, she had been lively and bright. But when Isen saw

her on Sunday morning, she looked at him with accusatory eyes, and it dawned on him slowly that she blamed him for the invasion of her secure, predictable child's world. He was the destroyer, and this role rattled the man who had grown to think of himself as a protector of his men.

"How are you today, Angela?"

No response.

"Is that a new dress you have on? It's very pretty." Isen was fast running out of child pleasantries. With no children of his own, he was not well versed in the special talent of talking to them. He reached over to touch the fine blackness of hair on the top of her head, but she pulled away. Isen smiled awkwardly at the child's mother, who returned a blank stare. As he moved away toward another family he thought he recognized, Isen heard Angela ask him if, please, would he please let her daddy come home today?

DEFENSE INTELLIGENCE AGENCY

10 April

Background Paper for Director, East Asia Pacific Region, Office of the Assistant Secretary of Defense, International Security Affairs.

SUBJECT: Faction Split in North Korean Government

1. PURPOSE: To support Joint Chiefs of Staff decision process with regard to tensions in Korea.

2. POINTS OF MAJOR INTEREST:
   A. A strong military faction in the government of North Korea is trying to provoke a conflict with the Republic of Korea (ROK). Satellite intelligence dated 9 April shows that mobilization is under way. Goals of the military faction are:
      1. Solidifying military control of the government by instituting wartime emergency measures; perhaps even including the dissolution of civilian government agencies.
      2. Capturing the industrial base of the ROK.
   B. The military's timetable has several major components:
      1. The North Korean People's Army (NKPA) must win a victory with substantial world-wide propaganda value before the US can reinforce the Eighth US Army, Korea, with armored and mechanized forces. Final NKPA

victory will then appear to be a foregone conclusion. The military faction believes that American public opinion will not support a land war in Asia in the face of such an apparent coup by North Korea.

2. Although the NKPA currently has an edge in force ratios on the peninsula, the ROK Army is closing the gap. The buildup of the ROK Army is in anticipation of a withdrawal of US forces from Korea sometime in the next three years.

3. Political unrest and student revolt in South Korea, though largely financed by North Korea, has some basis in genuine public dissatisfaction with the South Korean government. If they move quickly, the North Koreans can take advantage of this climate to contribute to the appearance of a "people's revolt" in the South. The NKPA would then appear to be intervening on behalf of the people of South Korea against a repressive South Korean government.

C. The moderate civilian faction does not want a war with South Korea or the US. They appear to be taking steps to delay military actions until the ROK Army is in a position to thwart the NKPA, or until US reinforcements change the balance of power in Korea. To this latter end, the civilian faction may take steps to force the US to build forces in ROK. They may even go so far as to support violence against Americans, in the hope that the US government will respond.

D. Rapid reinforcement of US forces in Korea may preclude an invasion. Such a policy may be just as likely to play into the hands of the militarists, who will point to US moves as a threat to 1) North Korea, and 2) the "people's movement for democracy" in South Korea.

E. Failure to reinforce US forces in Korea is a *de facto* abandonment of the ROK. US treaty obligations make rapid reinforcement necessary.

3. COORDINATION: National Security Council

PREPARED BY: E. Harrison Wheeler
Eastern Division
APPROVED BY: A. C. Palmeter
Colonel, USAF
Vice Assistant Deputy Director for
Research

Washington, DC (AP). Monday, April 11: The White House announced today that additional US forces are being dispatched by sea to reinforce the American units already in Korea. White House spokesman Kevin Hamm admitted that the announcement was kept under wraps until the units, which will come from several stateside bases, could at least reach assembly areas on the West Coast.

Hamm denied that the US is trying to create a crisis where one does not exist.

"We have indisputable evidence that North Korea has been taking an active role in supporting antigovernment demonstrations and violence in South Korea, including attacks on US servicemen. Furthermore, satellite reconnaissance shows that the North Korean People's Army has begun moving armor and infantry units to marshalling areas along the Demilitarized Zone.

"The steps we are taking to reinforce United States Army units in Korea are legal under the treaty agreements between our country and the Republic of Korea. We want to preserve the peace in South Korea, and protect our troops already stationed there."

Pressed for details on the timetable, Hamm would comment only that the long ocean voyage was of critical importance in handling the situation in South Korea. He stopped short of saying that the US position was tenuous until heavy reinforcements—tank and mechanized infantry units—could be landed in Korea.

A spokesman for the Seafarer's International

Union said that, although all union members stand ready to do anything necessary to assist American troops, the current deplorable condition of the US Merchant Fleet will make "extraordinary measures" necessary.

"Congressional coddling of foreign business concerns and neglect of domestic industry have brought about the decline of the American Merchant Fleet, once the world's largest." He later added that only a "handful" of American-flag carriers were ready to transport US forces across the Pacific.

"Maybe the Japanese will let us borrow some of their car carriers," the union spokesman added.

A Pentagon spokesman later announced that the armored and mechanized infantry units enroute from their home bases include the 1st Cavalry Division and 2d Armored Division, from Fort Hood, Texas; the 9th Mechanized Division from Fort Lewis, Washington; and elements of the 4th Mechanized Infantry Division from Fort Carson, Colorado. Deployment of these units, which must move by sea, could take three to six weeks. The spokesman refused to comment when asked which American units are already in Korea. The US 2d Division is permanently stationed in Korea along the Demilitarized Zone, and it is believed that the air force has begun the rapid deployment to Korea of two of the army's new Light Infantry Divisions, or LIDs: the 7th Infantry Division from Fort Ord, California, and the 25th Infantry Division from Schofield Barracks, Hawaii.

4

Fort Hood, Texas

11 April · Monday

Staff Sergeant Jeb Stuart Bartow stood on the hood of his small pickup truck and surveyed the traffic jam that had him trapped. For as far as he could see along Park Avenue, which ran for almost six miles along the southern side of Fort Hood's vast collection of motor pools, there was nothing but dust and confusion.

He had wanted to bring his truck right down to his unit's motor pool, where he could then load his duffel bag of personal gear onto his tank. His crew would already be on board, well into the systems checks and preparations necessary to get them moving. But he was stuck a good mile and a half away. And all he could see between Hood Road, which intersected Park to his right, and his own motor pool, somewhere off on the left, was a sea of green vehicles. Hundreds of trucks, HMMWVs, tankers, ammunition carriers, stake and platform trucks, and Military Police vehicles vied for space on the wide street.

"This is it," he said to himself. "The shit really hit the fan this time."

Bartow had seen quite a few roll-out alerts in his time in the army. On his first enlistment, as a tank driver in the 11th Armored Cavalry Regiment in Germany, he had learned to think of himself and his fellow cavalrymen as modern-day Minutemen. Once or twice a month the charge-of-quarters, a buck sergeant on duty at the barracks, would roust them out of bed and send them down to the motor pool.

Even at his most inexperienced, he was clever enough

46

to see the otherwise sobering pattern of the alerts—the tanks moving off to darkened assembly areas, the fuel tankers and ammunition trucks with their notional cargoes, the hurried officers and NCOs—as practice, a drill. There was a seriousness to it, but at times it seemed forced. He even remembered that, on occasion, some of the NCOs who lived in family housing would bring cookies or doughnuts from home for the troops to share. And the knowledge that it was all a drill, even before the commander came along and solemnly announced it was a drill, kept a lid on the emotions.

But this was dramatically different.

Bartow had followed the news reports of the rapidly deteriorating situation in Korea. Two nights earlier he had emptied and repacked his alert bag, taking out his older uniforms—which he kept in it just to satisfy the inspection requirements of the packing list—and putting in his most serviceable BDUs, coveralls, gloves, boots, socks, and underwear. He had stuffed the bag almost to bursting.

That afternoon he had been in the Post Exchange, absently flipping through the selection of cassette tapes, when the store manager had come over the public address system.

"The commanding general has asked me to inform all our military patrons to return to their units. All military personnel please report to your unit."

Bartow had known immediately that it had to do with Korea, but he didn't feel the weight of that realization until he inched his way out of the crawling traffic and into the parking lot of the barracks at 53rd Street, where he now stood on the hood of his pickup.

There was nothing to do but shoulder the duffel bag and walk down to his motor pool. He walked west along Park, his bag on his shoulder, breathing in the diesel fumes of vehicles that roared past as if the North Koreans were at the post gate.

All along the road lay the motor pools for the huge Second Armored and First Cavalry divisions, as well as for an air cavalry brigade and various corps support units. The most impressive thing about the sprawling post was the vast number of vehicles: hundreds, thousands of vehicles of every shape and size. The most familiar of these were the M-1 tanks and the cavalry fighting vehicles of the combat units. But there were plenty more: water tankers and fuel tankers and ambulances and supply trucks and command vehicles and communications vans, forklifts and cranes and tank recovery vehicles, engineer units with dump trucks and front-end loaders, and everywhere the darting Military Police vehicles, which buzzed around the edges of the swarm like unsuccessful sheep dogs, trying to create order where there was none.

Bartow stopped three times to shift the weight of the bag from one shoulder to the other. The noise of the vehicles was stupefying, but it was the scale of the confusion that really shook Bartow. Overnight, this community of tens of thousands had been thrown into a panic. Everyone seemed to be moving at once, and the concerns of everyday life here had suddenly disappeared.

Bartow allowed himself to believe that the confusion along Park was due to units that just didn't have their stuff together. Once he entered the haven of his own unit's motor pool, things would be different, calmer. There would be someone in charge. By the time he reached the gate, drenched in sweat, he was ready for the respite.

He was almost run over by an ammunition truck just inside the gate.

"Why don't you watch where the hell you're going?" he screamed at the cab of the retreating vehicle. Everything was lost in the noise.

He made it to his tank, where his crew was clambering inside and outside of the vehicle. He dropped his bag on the ground and stared up at the machine. Bartow had been a tank commander at Fort Hood for a year, and had worked with this crew for seven months. He had drilled them on every aspect of taking care of and fighting with this monster, and they responded well. He was proud of his crew, and believed, in his heart of hearts, that they would perform as well as any tank crew in the division. They were doing exactly what he had taught them to do, with the same intensity and seriousness that he brought to the tasks. But, following his lead, their work was tempered with a sense of humor that was essential in any group that worked in such close quarters and under such stress.

"Hey, Sergeant Bartow." It was Atwater, greeting him from inside the driver's hatch, low on the front of the tank. "What's shakin'?"

Bartow had a sudden mental picture of all of Fort Hood, shaking with might and confusion, making its way toward the sea and the western sky.

"Who the hell knows?" he answered, half truthfully.

Staff Sergeant Bartow, who had been in the army for just over six years, had no way of knowing that the same scene was repeating itself in motor pools and staging areas across the continental United States. The upheaval that Bartow felt was that of all the services having to overcome peacetime inertia. For the first time since the end of Vietnam, American military forces were deploying, in strength, to a foreign land.

Bartow and his tank crewmen, consumed by the immediate task of preparing their one tank for an extended rail movement, were ignorant of any history before the last roll-out, and beyond the hoped-for signal of the end of the current drill.

Behind them, the vehicles on Park Avenue began to switch on their headlights against the falling darkness and the thick Texas dust.

5

Near Pearl City, Hawaii

15 April · Friday

Adrienne was very much aware of the melodramatic potential of her situation as she roared down H2 toward Hickam. She was sending her man off to war. Or, more correctly, her man was being sent off to war. Forget that there was no shooting over there yet. Forget that the White House was talking in terms of American presence and its probable effects on North Korean intentions. Her husband was going someplace where he had a better than average chance of being maimed or killed.

After five years of marriage, of balancing both careers, of concession and compromise ironed out, of her fighting to maintain her identity as a professional woman in an army that was—in many respects—a throwback to the 1950s, and so expected her to stay at home, it all seemed to be coming apart, bursting at the seams.

More than once she had heard an edge on the polite questions at the cocktail hour: *So when will you and Mark be having children?* She had refused to be bothered by their comments, or at least she hadn't said anything aloud that might ruffle the feathers of the wives whose husbands outranked Mark.

But now Adrienne was very much the stereotype. She raced down the hill from Schofield Barracks to Hickam Air Force Base in the hopes of arriving before the trucks that were carrying the division soldiers to the airfield.

Her ID card and officer's blue vehicle sticker got her on the base, but she could get nowhere near the flightline. She parked her car on a side street near the edge of a block of metal warehouses and set out on foot, walking toward the sound of jet engines. Suddenly the block of warehouses ended, and she could see, through the grid of the cyclone fence, the bleak vastness that was the airfield.

Mark and Adrienne had flown Military Airlift Command flights all around the world, and had been to many of the air force's largest bases. But she never could have imagined the scene before her.

Stretched out on the concrete in the crystal-bright Hawaiian sunshine were *ranks* of airplanes. She recognized dozens of the stocky C-141s, and the huge bulk of the squat, droop-winged C-5A Galaxy, painted in dark green and blue-green camouflage. There were other planes, some that looked like smaller versions of the workhorse transports. Some were painted in sandy colors—these, she realized, must be used in desert operations, and must have come from Europe or the East Coast.

She was staring, open-mouthed, her fingers locked in the fence, when an air force security policeman came up on the inside of the fence.

"Excuse me," he said.

Adrienne noticed that the airman was being towed by a huge, ferocious-looking German Shepherd. He carried his M-16 across his middle, in the style that the Israelis affected on the American news programs. Mark always complained that they were ruining the weapons we gave them, something about pulling the sights out of whack.

The men were too far off to see, just a green blur in the hot distance, spilling out of the buses and trucks and separating into distinct blobs that she knew would be platoon and company formations. Her husband, her lover, her best friend, was also indistinguishable from here, lost among the rest.

Adrienne felt a welling in her eyes, swiped at them to clear her vision. She was by herself at this end of the field. Others had gotten closer to the offload point, but were still separated from the men by the fence. She suspected that being able to see Mark, pick him out and pick out the men in C Company, might be worse than standing way off down here.

"Ma'am?"

The security policeman had been trying to talk to her for several moments. "Yes?"

"You can get closer, you know, if you go over by the MAC terminal. They won't let you inside the fence, 'course, but you can see the troops."

Adrienne didn't trust her voice to respond. The airman, embarrassed at her emotions and his inability to say anything that might comfort her, sidled away.

It had come to this. The inextricable pull of the service and tradition had brought Adrienne—the MBA, the consummate professional woman in her linen suit—to stand by herself on the edge of a concrete airstrip under a broiling tropical sun, clenching the dirty fence, her makeup running and her nails breaking, crying as her man got off one of those buses and headed toward one of those planes. She hated the whole charade with a loathing that she hadn't known was possible. All the stereotypes came rushing to memory: Penelope and the mock heroism of her loom, the women waving good-bye from the sides of the streets at the foolish parades before they knew there could be such a thing as Verdun, the camp followers, the ridiculous parodies that were the patient women rolling bandages while Atlanta burned, or Berlin, or Troy, or Moscow, or Singapore. She had believed, truly *believed,* with the soul-deep faith of the elect, that her world was going to be different.

Adrienne had resisted becoming one of the tired women in shorts and T-shirts that she saw every day as she pulled into their cul-de-sac. She felt secure in her suit, in her profession, in the cool knowledge that she had her choices before her still: when to have children, when to make career moves, when to exert the power given her by education and brains and ambition. Her options were open, arrayed before her on the bright silver platter of her future. And now her control was disappearing with her husband in a shimmering mirage of heat on the tarmac at Hickam, boarding a plane for God knew what.

On the other side of the tarmac, Isen's soldiers were exhibiting a range of reactions as varied as their personalities.

"We're going this time, we're going this time, man," Isen heard a soldier chanting behind him. "We're outta here."

He turned to see one of the mortar gunners, an always enthusiastic Alabamian named Saltor who had great plans for a triumphant return to Alabama and Auburn University when his enlistment expired in seven months.

"This is it, ain't it, sir? We're really going this time."

"Looks like it, Saltor. We haven't been inside the gates yet this week," Isen answered.

They had been through the initial stages of the alert procedure several times since the initial call-out, and like the disbelieving witnesses in the story of the boy who cried wolf, they had become skeptical. They had even gotten to the point where they allowed themselves to joke about the situation, but they had always been called back before passing the gate to the vast concrete flightline. But there was an almost palpable change in the bus as the long lines of airplanes came into sight.

Saltor was standing in the aisle, bent over at the waist so he could see from the bus windows. He was smart enough to be nervous about what was ahead, but so glad to be finally through the waiting that he surged with excitement, shifting his weight from foot to foot in a dancelike shuffle, beating a drum roll on the seat back with his hands.

Isen could see another soldier through the frame of Saltor's arms now braced on a seat back. Sergeant Dennis, a team leader in the third platoon, was quiet, and perhaps the only man on the bus who was not looking out the window. Instead, he had his rucksack on his lap, and had hold of the nylon straps that, tightened, held the load in place. Every time Saltor said, "We're going," Dennis pulled hard at the straps. His face was impassive, but Isen could see the cords on the man's arms.

"Hey, Sergeant Richards," Saltor called to his section sergeant, "we gonna spend ten hours sitting around here today like we did before we left for Team Spirit?"

Saltor looked at Isen as he said it, and the commander shook his head.

The Team Spirit deployment had been planned in

excruciating detail, and still things went wrong. Men were scratched from or added to the flight manifests at the last moment. There were last-minute changes in equipment loads. The men hurried and they waited and they hurried and they waited some more.

But the careful planning of those days had given way, today, to a heady rush that was at once frightening for its seeming lack of direction, and exhilarating for its seriousness and its power. This was most definitely not a drill. Isen knew that they would, in fact, really get off this time, and the soldiers knew it too. He looked around at their sweat-soaked faces as they hauled the heavy rucksacks from the bus floor and got ready to unload as quickly as possible.

There were dozens of air force enlisted men and a single harassed captain waiting for the battalion as the buses made a quick circle to discharge the passengers. The tires on his bus screeched in the turn, and Isen couldn't help wondering if the civilian bus drivers were participating in the excitement vicariously by driving faster than they needed to.

As soon as his bus came to a halt, Isen pulled the doors open and stepped into the blast of heat on the concrete. A sweating air force sergeant came hurrying up to him, holding his brightly colored baseball cap on his head with one chubby hand, clenching a clipboard in the other.

"Charlie Company? Is this Charlie Company?" he said, almost tripping over his excited tongue.

"Yes, this is Charlie Company," Isen replied, resisting the temptation to point at the large cardboard sign in the windshield of his bus, which had a one-foot-square "C" marked in the center. Isen wondered about the need for all the running and shouting. There was no shooting going on at this end of the trip, and he wanted his troops as relaxed as possible for the long flight. They might not get any uninterrupted sleep again for quite a while.

The air force guide started waving the clipboard in an excited flurry, addressing the whole company as they began to move off the buses.

"Let's get over here in this marked-up area," he hollered, pointing in the general direction of an asphalt rectangle marked with white tape. "Come on, come on, let's get moving. Come on, I've got another battalion coming in and due here in just a few minutes."

A couple of the soldiers who had followed Isen off the first bus started to move toward the taped area in a cluster, but Isen froze them with a glance.

"Excuse me, Sergeant," he said, "I'm the company commander, and I have very competent NCOs who work for me who will move the company where I say and when I say." He paused to let that much sink in, as much on his own troops as on the hapless air force noncom. Isen almost felt sorry for the man; he was trying to do his job, he was just going about it the wrong way.

"I'll tell you what," he continued almost paternally, "you tell me where you want us and I'll get my first sergeant to move the company."

Isen couldn't tell if his words were having the desired effect; the NCO was looking frantically from his clipboard to the ground to Isen, his mouth working like a fish's, with no sound coming out. But Isen could see, out of the corner of his eye, his soldiers forming up by the buses, the platoon sergeants firmly in control. He put his arm around the air force sergeant, and walked him gently but firmly away from the company.

"This where you want us?" He pointed to the ground, to the empty rectangle of medical tape stuck to the tarmac.

"Yes, sir."

"What else?"

"Your people will conduct a manifest call from here, sir. Please don't allow any of your soldiers to leave this area, Captain. I'll be walking you to your aircraft after the loading call."

The man was calm now, and he tucked his clipboard under his arm and walked away to join the cluster of air force loadmasters who were standing a few yards apart from the soldiers. The gap between the airmen and the soldiers, now only a few yards, loomed larger. Isen's men knew where they were going, and the airmen, now still close enough to touch, knew they would be spending the night in Hawaii.

Isen wandered a few yards away as Barrow and Voavosa conducted the final manifest call. Barrow called off the last names, and each man answered with his first name. Isen could see the aircraft they would probably board, a dark green C-141B, the air force's workhorse transport that had been around for years. Some of the battalion's vehicles were being loaded on board the plane, where they would be secured in the center of the airframe. Nylon web jump seats lined the out-board sides of the plane's aluminum belly. The inside of the fuselage was a dark cavern of wires, cables, and braces.

In spite of his first brush with the air force that day, Isen couldn't fail to be impressed with what that service was pulling off. In a relatively short period of time, the air force had managed to shift the focus of its entire worldwide mission to support this movement of army troops and equipment to Asia. There were airplanes here that had been pulled from units across the United States and Europe. And the airplanes themselves were only part of the package. They came with flight crews and ground crews and maintenance specialists and fuel handlers and security police; they had their own repair parts stocks, fuel needs, Air Traffic Control Teams, and Aerial Port Squadrons. Air Force Operations in Washington had to locate, collect, move, and distribute tremendous amounts of people and materiel, all of which were needed yesterday. He couldn't tell by looking at them, but of the four planes nearest Isen, just weeks before, two had been flying out of Pope Air Force Base in North Carolina, one had been supporting pilot training in California, and one had been shuttling engines and spare parts around NATO bases in Europe.

In order to meet the immediate need and still maintain all the regular daily peacetime missions, several states' air guard units had been called in. Two of the planes closest to Isen had CALIFORNIA AIR GUARD stenciled in black on the fuselage. Isen wondered where the men in these crews had been just a few short weeks earlier. As startled as he was to find himself flying off to a potential combat zone, these men, weekend-duty civilians, had to be doubly shocked.

But he couldn't tell from their actions. They were professional and precise, and without being able to see up close the distinctive patches that identified the guardsmen, Isen couldn't tell them from the regular air force personnel. The loading crews on the nearest planes were moving quickly, without wasted motion. The loadmasters, senior NCOs responsible for the safe loading of the aircraft, moved through the shadows under the open tail assemblies of the great machines. With the practiced motions and authoritative airs of traffic policemen, they controlled their own men and the army drivers who sat in long lines of vehicles, waiting for the signal to drive aboard.

Isen watched as a line of quarter-ton jeeps pulled smoothly up the ramp of a C-141. He supposed that these vehicles had been stripped from the Hawaii Army National Guard, as the light divisions had long ago traded in the old workhorse jeep for what the troops called the "hum-vee," the much larger HMMWV, or High Mobility Multi-Purpose Wheeled Vehicle. The problem was that the HMMWV, which belonged to a new generation of equipment, wouldn't fit into the center of one of these planes and still leave room for the soldiers to sit on either side. Isen thought about his battalion's executive officer, Major Shelby, who, over the next few days, would have to try to gather up the unit's equipment, scattered somewhere between this single airfield in Hawaii and any of a number in Korea.

Only three months before, Shelby had taken all of the battalion's vehicles on a night-road movement around Oahu's perimeter highways to give the drivers practice in maintaining a convoy formation in the dark. That operation had been firmly and centrally controlled: Shelby in a trail vehicle and the supply officer in a lead vehicle. And it was, after all, conducted on an island. Still, the night was filled with frustrating adventures: stalled and disabled vehicles, breaks in contact, and wrong turns.

Now Shelby was putting these same drivers on various sorties as the loadmasters were able to fit them in: one vehicle here, two there, as the space became available in the tremendous rush to get the equipment to Korea. In some instances there was only one vehicle from the battalion, with a driver and assistant, on a flight. As the tensions on the Korean peninsula increased, so did the threat of unconventional operations against the airfields there, and the threat that aircraft would be diverted if a field had to be shut down. There was no guarantee that any plane would be able to land at its planned destination.

Shelby had done everything he could with the drivers, but finally it came down to putting eighteen- and nineteen-year-olds, with their own vehicles to take care of, on a plane for Asia, issuing them a map and a rally point, and wishing them well.

It was only a matter of time, Isen knew, before some of his men, including the ones unused to responsibility, would have their mettle tested in a similarly drastic way.

Barrow came up beside Isen and held out the computer-printed flight manifest. "Everything checks out, sir."

"Okay, Dale. You and Top did a great job over the last couple of days, getting the company ready for the move. I appreciated the fact that I could concentrate on the planning, 'cause I knew you guys would handle everything else."

"Thanks, sir," Barrow said, somewhat embarrassed. He looked off at the planes. "Sure is a shitload of aircraft, ain't it, sir?"

"Sure is," Isen said. "Looks like we'll be going on one of these." He indicated the nearest two transports. "I was kinda hoping we'd get a civilian charter, like the ones that took us to Team Spirit."

Barrow chuckled, but Isen was only half-kidding. He would much rather have seen these cargo planes carrying desperately needed ammunition and supplies, with the troops being transported on commercial aircraft. In a national emergency the Department of Defense could commandeer airliners, which were manufactured with the capability of reconfiguring for military cargo. But the President had decided, perversely, not to interfere with the airlines' business, though calling out the air guard had pulled a lot of pilots off the commercial lists.

Isen checked his watch when he saw their load guide coming at him in what he supposed passed for a run. They had been on the airfield for only fifteen minutes; the norm in peacetime was to provide hours of "buffer" time, in case anything went wrong or had to be changed. But no one was tripping over red tape today. He hoped the maintenance crews weren't cutting any corners.

"Ready to go, Captain?" the NCO puffed as he neared Isen. Voavosa, standing a few feet behind the commander, chimed in, "We were born ready."

Isen shouldered his rucksack as Voavosa gave the facing movements that would align the formation with the rear ramps of the aircraft.

"Column of twos from the left, for-ward . . ."

The platoon sergeants echoed the command, their voices fading in a sudden blast of noise from a nearby jet.

"March . . ." Voavosa snapped off the command even as the men were leaning forward in anticipation. Isen's company stepped off to the aircraft, to this marvel of twentieth-century technology that would carry them across the world's largest ocean in less than a day, urged by parade ground commands that had remained virtually unchanged for a hundred years.

Isen stood between the twin ramps that led up either side of the plane, trying to meet the eyes of each soldier as the company boarded.

"Looking good; keep it up; stay tight there; keep closed up. Good, good, good," he chattered like an outfielder.

Some smiled nervously at him; others appeared remarkably composed. The range of their reactions was as individual as the men.

Isen got on board last, and he sent Barrow climbing to the front of the plane along the aluminum piping that held up the jump seats. The plane was nowhere near full. Pallets of cargo filled the center, leaving only a few inches of clearance where the men sitting on the seats that lined the fuselage could dangle their legs. But there were plenty of empty seats. Nevertheless, the air force crew closed the big tail of the plane, swinging the doors shut like some great mouth. The interior of the aircraft, which had only a few small portholes, became suddenly dark as the Hawaiian sunshine was cut off from view.

The noise level in the plane swelled as the pilot taxied to the take-off runway, and the sound shut each soldier off by himself. There could be no more grab-ass and kidding around to relieve the tension. Each man was forced to be his own company, and Isen watched the faces of those nearest him as they sought comfort within themselves. He could see, just around the corner of the large pallet of ration cases that was in front of him, a soldier from second platoon who had joined the company with one of the drafts of replacements they had gotten so hurriedly in the last few days. The youngster (Isen thought his name was Santeos) was fingering some sort of medal that hung around his neck. His mouth moved quickly in prayer.

Isen saw the loadmaster, who was wearing a headset through which he could talk to the cockpit and vice versa, press the earphones to his head so that he could hear above the din. He waved his man back to the side door of the now-stationary plane, then motioned him to open it. When it was halfway open, Isen saw just the very top of a camouflage cap beyond the edge of the deck.

The crew chief and the airman got down on their hands and knees and started pulling in an odd collection of stuff: a duffel bag that was only half full, so that it hung limply from its straps; a flat, black vinyl case that must have measured three feet by four, then two smaller, padded cases. Isen saw what he thought was a slide projector in one of the cases, but couldn't imagine why someone would load a projector. The hat outside had disappeared, so that the gear seemed to be levitating, appearing on its own in the frame of the door.

Then Isen saw two hands, wrapped to the forearms in camouflage material, but unmistakably feminine, reach up to the crewmen, who exchanged a quick glance—*was that a smile?* They grabbed the disembodied hands and pulled hard, producing, from the space beneath the side of the aircraft, an air force captain.

She must have stood only five feet four, and couldn't have weighed much more than a hundred pounds with her boots on. Even with her face only backlit by the bright sunshine, Isen could see that she was an attractive woman.

She had a heart-shaped face, now set in concentration as she worked to get her equipment stowed. Her hair was up under her cap, but dark whispers of it had worked their way out from around the edges, some of them stuck to the frame of her face by a light sheen of sweat. She must have run the last few yards to the aircraft with all her gear.

Even if Isen hadn't been watching, he would have known something was going on by the stir her appearance created. The men on the end of the nylon jump seats across from Isen were suddenly shoving against their buddies, pressing to make room on the crowded seat, and making little effort to disguise their urgency. Isen had to laugh at how easily they were distracted from the worries that only moments before had them dredging up forgotten prayers from Sunday school.

The airman who was assisting placed the newly loaded equipment in the large space the men had created across from Isen. He strapped the stuff down, then nodded his thanks. The two soldiers nearest him, who had cleared the room for the passenger, not her gear, shot him acid scowls.

The late arrival walked the few feet across the width of the plane to Isen's side. He moved some of his papers, shoving them under the seat into the spot already filled by his rucksack.

She sat next to Isen, giving him a thin smile as she shuffled sideways into the few inches between her seat and the cargo loaded on the center of the aircraft floor. She was wearing the air force version of the army's battle dress uniform: the same brown and green camouflage pattern, but with incongruous blue name tapes. There was nothing the two of them could say above the noise of the engines, now speeding up for take-off. Isen pulled out his maps; but now there was the slightest hint of perfume, or perhaps shampoo, mixed with the odors of boxes and vehicles and men. The men across the plane were staring, and Isen gave them an exasperated look: *All right, so you've never seen a woman?* It worked, and the soldiers tried not to stare, at least not as obviously. Though they had certainly seen women in uniform before, they—especially the youngest soldiers—acted as if this were some terrific novelty. Even in the midst of all that was going on they had enough energy to preen and stare.

The air force crew, swinging on the superstructure of the jump seats, dropped small packages of ear plugs to the soldiers. Isen could just see out a porthole opposite him, and he caught flashes of green as the mountains behind Pearl City and Honolulu flashed quickly by the accelerating plane. He felt the nose lift slightly, and the pallets and vehicles in the center of the plane shifted almost imperceptibly to the rear. He could see Barrow at the front of the aircraft, now above him in this tilted, darkened world, and he wondered again how these behemoths could lift themselves from the ground. They rolled, and the wheels sent reports of the bumps through the aircraft skin. Isen found he was holding his breath as the plane moved down the runway and finally struggled into the air.

When he breathed again, he said a silent prayer that he would be up to the new task before him. He could make out most of the faces, even in the gloom, and he recited the names he knew, all but a few of the most recent replacements. He was taking a single rifle company, one hundred and ten men in this case, on a deployment of U.S. forces that involved tens of thousands of soldiers, sailors, airmen, and marines. But he was too close to think of them as markers in some big game. To him they were individuals, each with a distinct background, with his own needs and dreams, each with a family that was worried about his safe return.

As the aircraft carrying Charlie Company nosed out over the blue water, a mile and a half away an air force operations officer circled a "271" on a computer-printed sheet he had before him.

"Mark number two seven one," he said to his assistant, who kept a duplicate log.

"Two hundred and seventy-one sorties out, two hundred and fifty more for just this unit. Think we'll make the schedule, sir?"

"Yeah, I think so," the major said.

"That's a whole lot of folks going down-range," the assistant said, "a whole lot of folks."

Once the noise had died down sufficiently for Isen to hear himself think, he turned to his seatmate.

"I'm Mark Isen," he said, extending his hand.

"Rebecca Land," she said, studying his face as they shook hands. "You the commander of this group?"

"Yeah, this is my company. How about you? What are you doing?"

"I'm headed over to brief some of the air base commanders. I'm in intelligence."

Isen couldn't tell if she was going to offer more than that. In his experience, most intelligence types enjoyed being secretive as much as they enjoyed any other aspect of their work.

"They picked a helluva time for you to be doing some traveling."

As soon as he said it, Isen realized it might sound as if he were patronizing her, saying she didn't have any business heading for a trouble spot. He knew a lot of women in the army who were sensitive to such remarks, though not without good cause, since they had to listen to a lot of disparaging comments. But he didn't like the feeling that he sometimes got, of having to walk on eggshells. She didn't take it that way; instead, she seemed glad to have someone to talk to.

"Oh, I volunteered to go."

"Is that right?"

"Yeah, my husband was pretty upset. He's not really one for the 'stiff upper lip' and all that."

"Is he in the air force, too?" Isen asked.

"No, he's a schoolteacher," Land answered, looking at Isen. "A high school English teacher."

She was almost staring at him, and Isen wondered if she was waiting for some stereotypical macho-army response, like "Why didn't you marry a *real* man?"

He gave her a deadpan look.

"I don't think he ever really thought of me as being in the military," Land went on.

"How's that?"

"Well, I'm not exactly a fighter jock. I spend most of my time behind a desk, and in the three years he's known me I've kept regular hours. As far as he can see, my job is like a regular office job where I just happen to wear the same style every day."

Isen wondered how he would feel if he were at home and Adrienne were in his seat. *Nothing could be important enough for that,* he told himself—and he got a quick flash of how Adrienne must think of *him.*

"Anyway," Land said, "this *is* what I do. I'm a North Korean specialist. I've been over there a lot, actually. I spent two out of my first three years in the service in Korea. I've only recently moved to Washington."

Land took off her cap, revealing a thick rope of dark hair that was pinned up in the back. She stuffed the cap into the cargo pocket of her trousers.

"Too bad you didn't get to see Hawaii under better circumstances."

"All I got to see of Hawaii was what we could see from the flightline," she said. "I got off one plane and hustled over to make this one."

"Did you get a box lunch?" Isen asked.

"No."

"They probably have some extra on board. I can pass the word up to have the crew chief check."

Isen leaned toward the soldier to his right, intending to pass a request from man to man to the front of the aircraft, but Land stopped him.

"No, no; don't bother. Those things always make me sick anyway. If I get hungry, I'll ask."

Isen noticed she hadn't looked down the line of soldiers yet. He supposed she wanted to blend in, not call a lot of attention to herself. That would explain her not wanting every man on this side of the aircraft to become involved in a search for a meal for her.

They flew in silence for an hour or so, Isen studying his maps while most of his men slept. He was trying to commit to memory the list of codewords he had been given with the battalion's communications plan. He always tried to memorize as many as he could so that he wouldn't constantly be flipping through his notebook. Bock tried to help by making the codes sound as if they were connected with the message.

Rest Home signaled a withdrawal from forward assembly areas, a lessening of tensions.

X-ray Tonic indicated a move from one assembly area to another, with no change in the situation.

Lariat Advance meant move forward from assembly areas to defensive positions; hostilities imminent.

And finally, isolated at the bottom of the page as if banished, the last codeword was its own advertisement: a play on the thirty-eighth parallel that divides North and South Korea, and even a reference to American involvement. *Thirty-eight North Yankee* meant that the NKPA had crossed the Demilitarized Zone and that American units were to engage them.

Meanwhile, Land paged through a black loose-leaf binder that she kept hidden from Isen by turning her body awkwardly in the small area she had.

Isen, who might not have been curious but for her obvious attempts to be secretive, finally put his maps down and asked her, "So what can you tell an infantryman that might be useful?" If what she was doing was classified, she'd certainly let him know. Isen figured he had nothing to lose.

"Well, I don't know that I know too much that would be useful to you," she said, turning back toward him. She put the binder in her lap and stretched her arms over her head. There was no place to stretch her legs. She yawned, and Isen yawned too. A few seconds later, two soldiers across the way yawned. They were still watching her.

"Some of the army intell guys I work with in the Pentagon are headed over too, to brief the ground force commanders on the NKPA. I'm going to talk to the commanders of the bases over here about the North Korean Special Purpose Forces and the threat they pose to us, to the air force in particular, I mean."

"Are their special forces like ours?"

"Well, in a lot of ways they are, I guess. But they're a lot bigger overall."

"How big?"

She opened her notebook to a blank page of lined paper, on which she drew three rectangles, their long sides horizontal.

"The Special Purpose Forces make up somewhere between twelve and fifteen percent of the KPA, the Korean People's Army, depending on whom you believe and how you do your counting."

There was a definite change in her voice, from the conversational tone to the one Isen supposed she used when she was briefing. He did the same thing—unconsciously shifted tone—when he was talking about his own specialty. People love to talk about their work. That's what makes spying a listener's game.

"There are three different overall organizations to the combat side of their SPF, their Special Purpose Forces."

She drew, in the first rectangle, an "X" that filled the box and meant, in military shorthand, an infantry unit. Above the rectangle, she put another, smaller "X" to indicate a brigade-sized unit. In the U.S. Army, that meant about seventeen hundred men.

"First, they have between twenty and twenty-five light infantry brigades, each one about the size of one of ours. These include highly trained light infantry, like our Rangers; airborne infantry, like our parachute forces; some special reconnaissance elements, probably closer to our Green Berets, and some amphibious light infantry, similar to our marines and Navy SEALs."

"That's a lot of forces," Isen said, impressed.

"There's a lot more," Land said, moving her pencil down to the next rectangle. She marked the top of this one with another brigade marker, and wrote "CA" inside the box.

"They have five Combined Arms Brigades with upwards of three thousand men in each that they will use to spearhead attacks by the regular ground forces. These people, who have all their own supporting arms—artillery, communications, armor, and their own support people—will be the first ones we see coming across the DMZ."

She looked up at Isen, whose attention was riveted to the page.

"Don't you get any of this stuff in your briefings?" she asked.

"We got something about this before we went over for Team Spirit, but it seemed watered down. It wasn't in this much detail. And it seemed to me, at the time, to be more along the lines of those briefings we always get about how the Russians are such supermen."

Land shook her head. "The American intelligence community still has a fixation on the Soviets. For forty years our whole defense establishment was geared to refighting World War Two on the plains of Europe. But that's another story.

"Getting back to the problem at hand, I don't know about supermen, but these guys are pretty tough. More on that later. This last designation is the one you'd be most likely to encounter. These are the divisional light infantry battalions, and they're a whole different group. What they've done is give each commander of a regular division a dedicated battalion of his own Special Purpose Force guys to use kind of like a first string, the varsity, you know? They'll spearhead his assaults, isolate enemy units, infiltrate enemy positions, or conduct attacks immediately behind enemy lines. These guys will be operating from the front line to anywhere from fifteen to thirty kilometers behind the FEBA."

She drew a scalloped line across her page to indicate the FEBA (fee-ba), or forward edge of the battle area. Isen didn't know if she thought the army spoke another language, or if she thought he was just another dull, knuckle-dragging grunt.

"So your guys," he asked, "the base commanders, are worried about whom? The airborne light infantry brigades?"

"Yeah. The main mission of the airborne units is to hit the U.S. and ROK Air Force bases in South Korea. They don't have a lot of airlift capability, so we don't think they can get more than two brigades down south at any one time. Then once they get them there, they're going to have a hard time sustaining them. But these guys aren't unused to the idea of suicide missions. And it would take only a few units and a few days of operations to really screw up our ability to reinforce by air."

"We're supposed to get all our supplies—even ammunition—by air in the initial stages of this thing, until we can get some seaborne reinforcements," Isen said. He chewed his bottom lip. "Suicide missions, huh?"

"Yeah. These are the guys who tried to blow up South Korean President Chun Doo Hwan in 1983 in Rangoon. The whole team was wired with explosives so they could blow themselves up to avoid capture. And in 1968 they staged an attempt on the president's life right in Seoul, at the presidential residence."

"Kind of sounds like the stories of the Japanese in the Pacific in World War Two," Isen said. "You know, where they killed themselves rather than be disgraced by surrender."

He paused, thinking about a picture he had seen of a ragged Japanese soldier, not a Special Purpose Forces type, but a regular soldier, with his big toe stuck in the trigger guard of his rifle, the muzzle in his mouth. Defeat or surrender were too disgraceful to live with. *How can you fight people like that? How can you know what they're thinking?*

"So tell me about the guys we'll be facing," he went on.

"Wait," Land said, "let me get something out of my other case."

"Can I let my XO and first sergeant in on this? I'd like to have all the leaders hear this, but the room back here just won't accommodate us."

"Sure, I don't see why not. I'm only telling you stuff you could read about in a library. Call them back."

Isen sent word up for Barrow and Voavosa to join him. It took a few minutes to get the two men back over all the sleeping soldiers, then have those on the end move up to make room. When they were more or less settled, Isen introduced Land and said she had a lot of information about the North Koreans.

Voavosa studied Land intently. He couldn't get used to

the idea of women in uniform. In his assignments in the all-male infantry, he hadn't had occasion to work side by side with many women. And although all the women he had seen during his two tours away from the infantry, as a drill sergeant and at ROTC duty at the University of Michigan, had been very competent, he still couldn't get used to the idea. He knew all about the political implications and the arguments that women were more than capable of contributing to the defense, and on and on. But his outdated attitude persisted. Forcing himself to confront it one day, he'd traced it back to a memory from his adolescence.

He remembered that as a kid, during the war in Vietnam, he had seen a copy of *Life* magazine that showed pictures of all the GIs who had been killed during this one week of the war, the worst one for casualties that the conflict had seen. There were pages and pages of the tiny snapshots: high school pictures, photos from basic training, pictures with kid brothers and moms and dads. The young men stared out at him from the grainy photos and the oblivion of an early death, and he remembered wondering what they would say to him if they weren't silent. Years later, when he saw women recruits in basic training, he wondered if America, distraught as she was about seeing page after page of her wasted sons, was ready to see her daughters like that.

But if he was old school, he was smart enough to know when he had a shortcoming, and he knew his narrow view was his problem. So he kept his mouth shut about it. Still, he was curious as to what this young captain could tell him that he didn't know about Korea.

"There are two groups of the SPF you might see," Land went on. Then she remembered that Voavosa and Barrow hadn't been following all along. "I'm sorry, Special Purpose Forces."

She sounds like a teacher, Voavosa thought.

"The first units are these light infantry battalions, one assigned to each regular division of the Korean People's Army. These guys will operate from the FEBA to a depth of fifteen to thirty klicks. Their missions will be attacks in support of the division's scheme of maneuver: in other words, flanking, enveloping, or even leading. They'll also go after command and control centers, communications and intell gathering assets within their area. They don't have a sophisticated system for radio direction finding, but they're very good at operating the one they do have. They'll also cut LOCs, lines of communication and supply, to the front line units. They may even get behind us before an attack by the regular units to stop our reinforcements from reaching the battle area. They'll do some reconnaissance, and they're available for any other sticky missions the division commander wants to use them for."

Isen looked at Barrow and Voavosa, both of whom seemed impressed.

"What kind of equipment they got?" Voavosa asked. "I mean, how will we know when we're seeing SP forces as opposed to the regular guys?"

Good question, Isen thought. He turned to face Land, who looked Voavosa right in the eye and said, "I wish I had an airtight answer for you, First Sergeant, but I don't, and I'm not going to try to bullshit you."

Voavosa was impressed by her candor, and he suppressed a smile only by reminding himself that he didn't get a satisfactory answer.

"We don't have accurate tables of their equipment; at least we can't yet pinpoint what equipment will distinguish them from regular troops. We do know they've been modernizing with a lot of the stuff the Chinese and Soviets have been selling after reductions in their forces—the big Communist bloc garage sale."

Barrow smirked. Land wasn't smiling.

"One of the reasons I volunteered to go over there," she said, "is to try to get some picture of the organization and state of these forces."

Voavosa was genuinely surprised. *You volunteered to come over here, you little slip of a girl?* And he might have said it, too, not out of viciousness, but out of concern. But Land was an officer, so Voavosa kept it to himself.

"See," she said, "we're concerned about the worldwide capability of these SP forces. We think they might try to go after our bases in Japan and the Philippines. It's not inconceivable that they might even go after bases in Hawaii or the mainland, especially if they already have agents in the States. The problem is that we've only just been allowed to start working with the FBI on the list of suspects." Suddenly she caught herself rambling, and Isen could see the conscious effort she made to reel in her speech.

"The air base commanders are most concerned with the light infantry brigades, especially the airborne troops. They'll be used against strategic targets—like our bases. The other unit you might see," she said, going back to the diagram she had drawn, "is the Combined Arms Brigade. These are self-sustaining combat units with organic support elements. These are the guys who will lead the charge through the DMZ. They have self-propelled artillery and each brigade has a tank battalion. There are a couple of courses they would probably follow."

She turned to a small map that showed just the outline of the central peninsula. There were lines and arrows on the map, showing at least five avenues for advances across the DMZ. Most of the combat power was concentrated on the western side of the peninsula, pointed directly at Seoul or at the highway system that connected the city to the rest of the country. Seoul sits at the edge of a flat coastal plain that extends along the western edge of the peninsula, tucked against the sea to the west and the DMZ to the north. The shortest routes, Isen noticed, led through Uijongbu, a suburban city that sat on a critical crossroads northeast of Seoul. He had spent there the one day he had off during the last Team Spirit exercise.

"It all seems so *studied,*" Isen said.

"How's that?" Land wasn't following.

"I mean, they have these routes worked out and probably have informers in place and they probably know every foot of road in the south."

Land closed her book, holding her place with one open hand. "They've been preparing for this war—if that's what it's to be—since 1953. These are two countries with sizable armies and negligible military concerns outside this peninsula—a land mass about the size of Minnesota. They're packed in tight, and, yeah, I guess it *is* a studied scenario."

"So what kind of troops are we talking about here?" Barrow asked. He had been uncharacteristically quiet. Isen figured it was because Land was a woman, and because she obviously knew her stuff.

"In general, I guess the SPF soldiers are a lot like our own special operations guys: the SEALs, Green Berets, Rangers, what have you. They get training in infiltration, mountaineering, night combat, swimming, combined arms operations, martial arts, and intelligence-gathering methods. They have a very rigorous physical fitness program. None of that is news to anybody in the infantry, I guess, but their discipline is much, much more harsh. They expect instant obedience, and they get it. They know they're going to have to fight a numerically and technologically superior enemy, so they plan to do it fast. They know how to work alone, they can live off the land, they're used to physical hardships—going hungry, being cold, working without sleep. They live in a country where the norm for comfort among *civilians* would make a lot of American soldiers complain. And so they go a lot further in their training. As a result, they get tough, well-trained fighters who can travel farther and faster with more equipment and less food than just about any soldier in the world."

What a speech, Barrow thought.

Land looked around at the men she was talking to. They all had skeptical looks on their faces, just as she expected. She supposed that even if she were a man granted the privilege of talking about such things as physical toughness, she would still have trouble with an audience of army infantrymen. She found that they usually thought that no one could possibly have it tougher than they did.

"My bosses, after I give them an overview of all the skills, like to say that our guys get the same training. And because we have more resources, our guys get it more often, et cetera. But there's another side to this. One of the big things the Special Purpose units stress is the political indoctrination of their soldiers. A soldier can't get into the SPF unless he's politically reliable, and they even have to come from a politically reliable family. The problem is that westerners think that "political" means the same thing to the North Koreans as it does to us. It doesn't. It translates more closely to what we might think of as "religious." Because they don't have accepted religion, this struggle against the capitalists and their imperialist overlords is all they have. And they call it politics. But when they come across the wire, they're gonna have the same zeal that religious fanatics have. Remember all those drafts of volunteers the Iranians kept getting during the war with Iraq? The fools were clamoring to go out and get killed by the thousands because a holy war was a way to get into heaven. Well, these people don't have a heaven, but they sure as hell have a holy war."

Isen looked from the maps to Land, who was completely and remarkably absorbed in her words. And in that instant, staring into the face of this young woman with the terrible messages, he knew that she wasn't grandstanding or trying to impress them; it was all true. And something inside him, some unnameable sense, told him he would see it all. Everything that she had talked about in her apocalyptic vision would come to pass, and he would be there to see it.

6

Osan Air Force Base, South Korea

17 April · Sunday

The flight from Hickam to Osan was supposed to take thirteen hours. But because of delays in refueling at Guam, and thanks to a terrorist scare on the airfield, it was well over twenty-one hours before the plane touched down at its destination. During all that time, the men and the one woman had to share a single portable toilet located at the front of the cargo area. They had been issued only one meal, a box lunch consisting of greasy chicken, a stale roll, some crackers, and a heavily sugared juice that served only to make them more thirsty.

When they were forty-five minutes out of Osan, Isen had the men stow their field jackets and put on their load-bearing equipment: the pistol belts heavy with ammunition and hand grenades. They strapped on protective mask carriers and helmets, and adjusted rucksack straps. One soldier tied and retied his boots several times—anything to work out the nervousness. The small ritual of dressing, of a soldier's preparation—as familiar as it was, was somehow new. Isen had told his men that they could encounter anything from a warm welcome from the base commander to gunfire on the airstrip, and now the soldiers grimly prepared for the worst.

Land watched them closely. As the aircraft slowed and the noise level jumped dramatically, she mouthed "good luck" to Isen, who answered with what he hoped was a confident smile.

Osan Air Force Base, some forty miles south of the capital city of Seoul, is bordered on the east by a series of low mountains that only hint at the rough terrain to be found to the east, farther inland. The plane came in low, in order to reduce the time it was a ready target for any terrorist with a shoulder-fired surface-to-air missile, flying what pilots called "nap of the earth." In smaller aircraft this meant hugging the ground so as to stay out of sight. In the one-hundred-and-sixty-eight-foot-long C-141B, nap-of-the-earth flying was an approximation. The aircraft was not so maneuverable that the pilot could hug all the nuances of the terrain, but the ride was still plenty rocky for the men inside. The jinks, turns, and sudden loss of altitude on the rough approach, combined with the greasy lunch, the stale air, the single, inadequate latrine, the smell of all those unwashed bodies crammed on board, and the fact that almost no one could see the horizon (the horizon being a steady and traditional source of comfort for the airsick), and Isen soon had a planeload of very sick soldiers on his hands.

Men were heaving into their helmets, onto the deck, and into the pitifully inadequate airsick bags that the airmen had provided before they very cleverly got out of the way. Isen could see the loadmaster's crew, forced by their jobs to be at the rear of the plane, all turned toward the after bulkhead. They had no desire to watch the soldiers get sick.

A queasy Isen looked over his men, many of them pale and slightly green-looking in the dark light of the cabin, and thought about what a show they would make for someone on the ground expecting a group of military saviors to get off the plane.

Isen had flown into Osan Air Force Base several times, so he had some idea about what he was going to see when the plane's cargo doors swung open. But as the sunlight came flooding in and the airmen nearest him scrambled to get the narrow troop-loading ramps in place as quickly as possible, a wave of sound flooded the cabin.

For the sake of safety in what is inherently an unsafe place, most air force runways and flightlines are pictures of order. The men in the tower exercise iron-fisted control over everything that goes on. But it looked to Isen as if some madman were controlling what was going on.

There were vehicles parked all along the edges of the tarmac, many of them army vehicles being loaded by gangs of Korean civilian laborers. Other trucks were roaring by, dodging in and out of the groups of people moving on the flat blackness. As soon as the ramps were in place, the loadmaster gave Isen a curt nod, and Isen started down the nearest ramp, which bowed slightly under the combined weight of him and his equipment. He had told himself that the first thing he must do when he saw daylight again was to get oriented—find out exactly where he was on the vast base—so that he could move his company out of harm's way if they got hit. But Isen, map and compass out and balanced in his hand, could see almost nothing beyond the circle of swirling vehicles. Instead of the smells of new spring vegetation and jet exhaust, there was only the sooty flavor of burning plastic and rubber. When he looked back to see how his men were unloading, he saw the skeleton of a burning aircraft just in front of the plane he had left. There were several fire trucks around the wreckage, spraying the area with foam. Large wreckers waited to drag the remains out of the way of the base operations. Isen flexed his toes inside his combat boots, glad to be on the ground once again.

He could see that Barrow and Voavosa, at the other end of the company, were moving the men off in good order. The soldiers hustled down the ramp, rifles at high port, chinstraps fastened, the excitement of the moment making them alert once more.

Satisfied at the progress of the offloading, Isen turned to his front. Land had disappeared into a waiting air force sedan, but, surprisingly, there was no one there to meet Charlie Company. He looked for a place to lead his company off the busy airstrip, and saw what looked to be some sort of maintenance garage just beyond the terminal operations building. He turned and met Voavosa's eyes, then pointed to where he wanted the men to move. The first sergeant had them hustling within seconds.

This was the part of the base where they began the Team Spirit deployment, Isen remembered. At the end of that flight to Korea, they had been met by a welcoming committee from the brigade supply shop. They were told where and when they could eat, where they would meet their transportation, and how soon they could bunk down in a tent city already set up for them. Today Charlie Company breezed by the terminal, which was full of American civilians, presumably waiting to go back to the U.S. on the plane Charlie Company had just unloaded.

They skirted the edge of the terminal, Isen's company following him like a snake winding through the buildings, until Isen reached the maintenance shed he had sighted. There was no one inside. He instructed the first NCO in line to keep the rest of the company moving in out of sight, then he walked back to where he found Barrow.

"Any sign of anybody from brigade or division?"

"No, sir, I didn't see a thing, except that goat screw out on the flightline."

Isen's order, originating at division level, had been to get on the ground, where he would be met by a representative from a higher headquarters. Tilden, not trusting that everything would go smoothly, had worked out a contingency plan for his company commanders, selecting areas around the air base as possible meeting places for them to use if they got separated. But Charlie Company was the first of the battalion's units on the ground. Until Tilden and the other companies arrived, Isen was supposed to make contact with someone from the brigade staff. The staff would, presumably, let the battalions know where to go. Isen looked at his map, where he had Tilden's rally points marked in red grease pencil.

"The closest rally point is a good distance around this way," he said as he raised his arm. Barrow looked up at the sun to get his bearings.

"Around to the north, right, sir?"

"Yeah. What I want you to do is to find a vehicle, if you can, or a ride, and look for somebody from our battalion at the rally point. If that doesn't work, go find somebody from brigade or division. We've had planes landing here continuously for twenty hours. I can't believe there's nobody here to meet us."

"Okay, sir," Barrow replied.

"David is trying to raise somebody on the radio," Isen said, referring to his radio operator, a soldier with the unlikely name of Davis David. "But he's not having any luck; see what you can find out."

Barrow turned back toward the churning confusion of the main base area. Isen called him.

"Hold on there, Dale. You've got to have a contingency in case we're not here when you get back."

Barrow, who knew well that one of Isen's tenets was "Expect the unexpected," whistled through his teeth.

"Guess I'm getting a little ahead of myself, sir."

"That's okay; you'll do fine once you get in the swing of things." Isen held out his map, folded to show the northern edge of the base. "Now, if we're not here when you get back, look for us or a guide here." He made a mark on his map.

Barrow drew a small circle on his own map at the road junction Isen had indicated.

"Got it, sir."

"You have a radio?" Isen asked.

"Yes, sir."

"Okay," the commander went on, "good hunting."

Isen walked back to the shed. Inside, up against the wall nearest the airstrip, at least a dozen of his men were standing on what looked to be some sort of wooden platform. They were looking out the building's only window, and Isen could see, framed just beyond them, the column of smoke from the burning jet as well as the helter-skelter rush of vehicles that did anything but inspire confidence.

Isen saw the idleness as a potential problem.

"Okay, platoon leaders, let's get these men together and get weapons checked out. Make sure everybody has all their stuff. Supply," he called.

The company supply sergeant, Sergeant Geist, a fiery Arizona native who had just been promoted, answered immediately.

"Right here, sir." Geist and two privates were off to one side of the company, handing out some loaves of bread.

"Where the hell did you get those things?" Isen asked.

"The folks inside." Geist gestured back toward the large building that housed the terminal and a convenience store for the air force personnel. "They were getting rid of a bunch of stuff. I guess they figure they won't be needing it anymore, sir." He ended with a small smile.

Isen was surprised to see the loaves of bread, but not at all surprised at Geist. The supply sergeant had been on the ground for less than a half hour and was already scrounging extras for the men. He was never happier than when he was handing stuff—especially food—out to the grunts.

"I want you to start scouting around here for a water source, but don't get too far away," Isen told him.

The NCOs already had the men grouped by platoons and squads. They were checking weapons and ammunition loads, repacking the things the men had taken out of their already tight rucksacks. Isen put them to work because he believed that that was the best way to keep their idle minds from feeding on the fear already among them. They, and he, had been riveted by the sight of the aircraft burning on the runway. Isen wondered if that plane had also been carrying division troops.

Charlie Company stayed put for nearly two hours. Isen,

whose patience was at a breaking point after thirty minutes, would have left before that but for Barrow, who came back periodically to give his commander reports on what he was finding. First he told Isen that there was no one at the battalion rally point, but he thought he could get transportation. Then he came back and said he had lost the transport, but had found someone from brigade supply who was to tell them where their new assembly areas were. Then he left again. Finally, Barrow came back with a sergeant first class in tow. The NCO had a helmet, but no weapon or load-bearing equipment.

"Sir," he said to Isen as he approached, "I'm Sergeant Sellers from brigade supply."

"What can you tell me, Sergeant?" Isen asked.

"I have some trucks, ROK trucks, under my control until 1500. I should be able to move you to your assembly area in those if they get back from the run they're on now."

Isen glanced at his wristwatch. It was 1330. He had set it to local time almost as soon as they got on the plane, as if that would convince his body to get into synch with the hours on the Korean peninsula.

"Okay. Why don't you show me where that assembly area is?" Isen said as he pulled his map from his pocket. He squatted on the floor so he could spread the sheet out, but Sellers didn't follow suit.

"Er, I thought somebody from operations was supposed to brief you on the location, sir. Didn't anybody talk to you?"

"No." Isen stood up abruptly, dismissing the possibility of getting useful information from anybody on the ground.

"No sweat," he went on. "You just get me the trucks, and I'll tell you where I want to go."

"Roger that, sir. I can handle that." Isen noticed that Sergeant Sellers was greatly relieved. He had probably been set on the ground with little or no idea as to what was going on. Hell, he didn't even have a weapon. But, like a good NCO, he had probably worked his butt off to get hold of some trucks, no small feat in light of the confusion that was gripping the airfield. But he had no idea what to do with these infantry companies as they unloaded. Isen wasn't about to make him responsible for Charlie Company. "Thanks a lot, Sergeant," Isen said, ending the conversation.

Sergeant Sellers touched the brim of his helmet with his fingertips, turned on his heel, and trotted off to where another aircraft was unloading.

"Sir?" It was Barrow, who had been listening to the interview. "Do you know where we're supposed to go?"

"Well, no," Isen admitted. "I mean, nobody's at our battalion rally point yet, and no one from higher up can tell me where to go. But I do know that we need to get out of here, and get to someplace where we can defend ourselves, if need be, until we link up with our chain of command."

Barrow took the map from Isen's hand and began to study the area surrounding the base. Isen watched as another aircraft began to disgorge its cargo of infantrymen. His flight had held just his company, and there were a lot of empty seats. Isen had deployed with one hundred and ten men, and the aircraft was configured to carry one hundred and forty-three, up to two hundred in a tight situation. He watched as at least two companies of infantry squeezed out of the single plane. The load planning at the other end was that haphazard; some planes were leaving only partially filled, others overfilled. But in the context of what the air force had pulled off in such a short time, Isen couldn't find anything to complain about.

David interrupted Isen's reverie.

"Sir, it's the battalion commander," he said, handing Isen the radio handset.

"Uniform zero seven, this is alpha zero seven, over," Isen said into the mouthpiece. He'd consulted the card with the callsigns that David wore in a plastic shield that was strapped to his forearm.

"This is uniform zero seven, over," the handset said. Isen was grateful to hear a familiar voice on the radio, something he recognized amid the chaos that was engulfing the base.

"I want you to move to vicinity checkpoint one three, over," Tilden said, clearly and concisely. There seemed to be some order creeping into Barrow's "goat screw."

Isen took his map back from Barrow. Bock had given him several tracing paper overlays to apply to his maps, one of which had a series of checkpoints that the battalion operations officer had made up for their use. The points were numbered circles, placed over clearly identifiable terrain features, and different from the few rally points Tilden had designated. The checkpoints gave the company commanders a frame of reference so they wouldn't have to use the names of terrain features ("meet me at the bridge") over the radio. No matter who was listening, only the people with the overlays would know the locations they were referring to.

"Wilco, over," Isen said as he found the checkpoint, which was on a hilltop about five kilometers to the east. That meant they would have to go around the airfield and through the adjacent town, since they were now on the west side. He decided not to wait for Sellers and the trucks that might or might not arrive. They'd walk.

Isen did some quick calculating in his head, figuring how long it would take them to get there. "ETA nine zero minutes, over," Isen said, giving Tilden his estimated time of arrival.

"Understand nine zero mikes. This is uniform zero seven, out."

"One thing about old Colonel Tilden," Isen said to David, "he isn't one to BS around. Just get to the point and move out."

David didn't say anything. Radio operators were frequently privy to conversations that went beyond the concerns of their rank. Some commanders confided in these much younger soldiers. Others were given to angry outbursts on the radio, in front of their operators. But word of such histrionics always got back to the men in the ranks, and never did much for the officer's credibility. Soldiers, who felt it was their privilege to second-guess all officers, nevertheless wanted the officers to present a solid front of agreement.

Isen was in a singular position as commander. He had no peers in the company with whom he could talk about his personal concerns. Every other soldier had someone close to a peer to talk to, to unburden with. Even Voavosa had the platoon sergeants, who were close to him in age. But Isen had to be completely self-reliant when it came to handling his own doubts and fears.

Isen didn't show off for David. He treated the younger man with respect, and knew when to draw the line with how much he revealed. Nevertheless, Isen appreciated having David, who was bright, articulate, and knew when to keep quiet, to talk to.

For his part, David was thinking how similar Isen was to Tilden, and he took comfort in that. He had a great deal of trust in Isen, and he liked knowing that the boss one echelon up had the same kind of common sense.

Isen sent runners to round up his platoon leaders. Within a few minutes his four lieutenants; his mortar section leader, a staff sergeant named Arthur Richards; and First Sergeant Voavosa gathered around. Isen spread his map on the concrete floor.

"Okay, this is what we have. Colonel Tilden is somewhere on the east side of the airstrip. We're going to move out along this small access road here"—he indicated the track, a solid black line on the map, with his finger—"and make our way to the east. We should be able to get out through this gate, though it might be crowded if there are a lot of civilians trying to get on the base. There's a town, a city really, just outside the gate here. Once we're clear, we'll head for checkpoint one three, which is here." Isen pointed to the spot with the tip of his pencil, and he looked around at his subordinates as he did so. They were all busy making notes on their maps, and as Isen looked at them, the thought occurred to him that he was about to lead his company on their first move in what might, very shortly, turn out to be a combat zone. He wiped his mouth with the back of his hand, then hesitated for just a moment, until all eyes were on him again.

"We're in the big leagues now. I think the men will be alert, because they're pumped up with what's going on. But that won't last long 'cause they're tired. That's when we start to do stupid things. Let's be careful. Make sure that every weapon is on safe. Pass the word as to where we're going and how long it's going to take us to get there. Let's stay alert; I have no idea what to expect when we hit the ville and the countryside. Any questions?"

There were none. They were all anxious to get moving, to put as much distance between themselves and the chaotic base as they could. Isen wished he could promise them that things would be more sane once they left the airfield. "The order for the march is one, two, mortars, three. I'll be with the lead platoon." He checked his watch. "We move in ten minutes."

Nine minutes later, Isen was standing by the west-facing double doors of the building. He checked the set of his rucksack, and turned to look back over the company. They were ready to move because he had taught them that move time is move time, and it doesn't mean you're ready a half minute later.

But he was more impressed with something he hadn't expected. There was a calmness to their posture that he guessed belied what they were feeling inside. They stood casually, their rifles across their middles, resting comfortably still against the weight of the rucksacks that had not yet started to bite into shoulders. He knew, as he gave a one-finger "go ahead" signal to the lead platoon, that the men were performing for one another, for the group. Isen hoped the calm was infectious.

They swung out onto the narrow service road, past an overturned forklift and some abandoned crates. It was obvious that the base was straining just to get the aircraft in and out. All other operations were suspended.

As they moved around and out from behind the warehouses, Isen and his soldiers could see more of what was going on. Isen supposed that the Korean civilians he saw loading the trucks had been pressed into service by the ROK military. There were South Korean soldiers helping pass crates from the aluminum air force pallets, and South Korean officers were supervising. Isen wondered how American civilians, so used to their day-to-day independence, would react to such a demand, even in the face of an obvious national emergency.

The company moved in two files, one on either side of the road, staggered along the sides, weapons facing out. Voavosa walked up from the rear of the formation, where he had started the march. He had been talking to the soldiers all along the sides of the road. Isen could hear his progress as the soldiers traded banter with him.

"Hey, Top, where do you reckon we're going here?"

"Hell, I don't know. I thought I signed up for the cruise package."

Isen turned as Voavosa got closer. "How you doing, First Sergeant?"

"Pretty good, Captain. I'm just glad we heard from the old man. Wasn't nobody at that base who could tell us which end was up. I wonder if the whole division's this screwed up."

"I wonder if the whole country is this screwed up," Isen added.

"Yeah, and the shooting hasn't even started yet."

Isen nodded toward the runway, where they were now abreast of the burning wreckage of the plane.

"Well," Voavosa continued, "not officially. I wonder if they had a crackup."

"My guess is that everybody is in such a hurry that there are going to be a lot more accidents. We'll have to be careful ourselves."

Voavosa didn't answer. He was staring ahead at the gate to the American base. Lines of Korean civilians stretched away from the gate for hundreds of yards in either direction.

"I wonder what they're doing there," Voavosa said.

"I heard that the South Korean government isn't letting people leave their homes, even Seoul."

"They're *making* them stay?" Voavosa asked, the surprise evident in his voice.

"Yeah. Major Bock told me that our side expects the North Koreans, if they come across, to head for Seoul. And that fits with what that air force captain told me on the plane. So the ROK government is taking drastic steps to keep the roads south of the city clear of refugees. You know, so they can move reinforcements around."

Voavosa shook his head. "Can you imagine our government telling New Yorkers they couldn't leave the city, even though they were expecting an attack from Long Island?"

"It's pretty wild. But these people have been living with

this possibility since 1953. And, in spite of what we see on the American news, most citizens here are used to obeying the government. Compared to the U.S., this place is like an armed camp."

"That's true," Voavosa agreed, "but compared to how the comrades up north live, this place is Disneyland."

Voavosa had been stationed in Korea twice during his career. The first time, as a young private, he had been up on the DMZ, running patrols and trading shots with the North Koreans in exchanges that the American public rarely heard about. He had been married—for a short time—to a Korean woman. He had a fine appreciation for the people; for a westerner, it was a remarkable appreciation.

"'Course, you know what the news will show back home," the first sergeant continued. "They'll show something like this business of keeping the refugees out of the way and call it oppression, an example of why we shouldn't support the South Korean government."

Before he had joined the army, before he volunteered to become an infantryman, Isen had wondered how he would feel in just this position. He had suspected then that the most likely conflict he might encounter would be in Central America. Criticism of the governments the United States supported in that area of the world seemed, to him, justified. He had been wary of rushing into the army without at least trying to anticipate the moral problems that might face him: could he fight to sustain an allied government that he, personally, found repulsive? He found few chances to talk about such concerns in the company, and he was wary of sounding preachy.

"So what do you think?"

"I think that when the bad guys are ready to come across the border, all that debate about the finer points of civil rights is a luxury. These people aren't in some constitutional debate. They're talking about the survival of their country, their way of life." He paused, and Isen saw him staring at the Korean people closest to them as they approached the wall of civilians.

"I think we got a lot of damn nerve," Voavosa went on, "pretending that we can understand what's involved with their problems, sitting back there all safe and warm in

Washington and trying to make decisions for what's going on here."

As they got closer to the fence, Isen saw that the crowd was made up of women and children, with only a few old men mixed in. The adults remained quiet as the Americans approached, but the children waved enthusiastically, and Isen's soldiers responded as they always did, calling back to the children and digging into their pockets for candy or gum. He saw a few bright packages flash through the air as the soldiers tossed their gifts. The children squealed in delight, the screeching adding to the disconcerting noise coming from the tarmac behind them.

The area just beyond the gate was packed five deep with Korean civilians. Charlie Company would have to pass through the press of people, who formed a silent gauntlet from the gate. Isen thought it would be a perfect time for a terrorist to strike. A few of his soldiers, perhaps thinking the same thing, moved their weapons so that they had a better grip on them. But the crowd welled backward and parted, the people only a few feet away, staring at them quietly, intently. More than ever, Isen felt that he was stepping off into a situation he didn't, perhaps couldn't, understand.

The air security policeman at the gate gave Isen a sharp, almost exaggerated salute.

"Well, that's it, Top, we've left the world."

"Yeah, we've left something, anyway. Like the lady said, 'This ain't Kansas, Toto.' But I sure as hell don't know what it is yet."

The town that depended on the air base comprised two or three square miles of crowded concrete buildings. They moved through the narrow streets lined with shops that catered to the base's American servicemen. There were steamy laundries; seedy-looking bars; tailor shops that copied suits from pictures in dog-eared American magazines; barber shops where, for a few dollars, one could get a haircut, a shave, a massage, a manicure and, in a few of the establishments, a considerably more personal service, all without leaving the chair. There were food stands that occupied little more than a few feet in front of some shops. On most nights, garish yellow lights shone down on pots of seafood, mussels and sea cucumbers, tangles of yellow noodles, and the pungent, ubiquitous pickled cabbage, kim'chee. Isen, in deference to a weak stomach, avoided eating at those kinds of places. Still, he'd loved to stand in front of them and watch the hurried cooks and smell the thick, sweet aromas that he would forever associate with Korea, with his travels, with his youth.

The buildings were wood frame or concrete, and they were tightly packed to make use of all the available space. Isen remembered a ride on a Korean train—the houses that lined the tracks were shoved as close as possible to the right-of-way, so that it always looked as if the passing cars would take down building parts with every pass. This same parsimony was the rule in the countryside, where every foot of available flat space seemed to be cultivated.

The few trees spaced in planters along the municipal street were just starting to show green, and the air had a warmth that belonged only to the afternoon. Isen knew from experience that it could still turn cold at night, with the thermometer dipping as far as the low forties, even as late as mid-April. But the overwhelming colors were grays and blacks: the light gray of concrete construction, the black and white uniforms of the schoolchildren, even the signs were uniformly black and white.

Even here, in the city, Korea was a land of strong smells. In the countryside it was the smell of fresh-turned fields and manure fertilizer and animals kept in the very courtyard of the country farmer's house. In town the smell was of ondol, the charcoal that Koreans used to heat their houses. The fuel—cylinders of charcoal—burned in braziers along the foundations of buildings, and the hot exhaust was channeled under the floors of the houses. But if there was the slightest leak in the varnished covering of the floor, the house would quickly fill with carbon monoxide, suffocating the sleeping inhabitants. Every year these accidents killed several American servicemen and dozens of Koreans. Despite warnings, GIs always wound up sleeping in women's houses in town. One of the companies in the division had lost a soldier—he and his girlfriend asphyxiated as they slept during the most recent Team Spirit exercise.

* * *

As they walked, the men watched the few civilians that were on the streets. The Korean reaction to seeing Americans had previously been confined to two extremes. During the parades orchestrated by the local government to welcome the troops participating in Team Spirit, the people had lined the streets and waved their little Korean and American flags. And although Isen knew that such parades were staged, there still seemed to be something genuine in the enthusiasm. Many Koreans recognized that without U.S. support, South Korea would not be able to hold off her aggressive northern neighbor.

Whenever the GIs moved about the streets off duty, the locals affected an air of studied indifference. Many Korean civilians, particularly the younger ones, ignored the American presence, or tried to.

But as Charlie Company moved through a section of town toward the rendezvous, Isen noticed another bent to the civilian interest. Now they looked at his men as if the soldiers were aliens. These were men who were most likely going into combat, and Isen thought he saw an odd curiosity in the people on the side of the road as they stared and tried to divine what would make these men, these Americans, come halfway around the world to get involved in another country's plight. Instead of the gratitude that he might have expected, Isen saw bewilderment on the faces of these people whose lives were about to be shattered and changed by things completely out of their control. They weren't sure that the Americans weren't to blame.

And so the civilians kept a distance between themselves and the men, and even the soldiers who had made this trip before and enjoyed going to Korea sensed the difference.

As they moved toward the eastern edge of the town, heading toward their rendezvous with, Isen hoped, the rest of the battalion, the buildings started to thin out and the views open up. The land here was not as mountainous as it was farther inland, and it was a good deal flatter than it was to the north. Isen knew that twice during the war here, UN forces had been forced to abandon the South Korean capital: once to the North Korean People's Army, the NKPA, and once to the Chinese Communist Forces, or CCF, when they entered the war late in 1950.

He also knew, just from his association with the ROKs on two Team Spirit exercises, that the South Koreans had no intention of allowing the North Koreans, in any future combat, to fight in the relatively open areas south of the capital. The South Koreans were very much aware that the Americans would not cross the thirty-eighth parallel into North Korea; that move, in 1950, had brought China into the war. Such an extended war, with no clear objective in sight, was politically unthinkable in a United States grown so wary of involvement in foreign, and especially Asian, wars. The battle would be fought north of Seoul, where the shortest distance from the city to the DMZ was less than fifty miles. The South Korean Army would win there or be destroyed in the process.

Isen had seen, firsthand, some of the remarkable—to Americans—preparations that marked this whole country that lived with the constant threat of war. He remembered in particular driving on a mountain road northeast of the capital and noticing that there were dozens of wooden stakes thrust into the rock wall along the side of the road.

"What are those for?" he asked his guide, nodding upward at the sheer rock face above them.

"Dynamite holes," the guide said, smiling. "The NKPA come over, we put explosives in the hole. Take thirty minutes, maybe an hour, to close all these roads."

It seemed to Isen at times that the country was one vast civil defense establishment. He had been in Chunch'on, a road and rail center northeast of Seoul, after the field exercise less than a month before, when the town had its air raid drill. Shrill whistles cut the morning, and the bustling streets quickly emptied as the civilians went about their practiced routes to the shelters assigned to them. There were small military stations sown thickly through the country-side, so that the American forces were never more than a dozen miles or so from the nearest ROK compound.

But if the country seemed on the brink of war, there was no denying its economic vitality. During a two-day standdown period on his first trip, Isen had gone touring in Seoul. He had been amazed to find glittering skyscrapers and fast-moving traffic that rivaled anything in Los Angeles. He had read somewhere that one out of every four South

Koreans lives in Seoul, and it seemed to Isen that they all seemed to want to drive at the time that he wanted to cross one of the wide boulevards. The Korean people, so friendly and industrious out in the countryside, in the city seemed to be just industrious. The men were physically aggressive, and thought nothing of shoving past even the much bigger American GIs, who were sorely outnumbered and frequently lost amid the welter of signs in Hangul, the Korean language.

When they had less than a kilometer to go, the pavement suddenly ended, just a sharp drop off the concrete pad, and they moved onto a dusty road. The hills, imperceptible among the buildings outside Osan Air Force Base, were becoming more visible as they moved out of the built-up area. When he could see the hill that marked the checkpoint they wanted, Isen picked out on his map a road intersection that was just below the hilltop. He put the company in a perimeter in some sparse woods just to the near side of the road, and told Voavosa and Barrow that he was soon going to go look for the command party. He gave instructions to Marist, his third platoon leader, to send a few soldiers to him in about thirty minutes. They would go along with Isen and provide security.

They had not been stopped for five minutes when a small Korean cab pulled up. The car was an older model, made by the company that had broken into the American market in the mid-eighties. But this one, sold in Korea, had the distinctive dull brown paint job of all Korean cars that were more than a few years old.

"When I was here as a young soldier," Voavosa offered, "that was the only color car you ever saw. It was like they were working so hard to make the car and to make it good that they didn't bother with the superficial stuff, like looks."

"And now they're one of the biggest exporters to the U.S.," Isen added.

"I'm telling you, sir, these people make the Japanese look lazy. On my first tour here," Voavosa went on, "I bought this radio out in the ville, 'cause mine broke and the PX was out of 'em. I looked inside the back of it one day, and you know what I found?"

Isen shook his head.

"The radio was built with scrap electronics parts, American parts. They had a damn GI flashlight battery, a burned-out one, fit in there as a resistor. And do you know what?"

Isen shook his head again. Voavosa had an annoying habit of punctuating his conversations with rhetorical questions.

"Now you go into the PX, the PX, mind you, and a third of the electronics stuff on the shelf is Korean." Voavosa shook his head at the significance of his observation. He respected few things more than hard work, and these people redefined the work ethic.

Two women got out of the back of the cab, one dressed in western-style jeans with a nylon windbreaker, the other in jeans but with an embroidered, distinctively Korean coat, tied across the front with string. They gave nonstop instructions to the driver, who hurried from the front to open the trunk, from which the women pulled two cases of Coca-Cola and a case of what looked like a Korean version of a Moon Pie. The cab driver left in a hurry, as if he couldn't wait to get away from the women.

"Looks like mama-san's here," Voavosa said.

All through any field problem that the Americans were on, the units were followed by these entrepreneurs, who proffered everything from American soda and junk food to Korean rice wine to prostitutes. The joke among the American forces was that if you wanted to know where you were going to be moving the next day, ask mama-san. Isen, who admitted that he was naturally suspicious, once had tried to give the slip to one of the women, whom he suspected of casing his company position for the location of such easily pilfered and expensive items as radios. But after two successive moves, she still showed up in her taxi cab, hawking her wares. Voavosa had intervened on the woman's behalf, and had told Isen what the score was.

"Sir, if you treat mama-san good enough, she'll make sure we're not bothered by any of the slicky-boys."

"Slicky-boy," Isen knew, was the slang for the roving bands of youthful thieves that wandered the countryside, stealing radios, sleeping bags, food, and even an occasional vehicle from the too-trusting Americans. So the company commander had relented. Isen knew that, ideally, he should keep all civilians away from his unit. The American intelligence community knew that quite a few of these people, throughout South Korea, were in the employ of the North Koreans. Their use was an easy way to gather information on the whereabouts of American troops: what units were on hand, where they had come from, where they were going— all sorts of information that would help the North Koreans determine the troop strength facing them.

Now that the stakes were higher, and Isen's men were carrying live ammunition and seemed to have at least an even chance of getting shot at, Isen was less willing to make concessions.

"I don't like it, Top. I don't like it one bit."

"But, sir, you know as well as I do that these people are as much a part of going to the field here as getting rained on."

"Yeah, but we're not just going to the field. There's a good chance we'll be facing some pop-up-shoot-back targets real soon. And I'd just as soon not have to worry about these women knowing everything about my company just because our guys are used to having mama-san around to sell Cokes and to wash their dirty shorts."

Isen's tone hadn't changed; he hadn't taken his eyes off the women, but Voavosa knew his commander had decided. The first sergeant watched the nearby soldiers on the side of the road, who had already collected enough money to buy almost a case of Cokes for their platoon. He knew that Isen was right about the intelligence operations.

"I tell you what, sir, old habits die hard. I'm not sure we can keep the men away from the mama-sans, especially after we've been here awhile and they start bringing out those twenty-dollar whores. All during the time we were over here, we gave these people practically free rein with us. But, and you're right on this, of course, now there's some real good reasons why we shouldn't."

The first sergeant paused thoughtfully. "This is gonna be a tough one."

Isen didn't answer. He knew the soldiers were going to be upset, but he cared more about the operational security of his company than he cared if the troops got soda.

Voavosa finished his thought. "But that's why you and me get paid the big bucks, right, sir? To make the tough calls."

And with that he stepped away from Isen and toward the small crowd that had gathered around the women.

"All right, you people! Just what in the hell do you think you're doing?"

Before the first sergeant even reached them, the Korean women were on their feet, protesting in Hangul. Voavosa spoke to them in English.

"Yeah, yeah, I know. Your kids are gonna starve if you don't unload all this stuff, and besides, we've always let you do this before, right?" He paused, not because the women would understand, but because he knew the troops were listening.

"But all that's ancient history now," he continued, looking around at his soldiers, "'cause somebody went and changed the rules to this here ball game."

"Top, you mean to tell me we can't even buy a soda after we've been humping around the boonies?"

First Sergeant Voavosa froze.

Someone was back-talking him. Worse, someone was back-talking him in front of a group of his soldiers, challenging his authority in the worst possible scenario. His head swiveled on his powerful neck as he turned to the sound.

The voice belonged to Staff Sergeant Stahl, a squad leader in Marist's third platoon. He spoke in a joking manner, much as Voavosa's tone seemed to be joking. The staff sergeant assumed two things: that he could maneuver the first sergeant into a corner, and that the Samoan would see how small a thing this was. Stahl was correct on only the first count.

Some of the men, the more perceptive ones, took an almost indistinguishable step backward, knowing that Stahl was pushing the envelope. Voavosa's eyes had narrowed to two slits.

"You let us do this stuff a couple of weeks ago," Stahl said, oblivious to the warning signs that more of the troops were becoming aware of. Voavosa's already wide nostrils flared violently, as if he were gathering air for some explosion. Stahl missed that signal, too.

"Why, we're doing these people a favor," the younger NCO continued. "This is the only job they got. The only job they can get, I guess."

Stahl was playing for a laugh, but he got only a smile out of a couple of the youngest troops, who were far from seeing what was about to happen. Even the soldiers who wanted to be able to buy Cokes and junk food and maybe even women, who wouldn't begin to understand that these people, these harmless-looking women could be gathering information for the NKPA, even those men could see that Voavosa was barely containing himself.

Incredibly, Stahl reached into his pocket and pulled out a few wrinkled American dollars.

"Can we at least grab a couple of Cokes before they go anywhere? I mean, they're already here and everything."

He made as if to step toward the women, who, though they couldn't understand what was being said, clearly understood the signals coming from the gathered men and from the short, thick-necked man who stood in the center of his very own clearing in this crowd.

Voavosa stepped between Stahl and the women. Inside, he was saying to himself, *Unless you want to walk around with that case of soda sticking out of your backside, I'd suggest you take a giant step backward.* But he knew that it was more important for the men to understand that this was more than a showdown for control. Some of the soldiers would be first sergeants or even company commanders one day, and there was a point to be made about laxness in security. Even as he thought about these things, Voavosa congratulated himself for his presence of mind. A few years back, even this limited display of resistance would have been enough to bring him to blows.

"Sergeant Stahl, I know you know that these women, or some just like them"—Voavosa turned toward the women, who were standing meekly, their hands folded—"some just as innocent-looking, could be collecting information for the North Koreans. So they won't be hanging around anymore, and we won't be buying stuff from them."

As the words rolled off his tongue, he could feel himself relax. He relished the fact that, talking as he was in a low voice, the soldiers were obliged to hang on his every word. "You get the picture now?"

The light finally came on for Stahl, who shoved his money deep into his pocket. From where he stood, although he couldn't hear anything distinctly, Isen saw the little knot of soldiers break up. The two women were left standing there, looking sheepishly at Voavosa. Isen had expected them to fight with the first sergeant, which was their normal mode of operation when someone tried to get rid of them. But they must have sensed that Voavosa wasn't a man to be trifled with, or perhaps they knew and understood the American suspicions.

Voavosa pointed to the few buildings that were down the road about half a mile to the west. The women picked up their crates and walked away. Voavosa was also surprised that they didn't resist, and said so when he rejoined the commander.

"They didn't put up much of a fuss, did they, sir?"

"No. They were less trouble than Sergeant Stahl."

Voavosa had to chuckle at this. "Did you see how calm I was, sir?"

"Yeah, I saw it." Isen looked at Voavosa, trying to gauge just how much ribbing he could take. "Maybe you *won't* get high blood pressure in the prime of your life."

Isen watched the two women walk slowly away. They stopped to look back at the company, then, when they were only about five hundred meters away, they sat down by the side of the road.

"They're either waiting for a cab or they plan on coming back here as soon as they can."

"I hope they're waiting for a cab," Voavosa said. "I don't know how long this new patience thing is gonna last with me."

Isen and the two security soldiers left the company at the crossroads and moved around the base of the hill, looking for signs of the rest of the battalion. David, following a few feet behind Isen, was able to raise Tilden.

"Uniform zero seven, this is alpha zero seven, over," Isen called.

"This is uniform zero seven, over."

"I am vicinity checkpoint one three, over."

"Roger, alpha zero seven. I just linked up with the tango element. We'll be at your location in one five, over."

David, hearing the third callsign used, held up his wrist so that Isen could see the card there. The tango element was Alpha Company. Tilden came back on the net.

"Be ready to move to an alpha when we get there, over."

"Wilco, over," Isen replied.

An "alpha" was an assembly area, a spot where the unit could hole up for a time—anywhere from a few hours to several weeks—and prepare for future operations.

Tilden finished the transmission. "Zero seven, out."

Within the hour Charlie Company had linked up with the other companies and the battalion's very limited supply trains. A short while later the support platoon leader, a fiesty first lieutenant named Journey, came pulling up with a convoy of South Korean two-and-a-half-ton trucks.

The company first sergeants rounded up the men to prepare for boarding as the company commanders met with Tilden and Bock. The operations officer briefed them as to where they were going.

"We'll be moving north on highway one, then we'll swing east so that we avoid the metro area around Seoul. We'll be stopping somewhere west of our Team Spirit staging area at Chunch'on. That'll put us forty or fifty miles east of Seoul. I'll be flying ahead to do an aerial recon, and I'll meet the convoy at this spot." He pointed out a major intersection with his pencil.

Isen looked at Bock's map. The area he pointed to was a big rectangle of land bounded by the DMZ to the north, Seoul to the south, the Yellow Sea to the west, and the mountains of central Korea to the east. Uijongbu sat on a crossroads roughly in the center of the rectangle.

Tilden interjected something. "There's no telling how long we're going to be at this assembly area. You all know that there are a lot of things to work on."

Bock asked for questions, but there were none.

Isen, armed now with a map and overlay, a surer sense of where he was going, and in the company of men he trusted, moved back to his company quickly, glad that he was going to be able to tell them something concrete. There would be less certainty, he was sure, in the days ahead.

From the President's televised address to the nation
23 April · Saturday

North Korea has been among the most militarized nations in the world since the end of the Korean Conflict in 1953. This small nation of only eighteen and a half million keeps a standing armed force of over seven hundred and eighty thousand men. That means that there is one person in uniform for every twenty-four citizens of North Korea. Compare this with the per capita ratio in the United States, which has one person in uniform for every one hundred and nine citizens, or even the Soviet Union, which has a per capita rate of only one per seventy-two.

There is only one reason why the North Koreans maintain such a huge force. They have been planning the overthrow of the South Korean government for years. In recent months, the activities of North Korean agents in South Korea have intensified. Recently, as you know, North Korean–backed terrorists ambushed a convoy of unarmed American soldiers who were completing a joint service exercise, conducted annually with the Republic of Korea forces. We see this attack as part of a larger plan that is a prelude to an invasion.

At this grave hour, North Korean forces are massing along the Demilitarized Zone, preparing to invade South Korea and rob her of her freedom.

The United States has maintained a continuous presence in Korea since the end of the Second World War. We will not abandon our allies at this time. U.S. soldiers stand shoulder to shoulder with our Korean allies, ready to repel any attempt by North Korea to violate South Korean soil. And those American forces in Korea are just the point of the spear. The United States is prepared to back up, with its global military might, its obligation and solemn promise to defend South Korean freedom.

The United States will not tolerate an invasion of South Korea by the forces of the North Korean People's Army. We have no designs on North Korea, but we are determined to maintain the thirty-eighth parallel as the dividing line between North and South Korea.

Let me address, as directly as possible, the leaders of North Korea. This is the wrong war, at the wrong time, with the wrong adversary.

It is the intention of this administration to pursue every possible diplomatic channel in the hope of preserving the peace in Korea. It is also my intention, as the Commander-in-Chief of the U.S. military, to be ready for war if we are to have war.

Fellow Americans, I hope that you will join me in my prayers tonight for a peaceful resolution of this most serious threat to freedom in Asia. Pray with me that the guns remain silent, that our young men and women return home safely, and that the world recognizes us for what we are, determined protectors of peace and freedom.

Good night.

7

Near Chunch'on, South Korea

23 April · Saturday

Isen was afraid the men were losing their edge.

"Top, I don't know how long we can stay like this, all cooped up, I mean," he said to Voavosa.

The two men were leaning against the front of the HMMWV that Barrow and the first sergeant had been using to run supplies. Voavosa spat thoughtfully.

"They give us any news at all, sir?"

"Nothing except 'hang loose,'" Isen answered. "We keep getting the same information in our commanders' briefings, stuff about the ROKs and our State Department trying to talk to the North Koreans, to see if they can defuse this thing. But there isn't much more than that. I don't think the division staff is holding out on us; I just think nobody really knows what the hell's going on."

"That's not surprising," Voavosa snorted, "considering that the goddamned politicians are in charge."

The battalion had moved into an assembly area six days earlier. Isen had worked up a full schedule of intensive training, but was limited in what he could do because of the precarious diplomatic situation. The units had to remain close to the hastily established camp, so that their presence wouldn't be painfully obvious. The United States did not want to give the Communists any opportunity to accuse America of heightening tensions on the peninsula.

The Army would not be in a position to affect the balance of power in Korea until it had heavy forces on the ground. There was limited live firing of weapons and no helicopter training. There were no passes for the men and precious little free time and nothing to do when they had it. The 25th Division, to which Tilden's unit belonged, had flown two thousand miles, armed to the teeth, and was now trying to be as inconspicuous as possible in the hope that the diplomats could secure the shaky peace.

Personally, Isen would have been willing to stay sequestered for a month if it meant that he wouldn't have to fight—but he knew his soldiers needed to practice their skills constantly if there were to be any hope of staying alive once the bullets started flying. Their arrival in-country, even their presence there, seemed anticlimactic.

First Sergeant Voavosa went on, after pausing to let his remark about the diplomats settle with Isen.

"I'm just glad, with all this ammo and all these jumpy troops around, that we made it through another twenty-four hours without some dumbshit shooting his buddy."

Isen saw David approach, his radio on a pack board on his back, the handset pinched under his arm. He held an army-green memo book in his left hand, and was writing as he walked.

"Got a message here, sir," he said without looking up from the pad.

"What is it?" Isen asked, turning and placing his elbows on the vehicle's hood. David didn't answer, but just held out the book, opened to a page where he had written the deciphered codes.

Codewords are frequently sent in groups; lists of meaningless word combinations surround the actual message in order to further confuse eavesdroppers. David had deciphered seven three-word groups. The second from the bottom of the page was "thirty-eight North Yankee."

FLASH

TO: CHAIRMAN, JCS
    CINCPAC
FROM: CDR IN CHIEF, ROK-US COMBINED
    FORCES COMMAND
DTG: 240504 APRIL

1. THE NORTH KOREAN PEOPLE'S ARMY LAUNCHED A COORDINATED ATTACK THIS MORNING AGAINST US AND ROK FORCES AT SEVERAL POINTS ALONG THE DMZ.

2. ELEMENTS OF THE 4TH ROK DIVISION HAVE BEEN OVERRUN VIC KUMWHA.

3. COMMANDER, 2D US DIVISION REPORTS THAT SEVERAL OF HIS SUBORDINATE UNITS HAVE BEEN BYPASSED BY THE NKPA. HE MAINTAINS LIMITED FREEDOM OF ACTION AND CAN OPERATE AGAINST NKPA BELOW THE DMZ IN CENTRAL SOUTH KOREA.

4. ENEMY SPEARHEAD HAS PENETRATED TO VIC HWACH'ON RESERVOIR IN THE EAST, TONGDUCH'ON NORTH OF SEOUL, AND UIJONGBU.

5. USAF, USMC AND ROKAF AVIATION INTERDICTION MISSIONS HAVE SLOWED THE ENEMY ADVANCE AT SOME POINTS.

6. EXPECT 25 INF DIV AND 7 INF DIV TROOPS TO BE IN CONTACT WITHIN 24 HRS.

7. CASUALTY REPORTS FOLLOW

HALINGER
GEN, US ARMY
CINCCFC
CINC US FORCES KOREA

FLASH

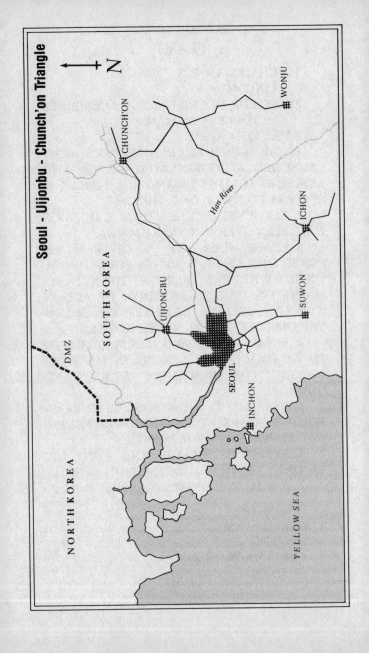

Seoul - Uijonbu - Chunch'on Triangle

8

West of Chunch'on, Republic of Korea

24 April · Sunday · 2310 hrs

Isen held the barrel of his rifle and stretched his cramped legs. He had given up trying to pick landmarks out of the rainy darkness outside the windows of the ROK truck. He watched the truck's speed and his watch. Every fifteen minutes he turned on his red-filtered, hooded flashlight and made another mark on his map, trying to estimate how far they'd come.

The battalion had been on the road since just before dawn, moving north and west from the assembly areas they had occupied for their first week in Korea. Intelligence must be good, Isen reasoned. The Americans had started moving at about the same time the North Koreans struck the Demilitarized Zone. Now, after nearly eighteen hours of stop-and-go truck movement north across the Korean countryside, he still had not seen much to confirm the bad news.

In spite of the dire warnings they'd heard every day in the command information briefings, the soldiers had been shocked by the order moving them to blocking positions. Even the gloomy reports on the worsening situation that appeared in the American press hadn't quashed Charlie Company's faith in a peaceful settlement. But the NKPA had finally decided, in spite of the growing American presence, to try to defeat the ROKs in a quick assault.

When Isen told the assembled company that they were moving into fighting positions, he'd been surprised at the reactions. There didn't seem to be a great deal of the exaggerated emotion he had expected. For the most part the men were calm. He had no soldiers trying to get out of moving north, nor did he have any unblooded plaster heroes spouting off a bunch of mindless slogans. They went about their tasks, grimly determined to get ready and to do the best they could.

The long days in the assembly areas, practicing and rehearsing their trade with live ammunition, had taken the edge off even his most gung-ho troops.

Isen saw the tiny blackout brake lights of the vehicle in front of his go bright, then the truck turned off into what looked to be a school yard. When he could see the rest of the convoy stopping, Isen jumped from the cab. He stood on the ground and reached inside to make sure that he hadn't left any gear behind. The ROK driver, a boy of no more than seventeen who hadn't spoken a word to him all day, flashed Isen a thumbs-up. Isen waved to the boy and shut the door.

The first sergeant was already at his side. Isen noticed that the rain had stopped, but they were standing in a soupy yellow mud that had been the school's playground.

"Top, keep the company on board 'til I find out if this is where we're going to dismount. I'll send a runner back as soon as I know. David!" Isen found his radio operator in the back of the truck.

"Grab your gear and come with me."

David handed down his rucksack, heavy with the spare batteries and the sleeping gear and the rain suit and the six extra meals and the two-quart canteen of water and the radio Isen would use to talk to the battalion commander. He jumped over the tailgate, swearing as he slipped in the mud.

Isen noticed that the first sergeant was still, intent on something beyond the school yard. Then he heard it, a sound like a far-off highway, a low rumbling that seemed a continuous murmur. Then David heard it.

Artillery.

The three of them stood there, frozen in the fading moonlight, a tableau of surprise and recognition. Isen knew that he would remember that scene for a long time to come: the small triangle of yellow mud, the first sergeant with his large head cocked to one side, his lips in a straight line, David scraping the sludge off his rifle.

For some reason, Isen thought of the expression "shots fired in anger." These were the first he had heard, and there was nothing angry about them. There was the pull of the sticky mud, there were the cold cramps in his back and legs, and there was even the new smell of fear—but there was nothing as positive as anger.

Isen found Tilden and Bock, the operations officer, huddled in the doorway of the school. He could see, in the unsteady red beam from Bock's flashlight, that the S3's map was marked precisely, the little unit symbols drawn as neatly as they might have been in a classroom at Fort Benning. He considered his own wet and leaky map case, which he folded under his arm.

Bock spoke without turning to face Isen. "Mark, I want you to move to the right of the battalion sector, establish contact with the ROK unit that's supposed to be out there, and establish a hasty defensive line on the north slope of this little ridge that runs east and west here."

Bock indicated an area hemmed in by an east-to-west-running river in the north, and a ridge that paralleled it a kilometer to the south. There was some flat ground around the river, and a smaller hill in between the ridge and the river.

"This isn't the area we had planned for, is it?"

Tilden entered the conversation. "No. Division just told us about an NKPA drive in the area north of here. It looks like they'll be crossing our front, going from right to left. An ROK unit south of us will be pushing through the battalion, probably right through your company, sometime tonight or tomorrow to hit the enemy penetration in the flank."

"The thing that looks fishy to me," Tilden went on, "is that the North Koreans are driving southwest, even west by southwest. Everything seems pointed toward the capital on a narrow front. It's risky."

Isen was studying the S3's map, which Bock held pinned to the wall with one extended arm. "Pretty hilly out there," Isen said. "How much flexibility can I have to, say, set up in the woods on the south side, the reverse slope? That way I'd be mostly out of sight of the river valley. I can watch it and keep out of range of anything on the north side."

Tilden was now straining to see the C Company area on the map. "Okay, Mark, you do what you think is best, but don't move back any farther than this trail here." He stabbed at the map with a gloved finger, indicating an east-west trail that ran parallel to and about one hundred and fifty meters south of Isen's ridge. "They'll be coming through with a beefed-up battalion or maybe a brigade, armor and mech infantry mixed. We're here to hold up the shoulders of this penetration the ROK corps commander is counting on making to our front."

"Our battalion is holding on both sides of the ROK advance, sir?" Isen asked.

"We're just about the only guys out here. Our brigade is spread pretty thin," Tilden said. "We're it, so we'll do it on our own."

"Roger that, sir." Isen waved at David, who sloshed back to the trucks to find the first sergeant and pass the word to unload. Charlie Company had found the war.

Isen had no trouble selecting the platoon that would anchor the company's and the battalion's right.

"Paco, you're moving out first. Take your platoon to this draw and meet me here." Isen used the tip of a mechanical pencil to point on the map. On the small-scale maps used by soldiers who walk, a fingertip will cover seven hundred meters. "We'll do a leader's recon. Pick a good man to look for the ROK unit that's supposed to be out there on our right. Take the battalion's KATUSA with you."

Each battalion had several Korean soldiers called KATUSAS, who wore American uniforms, lived and moved with the Americans, and functioned as interpreters. Their battalion had been assigned only one so far, a bright and energetic teenager named Yu.

Isen briefed the other platoon leaders and within forty minutes was scouting the hill where they would establish a defensive line until it got light enough to adjust the positions. There was not much threat from vehicles, except along a small dirt trail that ran north-south, perpendicular to the ridge, and led to the rear of the battalion sector. Charlie Company's position sat astride the most likely approach for enemy infantry.

Isen divided responsibility for the sector among the platoons and told the lieutenants where they should concentrate their efforts. He decided that the hill was low enough and wooded enough that they could put their position on the north slope, facing the enemy. Another small east-west ridge ran between them and the river, providing them some cover.

He took David, his other RTO, a kid named Murray, and an artillery lieutenant by the name of Christian who was his Fire Support Team (FIST) chief, and established a company command post just to the left and rear of Paco's platoon.

The men fought the mud and the darkness as they struggled to get ready for whatever might come pouring out of the night. Some of the men were spooked by the sporadic artillery they heard in the distance. Isen explained that it was "H and I," harassment and interdiction fire, blindly dropped on road junctions and hilltops and likely spots of enemy activity to keep the bad guys on their toes and to keep them from sleeping.

His lieutenants had done a good job, had security out and their crew-served weapons set in. They had arranged it so the men could get some sleep in shifts, lying in the mud in their shallow, scratched-out fighting positions.

Isen prayed that they'd see daylight before they had to fight on this ground. The character of a position looked a lot different in the daylight; setting in at night is a matter of best guessing. Around three o'clock, after he had checked the mortars, after he was satisfied that he could talk to battalion and to his platoons on the field phones, after he was sure that Christian had registered some target reference points for their supporting artillery and was ready to shoot if need be, Isen sat down. His boots and trousers were a thick mass of sticky mud, soaked from the rain running off the trees. He was wet to the skin under the portable sauna of his plastic raincoat. His protective mask carrier had rubbed a raw spot on his hip. He sat down on his rucksack, wrapped his hands and legs around his rifle, checked his watch, lowered his head, and fell instantly asleep.

Only minutes later, he woke with a start, sure that he had dreamed of great beating wings. David was squatting at his side, holding up the sound-powered telephone.

"Sir, second platoon thinks they got a tank out in front."

A tank. Isen was glad it was dark so he didn't have to worry if the expression on his face gave away his nervousness.

"Isen." He was glad to hear how calm his voice sounded.

"Sir, we got a tank or something out here."

It was Haveck, the second platoon leader. There was no mistaking the quavering in his voice.

"Calm down, Pete. Give me a sitrep."

"Right." Isen could picture the young man gaining control of himself as he went into the format he had been drilled in, as the training took over. "We have what sounds like one tank or light armored vehicle to our front, estimate about three to four hundred meters north of center sector. He sounds like he's moving on the road out there, moving in this direction. I got the first report about three minutes ago, and just heard it myself. No visual contact."

"Okay. Wake your men. Make sure you got your Dragons up. Don't engage unless it looks like he's gonna find us out. We don't want anybody to know we're here yet. I'll have illumination on call. Is he too close for artillery?"

"He will be in a minute or two if he keeps heading this way."

"Stand by." Isen was in his element now; the mantle of nervousness he had been wearing for days dropped away as he started to analyze what was now a tactical problem.

"David, ring up the other platoons. Christian, get some illum set in those tubes back there. We got company."

Isen turned the crank on the battalion phone, but as he lifted it to his ear, he heard the unmistakable *thwapp-*

thwapp-thwapp of a helicopter coming in fast. He sensed more than saw David, Murray, and Christian jump for their holes, and a half second later he did the same. He pressed his helmet down on his forehead and dared to look up to see the blackness explode with a white stream of fire that, he realized, must be coming from the helicopter. The source of the bright finger of light was moving parallel to the trace, or front line, of his company. He hoped that meant it was a friendly. The vapor *whoosh* of rockets confirmed it.

"COBRA," he yelled.

The ambush was over in a second, and the helicopter sounds were far behind him by the time he had regained his night vision.

"God*damn.*" David was wide-eyed, his voice cracking with the excitement. "Did you see *that?*"

The telephones were jangling crazily. He picked up the battalion phone first.

"Wait, out."

Then he grabbed the platoon hot loop. "Haveck, what'ya got?"

"We have one burning light tank out here, skipper. I don't know where that chopper came from, or how it knew what was out there, but it cooked that vehicle. Do you want us to go out and take a look?"

"Yeah, but don't get inside the circle of light, in case he had some buddies around. We still haven't been made in this position."

All the men were awake now, peering over the lips of their positions, weapons pointed at the bright orange of the shattered vehicle. The North Koreans hadn't even had a chance to react. They'd been jumped, caught flat-footed, cold-cocked, like an unsuspecting high school kid in his first bar fight. Knocked out with the first punch.

Isen reasoned that the helicopter, which was South Korean, was probably on routine patrol and had spotted this lone intruder.

And what if the tank had come ahead?

They would have been able to handle one, Isen was sure, and a lone vehicle operating at night was so unusual that it almost had to be an accident. There had been a moment there, when he wasn't sure whose side the chopper was on, when he felt helpless, naked. His company, his men, his responsibility—were out there on the bald hillside, subject to whatever the North Koreans might do to them. The thought chilled him, and he knew with perfect certainty that the next time there would be more tanks. As he gave his report to battalion, he was planning his countermoves.

9

West of Chunch'on, Republic of Korea

25 April · Monday

Isen was concerned that the uproar caused by the helicopter attack would only further exhaust the men. But the platoons were fully alert at stand-to, just before dawn.

Isen could see the platoon leaders and the squad leaders moving about, adjusting their positions in the daylight now that they could see what was in front of them. He could smell burning heat tabs, chemical fuel tablets, as the men warmed up coffee or water to make their rations palatable. He reached into his rucksack, rummaging around for a candy bar he had stashed there, when two jets passed over, splitting the morning sky.

Isen looked up in time to see the planes—American F15s—dip their wings. The pilots had seen the company, or at least knew that there were Americans out here.

Seconds later, he heard explosions off to the north. The land line from battalion rang. It was Bock, the operations officer.

"Mark, Jan. We got a call from brigade. The ROKs are going to pass an armor battalion through us to hit the side of an enemy penetration just north of here. Those planes were going in to soften things up a bit." Two more planes came out of the southern sky, and seconds later, several more explosions out to the north.

"Okay, I'll send my XO down to the road to show them through. Anything else?"

"No. This is going to be close by, right in our area, but it's gonna be their show."

Isen was already signaling Murray, one of his radio operators, to go get the XO. He patted his right lapel, where officers wear their rank, and pointed in the direction of company trains. Murray trotted off, his helmet and protective mask and load-bearing equipment jangling with every step.

"Call the platoon leaders," he told David.

Isen spent only five minutes with Barrow, telling the XO what he wanted. He made a quick drawing in his green memo book, and together they worked out the contingencies, trying to anticipate the unexpected. Isen watched as Barrow made studious shorthand notes. He trusted his XO completely and knew that Barrow, confronted with a situation he hadn't been trained for, would make a sound decision based on his mission and what he thought would be good for the company.

"Okay, Dale, this is it." Isen resisted the temptation to sound like an actor in a B-grade war movie, but he stuck out his hand to Barrow.

"See you in a little while, skipper," Barrow said. If he was nervous, he was doing a good job hiding it.

By the time Isen finished briefing his platoon leaders on his plan, they could hear the approaching tracks. Barrow met the first tank, which turned out to be commanded by the ROK captain whose company would lead the attack. Hard behind the captain were two AVLBs, armored-vehicle launched bridges, sixty-foot scissor bridges that could be launched from their tank-like chassis. Behind the bridges, Barrow could see the armored personnel carriers of the infantry unit that would attack with the tanks. The infantry soldiers, when they got across, would clear the woods on the far side of enemy anti-tank gunners. Barrow saw a wide-eyed driver pop his head up to get his bearings, then drop back into the vehicle.

* * *

Several hundred meters away, Isen sat with the battalion phone in his lap and studied his map. It wasn't hard to see what the ROKs were up to. The road—a mere trail by American standards—that ran through C Company's sector led to one of the few flat areas along the small river that was to the north of them. The ROKs would use the AVLBs to cross the water, hitting the other side quickly with armored vehicles, instead of waiting for the slower and more deliberate—but for Isen's money, safer—infantry assault. Isen couldn't imagine riding in an armored vehicle across the wide open field at that riverbed. Even with the hot-shot American-made and ROK-manned M-60A3 tanks overwatching by fire from the near side, the whole operation depended on surprise. The ROKs were gambling that the NKPA units on the far side would be running hell-bent-for-leather southwest toward Seoul, moving too fast to bother to check their flanks for obvious counterattack routes.

Isen wondered how much of an effect the U.S. Air Force was having on the NKPA advance. He sat down on his wet backside, satisfied that he had figured out most of what was going on. The only thing he hadn't guessed was that the ROK attack, scheduled to go off before dawn, had been delayed by problems getting the fuel up to the tanks over the clogged roads. The attack was going ahead anyway, without the protective cover of darkness, because it was a linchpin for the ROK Corps counterattack plan that was unfolding that day.

Barrow's voice came over the company net radio. "Foxtrot four three, this is foxtrot zero seven, over." Isen had been expecting the call.

"This is four three, go."

Both men were painfully aware of how quickly an attentive enemy radio-direction finding team could pinpoint a talkative radio net and put artillery rounds on a command post.

"Four three, this is zero seven, globetrotter, over."

Isen checked his notebook. This was the first of the codewords he and Barrow had worked out. Isen now knew that his XO had talked his way into accompanying the ROK advance down to the near side of the stream to watch the attack and report back to Isen. Isen could hear the vehicles over the sound of Barrow's voice on the radio.

"Globetrotter, out."

Isen now had his own man out front, keeping an eye on the most critical point in the battalion's sector. If he had to sit here with his hands tied, he didn't want to do so in ignorance. Content that he had provided for his company's security, Isen shouldered the radio and went out to see how his platoon leaders were putting his plans into action.

Barrow wanted to observe the attack from the ridge that paralleled the river on the south bank. When they were close, he tapped the shoulder of the ROK infantry platoon leader who had given him a lift. The lieutenant said something to the driver, who slowed down just a bit, then motioned to Barrow to jump.

Barrow climbed out on the deck of the M113 personnel carrier, then thought better of jumping with his rucksack on his back. He shrugged it off his shoulder, tossed it to the ground, and jumped after it. He tried to do a parachute landing fall, as he had learned at airborne school, but he had never been moving this fast before. Instead of a controlled landing on the large muscle groups of his buttocks and side, he hit feet, butt, head. His helmet slammed down on the bridge of his nose, and he heard a sickening crunch as his vision disappeared for a few seconds. He had broken his nose. There was blood running down into his mouth and onto his shirtfront, and he could feel the swelling start to spread under his eyes. He pulled an olive-drab scarf, what the troops called a "drive-on rag," from his pocket and pressed it to his face. He picked up his rucksack and jogged off in the direction of the river, spewing blood and saliva on his shirtfront with every deep breath.

Barrow moved to his left, away from the road toward a point on the ridge about a kilometer from the river from which he thought he'd be able to see some of what was going on in the valley. The ROKs were planning to use their attack positions for only a few seconds, long enough to deploy and get the overwatch vehicles into shooting position. He ran along, his map and compass clutched in one hand, his head pounding with the sudden blow he had taken in the face, running to a point on a small hill so that he could observe the crossing.

Isen was back in the C Company command post. He had waited for the warmest part of the day to indulge himself in his ritual. First he pulled off one boot and one wet sock. He patted that foot dry with the top of the dirty sock, then inspected the pale foot for signs of blisters or immersion foot. Satisfied that he'd found nothing to be alarmed at, he dusted the foot liberally with GI foot powder, put on a dry sock and the wet boot, then repeated the procedure for the other foot. He was thus engaged when David brought him the field phone.

"Mark, it's Bock. I got the info you wanted on that ROK attack."

Isen pinched the headset between his shoulder and ear and tied his boot. "Go ahead."

"That operation was supposed to go off at 0445, but they got held up by some logistics snafu. The ROKs were counting on last night's H and I fires to cover the sounds of those vehicles moving up."

"Roger. Thanks for the word."

"What are you doin' up there?"

"Well, I was just wondering why they were trying this mounted attack in broad daylight, that's all. It was a good plan for darkness—but it needed to be called off or changed for daylight. We're trying to anticipate contingencies up here in Charlie Company. I'd like to talk to you and the old man about what might be going down up here. Are you headed this way?"

"We were going to start with Bravo Company, but we'll come out to your position first, okay?"

"Sounds good," Isen said, and in his head he started to frame the case he would make to convince Tilden to dedicate some of the battalion's most important fire support assets to Charlie Company.

First Sergeant Voavosa walked up. He had been out to the listening post positions the platoons had selected for the night.

"Top, how does it look out there?" Isen asked him.

"Good, sir. We'll be ready in a couple of hours, maybe ahead of schedule even."

Voavosa noticed Isen's preoccupation. He was older than Isen, with a lot more time in the army, and he had a natural instinct to take a fatherly stance with this younger man whom he liked and trusted. But there were limits to what the first sergeant could share. Isen was always willing to listen to the intelligent input of his subordinates, and he had solicited comments on the plan they were putting into effect now. But this was new territory. On the surface, what they were doing looked the same as what they did in training, but every man felt the palpable distinction. This was for real. And no matter how they cut it, how they performed in their test, everything came back to Isen, to this twenty-seven-year-old commander. The decisions and responsibility were his alone.

"You and me can go over it on my map here, sir," Voavosa continued, "before you go out to the platoons. Any word from the XO?"

"He's out there with the ROKs. He'll keep us posted."

Voavosa nodded. "He better. We might get caught with our ass in the breeze."

Barrow expected to hear artillery fire at any moment, but nothing was happening. When he heard the screech of the unfolding AVLBs, he crawled on his belly up the final few feet of the slope, so that he could see the valley on the other side.

He was startled at how clear the valley looked, like a sand-table exercise in river crossing operations. There was virtually no cover down along the small river, and he could see the AVLBs, one already deployed, and all the way north to where the terraced fields on the other side reached up to a woodline, about two thousand meters away. He knew immediately that the ROKs were relying on surprise, otherwise there would have been artillery fire on that woodline. Below him and to the left he could hear the shouts of the vehicle commanders, barely audible above the idling of the halted tanks as they hurried to get into position, anxious to get through the dangerous bottleneck that the two bridges created. The first tanks were across the river and beginning to fan out on the far side when Barrow saw the puff of smoke from the far, wooded ridge. He saw the hit before he heard the crack of the tank cannon as a spout of mud and water jumped into the air next to one of the AVLBs.

Barrow pressed his belly to the earth as the four ROK tanks arrayed on either side of him answered with a volley, looking for a target in the dark curtain of woods over a mile distant. He reached for the handset, and licked his lips with a cotton-dry tongue.

"Foxtrot four three, this is foxtrot zero seven, over."

Isen answered quickly.

"This is zero seven. Black sox, I say again, black sox, over."

"This is four three, understand black sox, out."

Isen now knew that the ROKs were making an opposed attack across the river. They had failed to gain surprise.

Barrow watched, fascinated and enthralled as the ROK tanks bulled their way across the stream. He could hardly believe that he was about to witness, indeed, had a ringside seat for, a battle involving modern armored units. The NKPA gunners still hadn't exposed themselves, but they scored hits on two ROK tanks that were now burning and belching black smoke on the far side of the crossing.

Barrow wondered if he should butt in and call for American artillery on his radio. The fire planning for this kind of attack would allow only the attacking unit to call in fire. Such control was necessary, Barrow knew, to keep friendly artillery from hitting advancing formations. But the ROKs clearly needed help. Just as he finished working up the location, the first rounds of South Korean artillery started coming in on the NKPA positions.

An ROK tank broke from its hide position alongside a paddy dike on the near side and raced for the nearest AVLB, its gears whining as the driver pushed it as fast as it would go. The attack was falling apart because someone up top had pressed what had been planned as a night attack, even though the sun was up. The ROK soldiers couldn't be faulted. Barrow was amazed at how they threw themselves at the crossing, trying to force their way across the mass of burning metal that was piling up on the far side.

A tank on the AVLB exploded, the turret popping up and spinning over the side, landing upside down in the water. The AVLB buckled, reaching with its new V shape for the surface of the river. That left only one bridge intact.

But now the ROK attack started to come together. The South Korean artillery poured smoke and high explosives on the woodline, and the North Korean gunners, without the benefit of thermal sights that enabled the South Korean tankers to see through the smoke, were blinded. Barrow watched as a platoon, then two, then nearly a company of ROK tanks made it across the AVLB. They stopped on the far side, hunkering down behind the limited protection the terraced paddies afforded. Only a few of them were firing. Barrow thought that these monstrous weapons were doing just what individual soldiers would do in the same situation and without leadership. The tanks sought cover, trying to escape the direct fire that was still coming, through the gaps in the smoke, from the NKPA positions on the hill.

If those were troops, Barrow thought, *I'd get them up and moving. They're sitting ducks behind those paddies.*

Barrow's view was suddenly blocked by artillery exploding on the near shore. He let himself slide backward a bit as he heard the high whine of shrapnel singing through the air above his head. The barrage intensified as the North Korean gunners found the range and worked to separate the ROKs already on the enemy side from the rest of the South Korean force. Barrow was on a ridge almost a kilometer back from the crossing site, but he felt his bowels tighten as the *slamslamslamslam* of the rounds reached him. The North Koreans were now mixing smoke in the rounds they were dropping on the site.

Now I can't see a goddamned thing, Barrow swore. He watched for a good sixty seconds as the scene below him drifted in and out of his field of vision with the passing smoke. He wondered why the North Koreans would obscure their own targets, the fourteen tanks in the lower part of the valley. The realization came to him at once with the sound of tracks off to his right.

Barrow rolled right, then pulled himself up on his elbows and scanned the sparse trees and small hills that were off to the right flank of the ROK tanks that had made it across the river and were now holed up on the far side. Nothing. He swung his binoculars back to the stalled attack. Still no movement. *Get moving, you sorry suckers.* He was trying to force his thoughts, like a radio transmission, across the space to the Korean tankers, when he saw the rightmost ROK tank lurch sideways. A split second later there was a terrific explosion inside the vehicle. Flames shot out the blown hatches like hot white water from a hydrant.

Barrow looked right again and saw a sharp tongue of flame in the woods. The North Koreans, far from being surprised, were counterattacking.

Below him on the far side, the ROK tanks whose commanders realized what was happening started to back out. Another on the line took a hit that jammed the turret. With its gun tube stuck straight ahead, it tried to spin backward and to the right, but it only managed to bury the cannon in the soft mud of the paddy. It had used all its time and luck, and a North Korean gunner found his mark, exploding the bucking and helpless tank before it ever got a shot off.

Now several of the ROK tanks had backed away from the paddy wall and swung to the right. They managed to get off a shot each as they punched their smoke generators and moved for better positions.

The North Korean tanks started to show themselves. Three raced from their covered positions behind the low hills, on the South Koreans' right, to get behind the ROKs, between them and the remaining bridge. A South Korean tanker hit one of the end runners, but the other two made it to the edge of the river. They dropped over a small dike that was made to contain the swollen river, and were suddenly in a hull-down position, all but their turrets hidden, firing at the exposed ROK tanks, some of which were still facing uphill.

Barrow saw one of the two NKPA vehicles near the river bracketed by geysers of mud as the ROK tanks in the overwatch positions on the south side tried to join the fight through the drifting smoke. But their line of sight—and their shooting—was erratic. The North Koreans continued to move until they found sheltered positions amid the gullies and washes along the river.

Although four ROK tanks caught in the counterattack were now burning, the remaining vehicles looked like they could fight their way back across the AVLB. Instead, the ROKs chose the more aggressive course, maneuvering their tanks against the North Koreans hidden along the river. But the enemy had the advantage. The South Koreans, perhaps shaken by the sudden counterattack, advanced piecemeal across the little river valley, and were chewed up by the outnumbered but invisible NKPA tankers.

In the space of perhaps seven minutes, Barrow had witnessed the slaughter of over forty men in ten tanks. He was dumbfounded at how quickly it had all taken place. He had barely realized the mistake the ROK tanks had made by huddling on the far side when all hell had broken loose. He wondered if, under the pressure of conducting the attack himself, he would have realized the mistake in time to save his own men. This was to be a game of minutes—seconds— and evidence of the high stakes burned and crackled in the valley below him.

If the battalion commander had any reservations about Isen's plan, the distant crunch of artillery and the close-by snap of tank cannons swayed him to Isen's point of view.

"Okay, Mark, we're gonna go with it," Tilden said. "Jan, get the Fire Support guys down here. You brief the battalion XO and have him pass the word to the S4 to shake out the ammo."

Isen had always thought of his commander as an overly cautious man. But in the face of a real threat to his command, Tilden's decisions were careful and prompt, his orders clear and unmistakable.

Bock, on the other hand, was dead set against Isen's idea. It would tie up many of the unit's critical—and limited—assets, and depended on a combination of factors, all of which were under the control of the North Koreans, who might or might not advance.

"Sir," Bock addressed Tilden, "I think we'd be making a big mistake with this. We just don't have the assets to commit here. We're denying ourselves flexibility if the situation changes. Mark is arguing for nothing less than us putting all our eggs in Charlie Company's basket."

Isen wondered if he would have been as controlled as Bock was now if he were arguing against something he felt that strongly about.

Tilden looked at Bock, then surprised him and Isen by placing his hand on Bock's arm.

"I see your points, Jan, and they're all good ones. But we're going to make our tradeoff right here."

And so it was. Isen would get the assets he wanted, and the battalion's defense, the security of five hundred men, now hinged on his company and how well he could do his job. He experienced a flash of doubt—what if his assessments had been wrong? But he couldn't let unfounded worrying sway him. He still felt that he was right, and they had to do something; they had to be proactive, not reactive, faced as they were with a dangerous mounted enemy. He wished he knew with some certainty that things would work out.

Isen wasn't in the command post when David took the call.

"Foxtrot four three, this is foxtrot zero seven, over."

It was the XO's callsign, but it sure didn't sound like the XO.

"Foxtrot four three, this is foxtrot zero seven, over." The voice was starting to sound frantic, and less and less like Lieutenant Barrow. David reached inside his shirt, to where the communication book, thick with callsigns, frequencies, and codes, hung on a cord around his neck.

"This is four three, over."

"This is foxtrot zero seven, Black Friday, over."

David hadn't been privy to the CO's and XO's conversation, and he had been given no list of codewords. He had no reply for this voice.

"Foxtrot zero seven, authenticate mike uniform, over."

There was a long pause at the other end, such as there always was in response to an unexpected challenge. Authentication required the challenged caller to respond using the correct sheet of letters from among the dozens of possibilities. David had himself been slow at times in responding.

Nothing.

He wondered who could have gotten the callsign—who

was listening in and sending this weird signal. The strange voice, coming through the very handset that David carried, made the enemy seem a lot closer.

"I authenticate, X ray, over."

David still didn't recognize the voice, but the reply, above his dirty fingernail on the encode-decode sheet, was correct.

"I copy Black Friday, over," he said to the handset.

"Roger, over."

"Foxtrot four three, out."

Black Friday. Wonder what the CO is up to now?

He called Perreira, the second platoon RTO, who told David that Isen had just left for the first platoon area in the center of the company sector. David thought he should catch him on foot, so he picked up his weapon, shouldered the radio, which he had removed from his rucksack, and set off to find the commander.

Third platoon's positions were spread along the north slope of the small ridge that defined C Company's position. On the side nearest the CP, some men were resting behind the line, taking advantage of the cover and sitting on the ground.

"Yo, David, how's it goin', man?"

David recognized a soldier named Turney who was, like David, from North Carolina.

"Good, man. What'cha doing?"

"Getting ready to throw a party for the North Koreans, if they try to come this way."

Turney and another man that David didn't recognize were cleaning their weapons. Behind them, farther up the slope, another soldier was cutting salvaged commo wire into lengths of eight feet.

"What's this for?" David asked as he came closer.

"Don't know, yet. Top told me to cut this stuff up, then bring it up to the front of the platoon sector and meet him."

"Where's the CO?"

"I saw him down there"—the soldier raised his arm—"by second squad."

David caught up with Isen, who was crouching among the trees on the north side of the slope.

"Sir, we got a call from foxtrot zero seven. It didn't

sound much like the XO, but he authenticated. He gave me the codeword 'Black Friday.'"

"Thanks, David."

David had been hoping to find out what was going on up here, but Isen was either too distracted to let him in on it, or he didn't think David needed to know yet. The RTO stood still for a few moments, hoping to hear some news, any news about what was going on.

"Go on back to the CP, David. Keep your ear on that radio. The next transmission from the XO is an important one. I'll be along in a minute."

David, clearly disappointed, turned to leave.

"You're doing a good job. Keep it up."

Well, that wasn't much, but it had to be enough for now, David thought. Isen was a good guy. David figured he didn't *need* to know as much as he *wanted* to know. As he walked back down the hill, he watched as a detail from the platoon carried armloads of claymore mines up the hill to the platoon leader's position. *Wonder where they got all those claymores? Must be more than a battalion's share there.* David, unsettled, took his rifle off his shoulder, pulled back the charging handle to make sure there was a round in the chamber, and walked the rest of the way with his rifle in both hands, slung low across the front of his body.

Barrow stayed at his spot, perched above the little river valley, for almost a half hour after the North Korean ambush had taken the edge off the ROK attack. The four surviving tanks that remained on the other side of the river traded desultory shots with the North Koreans, who seemed content to let the South Koreans stay put. Although the carnage he had witnessed had rattled him, he had no trouble at all seeing what the ROKs should do. To push forward at this point, with the North Koreans so obviously in control of the crossing site, would be sheer stupidity. Even though the ROKs had at least a half-dozen tanks, as well as the still-uncommitted infantry, left on the south shore, it was clear that the South Korean commander needed to get his men off the north side of the river. If the North Koreans were at all interested, they could shove the South Koreans back over the river, or pin them down in the valley and carry the counterattack south, eventually running into Charlie Company. But if this was clearly a decision point, there didn't seem to be much activity going on.

What Barrow couldn't see on the far side was that the North Korean battalion commander whose troops had responded with the limited counterattack was arguing for reinforcements. Lieutenant Colonel Tae Kil was the forty-one-year-old commander of the Second Tank Battalion of the 58th Combined Arms Brigade. The brigade, a thirty-five-hundred-man unit, was one of five such independent forces in the VII Corps of the North Korean Special Purpose Forces. These troops, the cause of so much concern to Captain Land and her counterparts in the army intelligence community, were the elite strike forces of the Korean People's Army. Favored with modern equipment and training opportunities that were the envy of commanders in the regular forces, these units were the shock troops of the NKPA. In addition to the intense physical and ideological training that all Special Purpose Forces soldiers underwent, members of the Combined Arms Brigades were experts in coordinating the vast array of combat power—artillery, tactical aircraft, engineer assets, tanks, motorized infantry, chemical weapons—and bringing that fighting power to bear at the critical point on the battlefield.

Tae, like most of the commanders in these units, was highly competent and extremely aggressive. He had been particularly unhappy when, several weeks earlier, he learned that the whole brigade would be kept in reserve while other units spearheaded the thrust through the demilitarized zone. The 58th Brigade had remained in an assembly area near their headquarters at Namdae-ch'on, near the east coast port of Kuum-ni, for several days during the critical buildup before the first attacks. But, frustrated as he was by his initial limited role, Tae was thrilled with the mission that had been given him the previous evening.

North Korean intelligence had learned of the ROK attack—the one witnessed by Barrow—planned along this corridor. Tae's tank battalion had been ordered to rush to the spot and deflect the attack. He had arrived with a single company—the rest were some twenty kilometers behind, waiting for ammunition—in time to get a thorough look at the area, and his soldiers had carried out his plan flawlessly. Their aggressiveness in the counterattack mirrored his own; they were extensions of his personality, he felt. He fed upon their energy and drive, and they fed upon his. They responded instantaneously to his commands, and he used them—their skills and their lives—wisely. That was the deal he had worked out in his mind (the soldiers had no say); they would fight and he would keep in mind that they wanted to live. But mostly, he would fight.

Tae, like Barrow, saw that he could push into the ROK sector south of the river if he seized the moment. Since it was already past two in the afternoon, he realized that there was a chance that any attack started now would have to be pressed after sunset. But he did not want to send his tanks into the wooded ridges on the south side of the stream without dismounted infantrymen to clear the woods of enemy. In the dark his tanks gave up their advantage of speed and range to the lowly infantryman. They could be ambushed in the close quarters of a woods.

The closest 58th Brigade unit was a light infantry company that had been marching since midnight of the night before, and was still nearly two miles away. All the brigade's truck-mobile infantry, as well as their artillery, had already moved closer to the spearhead of the attack, well to the west of where Tae was fighting, and he could not call them back. Only the light infantry, moving on foot and lagging behind the attack, was close enough for Tae to use. He cursed the timing of the attack, cursed his army's lack of motor transport, their insistence on the ascendancy of the foot soldier in a peasant army. He knew that in the last war for Korean unity, the Chinese Communist Forces and the NKPA had always suffered mightily for their lack of mechanization. The UN forces had been able to mass more quickly, and so had inflicted great casualties on the communists.

Tae believed that his soldiers were better than their enemies in every measure. He sometimes wished that they had the resources that the other side had. But plenty, he reminded himself, was a double-edged sword. Tae knew from years of firsthand observation that the Americans in

South Korea were soft, and missed the comforts of home. As part of the training that many Special Purpose Forces officers received, he had several times roamed the South Korean countryside during American maneuvers, disguised as a farmer and talking to the friendly American GIs. He had seen the great lengths they went to import their own culture here, spending untold riches babying their troops, bringing them soda and candy in the field, musical shows in the camps along the demilitarized zone, hot food in the most remote training sites. He hated them for their wealth, for their endless supplies, for their fine equipment. And soon, somewhere miles below the river to his front, he would get his chance to prove to the world how weak the Americans were.

Several miles to the south, Captain Mark Isen was hurrying his company, racing against the failing of the long afternoon. He had gotten an "up" from second and third platoons, now he needed word from first platoon, signaling that they, too, were ready.

Until now he had resisted returning to the platoon sector because he didn't want to be breathing down the platoon leader's neck. He was fairly confident that the lieutenant, a new West Point graduate named Mike Lake, could handle the mission, but he could wait no longer. He had given Lake's platoon the center sector. Although he knew they might have the toughest job if the North Koreans came through mounted, he thought that Lake's platoon could handle it. In just the short time that Lake had been with the company, he had proven himself competent, and his platoon sergeant was one of the strongest in Charlie Company. Still, Isen planned to be nearest Lake's sector during a fight.

As he crested the ridge, just to the right of the road that split the company's position, he saw that the men were working as fast as they could.

"How's it going, Mike?"

"Good, sir. We got about three or four more spots picked out, and we got men up there now, tying the claymores in with commo wire."

Isen glanced to where Lake pointed, and could just

make out the dark forms of soldiers up in the trees a couple of hundred meters down the slope, along the trail that led toward the river.

"How long before you're finished down there?"

"I'd say about twenty minutes, sir."

If Lake was rattled by the urgency, he didn't show it. He was the youngest officer in the company, had been one of the youngest members of his class at West Point. He was tall and well built, with the easy athletic grace of a baseball player. Isen knew that in fact Lake had boxed at West Point. A lot of his quiet confidence, Isen had always thought, must come from knowing that his physical presence was intimidating. The young man's easy calmness was paying off now, helping the troops resist the urge to panic as they hurried their preparations.

"Okay, Mike. Your men know the score? When to hold and when to shoot?"

"Yessir. Sergeant Bladesly and I each briefed half the platoon, then debriefed the other half. They know what's going on. They're ready, sir."

Barrow watched the far side of the river, trying to divine what was going on in the woodline. He checked his watch, then looked again at the valley below. Only in his ignorance, now, did he begin to worry, wondering what would happen next. For the first time that day it occurred to him that he was isolated, a good half-hour's run from the company position. And now that he had seen the display of firepower in the valley, he began to wonder if even the Charlie Company position offered that much of a refuge.

Barrow pulled his rucksack toward him and fished around inside it for something to eat. He found a couple of crackers that had fallen out of one of the plastic bags from his MRE (Meal, Ready-to-Eat) combat ration. He crunched on them and took a swig of water. His nose was swollen and tender, and if he looked down he could see the half moons of thickening flesh under his eyes. It had stopped bleeding, but it hurt like a sonofabitch. He wondered if it would be crooked.

As he probed his cheeks with his fingers, he heard the five or six ROK tanks that were still in overwatch positions to his left and right gun their engines. The ROK infantrymen who had dismounted were now yelling at one another and scrambling into their hatches. Barrow looked up over the ridge, but could see nothing happening on the far side. The ROK tanks stranded over there were still, there was no movement in the distant treeline, and the two NKPA tanks that had come from the right flank to cripple the attack were nowhere to be seen. It was as if they had fought to a draw. But the ROKs on both sides of Barrow were definitely scurrying. As he watched, he saw blue diesel smoke blow from the exhaust grilles of the South Korean tanks on the other side of the river. They popped smoke grenades and looked like they were getting ready to move. A few rounds of artillery came in on the North Korean positions, smoke, but not enough to cover anything. He wondered if the South Korean artillery units were running out of ammunition.

Barrow watched the vehicles stranded on the north bank. The first of the ROK tanks to move out of its cover was hit immediately, its turret swinging crazily as it stumbled like some hard-struck and wounded animal. The ROK tanks on both sides of the river answered with an immediate volley. The tremendous crack of all the cannons at once smacked Barrow's ears, but there were no obvious hits on the far side. The three remaining South Korean tanks then hesitated, and for that they paid dearly. The two North Koreans that had counterattacked and had been hiding all along on the right flank of the crossing site showed themselves again. One of the NKPA tanks was hit by fire from the overwatch position, but the last one moved forward doggedly, hugging the folds in the earth as it stalked the exposed ROK tanks. The North Korean fired five rounds, striking each of the three South Korean tanks at least once. The single NKPA tank was finally struck by fire from the overwatch, and the carnage was complete.

Barrow could see the crewmen of one of the stricken ROK tanks climbing out of the hatches. Only two of them made it to the ground; the vehicle commander sprawled from his cupola, his arms reaching limply downward to the ground, his back stitched with red.

As if on cue, the South Koreans who occupied the ridge with Barrow began a hasty withdrawal. The vehicle commanders maintained control, keeping the proper interval between vehicles. But there was no mistaking the urgency. Before he could grasp what was happening, they had cleared the ridge, leaving Barrow stranded, alone on foot at what was now an unprotected crossing site. He picked up his rucksack and weapon and started down the hill at a slow run.

Three-quarters of a mile to the north, the North Korean light infantry company that Lieutenant Colonel Tae was waiting for finally reached the crossing site. They were exhausted, panting, and sweating profusely.

Tae, conscious of how quickly the opportunity to exploit might slip away from him, gave the arriving unit no time to regroup. He hollered at them to climb on the tanks. He would take them across the river on the bridge.

The infantry commander was horrified. Captain Lee Jae Hyung had received three sets of conflicting orders in the last five hours. He had marched his men hard trying to comply with each new directive. But even as his soldiers obeyed, he felt his credibility slipping. Every time he changed the orders, it looked to his men as if he didn't know what he was doing. He was not as concerned with saving face as he was with the wearing away of the trust they had in him.

The situation was worsening quickly. His men were winded and disorganized. Riding the tanks, they would be exposed to the South Korean artillery that was sure to oppose their crossing. But orders were orders, and he got his men on board. He had started out the two-day forced march with a total of one hundred and twelve men. They had been moving almost continuously, and he'd lost some to injuries, and nearly a platoon had been wounded or killed when an American jet, on its way back from a bombing mission with unexpended ordnance, had chanced on the column. Only sixty-seven North Korean soldiers climbed on the tanks, grabbed the handrails, and squatted so as not to be thrown under the treads of the tank behind when the drivers accelerated. Lee ran toward the colonel's tank, hoping to get a chance to talk to the man as they rode, to find out where they were going and what the plan, if one existed, was.

But Tae's tank accelerated just as Lee got within

shouting distance, leaving the captain stranded and forcing him to catch a ride on the last tank. It would be hours before Lee—who was even now cursing the colonel and kicking the ground in rage—would appreciate how fortunate he had been to miss the ride he wanted.

Barrow made his final call to Isen as he trotted back toward the C Company position.

"Foxtrot four three, this is foxtrot zero seven, over."

"This is four three, over," David answered.

"Let me have the actual." Barrow wanted to talk directly to Isen.

It took a few seconds, but Isen was close by.

"This is zero seven, over."

"This is foxtrot four three, war dog, I say again, war dog, over."

Barrow was coming in. Somewhere behind him, he was sure, the North Koreans would be following.

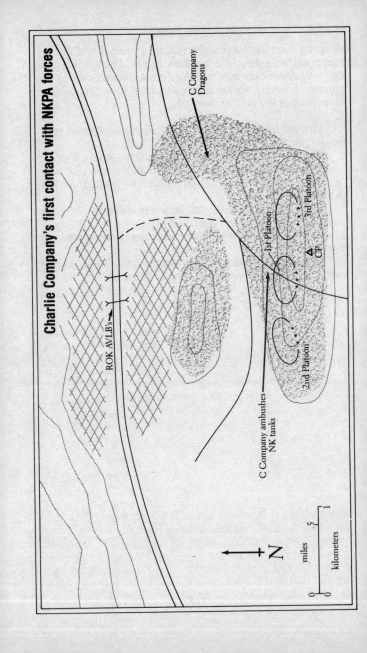

Charlie Company's first contact with NKPA forces

ROK AVLB's

C Company Dragons

1st Platoon

3rd Platoon

CP

2nd Platoon

C Company ambushes NK tanks

N

miles
.5
1

kilometers
0

10

The first North Korean tanks rolled across the remaining bridge under the cover of the NKPA tanks that watched from the ridge north of the river. Lee and his infantrymen, clinging to the handrails on the tank decks, cringed as they waited to hear the incoming artillery. But none came. Perhaps the South Koreans were that disorganized. When they made the south bank Tae didn't hesitate, but drove straight for the cover provided by the ridge just vacated by Barrow and the South Korean elements. The most dangerous part of his attack, Tae believed, had been crossing the bridge in the exposed river valley. He had crouched low in the commander's hatch of his Russian-made T-55 tank as they moved across the bridge. When they made the south side of the river, he stood straight up on the seat below him, so that he was exposed from the waist up. He took a deep breath, convinced now that his attack would succeed. Off to his right, the sun was slipping down the sky.

As Barrow ran along, he heard the South Korean vehicles race toward their own lines. They had decided, for whatever reason, not to make any stand at the river. That left the Americans exposed, but Barrow wasn't sure if the North Koreans even knew that there were American soldiers this far north. With nothing to keep him from being overrun by any North Korean vehicles that had made the crossing, he decided that he wasn't moving fast enough. He dropped his ruck, pulled the radio and its flat harness out, and put that on. He left his forty-pound rucksack, with all of his warm clothing, his chow, and extra ammunition, in some bushes and started running. He hadn't heard any demolition from the direction of the river, and he wondered if the South Koreans had managed to blow up or remove the AVLB that remained.

Isen watched the woodline of the small ridge between his company and the river, looking for his XO. The company was as ready as he could make it; all he needed now was a few breaks. He was counting on the North Koreans to try to push at least as far south as Charlie Company's position before dark. He was also counting on the North Koreans not knowing that the Americans were waiting.

Lieutenant Colonel Tae was ecstatic. The ROKs had abandoned their positions on the nearest ridge south of the river rather than be slaughtered by his battalion's accurate tank fire. He believed in leading from the front of his formations, so his vehicle was the first to reach the ridgeline that had been the South Korean overwatch position. With no enemy in sight, he was now playing against only the fading light.

He pulled out his map and marked a limit of advance for his force, the second ridgeline below the river, about two kilometers to the south. There he would let the infantrymen off the tanks, let them catch their breath, and regroup. He was not happy that they had had to ride over here in such a disorderly manner. He would have greatly preferred to have given the infantrymen time to regroup, to at least get on vehicles with their own chain of command. As it was, the soldiers had jumped on the nearest tanks. The junior leaders did not necessarily know where their men were located, or even which men had made it to the crossing site. But there would be time to sort all that out. The South Koreans didn't look like they were interested in interfering. He was flushed with the excitement of the chase, and though he considered having the infantry dismount to clear the woods on the second ridge, he decided to go for speed instead. When he had only a platoon of tanks on the south shore, he radioed to his second in command to bring the rest of the element across the river. The second ridge, which he suspected had also been abandoned, was split by a trail that ran perpendicular to it, due south over the small rise. He signaled his driver, and the tank rolled ahead into the lengthening shadows.

Barrow reached the Charlie Company position at the same time the North Korean Commander was picking out this ridge as his limit of advance. He went to the CP and fell, breathless, his nose bleeding again, and motioned for David to get Isen.

At first Isen thought Barrow had been shot, because there was so much blood. But when he saw the swollen nose, he knew that the man had been struck somehow. That at least explained why David hadn't recognized the XO's voice.

"The ROKs left the crossing site, sir." Barrow's voice was a honk. "They got their butts whipped down in that valley by a handful of North Korean tanks, and they wound up having to pull back. The bad guys got some hellacious gunners."

"Did you see the North Koreans coming for our side of the river?"

"No. I left when the ROKs did, but I don't think they blew the bridge. The guys on the other side are aggressive. If there's a way across the river here, I think they'll be coming."

"How long?"

"Well, the earliest they could be here is in a few minutes. More likely, they'll be here around dusk."

"Good job, Dale. What happened to your nose?"

"I broke it—can you believe this?—jumping off the ROK vehicle I was riding before I even got up there. Pretty heroic, huh?"

For the first time in several days, Isen felt himself smile. "It does wonders for your looks, it really does."

As he rolled south, Colonel Tae could clearly see the ridgeline he wanted to reach, and realized that he would make it just before dark. He had many things on his mind, nagging questions that buzzed around in his head like disturbed bees, angry and unanswerable: Did these infantry-men have shovels for digging in? Did they have wire and communications equipment? How much ammunition were they carrying? Did they know where their leaders were? How many of them had so much as a single dry shirt to exchange for the sweat-soaked ones they were wearing? He slapped his hands together and turned again to face the front. Creature comforts would have to wait. The eyes of his corps commander were now focused on his efforts here. He would not allow his men to be as soft as the Americans. They would push through to find the South Koreans. They would be sustained by the evidence of the enemy's headlong retreat, reeling before his advance as he sliced through this rich country. He wondered how long it would take to consolidate his gains, set in a defense for the night, bring up fuel and ammunition, and complete any minor repairs the tanks needed. At any rate, he planned to press the attack in the morning, at the latest.

Two hundred and fifty meters north of C Company, three men of Lake's first platoon crawled to find a position from which they could get a good view of the road without exposing themselves. The tall grass along the edge of the woods limited their view, so they had to settle for good close-in observation. They couldn't see the hill to the north.

As the shadow of the ridge behind them stretched up over the next rise, they checked and rechecked the batteries on their night-vision scopes, tested the sound-powered telephone, double-checked the frequency on the single radio they had between them. They were all three conscious of an unspoken, yet clearly recognizable commitment they had to one another to appear calm and to perform well.

Sergeant Keith Lamson was a twenty-two-year-old team leader in the first squad of the first platoon. He was the best man—in the opinion of his squad leader and platoon sergeant—to be in charge of the forward observation post on this crucial evening.

Lamson, in his turn, had only four men to choose from. He left his best soldier in charge of the team's portion of the platoon position. Only later, when he was lying still on the forest floor, did he think that perhaps he had been picking his successor.

Lamson had with him a nineteen-year-old PFC from Philadelphia, Tony Cipriotti, and a twenty-year-old Floridian named Brian Boste.

Boste was a rock, a little too quiet perhaps, but one of the most technically competent soldiers in the squad. Boste was armed with a SAW, or Squad Automatic Weapon, a small machine gun that fired the same 5.56 millimeter ammunition as did the standard M-16 rifle. Boste thought he looked gangster-like with the weapon, which sported a plastic drum of ammunition on the side. As a kid he had seen *The St. Valentine's Day Massacre,* and he could easily be encouraged to do an imitation of Capone's henchmen, swinging the weapon from side to side like the old .45-caliber submachine guns popularized by Hollywood.

Cipriotti was another story. A small, wiry Italian from South Philadelphia, he had been in trouble once a month for each of the six months he had been with the unit. On two occasions the trouble had involved a barfight, a woman (a different one each time), and the business end of a military policeman's nightstick.

Lamson didn't like Cipriotti, and he kept hoping that the CO would remove the headache from the squad and from the army. It didn't take Lamson long to figure out that Isen liked Cipriotti's spirit. But the CO didn't have to listen to him on a daily basis.

"Yo, Sarge, what's going to be coming up this here trail?" Cipriotti had an elaborate stage whisper that did nothing to hide his thick accent. *Yo, Sahge, whutz ganna be cummin' up this heah trail?*

"Don't call me Sarge, Cipriotti," Lamson replied.

"Yes, Sergeant."

"Well, could be nothing will come up the road." Lamson paused and looked at Cipriotti, who was studying him intently. "Or could be some North Koreans."

"Don't worry, Sip," Boste added, "we ain't gonna fight 'em, just spot 'em."

Boste was sighting his weapon along a small log he had placed on the ground under the barrel. When he had the gun aligned on a good target area, he used his bayonet to cut a small notch in the log below the barrel. Later, in the dark, he would merely have to lay the barrel of the weapon on the log and he'd be firing into his target area.

"Don't forget what the CO wants in the report," Lamson said for the tenth time. "What is it, Cipriotti?"

Cipriotti had taken three hand grenades from his web gear and laid them, with exaggerated care, on the ground in front of him. He had removed the packing clips and was now straightening the pins for easier pulls.

"The old man needs to know how many tanks, how many other vehicles, how much infantry, and . . . umm . . ."

Lamson was amazed at how dense the man was. "Well?"

"Oh, yeah, he wants to know if the vehicle commanders are riding exposed, you know, outside the turrets."

"They're never gonna know what hit them," Boste added.

If we get to hit them first, Lamson thought.

Lamson heard it first—armored vehicles on the road below them, toward the north and the river. There was a tremendous crashing close by that threatened to drown out the noise from the road, but it was only his heart, thundering against his rib cage. He looked over at Cipriotti and Boste. Boste gave him a thumbs-up, but Cipriotti looked at him with a wide-eyed, animal stare. Lamson could see that Cipriotti was glistening with sweat. He reached out to touch the youth on the shoulder, hoping that his hand wouldn't tremble.

He unsnapped the chinstrap of his helmet and pressed the telephone as close to his face as he could get it, then studied the empty road. Sergeant Keith Lamson, fire-team leader, was the most forward man in the division, and he would be the first man in the American relief force to square off with the enemy. His being there was evidence that America was ready to put its money where its mouth was, one young man at, in the words of his Commander-in-Chief, the point of the spear, representative of the commitment of the most powerful military forces the free world could muster. But Keith Lamson was oblivious to all of this. He was conscious only of the labored breathing of the two young men with him, of his own vulnerability—even mortality—and of the responsibility he had to warn the other soldiers in C Company. His generation wasn't raised on words like duty, and honor, and he would have insisted that he was only doing his job, but every atom of him was focused on divining what might be coming up the road.

He saw the gun tube of the lead tank first, peeking around a slight bend, hesitating, then pulling completely into view. There was a rush of panic as he couldn't identify the tank as friend or foe. He couldn't see its shape. But then he realized that there were infantrymen crouched all over the tank's deck, trying desperately to hold on as the vehicle dashed from side to side on the small road.

North Koreans.

Lamson depressed the push-to-talk switch, signaling his platoon leader that he had a report. Once he had an answer, he began to speak.

Colonel Tae was annoyed with his tank commanders. They weren't closing in on him fast enough—they were driving slowly because they were afraid the infantrymen clinging to the sides of the vehicles would fall off.

He considered having the soldiers dismount and advance on foot, but he didn't want to get to the ridge without the foot soldiers there to clear and occupy the ground. He also considered slowing down enough so that the straggling tanks could close up, but he knew there were only twenty minutes or so of daylight left. He was afraid he wouldn't be able to reconnoiter the ridge properly in the dark.

It is only another half kilometer to the ridgeline. I can press on like this and fix the formation when I get there.

He leaned farther out of his turret to better see over the

infantrymen on his tank. The ridge he was climbing had a gentler rise to the east, on Tae's left. There, the hill and the woods on the hill reached farther down toward the river, which was now behind the colonel. The ridge was steepest on its western end, off the front right of Tae's tank. The trail he followed entered the close quarters of the woods near the ridge's center. As his tank entered the bottleneck, he was too preoccupied with thinking about the best way to consolidate his gains, to study those woods. He wouldn't have seen anything anyway.

There was only one tank immediately behind him. He turned to wave at the vehicle commander, relieved that at least one had caught up to him. Down the hill to the north, he could see five more tanks, all likewise covered with infantry. They were only minutes behind, but he decided to radio his second-in-command to see how many of his vehicles had made it across the river on the South Korean bridge.

As he turned in his hatch, he noticed the outlines of a dozen or so rectangles in the trees, just off the trail and above his head. His last thought before the daisy chain of claymores went off was *I wonder what those are?*

Sergeant First Class Martin Bladesly pressed the firing device that controlled the claymore mines when he saw that both of the lead tanks were well within the kill zone of the ambush. He had put his head down and buried his face in the loose soil so the sudden bright flash wouldn't blind him, but the sound and the shock wave from the explosion still rocked him.

Nearly two dozen claymores went off simultaneously, over fifty pounds of plastic explosives and thousands of steel pellets the size of large ball bearings ripping the North Korean infantrymen from the vehicles. Both tank commanders had been exposed from the waist up. There was no sign of the commander of the second vehicle, but Bladesly could see the commander still in the hatch of the lead tank, his body pinned across the top of the blood-slick turret.

Bladesly's machine gunners opened up immediately, as they had been instructed to do. They were almost directly in front of the tanks in this L-shaped ambush, and their disciplined six-shot bursts caught the column head-on, spraying rounds along its length. But there were no surviving soldiers to worry about.

Now Bladesly had two tanks, without commanders but otherwise unscathed, to deal with. The vehicles were still moving in the kill zone, and the trail tank had picked up speed and was rushing up the little road. The lead tank was still moving at the same slow speed, but at an angle to the road that would run it into an embankment that was probably too steep to climb. Bladesly saw that the driver's periscopes were blocked by the body of one of the soldiers that had been riding on the tank. The second tank would not be able to maneuver around the lead vehicle on the narrow road. Bladesly had a slight advantage that would last only a few seconds. He had to win the fight in that time or the tanks would back up and find another way to attack, rolling over his platoon.

In the woods to the north and east of Bladesly's position, set a few hundred meters off the trail, five Dragon teams from second and third platoons tracked their targets —the five North Korean tanks that had fallen behind their commander. The American gunners were to take out these tanks when the ambush was sprung.

Corporal Bernie Parrish was not one of the assigned Dragon gunners in third platoon; he was a fire-team leader, recently promoted, with three men under him. But he had been the best gunner in Charlie Company for the last eighteen months—always firing the highest scores on the simulators. Twice during that time he had been chosen to fire live Dragon rounds, the only two live rounds that the battalion had seen fired in over two years. The Dragon was an expensive missile.

The Dragon, the army's medium range anti-tank weapon, was another in the family of wire-guided missiles. The gunner held the disposable fiberglass launcher and most of the weight on his shoulder; a folding metal leg at the front of the tube helped stabilize it. In theory, the gunner need only keep the scope's crosshairs on the target. A computer brain in the reusable tracker sent flightpath corrections to the missile through the wire that played out from the tube. Small motors on the sides of the missile fired, like the boosters on a spaceship, to correct the missile's flight, even to the point where it could hit a moving target.

In practice, the trackers and the rounds got banged around as the infantrymen carried them for days over all types of terrain. The sensitive electronic components, the small computer chips and tiny wires, could not withstand the jostling.

Bernie Parrish, the best shot in the company, was the only man to have fired the missile live—and both of his shots had missed, nose-dived into the ground. The civilian technicians that had come out to watch the last shoot, representing the company that charged the government ten thousand dollars per missile—weren't sure what happened.

"Just a bad lot of missiles, I guess," one of them had said.

So the army had gotten soaked on the Dragon, a piece of equipment that was too complicated for its own good. Replacement weapons were on the drawing boards—but in the meantime, ten American soldiers were out in a darkening woods six thousand miles from home, facing the first armored enemy American soldiers had seen in a long time, all the while wondering if the goddamn thing would even reach the tank, much less kill it.

When the golden flash of the exploding claymores rolled down the hill, Parrish squeezed the trigger mechanism. He watched in agonizing slow motion as the tank commander dropped inside the vehicle, and a few infantrymen riding on the tanks leapt to the ground, warned by the explosions up the hill. Then came the loud, windy rush as the rocket motor ignited. He felt the missile jump inside the tube, then lost the sight picture as the weight suddenly left his shoulder. He recovered quickly and regained the target.

Parrish wasn't conscious of the other gunners firing, but they had all picked out their targets ahead of time so as not to waste missiles. Unfortunately they did not have enough trackers to engage the tanks with multiple rounds as they would have liked. They were firing one round at each tank. The gunners were back far enough in the woods so that the signature blast of flame and smoke would be hidden from view. Unless the tankers had been looking in this direction, which was to their left and sightly to the rear, it was unlikely that they saw the shots. The Americans would have a few more seconds before the tankers would see the slow-flying missiles.

Parrish could see the rocket's corrective charges firing as the tracker sent flight-path corrections to the missile through the thin wire that was trailing from the tube on his shoulder. His target tank went into a small dip in the trail as it accelerated, but Parrish quickly regained the sight picture as it came out.

On target, on target, he muttered to himself through clenched teeth, wondering if they would see the missile. *On target.* The missile drove home just below the level of the tank deck. The effect was not immediately obvious as the missile's shaped charge burned through the tank's steel side, creating a hole not much bigger than a silver dollar and sending molten steel flying through the crew compartment, incinerating everything in there. Parrish took his eye from the sight just as the tank's ammunition cooked off, separating the turret from the hull at the back of the turret ring. He had killed the lead tank.

He yelled to his assistant gunner for the next round as he tore at the tracker, separating it from the now-useless tube.

Only one other missile had found its mark. Parrish watched as the other tanks swung their turrets around even as they ran for cover—firing off the main gun rounds that had been in their tubes. The three tank rounds, probably the solid steel spikes used against other tanks, went shrieking overhead, scary but harmless.

The North Koreans moved from the trail, driving off the west side where the path was raised above the surrounding paddies. The tankers, knowing that they were being engaged by infantry, opened up with their machine guns. In the failing light, they had no targets in sight, but they poured a deadly volume of fire into the dark treeline. One team was hit, the men caught full in the chest and back as they worked to load the next Dragon round. Parrish hollered at the other gunners to reload. The gunner in the position next to his was yelling at his assistant for the spare round, but the young soldier stared at the spot downhill where he could see, among the trees, the motionless legs of the first two Charlie Company soldiers to be killed.

Farther up the hill to the south, Bladesly watched the blinded lead tank career into the ditch on the near side of the road. The slight downward tilt was enough to keep the vehicle from climbing and getting at its tormentors. The gunner fired the coax, the machine gun mounted along the axis of the main gun, but its rounds went harmlessly into the dirt. Bladesly saw the legs of the dead tank commander suddenly appear as he was pushed from below. Another soldier—the gunner?—appeared, grabbed the commander's machine gun, and fired a long but not well-aimed burst uphill. He yelled something into the tank, which began to back up. Down and to Bladesly's right, several riflemen opened fire, killing the exposed tanker instantly.

The second tank was firing its coax as well, also with little accuracy. On flat ground, the tank would have driven through the line of infantrymen unscathed. But here, in the close quarters of the woods, with a blocked road ahead of them and the tank crew buttoned up inside and unable to see very well, the odds were considerably evened.

The ragged firing of four or five LAWs drowned out all but the whine of the North Korean's engine. Bladesly's troops were firing volleys of the small rockets. The increase in number gave them a better chance of getting a hit.

Bladesly saw the trails of two rockets that bounced off the second tank's turret. One of his soldiers worked around behind the tank, and his rocket found the lightly protected engine compartment. The tank lurched, then halted, immobile but still dangerous. Its front plate was almost touching the rear of the lead tank. Thick black smoke curled up from the stricken second vehicle, giving Bladesly an idea.

"Smoke," he screamed, pulling at a smoke grenade he had on his web gear. He tossed the canister down on the tanks. One of his squad leaders added a few more, and soon the tanks were swathed in smoke from the grenades and the burning engine fluids. Whoever was left inside the vehicles wouldn't be able to see their attackers.

Bladesly saw three of his men crawl slowly down the hill

and set up deliberately, taking careful aim from just behind the tanks. Two of the rockets went through the deck of the rear tank. Then, as calmly as if they were on a firing range back at Schofield, they extended two more of the collapsible fiberglass launchers and took aim at the lead tank. The driver of that vehicle started to climb out, thought better of it, then extended his hands through the hatch in surrender. The riflemen, who by this time were in position to kill the tank if it resisted, helped the wounded man out of the small hatch.

Through the crackle of flames and the explosions of tank ammunition, Bladesly heard the sound of a helicopter.

Isen was in the first platoon sector, just uphill from where Bladesly had positioned his machine guns. He was kneeling; David and Murray were lying flat out next to him. Isen held a radio handset in one hand, a wire telephone in the other.

"This is kilo four foxtrot four three. We have three enemy tanks at checkpoint three zero; I say again, three enemy tanks at checkpoint three zero."

His voice crackled with the excitement of the battle. He had a report from his Dragon teams that the three tanks that survived the initial ambush were on the loose somewhere downhill from Charlie Company. Isen knew that if the tankers figured out that they were facing a light infantry company, they wouldn't hesitate to break through, and would probably be successful. But he suspected that the violence of the initial contact had shaken them, and they had no idea what was in front of them. The voice that came back to him over the radio was calm, slow, and obviously coming from a helicopter. The speaker's voice vibrated with the pounding of the blades.

"Foxtrot four three, this is uniform one one. I understand three tanks at checkpoint three zero. I can see some vehicles burning in the woods. Are those the targets? Over."

"Negative," Isen shot back. "We got those. There are three more down the hill somewhere. I have some friendly troops in the woods. Watch your shooting, over."

Isen was talking to the section leader of a light attack

section, part of a three-helicopter team that had moved into the area to help even the odds as Charlie Company struggled to fight a platoon of tanks. The mainstays of the team were two Apache helicopters, twelve-million-dollar, all-weather, flying weapons platforms that were specifically designed to kill tanks. A lot of tanks, quickly, and from well beyond the range that the tanks could shoot back.

"Roger, four three, my shooter will be on station in one minute, over."

"Good hunting, one one," Isen said, "out."

The scout helicopter was just behind the ridge occupied by Isen's company, hovering low to the ground so that he was invisible from the north. One killer would come up on the right flank, two and a half miles southeast of Isen. The other Apache held back, in reserve four miles away.

Fifty seconds later, the scout helicopter slowly raised itself, unmasking the electronic eyes that were mounted in a black ball above the rotor head. The body of the helicopter was still invisible behind the hill mass. But now the pilot and the AFSO, aerial fire support officer, could see the terrain in front of them through the eyes of the MMS, the mast mounted sight. One tank showed up immediately on the twin screens in the cockpit, its hot engine plates showing green on the tube. The AFSO pressed the laser trigger, sending an invisible beam out to touch the target. The Automatic Target Handoff System sent all the target information: location of spotter, direction and distance to the target, target movement, and target elevation, from the Scout's on-board computer to the Apache's, in a burst of coded radio waves.

"Target identified."

The Apache responded simply, "Accept." He was ready for the engagement.

The AFSO, a young artillery lieutenant, adjusted the crosshairs on his screen, placing them on the center of mass of the green target. Three-quarters of a mile away, the tank crew was desperately seeking targets in the treeline from which the missiles had come just a few minutes earlier. They had no way of seeing the helicopter, no way of knowing that the invisible laser beam had singled them out. The lieutenant's finger was poised above the laser trigger as he spoke into his headset. "Ready."

In the Apache, twenty-five-year-old Lieutenant Paul Walthers was in a near trance-like state, holding the joystick control of the chopper by the slightest pressure. The helicopter was as near still as it could be, hovering sixty feet off the ground behind a ridge. As a slight wind nudged it to the side, Walthers simply *thought* about increasing the pressure infinitesimally, swinging the great machine as if against a gossamer web.

Walthers had only recently been in simulated combat at the army's National Training Center in Fort Irwin, out on the hot skillet of California's Mojave Desert. There the Apache had enjoyed great success, when it flew.

The National Training Center, NTC to the soldiers, is a training ground for mechanized forces, and is hailed by army brass as the closest thing to combat that modern technology can create. All vehicles and weapons systems are tied to a gigantic computer complex, so that controllers can keep tally of movement, maneuver, mistakes, and kills. In his unit's first go at desert warfare, Walther's performance and that of his platoon had prompted the senior controller to remark that "whoever has the Apaches—wins."

Then the maintenance problems set in. The fine desert dust blew in great tan clouds across the hills, and was sucked up by the Apache's greedy air intakes. The talcum-fine sand wore away the sensitive mechanical and electrical equipment. After a week, Walther's unit had more aircraft grounded than flying. He had experienced few things as humiliating as having to sit at the repair point, his helmet and his flight gear in a heap at his feet, while he waited for the technicians to service his helicopter. He was passed there by several officers from the opposing mechanized infantry unit, who couldn't resist a cut at the fly-boy. They reminded him that the tables do sometimes turn, and that, even though they were mere diesel jockeys, they weren't going to be walking anywhere that day.

Walthers felt he had something to prove here about this machine and its believers. But for now he had emptied his mind of everything except the feel of the great aircraft through the thin gloves on his hand, and the voice of his co-pilot/gunner, who nodded to Walthers as he spoke through the intercom.

"Shot, over," the gunner in the Apache said.

"Shot, out," the AFSO in the scout said, confirming that the machines were communicating. He pressed the laser trigger.

The Hellfire missile is capable of climbing over trees and hills on its own, so that the Apache never has to expose itself to the target. But Walthers was overcome by curiosity, and he raised the nose of the helicopter slightly. The valley below was visible just for a few seconds, long enough for the pilots to see the burning tanks that Bladesly's men and the Charlie Company Dragon gunners had destroyed. They could not see the target tank, but didn't have to. The gunner fired the missile, which left the chopper in a *whoosh* of white smoke. As soon as the missile was away, Walthers brought his aircraft below the ridge again. The North Koreans had not seen him.

Now the Hellfire missile was streaking toward the target, the photo sensor cells in its head picking up and homing in on the reflected laser beam that the scout helicopter held on the target. It reached its top speed of Mach II in the first half mile, and as its rocket motors were in the rear, it became all but invisible. The target tank, unsuspecting to the last, disappeared in a white spray of fire.

The commanders of the last two North Korean tanks remaining on the south bank did not see the explosion, but they heard it and felt the effect on their vehicles. They both backed into a small wash that they hoped would lead down to the riverbed, frustrating the Scout helicopter's efforts to find more targets. One tank swung just in time to catch a Dragon round square on its front glacis plate, the thickest part of the tank's armor. The blast stunned the driver, but as he was protected by four inches of rolled steel, he was unhurt. Two more of Parrish's men fired Dragons at the retreating tanks, but the rounds were high, and one of them exploded in the trees.

The tankers popped smoke grenades, turned toward the river, and made for the bridge, hugging the low ground as they went. The helicopters, low on fuel and under orders to stay south of the river, did not pursue.

Charlie Company and the supporting helicopters had destroyed five tanks in twelve minutes of furious shooting. When Lieutenant Lake, who by now was out front with the forward-most observers, called Isen and told him the remaining tanks were retreating, Isen was almost afraid to believe his first platoon leader.

"Foxtrot, one two, this is foxtrot four three, get me a status on those Dragon gunners, over," Isen instructed. He had a feeling it wasn't nearly over yet. The North Koreans would never leave them with that easy a fight. He had to get his company ready for the next onslaught.

Isen turned to David. "Get on the wire and tell Top to get some more Dragon rounds ready."

David was beside himself with excitement. He fumbled at the field phone, almost unable to turn the small crank that would ring the other end.

"We took care of 'em, didn't we, sir?" David said.

Isen called Lake and told him to move the Dragon gunners from their position in the woods.

Lake was incredulous. "But we got great shots from here, over."

Isen cut him off. "I say again, move those positions, out."

Lake moved over to where the gunners had been concealed in the woodline. He was on an adrenaline rush from the contact, but came up short when he saw the two bodies wrapped in ponchos. Corporal Parrish was standing nearby, giving orders for the men to get ready to move. When he saw Lake looking at the bodies, he came up.

"It's McCreavy and Bartkowski, sir."

Parrish was calm, calmer even than usual, and this made Lake all the more aware that he was about to throw up. He looked from the ponchos to Parrish, then to the ground. There seemed to be something he should say, but for the life of him he couldn't imagine what it was.

Parrish continued. "We're gonna move them back now, sir. Did the CO say we should be moving or anything?"

Lake grabbed hold of his reason. "Yeah. How did you know?"

"Well, if I was those North Koreans, I'd be calling in some artillery on this woodline, pronto. They might not know who's out here, but they know where we was shooting from."

Lake felt a sinking feeling. *Of course the enemy would call in artillery.* He had been a fool not to have known that, a bigger fool to question Isen's decision to move these gunners. "Let's get out of here. You have enough guys to carry everything?"

"We got it under control, el-tee. Are you bringing the other guys in?" Parrish asked, meaning Lamson and his crew.

Lake didn't know, and though he desperately wanted to look like he was sure of what he was doing, he knew that there is nothing to be gained, and a lot to be lost, by play-acting for your subordinates. "I gotta call the CO on that."

As they spoke, four of the men who had been with Parrish picked up the two bodies, struggling to keep their footing as they found the balance. They were skittish and obviously ill at ease with their strange burdens. Lake thought he had never seen young men so sad. Parrish and a couple of others brought up the rear of the little group, making their way back to Charlie Company in the last light.

Isen told Lake to move Lamson and his men in closer to the company position, check their communication equipment, then come back to the company himself. Lake had just cleared the woods where Parrish and the gunners had been when several rounds of artillery burst among the trees. Lake crouched over in his run, his breath coming in sharp, shallow gasps, and muttered a quick prayer, thankful that he was being trained by Isen.

Lamson was ready to move when Lake arrived. He knew that the standard operating procedure, the SOP, called for observation posts to be pulled in closer at night, when they became LPs, listening posts. Lake led Lamson and the two other men to a site they had picked out in the daytime, in the woods north of the center of Charlie Company's sector, just downhill from where the tanks that Bladesly had destroyed in the ambush were still burning fitfully.

Lake talked to the three men for a while about what they were expected to do out here in the dark. Lamson was as coolly confident as ever, maybe even more so after what had happened that afternoon. Cipriotti was strangely quiet, Boste profoundly morose. Lake sensed that Boste was angry at having to pull duty out here again, but the men didn't say anything. As he was leaving, Cipriotti flashed him a wide smile, but said nothing.

Back in the company CP, Isen and the KATUSA questioned the captured tank driver. The North Korean had been stunned to find that his captors were Americans. He was terrifically frightened, sure that he was to be killed. Once he believed that Americans did not, as a matter of course, kill their prisoners, he started talking. They had been told, he admitted, that they would encounter no Americans for at least several days. He also told them that the tank soldiers had been angry that they had not been allowed to wait for the infantry to clear the woods. The infantry should have crossed first. Now all his friends were dead.

One of Isen's soldiers helped the man, whose hands were bound, get to his feet. Voavosa, who had just returned from distributing ammunition, told the medic to put a dressing on a burn on the man's neck.

"Anything else, sir?" Voavosa asked Isen.

"No, Top. You going back?"

"Just to the pick-up point over the hill behind us here. I want to make sure that McCreavy and Bartkowski are put on the trucks."

Voavosa and his little group shuffled away under the heavy load of two dead men. Isen watched them, wondering what he would write to the families of those soldiers when he got a chance. He wondered, too, if the enemy infantry that had survived the fight had headed north across the river, or was even now moving through the trees on this ridge toward Charlie Company.

* * *

Lake reached his platoon CP, in the center of the company sector, an hour later. He found SFC Bladesly sitting with two canteen cups of coffee.

"Have a seat, sir, and I'll give you a rundown of what's going on."

Lake dropped to the ground, letting his feet dangle into the fighting position, and took the cup. He burned his tongue on the first gulp, but savored the warmth as it went down.

"Thanks." Lake had been moving continuously since four o'clock that morning, nearly nineteen hours. He had been moving when the North Korean tanks appeared, down checking on Lamson's position, which was why Bladesly ran the ambush. "Okay, what have we got?"

"First thing is the platoon. I had the two squads that stayed back spread out among the positions, improving them for tonight. Sergeant Mickson checked all the positions himself, and I checked the crew-served weapons. We got a resupply of ammo, we got trip flares out, and claymores, and we got a sleep plan ready. Most of the men had time to get something to eat. I rustled you up some coffee and an MRE."

"Thanks. What's the word from the CO?"

"I think the colonel is coming down," Bladesly continued. "Him and the CO are going to be checking the platoons. I figure you got time to knock back some chow before they get here."

"Great." Lake was immensely relieved. He was sure he would have been able to think of all those things by himself, but he certainly wouldn't have been able to do them all. He grabbed a plastic-wrapped MRE and cut it open with his knife, looking for something inside that he could eat as he walked.

"Let's take a look around now," he said, pulling himself to his feet.

"Okay, sir." Bladesly got up and nudged a figure that was sleeping beside the fighting position. It turned out to be Janeson, the platoon RTO.

"Tune in, Janeson," Bladesly told him after making sure the man was fully awake. "The el-tee and I are going around the sector. You listen for the horn."

Lake moved in the direction Bladesly indicated. He had been unsure of himself when he was setting the platoon in—when was it, yesterday? But now he was confident that he knew what to look for as he checked the positions. The moon was up and provided enough light for them to find the holes fairly easily.

Lake checked the fighting positions, climbing down into each, careful not to step on the man whose turn it was to sleep. He questioned the squad leaders and the team leaders, asked the soldiers about what was to their front, now hidden in the darkness.

Each position had a range card, a schematic of what the sector front looked like. The machine gunners and the grenadiers had the most elaborate, with ranges, directions, and elevations all noted at the bottom of the luminous piece of plastic. The card had been Lake's idea, and he was glad to see that the troops had adopted it, both because it made sense in the dark, and because it had been his idea.

Lake felt better as he moved from hole to hole, as he saw the results of the discipline and the training. He had inherited a good platoon when he came to the unit only three months earlier. His first field problem had been the Team Spirit exercise; he had been nervous then, but in a decidedly different way. By the time of their return to Hawaii, Lake felt like he fit into the unit.

Now his concerns weren't that simple. There was a new twist to things, spelled out in the memory of the two poncho-wrapped bodies he had seen late that afternoon, and underscored in the calm trust of the men he talked to as he made his rounds. They believed he would do his best for them. Whether his best would be enough was another question. As he walked back to the CP, he formed an awkward prayer in his mind.

Dear God, let me do okay. Don't let me let them down.

He wondered if it would be sacrilegious to pray for a victory in this small battle—for success in the killing that was coming.

When Lake and Bladesly got back to the CP, Isen and Tilden were already waiting for them.

"Mike." Isen surprised Lake by shaking his hand.

"Mike, we're making the rounds of the platoons, but

we're not going to have time to go out to each position. Why don't you just show us what you have? You have a platoon sketch?"

"Right here, sir." It was Bladesly, stepping up and offering a notebook. He unrolled his poncho as Isen, Tilden, and Lake got down on the ground, their heads close together, their bodies splayed like the spokes of a wagon wheel. When Bladesly covered them so that no light would show, Lake turned on his red-filtered flashlight. Under the poncho, Tilden addressed Isen.

"These guys did a great job up here today, Mark. You know that. As far as we know now, that bridge is still intact, and we're not sure what they've got on the other side."

"Most of my second platoon wasn't engaged today, sir. They'll be running patrols pretty far down toward the river tonight. My third platoon lost two men—one of the Dragon teams. And of course we'll have LPs out in the thick woods."

Tilden pulled his map into the small circle of red light, checking Bladesly's sketch against the terrain.

"We have some GSRs available tonight. I think I'll send them up so you can use them out here on your right."

The GSRs were man-transportable ground surveillance radars that were particularly useful at night for keeping an eye on terrain that was supposed to be quiet. When set up, they were about the size of a kitchen chair. Good operators could also "vector" a friendly patrol, listening to their progress and keeping them on course by sending corrections over the radio.

Lake looked on as Tilden and Isen formulated the plans for Charlie Company's defense of the battalion's right flank. Although the ROKs had sent a liaison to the battalion CP, Paco's third platoon still had not made contact with the ROK line that was supposed to be off to Charlie Company's right. As far as these men knew, there was a dangerous gap on that side.

Lake tried to anticipate how his bosses would lay things out, tried to figure how he would do things if he were in charge.

"I'm going to plan for my defensive fires to cover out as far as the small hill between us and the river," Isen went on.

"What would you think about our trying to get a patrol with a GLD down near the bridge to take it out, sir?"

The GLD, or Ground Laser Designator, could guide in "smart" bombs such as the Hellfire that the Apache had used against the tank earlier that afternoon. The newest version of the system, developed for the marines, was man-portable. It looked harmless enough, like an overgrown olive-drab video camera. But it could pick out a target for a pinpoint hit by a laser-guided round fired from an artillery piece thousands of meters behind the front lines. If Isen could get Christian, his Fire Support Team leader, up into the river valley with one of those, he could eliminate the AVLB that the South Koreans had put in place there. Since the North Korean spearhead was well to the west of them, chances were that there wouldn't be any bridging equipment nearby. Isen liked the idea of having the river to protect him from more tanks.

"I'll have to talk to division on that," Tilden said. "That bridge still belongs to the ROKs, and they might not want us to blow it up just yet."

As the battalion commander spoke, Lake wondered what might be coming over that troublesome bridge in the darkness, making its way toward the ridge, guided by the beacons of the still-burning tanks.

11

26 April · Tuesday · 0001 hrs

A kilometer to the north of the crossing site, a North Korean major, Chang Kang-Su, had inherited command of the independent tank battalion when his commander, Lieutenant-Colonel Tae Kil, had been killed by Charlie

Company's ambush. Most of the battalion was still somewhere off to the northeast, and Chang was profoundly disturbed that he could not raise those companies on the radio. A large part of the tank company that had fought so well against the ROKs that day had been decimated on the south side of the river. Although he had just been reinforced by two companies of light infantry, he was short on armor, his most critical weapon, and on intelligence about what had happened on the south bank. Chang was trying to piece together what had happened by questioning the commanders of the two tanks that had made it back to the North Korean side.

One of the tankers, a lieutenant who appeared to be the younger of the two, was doing most of the talking. He had a long, deep cut over his right eye, and his face was covered with dried blood. He had opened the wound when his tank had jerked back into the streambed that had allowed them to escape the last volley of anti-tank missiles. A few hours earlier he had been exhausted, almost able to fall asleep in his hatch when they were waiting for the infantry and the chance to sprint across the South Korean bridge. Now he was nauseous with nervous energy and adrenaline, anxious to get his tank ammo uploaded and the fuel topped off, and eager to get back to the south side of the river. He made no effort to hide his desire to take the fight back to the enemy.

"With the newly arrived infantry, Major, I think we can clear those woods and gain the ridge before dawn. That would put us in a position to exploit the better roads on the south side of the river when the sun comes up."

He wanted to add that every moment that they spent debating the issue was wasted time, that they needed to get the infantry across, but he was aware of how easily the major could silence him. The new commander was a little man with thick glasses who did not fit the dashing image of the Special Purpose Forces. The young lieutenant mistook his new commander's deliberateness for timidity.

"I'm not sure we can go again," the new commander said. "We took grave losses in that action over there, grave losses."

The lieutenant almost spoke, but then realized the major was talking about the death of the colonel. *Merely the price of victory,* he thought to himself as he bowed his head in mock sorrow.

"We can send the infantry across to get into those woods, see what is there, then move again when they tell us it is clear," Chang said, as if considering the plan for the first time.

"Sir, there were no tanks on the south side. We took fire only from infantry," the lieutenant continued. He wanted to throttle the man. Couldn't he see that they were throwing away an opportunity here? He decided not to mention his suspicion that some of the enemy missiles had come from helicopters. Instead, he pressed on, sensing that his new boss was weakening.

"I would like to take my company across."

"What's left of your company, you mean," Chang added.

The aggressive posture and the reputation of the Special Purpose Forces were working against Chang at the moment. He wanted to conduct a better-planned, more deliberate move to the south side of the river, so as not to repeat the mistakes made by his late boss. But he had little choice, really. He was very much aware that his brigade and corps commanders had expected this attack to work, had been promised, by the now-dead colonel, that it *would* work. And he would be the one explaining what happened if nothing came of it.

His immediate superior, Senior Colonel Ch'oe Chon Hwang, commander of the 58th Combined Arms Brigade, was rabid for some measurable success. As the days went by, the brigade was being committed piecemeal, while other parts were being held in reserve. This would never do for the ambitious senior colonel. A successful local counterattack that opened a new avenue south would steal some of the limelight from the brigades now spearheading the main attack. Colonel Ch'oe wanted attention, he wanted resources, he wanted to be the hero of the moment in this, the only show in town.

Major Chang did have the option to resist. He could drag his feet for a few more hours, perhaps stall the attack until dawn. But he would no doubt be relieved, perhaps even shot by the mercurial colonel. And that would leave his men in the hands of officers such as the tanker lieutenant standing in front of him.

He turned to his runner and sent for the senior company commander of the two late-arriving infantry companies, then turned back to the lieutenant.

"Prepare your men, Lieutenant, then meet me back here to discuss the attack plan with the infantry commander."

The lieutenant, sure now that he would get his way and would be well behind ROK lines before the sun set again, snapped a salute.

Just a few minutes after Tilden and Isen left, Lake was wrapped up inside his poncho, lying beside his fighting position. Bladesly had completed the checks of the communications—both wire and radio—while Lake was with the commanders. Now it was time to get some rest.

Lake was not one of those officers who thought it macho to try to go without sleep for days at a time. He had learned, while a student at the Army's Ranger School, that without sleep, even the most competent soldiers quickly degenerate into useless wrecks. He had been asleep only seconds when Bladesly nudged him.

"Hey, Lieutenant, you need to get down in the hole."

"Huh?" was all Lake could muster. His tongue felt swollen and scaly, as if someone had put a fish in his mouth. He recognized the figure of his platoon sergeant, but was unable to communicate anything. Bladesly crouched closer.

"You need to sleep inside the fighting position, el-tee, in case we get some incoming rounds."

"Oh, right." *How could I be so stupid?* Lake thought to himself. He had heard many times that soldiers will fight the way they train, that bad habits picked up in peacetime will carry over to combat, and here he was, a case in point. They never dug fighting positions back on Oahu, because all the training land was privately owned, leased by the army. And they didn't dig when they trained on the big island of Hawaii, because the soil was volcanic rock. So here they were, with the threat of enemy artillery, and they dug, but then slept above ground. All Lake could think about was that he should have known better. He was embarrassed, but more concerned about the platoon than he was about saving face in front of Bladesly.

"Sergeant Bladesly, are the rest of the men sleeping in their holes?"

"Roger that, sir," Bladesly said without irony, as if it were the most reasonable question in the world.

"Good."

Lake worked his way to the bottom of the hole and propped himself up on his ruck in a sitting position, his back up against one muddy wall, his shoulders pinched by the narrow hole. He was numb, his limbs heavy with exhaustion. His head ached from the helmet, but he pulled it low over his eyes and, wet and muddy from the waist down, with his feet shoved in the sticky mess at the bottom of this too-small fighting position, he closed his eyes and let sleep come. Just before he went under, he remembered that he hadn't eaten that day.

When he reached the company CP after walking Tilden over to the eastern edge of Bravo Company's sector, Isen sent Murray to look for Christian, his fire-support officer.

Each platoon had an artilleryman, a noncommissioned officer who advised the platoon leader in planning and using fire support: mortars, artillery, and, when available, naval gunfire, tactical aircraft, and helicopter gunships. The fire-support teams were supervised by Christian, whose job was to advise Isen on the same concerns.

Christian came up in a few minutes, almost stumbling on Isen, who was sitting on the ground.

"Jay, I want you to take the GLD out to the bridge with the patrol from second platoon."

"Sir, that's Sergeant Munro's job."

Christian was surprised at the urgency in his own voice. He tried to soften his answer and added, as if Isen didn't know, "He's the FIST for that platoon."

"I know who the FIST is. I want you to handle it," Isen continued in the same even tone without looking up.

Christian saw how the lines were now being drawn. He knew that it wouldn't be the right thing to do to take the job away from his NCO, but he also knew it was starting to look like a question of his personal courage. He plunged ahead.

"Captain Isen, as your FIST chief I think I should be able to say who can handle the mission, and I think—"

Isen stood and took a step toward Christian, so that his face was only inches away. Christian was reminded that none of them had bathed in days.

"Listen, Jay, I appreciate your concern, but you and I both know that old Sergeant Munro didn't do squat on the Team Spirit exercise. You're the man. Any questions?"

Christian didn't think the question needed a response. He remained silent.

"Good." Isen went back to his map.

Now Christian was really confused. He had wanted to do the right thing by trusting his subordinate, letting Sergeant Munro do what he got paid to do. That was good leadership, right? That's what he learned at the Artillery School. But he also knew that now Isen had reason to think he was afraid of going out. For that matter, he was afraid, only a fool wouldn't be. And then there was the business of operating the GLD. He hadn't done all that well with the gadget at the Artillery School at Fort Sill. He hoped the blasted thing worked once he got it out there. He hoped he didn't choke.

Over in second platoon's area, on the left, or western end of Charlie Company, Lieutenant Pete Haveck was watching one of his squad leaders inspect the eight soldiers who would be going out on patrol. They would comb the woods and hills between Charlie Company and the river for signs of North Korean movement.

When Isen had told Haveck to send a squad out to see if the North Koreans had anything left on the south side of the river, Haveck immediately decided to send Staff Sergeant Hector Padilla. Padilla was Haveck's premier squad leader, one of the best in the company. The twenty-five-year-old from San Diego had just last year graduated from the army's best school for leadership and small unit tactics. Like the majority of officers and a growing number of the young NCOs in the light divisions, Padilla wore a small crescent-shaped tab above the division patch on his left shoulder. In the daylight, one could see that it said "Ranger."

At five-feet-eight and one hundred and sixty pounds,

Padilla had the wiry, compact build that served so well when it came to physical exertion and sheer stick-to-it-ness. He had a thick shock of dark hair, almost black, with fine skin and delicately chiseled features that gave the lie to his true nature. His troops called him "Sergeant Rock," but only behind his back.

Padilla walked along the rank of men, quietly asking each one questions about the mission, their orders, where they were going, what they were to look for, what they were to do if they made contact with the enemy. To a man the soldiers were able to answer correctly; they had all paid attention in the briefing he had given them. If their nervousness about going forward of friendly lines in the deep black of night wasn't enough to keep them awake in the brief, Padilla was not at all shy about using the palm of his hand on the side of a helmet to get a man's attention.

"What do you do if you get separated from the patrol?" Padilla asked one of the men.

"I make my way to the rally point just in front of the company and wait for the rest of you guys, then we come back in together," he answered confidently.

"And what if the rest of the patrol is already back inside?" Padilla continued.

He hadn't addressed this contingency in tonight's order; he was questioning the man's common sense and skill as a soldier. The shadow shifted uncomfortably from one foot to the other and stared off at a point over Padilla's shoulder.

"I guess I'd stay put there until it got light, then try to come in by myself."

"Good." Padilla was pleased. Just minutes before going out beyond friendly lines on his first combat patrol in the pitch dark that followed moonset, this nineteen-year-old soldier was capable of thinking on his feet.

Padilla stepped behind the next soldier and jostled the man's canteen to see that it was full. When he looked up at the back of the man's helmet, there was nothing there but darkness.

"Where's your cat eyes?"

"They're right there, Sergeant." The soldier placed his rifle between his legs and reached around to the back of the elastic band that encircled his helmet. On the flip side of the band were two small rectangles of luminous tape. He twisted the band so that the tape showed, the only things visible to anyone behind him, the only way the men in the patrol would be able to see one another. Walking through a darkened countryside with an infantry patrol was a game of following these dull sets of beacons. To lose them meant to break contact, to risk splitting up the patrol and blowing the mission.

Padilla put his patrol in a small circle not far from the platoon CP, then went to find Haveck. He was less than fifteen minutes from his departure time when he found his platoon leader and Lieutenant Christian, the fire-support officer, sitting on the ground.

"Ready to go, Sergeant Padilla?" Haveck asked.

"All set, sir." Padilla studied Christian's dark outline, trying to figure out why this officer, who belonged with Isen in the company CP, was down here. *He must have come down to help double-check my fire-support plan,* Padilla thought. *That's pretty squared away.*

Christian and another soldier that Padilla hadn't noticed in the darkness stood up.

"Lieutenant Christian will be going out on patrol with you, Sergeant Padilla. He's carrying a GLD and we're waiting for word to take out a bridge that the South Koreans left standing at the river," Haveck said.

"Okay, sir." Padilla wasn't one to complain, though he felt as if control were being wrested from him even before he left friendly lines. "Who's this?" he asked, gesturing to the other figure.

Christian spoke, whispering loudly. "This is my man, Kramer. He provides security for me when I operate this thing."

Padilla addressed Haveck. "If it's okay with you, Lieutenant, I'll just take the one addition. We got enough people going out already. I'll make sure he has somebody to cover him."

If Christian knew Padilla wasn't talking to him, he didn't show it. "I'd like to have my own guy out there." He stopped short of saying *someone I can count on.*

Padilla decided he didn't much like Christian, wouldn't

be taking him if he had a choice—but the fact was that he didn't. The ball was in Haveck's court now. Padilla turned to his platoon leader.

"I'm sure Sergeant Padilla will take good care of you," Haveck told Christian. "He just wants to keep the size of the patrol down to a manageable number."

In the darkness, Padilla couldn't gauge Christian's reaction, but the soldier who had just gotten the reprieve let out an obvious sigh.

"If we get a call from the CO," Haveck continued, "to take out that bridge, I'll send the codeword 'boxer.' That mission then becomes the priority. Lieutenant Christian will show you on his map the area he thinks he can get a shot from. Make sure you pass the changes on to your squad."

Haveck looked at his watch, the luminous dial making a quick arc as he brought it close to his face.

"You've got a little more than ten minutes. Good luck."

Padilla turned on his heel, and without saying anything to Christian, walked back to where his patrol waited for him. Christian grabbed the GLD, pausing just long enough to say to Haveck, "Looks like the start of a wonderful relationship." He set off in the direction Padilla had taken, happy to be moving, but more than a little apprehensive about what was going to happen, and about his relationship with this group of strangers who would be taking him closer to the enemy.

Captain Lee Jae Hyung, the North Korean infantryman whose company had ridden south with the attacking tanks, had survived the ambush on the south side of the river by sheer luck. Almost left behind by Colonel Tae, he had been riding on the last tank, on the side nearest the ambushers, and so saw the flash from the missile launchers in time to jump clear of the doomed vehicle. He had made it back across the river with only a dozen of his soldiers. When he found that he outranked the commanders of the newly arrived infantry companies, he went to see the new tank battalion commander, hoping to talk some sense into the man.

"Major, I respectfully request that we conduct this assault according to our operational doctrine," Lee said.

With this one deft move he maneuvered the ambitious lieutenant, who was standing by the major, into a position where the younger officer seemed opposed not just to common sense, but to army dogma. The implication was not lost on the major, and Lee thought he saw a slight up-turn at the corners of Chang's mouth.

"What do you propose, Captain?" Chang asked.

Lee felt, without seeing, the lieutenant's sneering glance.

"Let me take a scouting force across, followed at a distance by the larger body of infantry that has just arrived. Let us find what is on those ridges to the south. Then we can call for the tanks when the ridge is clear."

"We do not have hours to wait for the infantry to reach and clear the ridge," the lieutenant said.

Lee turned on him, and saw the lieutenant struggling to control his anger.

"Excuse me, Captain," the lieutenant said, trying to placate Lee. He addressed the major. "We must strike while the enemy is on the run."

"You are confused, Lieutenant," Lee said, with an obvious emphasis on the man's rank. "The enemy you met this afternoon ran. The enemy you met at dusk was not running. That ambush was too carefully planned and executed to have been a rear-guard action."

The lieutenant said nothing. The decision now rested with Chang, who stood with his hands thrust into his pockets, scowling at the ground. He now had the assets to develop the situation. The infantry worked best at night, and even though these units were tired from days of hard marching, they could find out for certain what was to the south. He could then exploit the situation in the morning, when he would—he hoped—have the rest of his tanks with him.

"When the enemy attacks, retreat; when the enemy retreats, pursue; when the enemy halts, attack," Chang said, quoting the Maoist philosophy which had served the North Koreans well in the Fatherland Liberation War. He looked at Lee.

"Captain, the enemy has stopped. We must find out

where he is before we can attack. And for that, we use the infantry."

Lee would lead with one platoon, followed at a distance of four or five hundred meters by the bulk of his force—the two companies of foot soldiers who had just arrived, winded but in good order, and who were anxious to join the fight. The tanks—there were six of them operational on the north bank—would wait for his call.

Unlike the tankers, whose effectiveness diminished after dark, these light infantrymen preferred operating at night. The North Korean Army had long ago recognized that swift, aggressive night attacks helped negate the advantages enjoyed by a technologically superior foe. More than half of North Korean tactical training was done after sunset, where simple tactics and memorized drills worked best. Though there was no room for flexibility or individuality in North Korean operations, the lock-step predictability of their tactics served them well after dark.

Lee moved the whole force down by the remaining bridge, and positioned himself with the platoon-sized scout force. He had recognized a dangerous impetuousness in the lieutenant who was now commanding what was left of the tank company. Lee would not squander the lives of his men the way the now-dead armor commander had wasted his tank crews. He believed in the careful and deliberate movements of the foot soldier, and felt that the flashy audacity of the tankers was not only dangerous, but ineffective. He had no way of knowing that his personal philosophy was similar to that of his enemy across the river to the south. Mark Isen also believed that finally, the battle was won when an infantryman stood on the contested ground.

Lee planned to cross the bridge with the scout force of one platoon, followed after a fifteen- to twenty-minute interval by the rest of the infantry. They would travel light, their personal equipment tied down so that it would not jangle, their faces darkened with mud. The small group would move silently, guided only by hand signals passed from the sergeants to the men. The commander was pleased with their preparations and camouflage. As he moved from the rear of the little column to the front to lead them across the bridge, the soldiers he passed dipped the muzzles of their weapons so that Lee wouldn't brush the sharp blades of their bayonets.

Silently, confidently, they moved across the river and toward the outline of the long ridge they could just see against the southern sky.

Sergeant Padilla's patrol passed through Charlie Company's lines at the same time the last of the NKPA soldiers in Lee's scout element crossed the bridge.

Padilla had asked Christian to walk right behind him. The artillery officer was the only soldier in the patrol that Padilla hadn't trained—and he wanted him close in case Christian started to make noise.

The ten men moved in two narrow wedges, like Vs of migrating geese one behind the other, through the woods in front of second platoon, down the slope of the ridge, to the left and parallel to the north-south road where Bladesly's men had ambushed the tanks. Padilla checked his compass periodically, the floating luminous dial bouncing comfortably in its case as he steered the formation almost due north.

They reached the low ground between Charlie Company's ridge and the one to the north from which Barrow had watched the ROK attack earlier that day. Here the woods thinned out, and though there were some trees on the slope ahead of them, they were about to leave the best cover behind.

Padilla touched the shoulder of the man in front of him, the point man, who stopped immediately. The rest of the patrol halted within a few steps. Padilla allowed himself a measure of pride that his men, these men that he had trained, automatically formed a small cigar-shaped perimeter, turning their weapons and their attention outward, like an Old West wagon train circling for protection.

Padilla was carrying a night-vision scope and his own radio. When his assistant patrol leader found him, Padilla left the radio, took the scope and one soldier along to provide security, and moved close to where the trees thinned out. The gate-like rubber eyepiece on the scope popped open as he pressed it to his cheek and swept the rise in front of him, the hill that lay between Charlie Company and the river. The view through the scope was fuzzy, with no distinct shapes visible in the light green haze. That was good.

He put down the scope and paused to listen, opening and breathing through his mouth because he had once been told you could hear better like that. He kept his eyes moving, looking for the indistinct flash, just a change in the composition of the deep shadows that a man's silhouette makes at night. There was nothing there.

He returned to the patrol and whispered to his assistant that they would move on to the thinner woods of the second slope now. The men would have to spread out more since the vegetation wasn't so thick. They were a little more than six hundred meters north of Charlie Company. Just north of the ridge that Padilla and his men were about to climb, the North Korean scout element was climbing also, moving south, hurrying through the night to see what they might find on the second ridge to the south, where the tanks had died.

Lake woke with a start, clenching the pistol grip of his rifle. He could see only a rectangle of sky above his fighting position, and it took him a few seconds to remember where he was. He pulled his legs from the drying mud, and the dream came back to him.

He had been in some sort of ditch, a drainage ditch or roadside culvert. It was broad daylight, and he could hear the voices of North Korean soldiers walking down the road toward him. He had no idea how he had gotten there. He could not see the soldiers. He was facedown in the ditch, wondering if his back was visible from the road as he fumbled to pull the pins from three fragmentation grenades.

He remembered his dream-self thinking *How did I get here? How, for that matter, did I get to be a soldier?* and as the North Koreans got closer and it became clear that they would see him and shoot him or he would throw the grenades and kill all of them or maybe only get some of them, he thought *I wish I'd never heard of West Point.*

Lake stood up in the position, which was not quite deep

enough for him; most of his chest was exposed when he stood.

The platoon sector, which was the company center and which included the trail that split the ridge, was quiet. Through his night-vision scope, he could see the silhouette of Janeson, the RTO, just above the ground at Bladesly's position, about twenty meters away. He did a mental inventory of the platoon's positions, picturing each of the men in turn. It occurred to him that some of them might wind up as had those two men from third platoon, boots sticking out from under a poncho.

As they approached the crest of the final ridge before the river, Padilla halted his patrol. If the North Koreans had night-vision devices, they would be able to see men who silhouetted themselves on the crest of the hill. He tapped Christian and motioned for Heming, the point man, to follow him as he bent over in a crouch and continued up the slope. As they neared the top, the three men got down on their stomachs and crawled to the crest. The river valley below was dark as velvet, as if the low ground swallowed up what little light was available. Padilla could not see the bridge through the scope. He passed it to Christian, then with his lips almost touching the lieutenant's ear, whispered, "See if you can find that bridge for me."

Christian took the scope, and Padilla could just see the lieutenant's shadow moving as he traversed the sector. "Nothing," Christian breathed.

"I think we're masked by the trees down there. We have to move to the right," Padilla said. "I'm going to leave the patrol in place for now."

With that he began to move to his right, eastward, staying just below the crest of the ridge as Heming hustled to take his place in the lead. Christian's GLD clinked and jingled against his body as he moved. Ten meters away, two North Korean soldiers, point men for the scouting element, froze when they heard the noise.

Jay Christian was looking down, adjusting the strap that attached to the GLD, when the first North Korean soldier opened fire just ahead. Christian was not blinded by the sudden flash of muzzle blast, nor was there enough time for him to think about being afraid. The overwhelming sensation was surprise; the last thing on earth he expected to hear was rifle fire.

The North Korean soldiers had seen Padilla's point man just after hearing the Americans. They froze, but realizing that they would be seen in a few seconds, opened fire at the shadowy figure that was just a few meters away across the shallow flat top of the ridge.

Padilla was watching Heming, his point man, and saw the luminous cat-eyes disappear as the soldier crumpled in front of him. Padilla had the thumb of his right hand on the selector switch of his M-16, and he pushed it over to full automatic as he dropped to his knees and swung the rifle to his left. He fired a long burst at where he thought the muzzle blast had come from, then fell to the full prone, catching his stomach on a limb that was on the ground. Christian, immediately behind him, hadn't fired yet.

Padilla could see nothing on the few feet of slope above him, but heard something scrambling farther off to the right. He groped for a hand grenade on his ammo pouch as he rose and skidded on his knees to find his man. He pulled the grenade free, snapped the clip, and tossed it when he found his soldier. Covering Heming with his body, he tensed as he waited for the explosion. Remembering that he was supposed to be counting, he started in the middle at one thousand two, one thousand three, one thousand four, one thousand five. Nothing. *I forgot to pull the friggin' pin.*

Christian reached him as Padilla rolled Heming over onto his back. Padilla noticed that Christian was also arming a grenade, and he had just enough time to register surprise that Christian would know that the grenade—which doesn't have a signature flash and doesn't betray your position—is the preferred weapon for close-quarter grappling in the dark.

He placed his hand on Heming's throat to check for a pulse, and felt only a warm give of torn flesh. The rounds had caught Heming high on the chest and in the neck. He was dead.

"Toss it," he told Christian.

Christian pulled up to a kneeling position. Padilla

could just see, against the sky, Christian's free arm held in front of him for balance.

Afraid that the grenade might roll down on top of him, Christian let the spoon go before he threw, allowing the grenade to "cook off" in his hand for two long seconds. The shock of the firing had calmed him, like the initial contact in some vicious football game. As he threw he grabbed Padilla and they scrambled back down the hill after the blast.

When Captain Lee Jae Hyung got his point man calmed down, he figured, correctly, that they had encountered only an enemy patrol. Lee was sure that the enemy grenade was meant to cover a withdrawal. The question was whether his enemy would be aggressive enough to run counter-patrols, trying to find him and snuff him out before he could get back to his lines. He did not yet know that he was facing Americans, had no idea where the enemy was or how large a force was south of him in the darkness. But he had no real choices, and the only way out was ahead. He decided to push on, and so put the trail squad in the lead, told his NCOs to move more quickly, and gave the word to move out.

Padilla and Christian stopped when they reached the relative safety of the patrol. Padilla cursed himself for what had happened. He'd lost a good man blundering around in the dark, had forgotten how to use a grenade, had compromised his patrol and still had no idea what it was he had run into out there in the blackness. He was determined, however, to salvage his mission.

Padilla radioed Haveck. Regaining some of his composure, he gave the report in an even tone. Haveck took the information, then told him, "Wait, out."

Padilla figured that his platoon leader was calling for instructions, and he used the few-minute wait to check his patrol, tell the men what had happened and where, get a new point man, and make plans to recover Heming's body. He had decided that they would pull back off the slope and continue to move to the right, to the east, trying to find the patrol they'd hit.

Haveck came up again.

"Sierra five four kilo, this is Sierra five four, over."

"Five four kilo, over."

"This is Sierra five four . . . 'boxer,' over."

"I understand 'boxer,' over."

"Five four, out."

That was it. Haveck—and probably Isen had a part in it too—had absorbed what had happened to Padilla and had not only decided that he could handle it, but could go on to complete a more difficult mission, even given that there was a hostile force out there somewhere.

Now it really doesn't matter if we make it back, Christian thought. *Now we just have to blow that bridge.*

He allowed himself no more philosophizing, but ran a systems check on the GLD as Padilla and his assistant patrol leader passed the word from man to man, crawling on their stomachs and whispering to each soldier. A single codeword had come over the radio and now the eight men were all intent on making sure Christian had the chance to destroy the bridge.

Padilla was shaken by Heming's loss. But the effect on him was to focus his concentration, so that he saw exactly what he must do, saw with a startling clarity that he had never before experienced. He approached Christian last.

"Ready, el-tee?"

"Ready."

As the patrol, nine men now, began to move to the east, the last of the NKPA soldiers that made up the scout element crested the ridge. Padilla's group, two hundred and fifty meters to the west, would just miss the tail of this element, would pass just behind them and into the gap between Lee's scouts and the main body of North Korean infantry, which moved steadily toward Charlie Company.

Paco Marist went down again to his first platoon's LPs in front of the right, eastern end of the company to see if the radars were operational yet. Isen had given the radars to Paco because the right flank of the company provided the best chance of "seeing" all the way to the river.

The operators had arrived just an hour earlier, but the young soldiers had been eager to show what they could do, even when Marist told them they would be forward of friendly lines. He picked the two positions himself, and set them some distance apart, so that he could use reports from the radars to vector in on anything they heard. He would draw a line on his map through the position of each radar, in the direction they indicated they heard a sound. The intersection of two such lines would be the location of what they heard.

He set two of his troops with each operator, tying the positions in with his by telephone land-line. The radar operators had brought their own sound-powered phones.

Moving along his sector, Marist found all the soldiers alert, and was pleased with the security his infantrymen were providing. They had, of course, heard the exchange of gunfire and the single grenade go off in the distance, so they were wide awake, staring into the darkness. Marist checked the rightmost radar position. The soldiers there were also alert. He moved to the second position and spoke to that operator. Just as he was about to leave, the radar man hissed at him.

"Got something, sir."

Marist moved next to the man, straining his eyes as if he could see what the radar might be picking up in the darkness.

"We got our own patrol out there, too, you know," Marist said.

The rustling sound faded in the soldier's headset.

"Could be them, I guess, moving on that hill between us and the river."

"Yeah." Satisfied that these men would help him with security, Marist moved back in the direction of his CP.

Christian located the bridge easily from the new vantage point they found on the ridge, then handed the night vision scope back to Padilla. As Christian adjusted the GLD, Padilla prepared a call-for-fire that would be patched through his battalion fire-support team.

Miles behind them, an American artillery gun crew waited by their howitzer, a single Copperhead round in the tube. The round, obscenely expensive and complex, would home in on the laser beam fired from the GLD reflected off the target. The round would then correct its flight path, all in the space of a few seconds, finally hitting the target within a foot or two of the point where the laser beam was striking it. Near the gun, the battery commander and his boss, the artillery battalion commander, stood by the battalion commander's vehicle, waiting for the call from some GI that would put this unit into action.

Padilla rested his night-vision scope in front of his face as he waited for Christian. He eased forward on his elbows to see if he could sight in on the bridge, still very much aware that the enemy also had at least one patrol out here also. What he saw pushed the air from his lungs.

Below him, at least seventy-five soldiers—they had to be North Koreans—had crossed the bridge and were hurrying from the river to the ridge he was on—he and his eight men. Before he could speak, Christian touched him.

"Call for fire."

Padilla hesitated. "But . . ."

Christian did not turn from his sights, but his low voice was insistent.

"Call for fire. *Now.*"

Padilla pulled the handset to his ear. Before he depressed the push-to-talk, he told Christian, "Company of North Korean infantry, heading this way, distance about three hundred meters." Then he made the call.

Christian digested the new threat without flinching, saw immediately what he had to do. Destroy the bridge, then call for conventional high explosives on the infantry so that they could stop the push toward Charlie Company and get out of there.

"Shot, over." The artillery fire direction center reported that the round had left the tube.

"Shot, out," Padilla acknowledged.

Christian held the bridge in his sight. *Steady.* He wondered where the North Korean infantry was.

"Splash, over." The round was seconds from impact.

"Splash, out." Padilla dropped the handset and pressed the night-vision scope to his eye. He could make out several distinct shapes moving on the slope below them. They might even have to engage the North Koreans with rifle fire in order to slow them down a bit and get the artillery on them.

Christian forgot to close his eyes, and the flash from the Copperhead burned a bright orange disc on his retina. He couldn't see the bridge, couldn't see anything as he pressed the palms of his hands into his eye sockets and listened to what was going on around him.

Padilla called for his two grenadiers to open fire, calling out the range for them. "Enemy infantry, two hundred meters, grenades." Then he called Haveck and gave a five-second report that riveted the platoon leader and the company commander, who was also listening to the net.

The grenadiers must have had their fingers on their triggers; their response was immediate and Padilla heard the *ploop ploop* of the forty-millimeter grenades leaving the tubes.

Christian regained his eyesight as the grenadiers got off their fifth and sixth rounds. Padilla was beside him, pulling his arm.

"We gotta move!"

But Christian pushed his arm away and looked for the bridge again.

It was intact.

The round had landed a dozen or so meters to the right, where Christian could just see the smoking crater on the far bank.

"Call for a repeat," he told Padilla.

"The fucking thing didn't *work?*" Padilla was almost screaming. "We're gonna get overrun here in about two minutes—and you *missed?*"

Padilla was at the edge of panic, so Christian told him the first thing that came to mind.

"The sight must be off. I'll use some Kentucky windage."

But he wasn't sure if it was him or the sight. Christian's confidence in the weapons and gadgets was shaken. One thing that was certain was that the enemy infantry would be on them very soon.

He placed the reticle cross-hairs on the bridge again,

but knew that Padilla hadn't made the call. Down below them on the slope, he could hear an unfamiliar snapping sound as the North Koreans opened up with a light machine gun. The rounds sailed overhead, the surprisingly delicate glow of tracers arcing into the night behind them.

"Call for a repeat, Sergeant Padilla."

Christian felt somehow out of himself, and all his concerns about what the hell he was doing out here had become blurred, so that the only thing he was able to concentrate on was the necessity of destroying that bridge.

Padilla called for a repeat as his assistant patrol leader organized the other six men to try to hold the crest for just a bit longer—in the face of an advancing company of enemy infantry. The men were hurling grenades as Padilla repeated the call.

Isen and Haveck were monitoring the net. Whatever they had thought might happen, they had not thought the round would miss, or that Padilla would be holding off a company of infantry. It took Isen less than a minute to work up a call-for-fire. It took the mortar section just a bit longer to set the weapons and stand, rounds clasped in sweating hands over the ends of the tubes, waiting for the word from Padilla.

Isen broke into Padilla's net.

"Mortars ready to engage. You fire and adjust, over."

Padilla recognized Isen's voice, though the commander had forgotten, in the frenzy, to use his callsign.

The second Copperhead round took longer. The artillery hadn't been planning on firing two. By the time Padilla got the "splash" message, the men to his right were firing their rifles at the North Korean infantrymen who were now working their way deliberately up the slope.

Splash, out, Christian thought. Padilla didn't respond to the call from the artillery.

Christian remembered to close his eye this time, and when he opened it the bridge was gone. He grabbed Padilla's handset.

"Gimme the radio. I'll call for fire. You get your men out of here."

"The mortars are hanging," Padilla said as he slipped

out of the radio's shoulder harness. Off to the right of the two, a North Korean soldier stood for a brief second on the crest, illuminated by the muzzle blast from an M-16 almost immediately below him. He toppled over, but was replaced by two more.

The North Korean infantry, sure now that there were only a few enemy soldiers on the ridge, broke into a run. They came up the final few yards of the slope, weapons held low, firing as they moved.

Padilla's men were overwhelmed. There were too many targets. They hit six or seven of the attackers, but the North Koreans were coming too fast. Padilla heard a man scream, then another to his right let out a low *uunnhh* as a figure rushed up and thrust with his rifle. The North Koreans were using bayonets. He fired two quick rounds, taking careful aim at the nearest silhouette before the first mortar rounds came in. He shouted at Christian behind him.

"They're all over us!"

Christian looked up in time to see Padilla move forward, walking away along the side of the slope, firing from the shoulder at the North Koreans who swarmed on his men. Dozens of figures topped the crest, then dozens more. Though Christian's hands were shaking and his arms trying to betray him, deep inside there was a separate voice that was clear and in control.

Must be a whole company, his other voice said.

Christian had his lensatic compass out now. The odd calmness seemed to spread over him as he looked to the north and saw the first 105-millimeter rounds explode behind the enemy infantry. The center of mass of the NKPA unit was now spilling over the ridge, soaked with the blood of Padilla's patrol and headed for Charlie Company. Christian called in the adjustment.

Ten kilometers away, the artillery crews made minor changes to their guns, depressing the elevation ever so slightly according to the corrections Christian had called in. They fired off four rounds from each gun, and the shells landed in a pattern that mirrored the lay of the battery, inundating the crest of the ridge where Padilla and his men had made a stand.

12

Isen heard the rounds come in, saw the bright light on the ridge to the north, and recognized the signal for what it was—the war was reaching for Charlie Company.

He suddenly felt a tremendous isolation as he crouched close to the ground next to his fighting position. He had spent his whole adult life preparing for just this moment, and for the last year had poured everything of himself into preparing this company for combat. If he was unprepared for anything, it was for the sudden feeling of helplessness.

Out there, in the dark, the individual soldiers who made up this entity called Charlie Company would respond, or fail to respond, react correctly or incorrectly, and would, for the most part, do so as individuals. The final problem of command was just this: in the end, all the team-building and coordination and training produced just this group, ninety-eight men, in ones and twos, spread out in the night, each one waiting in fear to see what would happen. In the seconds before battle, each man was as alone as if he had been preparing for single combat in the days of mounted knights.

A short round landed behind Isen's position and sent him scrambling for cover. As he listened to the hiss of the shrapnel tearing through the trees above his head, he wondered where he would find the courage to get himself up and moving, above ground—when the rounds coming in were enemy and were aimed at him.

There was no guesswork involved in the decision the North Korean infantry captain, Lee, made next. He

175

couldn't get radio contact with the unit behind him, perhaps because he was now in the small valley just south of the hill where he had run into the enemy patrol. But the artillery he heard was no doubt aimed at the main body of his force. The very best situation that presented itself now was that he had been found out; the worst case was that the main body of his unit had been destroyed and he was cut off from reinforcement. Everything about the training of the North Korean soldier pointed to a moment such as this: tired, outflanked, with little or no chance of reinforcement or even withdrawal, and facing an alerted enemy. Lee decided to take his remaining troops into a hasty attack against the positions he was sure to find on the ridge to his front.

When Marist reached his CP, his platoon sergeant told him that Isen had called to tell them of the enemy contact. The artillery they could hear was engaging a company-size enemy element, but Isen suspected that there was another unit somewhere in the small valley to the front.

Marist called in his LPs, telling the men to pull back to the main line and ready for an attack. Then he and his platoon sergeant went out to the squads to check the positions one last time and to tell the men not to shoot at their comrades coming up the slope from the LPs.

Marist found the soldiers nervous, but alert and ready. He reminded the machine gunners to hold their fire until they got orders from him or one of the NCOs. He didn't want them giving away the positions of their most important weapons at the first few rifle shots.

His platoon was as ready as he could make them now. He was confident that whoever was coming toward them didn't know exactly where his platoon was located. He and his NCOs had done everything they could to prepare. But there was another element they could not control, something that lay beyond order and training. Clausewitz called it the "fog of war"; GIs call it luck. And luck, at least in the first moments of this impending collision, was on the side of the North Koreans.

The three soldiers who were at the farthest LP, in front of the eastern end of the company, left their position in good order. They hurried, but they did not panic. But as they made their way in the dark, the lead man lost his way, and they had to double back fifty or so meters toward the enemy, to the point in the faint trail where they had turned the wrong way. They lost precious minutes in this detour; worse yet, they lost their composure.

When they turned up the hill they weren't even heading toward third platoon, but had veered off to the southwest in the direction of the first platoon sector in the middle of the company. They were spread out with nearly fifteen meters between each of them. The radar operator had fallen behind and was in the rear, breathing heavily and making too much noise as he struggled with his burden. He passed within ten meters of a North Korean soldier who had halted when he heard the noise.

Lee moved in a low crouch to the point of his small element after the figures passed. He saw immediately what was happening, and he stepped out onto the trail behind the figures who were leading him to their position at the top of the ridge. He signaled for his men to follow.

As he approached the company position, the lead GI realized that he was out of his platoon area, but he was too eager to get back in to care. He was challenged and answered correctly, then moved behind the trace of friendly troops. The squad leader in that sector, anxious to set things straight, got out of his fighting position and approached the soldier to tell him he wasn't in the right platoon. The men in adjacent positions were distracted, and they watched their squad leader—instead of counting the figures that were coming back in.

Captain Lee Jae Hyung walked right up to the little knot of soldiers without slowing down. He held his breath, afraid that his runaway pulse would betray him.

The scene rushed at him quickly, and he saw a space to the left of where the men were standing and quickly decided to walk by and get behind them before he started shooting. He was next to them, gliding past in the darkness and amazed at his luck, when he heard one of the figures speak, almost aloud.

"What the hell are you guys doing here?"

Americans!

In spite of himself, Lee snapped his head to look, and the movement was enough to draw attention to him. The North Korean fired first, shooting from the hip, but hit nothing as the figures scattered. He felt the stock of his rifle jumping against his side, but in the next instant there was a tremendous crash as one of the Americans swung the butt of his rifle up to the North Korean's face, catching him flat on and full, knocking him back and up and up before he went crashing down to the ground.

The North Korean soldiers immediately behind Lee fanned out quickly when the shooting started. The Americans they confronted had only seconds to react, and only a few of the GIs found targets.

Lake was moving forward as soon as he heard the shooting, bent over in a low crouch, holding his weapon across his front. A finger of tracers reached for him, swinging like a glowing reed through the night.

"Sappers in, sappers in!"

Lake's soldiers were passing the warning that there were enemy soldiers in among the platoon positions and that all friendly troops should go to ground. Anyone left standing would be a target.

Up close now, Lake heard more than scattered rifle shots, the quick snap of M-16s, and the flat *thwapp* of AK-47s. The men in and around the fighting positions were struggling hand to hand. Lake hit the ground as a machine gun off to his left opened up, firing just a few feet off the ground, trying to scrape away the intruders. He crawled furiously, reaching the nearest position and tumbling in on top of an inert body. There was no sign of the second soldier who should have been there.

He was exactly where he needed to be, in the thick of the fighting with his platoon, but that fact, by itself, gave him no confidence. He could see no more than a few feet in any direction, yet he was supposed to affect—control, even—the struggle that tossed and strained about him in the blackness.

The North Korean scout element had the advantage of surprise, but Lake's platoon, already on full alert, had reacted quickly. The North Korean soldiers, each of whom had received many hours of instruction in the martial arts and in knife-fighting, fought viciously. But two things worked against them: they had not pinpointed the American positions before the machine guns had opened fire, catching many of them as they ran forward, and they were leaderless.

Captain Lee lay unconscious where he had been butt-stroked by one of Lake's soldiers, and both of the noncommissioned officers had been hit by machine-gun fire. The North Korean soldiers who managed to take cover were ready to fight to the death. But because they had never been encouraged to show initiative, they became confused without their leaders. They hesitated, and were lost.

Lake saw a figure running toward the platoon rear— sensed his presence, really, in the darkness. By the time he brought his rifle to bear, the figure had been swallowed by the tar-black night. Then he remembered that he had secured two hand-held flares, aluminum tubes a little more than a foot in length, in the cargo pocket on the side of his trousers. He had marked the illumination flare with a thick band of tape so that he could tell them apart in the dark. He pulled the illum out, snapped off the cap, and placed it on the other end of the tube, like the cap on a pen. This aligned the firing pin with the firing device. He held the flare away from his body at a sharp angle and slapped the bottom with the palm of his hand, sending the small rocket climbing a hundred feet or so above the platoon.

The one small flare did not do much to light the position, but it was a signal to Bladesly to call for more illum. In less than a minute, two artillery-fired illumination rounds were lighting the center of the Charlie Company sector.

Lake pressed his nose to the forward lip of the fighting position. Things had quieted down quickly. Nothing moved in the eerie light, except the shadows that swirled in tight circles as the flares swung at the end of their parachutes in slow, spinning descent.

Less than twenty-five meters to the east, off to Lake's right, Tony Cipriotti thought he saw movement, just before the flare burned itself out, between his position and the one to the right. By the time another flare popped, there was nothing there but his suspicion. He turned to Boste, who shared the two-man fighting position with him.

"I think there's something over there, next to Lamson's hole."

"Call him." Boste was cemented in position, his cheek pressed to the stock of his weapon, eyes front. He had been like that, without firing, since the shooting had started. Cipriotti called to his team leader.

"Hey, Sergeant Lamson, you there?"

"What a stupid fucking question—where do you *think* he is?" Boste said.

"Well, I saw *something* over there," Cipriotti said, wondering, even as he said it, if he was imagining things. "See? No answer."

"Yeah, well, there ain't nothing there now," Boste said, as if this would close the question.

"What if one got through?"

"Bladesly and Lake can take care of themselves. We're supposed to stay here."

"But Lamson didn't answer." Cipriotti hesitated. "What if he got shot?"

Boste turned on him. The shifting yellow light lit only the bottom half of his face under the edge of his helmet. The mouth moved again.

"So what're you going to do, waltz over there and say hello?"

"Look, that's the whole problem, I don't *know* what to do," Cipriotti said, wondering how Lamson would handle this. "But I don't like not gettin' an answer. What do you think we should do?"

Cipriotti recognized the familiar sensation of welling-up anger. He was angry at Lamson for not answering, or for what might have happened, and at Boste because he obviously wasn't going to contribute anything, and he was absolutely livid at his own indecision. This was the feeling —rage bouncing around inside him like a nasty ricochet looking for an out—that always got him into trouble, always came just before he shoved, or swung, or mouthed off to some MP.

Boste was in his crouch again, his back arched as he leaned over his silent weapon.

"I'm gonna have a look."

Cipriotti had hoped saying it out loud would make it seem the right thing, but the trick didn't work; he still wasn't sure. But he had said it.

He had one foot up on the step dug in the back wall of the position when Boste grabbed him.

"NO!" Boste shouted, pulling Cipriotti back by his pistol belt so that they fell into the cramped muddy bottom of the hole.

"What the hell are you doing?" Cipriotti pushed off Boste as he struggled to get to his feet in the two-and-a-half-foot-wide position amid a welter of straps and weapons and belts.

"Don't . . . don't . . . I mean, we're supposed to hold here. No one told us to move or anything."

"Yeah, but Lamson and Cordiel"—Cordiel was the man in the position with Lamson—"ain't answering. We might have a hole right through the platoon here and not even know it."

Boste didn't answer. It hit Cipriotti that his partner was afraid. Charlie Company's premier peacetime soldier: never in trouble, best in inspection and on the range and in the physical fitness tests; was afraid to stay alone in the relative safety of the position while he, Cipriotti, the company screw-up, was going to crawl across open ground, under the sputtering yellow light of the flares, to check on a man who couldn't stand the sight of him. He almost laughed.

"Look, man, just stay here and cover me. I'm just going over there." Cipriotti pointed, as if reassuring a child. He strained to see Boste's face, but the second flare went out at that instant, dropping them both into a darkness that was all the more impenetrable for their having been in the light.

"I'm going now."

Cipriotti pulled Boste to his feet and slipped over the edge of the position, keeping flat to the ground and rolling down a slight incline. Clear of the hole, he paused and listened. He could hear the men in the adjacent squad, off to the right, calling to each other, checking weapons and redistributing their remaining ammunition evenly between them. But the only sound close by was the sharp in and out of his own breathing.

Another illumination round broke overhead, and Cipriotti could see the fresh-turned earth just behind Lamson's position. He crawled on his knees and elbows, his rifle cradled in the crooks of his arms, his head up. He focused his attention on a small hump in front of him that he thought was part of Lamson's protective earth berm. He was conscious of an exquisite alertness; he felt energized, almost refreshed. The doubts he had had a few minutes before as to what he should do left him. It was good to be moving, to be doing something. Lamson, who knew how much Cipriotti despised the dark and the woods, would be surprised that he was the one to show some initiative.

Cipriotti could hear the hiss of the falling flare now, and knew he would be in darkness in seconds. The sound grew louder and the shadows swung crazily as he hurried the last few feet, wondering if the flare might land on him, burning his legs and back. As he approached the hole, he called out in a low growl so that Lamson wouldn't be surprised and shoot him.

"Sarge, *Sarge.*"

As the light failed, Cipriotti reached the hole and peered in, catching the scene as if in the stop-action of a strobe: the hunched back without the U.S. pattern camouflage or suspenders, the slow spin of the North Korean soldier as he rose and turned to face Cipriotti, the quick glimpse of the stained shirtfront sprawled in the bottom of the hole, and the vicious flash of the blade. As the light snapped out, Cipriotti saw that the soldier's face registered surprise.

The North Korean slashed at Cipriotti with his knife, and Cipriotti heard the blade sing through the air by his ear as he ducked and rolled right. He pushed his rifle forward to get to the pistol grip and trigger, but the North Korean grabbed the muzzle and pulled hard, trying to leap from the hole and almost jerking the weapon from Cipriotti.

Cipriotti managed to get to his knees, and he thrust his whole body forward, knocking the North Korean off balance so that he slipped and landed on his side, clawing the air, his feet still in the fighting position. Another illum round opened, and Cipriotti tugged at his rifle. He squeezed the trigger, but the other man had pulled past the muzzle, swinging his blade and slicing Cipriotti across the upper arms.

Cipriotti yanked hard at the rifle and swung his feet around, kicking at the North Korean's face, pounding with his muddy boots and working his legs like a jack-hammer to drive the man away. Remembering his own bayonet still buttoned in its sheath, he grabbed the handle, freeing the blade just as the North Korean got to his knees. Cipriotti let go of the rifle as the man slashed at him again. For a brief instant they seemed to pose, the Korean soldier with his shoulder turned to Cipriotti, his face invisible in the back-light of the flare. Cipriotti grabbed the material at the shoulder of the man's jacket and pulled him forward as he brought the bayonet up with a strength born of animal fear. The blade slid neatly between the man's ribs, and the soldier pitched forward, knocking Cipriotti down and locking them together as they hit the ground. The fight was over.

Cipriotti skittered away, hearing for the first time the low groan that had been coming from him the whole time. He retrieved his rifle and moved back to Lamson's position. In the sickening yellow light of the falling flare he saw Cordiel, face up and dead, his legs twisted at an impossible angle under him in the bottom of the hole.

Cipriotti moved Cordiel's body as gently as he could out of the position, then he called back to Boste.

"I'm here. No sign of Lamson."

"Okay." Boste's reply was feeble.

Cipriotti sat still in the dark, listening to the rush of his own breathing. He fought an urge to vomit by removing his helmet and bracing himself against the front wall of the fighting position. His throat was ashen and his knees limp. He was surprised to find the right leg of his trousers soaked and warm where he had urinated on himself out of fear. When the next flare opened, he turned behind him to where the two bodies, Cordiel and the North Korean soldier, lay crumpled and face down. Even at a distance of only a few meters, under the strange light and shifting shadows of the illum rounds, Cipriotti couldn't tell which body was which.

Isen's platoon leaders did a good job of keeping him updated through the night. At four o'clock he told Marist to organize and lead a patrol out to the river to look for whatever remained of the element Christian had engaged with artillery, and to look for Padilla's patrol.

Voavosa met Isen in the CP just before first light. He had been supervising the evacuation of the wounded and the collection of the dead since the shooting started. He and the company medic, a lanky and too-old-to-be-a-private Virginian named Carey, had taken two casualties out of Lake's platoon area while the shooting was still going on. They had crawled the last forty meters with their faces and their hands and knees and elbows pressed flat out as the platoon's machine guns chattered nearby and overhead and the wounded men called for help.

In the dim light, Isen could see the weight of Voavosa's burden. The first sergeant sat down next to Isen without speaking, fished in the breast pocket of his jacket, and pulled out a green army memo book, which he handed to Isen. Rubber bands on the cover pulled the book open as Isen placed it on his lap and read the names on the exposed, muddy page.

Lake's platoon had lost three men killed and three wounded. Marist's platoon lost the two men who had been followed by the North Korean patrol into Lake's sector. The radar operator who'd been followed in by the North Koreans was wounded, but would not have to be evacuated, Carey expected, beyond the battalion aid station.

Haveck's platoon had nine men missing, the entire patrol. Christian, who was attached to the company headquarters, made ten. Isen closed the book, but had no idea what to say to Voavosa. The older man spoke first.

"I moved the KIAs back behind your position here, sir. The XO will take them and the prisoners to the rear after he brings up some ammo. One of the North Koreans looks like an officer, but he took a shot to the head and can't talk."

"Thanks, Top," Isen mustered.

"I already distributed what we had on-hand; we used mostly M-60 ammo."

Isen was silent. Voavosa waited for the rapid-fire string of questions that Isen always had when he thought out loud, anticipating the company's needs. That was how he and the first sergeant checked each other.

But Isen was still. He had anticipated this moment all through the night, unsure of how he would react when he found out the casualties. He was most afraid of losing his concentration, of not being able to focus on the task at hand. But as he thought of Haveck's decimated platoon, he forced his mind back on the familiar track, and began planning how he would adjust his defensive position, what he would say to Haveck and his men that would allow them to function again.

Marist's voice came over the radio.

"Tango two five this is X ray seven seven, over."

Isen turned to where David's rucksack was tucked under the lip of the hole behind him.

"This is two five, over."

"We have three of the SIERRA element's people," Marist said, referring to Haveck's second platoon by the letter identifier for that unit. "Have recovered the rest of that element."

Marist let go of the push-to-talk to interrupt the signal, a precaution against radio direction-finding teams. Isen sucked in his breath. *Found three, recovered the rest. That meant seven dead.*

"We found where the enemy crossed back over; nothing but enemy KIAs on this side, over."

"Roger, seven seven," Isen answered. "C'mon back."

"Wilco, out."

Isen put the handset back inside the waterproof battery bag David had rigged up. It began to rain.

He looked through the trees behind his CP and saw Barrow watching two soldiers from the headquarters element load bodies into the back of a vehicle. The bodies were wrapped loosely in ponchos, which were slick now in the rain and swung free when they lifted. Barrow stood quietly to the side, his helmet under his arm.

There would be no sunrise, Isen thought as he watched the clouds spill on the low hills to the south. There had been no battle, really. No controlled movement, no maneuvering or orchestrating the entire company. There had been just the random violence of armed men crashing together in blindness, intent on destroying one another.

Isen had lost eleven men killed and had not personally

seen a live North Korean soldier. And, because he was hardest on himself, he replayed his every action in his mind, wondering what he could have done differently.

Somewhere to the north there was a force he would still have to reckon with. No doubt they, too, sat licking their wounds and planning their next move. Mark Isen thought about them as he sat in the rain, stooped under the weight of responsibility and the heft of dead men being loaded into the back of a truck, on the morning after his first night in the war.

13

26 April · Tuesday · 1000 hrs

The rain continued all through the long morning as Isen and his platoon leaders adjusted Charlie Company's position, and Voavosa and Barrow moved supplies and food forward and the dead and wounded to the rear. Slowly, cautiously, the men began to move about after the platoons had again established the forward observation posts that would protect them from surprise attack. They stepped gingerly, walking between positions as they worked, talking to their buddies about nothing in particular, just talking, as if to prove to themselves that they had, in fact, made it through the night.

The soldiers also looked for reassurance that there had been something going on that was larger than just what they had been able to see. There is a peculiar quality to close combat, especially in the dark, that leads men to believe that theirs is the only war going on. The engagement is made up of many small engagements, and the men who do the fighting are not sure, all the while it is going on, whether or not theirs is the only battle. So the men in Charlie Company walked about, checking on buddies and trying to piece together some larger view of what had happened to them during the night.

Isen walked the length of his company, talking to the men and drawing as much as giving reassurance. They expected to see him, and they even forgave his ignorance as they asked about what was in store for them.

"What's coming up, sir?"

"Well, for now we're staying here," Isen called back, "and you guys are pretty good at that."

"You got it, sir," another soldier added, trying to pick up the old optimism that they were all looking for. "We can hang here."

The other men in the squad joined the chorus, and Isen was surprised that with all that had changed, all that these men had gone through, they were still capable of some degree of the enthusiasm they had always shown. But the enthusiasm came from what they had proved to one another; the playfulness was gone now.

"You men did a good job here last night. You proved that you can handle yourselves."

Isen wondered if he should go on, wondered, as leaders do, how much is enough.

"We're not finished here yet," he said, taking off his helmet and wiping his face with his sleeve, "but we did, and will do, our jobs, I guess."

He looked at the men around him, each one in the eyes, wondering if they understood what he was saying, if they knew how much he was concerned about them. One of the men turned away, then faced Isen again.

"Hey, sir, want a shot of coffee?"

Another added, "Yeah, have some, Captain Isen," and still another said, "I even got some sugar here somewhere" as he fished through the pockets of his wet shirt. Isen stepped forward and held out his canteen cup.

Haveck's platoon had suffered the biggest losses; almost a third of the men in the platoon had not returned from the patrol. As he made his rounds, Isen saw the stacked rucksacks and the sad, scattered odds and ends of the dead men's personal gear that Haveck had had moved to the platoon rear. As he talked to the soldiers of Haveck's platoon, Isen found that there was an underlying sense that Padilla's men had protected the whole company. Isen had debated whether or not to tell them this morning that Christian had called down artillery fire on the patrol as they were being overrun by North Koreans. But word had already made its way back from the survivors, and the word was that without that fire, none of them would have survived. The incoming artillery, horrible as it was, had made things even on the hillside. Every soldier, American and North Korean, became instantly isolated, concerned only with survival, and three Americans had made it.

The soldiers who had accompanied Marist on the search were badly shaken by what they had seen. The artillery fire had smashed the bodies of North Koreans and Americans, scattering limbs and vitals throughout the wood. The witnesses were numbed into a sinister quiet. When he looked at them, Isen had nothing to say.

When he finished his rounds and got back to his CP, Isen called the battalion operations center to see what he might expect that day.

"To tell you the truth, Mark, I don't know what they've got in store for us today. The old man was called to a meeting with the brigade commander about an hour ago. He said something about having to go and meet the division commander and the ROK corps commander. I think the ROKs are frantic about what's going on west of here." Major Bock stopped at that.

"What's that?" Isen asked.

"I'm not sure, and it's not even something I can put my finger on. It's just that the colonel looked more worried about the meeting than about what's going on here. But I'm just guessing. I'll keep you guys posted about anything that comes up."

"Okay, sir," Isen finished. "Thanks."

Isen called Barrow on the land line and told him to bring up the rest of the company's set of maps. He wanted to take a look at what kind of terrain lay to the west of them.

* * *

Lake spent the first few hours of daylight moving around his platoon position and talking to his men. As he did so, he made mental notes on how he might adjust the platoon when he got the expected instructions from Isen to take over some of the responsibility for the sector to the west, his left, now that Haveck's platoon was so short-handed. He and Bladesly discussed the adjustments, then Bladesly set the men to work, redistributing ammo, and burying the commo lines that had been torn up or broken. Lake met with the squad leaders to talk about what had gone on in the early hours.

"All in all, I'd say we handled things pretty well," he started out. "The men reacted to the commands and cleared the ground. The machine gunners used their aiming stakes so that we kept the fire out of the adjacent platoons' sectors. Sergeant Lamson got caught out of his position, but there's nothing to be done about that. He took to ground as soon as he heard the word."

"He feels like he messed up, sir," said Staff Sergeant Hall, Lamson's squad leader. "He said if he hadn't been out of that position, Cordiel might not have gotten killed."

Lake was surprised that the first thing that came to his mind by way of response was something along the lines of *We have to expect these things to happen.* Instead, he said, "He was checking on his other positions. All we can do is do our jobs."

He was trying to strike a balance. The soldiers were upset about what had happened; their sector had been compromised and some of their buddies killed. Lake knew all this and felt as they did, but it was his place to remind them that the show was going to continue. He felt somewhat hypocritical, but knew he could live with that as long as his platoon was ready when the shooting started again.

The squad leaders had little to say when he asked them what the platoon might do differently. They had seen only small parts of the fight, but they each had some plan for making improvements in the individual squads.

Lake left them to Bladesly and moved along the ridge to a point where he could see, with his binoculars, to the north and the hill that spread across the front of Charlie Company. He swept the soggy gray woods until he saw the patch of splintered trees and torn earth, as if some giant had set foot on the small hill. He checked his watch and decided to give himself two or three minutes here to collect his thoughts.

Lake had resisted thinking about Christian's death, as if he could somehow backpedal through time and, by denying it, make it untrue.

Christian had been the first officer to give Lake more than a perfunctory welcome to Charlie Company. Even though Christian was an artilleryman and only attached to the rifle company, he went to the field whenever Charlie Company did, participated in all of the training exercises, and never missed a deployment. Compared to Lake, Christian was an old hand.

Their friendship dated from just before Lake's first meeting with Isen, who had been away when Lake arrived.

"Hey, West Point," Christian had told him, "when you go in to meet Captain Isen, he won't be playing any mind games with you, so don't try to play any with him."

"All right," Lake answered.

"And loosen up, man."

Christian encouraged him to relax a bit in his new role, and the relaxation allowed the human side of Lake into his dealing with his soldiers. Lake knew that he was no martinet, but after four years at West Point, he also knew he could stand a little loosening. Christian answered a need in him for a complementary personality. They became friends, Lake the straight man, Christian the joker.

There is a unique bond that develops between the lieutenants in a unit. When a new lieutenant is assigned to a platoon, he is the senior ranking and the most inexperienced member of the team. He has anywhere from six to ten months of schooling behind him, but doesn't know the first thing about the idiosyncrasies of how this platoon, *his* platoon now, operates. And from this benighted position, he is supposed to *lead*. The gods smile on some, and they go to units where the noncommissioned officers, men with six, ten, twelve years of service, see the training of lieutenants as part of their jobs. But even the most clever novices have bad days, and when they do, they turn to other junior officers.

Their conversations, held at mess hall tables and at the bar in the Officers' Club, are built around insecurities and mutual assurances that, yes, I did the same dumb things, and this is what I learned.

Junior military officers learn to swim by being thrown in the water. In this struggle there are bonds made that even the men who feel them most strongly have trouble explaining. The external trappings of the bonding are easy to see. The men share hard, physical work through long days. They are very much aware, even in the peacetime army, that the measure of their individual skills and the collective skills of the team might make the difference, in war, between coming home and coming home in a box.

The military is a hothouse for friendships. Far away from family, these people share Christmas dinners and Fourth of July picnics; they go in groups to the baby christenings and the promotion parties. They waste no time in getting to know neighbors. Move into a military housing area and the neighbors consider it a matter of course to come and introduce themselves, to bring the first night's dinner, to watch the kids so that they don't get under the movers' feet. In this environment, friends become family.

And now Lake was forced to see, in Christian's death, that relationships so carefully cultivated and prized, friendships that had in them the promise of lifetime connections, could be torn apart in seconds.

Isen got a call from Bock just before noon.

"Mark, this is a warning order," the S3 said over the field phone.

Isen pulled out his pad and a pen. "Go ahead."

"The North Koreans are pushing the ROKs south along the highway toward Uijongbu and Seoul. The ROK corps commander was trying an economy-of-force move— holding back units for a decisive counterattack."

Bock was speaking very quickly, and Isen stopped trying to take notes and just listened as the operations officer went on. "But the North Koreans are moving faster than anyone anticipated. The ROK reinforcements are not in place, and we are, so we, the division, that is, are being attached to the ROK 6th Corps. The old man and the brigade commander said they thought we'd be moved out on trucks or by helicopter no earlier than 1400. Be ready to move off your ridge on foot by 1400. After you pass the word, you need to get over here to the battalion TOC for an orders brief. I expect the old man will be back sometime in the next thirty minutes with more word."

Isen chewed his bottom lip, wondering what the surprises would be for him that afternoon. "Are the North Koreans leading with tanks over to the west?"

"I saw a couple of armored unit markers on the S2's map when I was at brigade. I'm guessing that they're being worn down by our air force, but there's definitely some armor up front," Bock answered.

"Has the S4 had any luck rustling up some more anti-armor stuff, Dragons and mines and road-cratering charges?" Isen asked.

"Not too much, I'm afraid," Bock answered. "We pretty much came over here with the shirts on our backs. The air force is flying in as much stuff as they can, but they can't keep up with our ammo use."

That was the answer Isen expected. He knew that the logistics of keeping a unit such as his light division supplied, almost totally by air for the first days and weeks of a war, were staggering. There were literally thousands of tons of supplies that had to be moved to Korea: repair parts and spare engines for all the equipment already in-country, as well as all kinds of supplies: medical supplies and socks and sand bags and radio batteries and protective-mask filters and communication wire and food. Then there was the ammunition. Even the light divisions, with their relatively limited firepower, could go through more than eleven hundred tons of ammunition in a day.

The units in Korea had quickly chewed up the limited stockpiles available in-country and on the supply ships of the Pacific fleet. And to make matters worse, army and marine supply officers were competing for priority in huge chunks of aircraft load space. The ROK-US Combined Forces Command supply staff was getting the first signals that the South Koreans would soon turn to the U.S. for supplies of ammunition. At ammo supply points such as the one at Schofield Barracks, civilian technicians who were used to handling thousands of rounds in a day were suddenly trying to come up with and process the hundreds of tons of ammunition that the front-line troops needed.

During his studies at the Infantry School, Isen had learned how to use a series of tables that predicted how many tons of ammunition a unit would go through in combat in a day. But as much as they bitched and moaned about the study assignments, trying to get the numbers to come out right, the infantrymen had never had to worry about the other dimension of the problem: how would all this ammo get to the theater?

Now, faced with the prospect of not being able to get the ammunition and explosives they needed, Isen remembered the narrow-focus complacency that had been such a luxury. It hadn't occurred to him before that they might run out.

Barrow came by in a few minutes, and Isen briefed him on exactly what the battalion S3 had told him. Isen's XO seemed a bit more frazzled than most of the troops.

"You okay, Dale?"

"Yeah, I'm all right, sir." Barrow pulled his rain jacket open, then ran his hand over his short, dirty hair. "I do feel like I have two socks stuck up my nose," he said, touching the tape on the bridge of his nose. "Why do you ask?"

"You're just low key, I guess. Not that you don't have reason. It's just that I'm not used to seeing you this way." Isen folded his map and leaned forward, elbows on knees, facing his XO.

Barrow recognized the pose; Isen was giving him the chance to talk. With everything else he had on his mind, the concerns of a whole company, Isen noticed and was willing to talk about what was bothering his XO.

"I'm not sure, sir. It's almost like I've scaled back, cut down on power usage or something. I don't know."

"Know what I've found over here, Dale?"

"What's that, sir?" Barrow said, looking up into Isen's face.

"Ain't nothing like what we expected, is it?"

Barrow shook his head. "No."

"But all the important stuff is still the same. We still

193

have to be careful in planning. We still gotta take care of the small stuff."

Isen paused, thinking Barrow might say something.

"Dale, you're doing a good job."

"Hauling ammo around, you mean."

Isen didn't answer.

"I'm sorry, sir. I just thought it would be different. Guess I have a lot to learn."

"Yeah," Isen said, "we all do."

Isen called Marist and told him to send a soldier down to accompany him, Isen, to the battalion command post. He didn't want to be walking around alone, even behind friendly positions, when there might still be some of those NKPA troops wandering around in the rear.

Isen secured his maps, leaving behind all the ones that showed the terrain to the east of them, taking the ones that showed the land to the west, and moved to a trail juncture where he was to meet the soldier from Marist's platoon. He had a limited view of the south side of the ridge, where his company was set in and was now moving about, rolling up commo wire and moving ammunition. The men were quiet in their work, but he could hear the soft jangle of equipment and the voices of the NCOs as they got ready to move off the ridge.

The set-piece battle he had foolishly anticipated had never materialized; no name would be given to what had happened here. Yet some of his men had died. Back in Washington, even back at corps or division headquarters, it probably looked ordered and precise. From the vantage point occupied by this one company commander, the reality was a lot closer to chaos.

Lieutenant Colonel Tilden was already back at the battalion CP by the time Isen got there. He and Jan Bock were looking at the collapsible map board that was just about the only furniture that made up the TOC, the Tactical Operations Center. Isen thought about peering over their shoulders, but saw that the other commanders were sitting cross-legged on the ground, so he joined his peers instead.

Tilden turned and spoke without greeting them.

"The shit is starting to hit the fan to the west of us. The ROKs were spread pretty thin, trying to cover the whole width of the country. They put a lot of their air assets between the DMZ and Seoul, to slow the North Korean advance to the point where they could handle it with their ground forces. But the North Koreans didn't oblige them by coming across on a wide front. It looks like they're going after Seoul instead of the ROK Army. The NKPA is punching through with two strong columns, both headed at Seoul, one from directly north of the city and one from the northeast. Our division is sitting just south of where that second column, we're talking four or five divisions, has to pass."

Bock was behind Tilden, hanging a piece of clear acetate over the map. The plastic was marked with two large red arrows, each seven to ten kilometers across. Spread along the length of each arrow were unit symbols, also in red, that indicated how the intelligence folks thought the NKPA units stacked up. The picture was put together in a process called templating, which was really just an educated guess that took into account all sorts of known factors: NKPA doctrine for the offensive, what the road network could support, what aerial photographs revealed, confirmed sightings of types and numbers of vehicles and artillery pieces, and a host of other, more difficult to quantify measurements.

Tilden went on. "Our division commander isn't sure that the ROKs will be able to stop them with what they have in the area. The South Koreans are having a hard time reinforcing and moving behind their own lines because North Korean agents keep ambushing convoys on the roads. The 25th Division is about the closest reinforcing unit to the hot spot; and yes, the old man pointed out that we're not configured or equipped to fight tanks." Tilden turned to the map to get his bearings, then picked up a collapsible pointer.

"So the ROK commander said he's going to use us in one of the built-up areas on the far northeastern outskirts of the city." He touched the map in the vicinity of what looked like a series of low hills, like the ones they were getting ready to leave. Seoul was nowhere in sight on the small scale map, but one of the major highways into the city from the northeast was about two klicks north of where Tilden was pointing.

"The only thing we have now is a set of orders making the division OPCON to the ROKs and telling us to get ready to move, by truck, as soon as possible. Since we're only under operational control, we're responsible for our own logistics. Of course, the ROKs know we don't have enough transportation to move ourselves, so they said they'd take care of that."

"The S3"—Tilden indicated Bock, the operations officer—"is going to talk about the move. Where's the S4?" He looked around for the supply officer, who raised his hand. "The four has, I believe, the information you need to start planning. Our battalion will be the first in the brigade to move, generally west of where we are now. Questions so far?"

Isen noticed that the other commanders wore the same flat expression he supposed was visible on his face. They were waiting for confirmation of their suspicions that they were out of the role of actor, things were now being done *to* them.

Isen couldn't shake the feeling that what they were seeing had an importance beyond the immediate, but he couldn't put his finger on it. *Intelligence on enemy intentions has been excellent so far,* he thought, remembering that his company had moved out on the first day of the war just as the NKPA was coming across the DMZ. *How did we suddenly get fooled? Or maybe the North Koreans just changed their plans.*

Tilden continued. "I'll be heading out of here in about a half hour with Jan to get a look at the area we'll be going into. The XO will honcho the move as far as battalion goes, but as you'll see in a few minutes, you'll be pretty much on your own."

"Sir." Isen lifted his hand off his lap.

"Yes, Mark?"

"What do you make of the North Korean move toward the capital?" *Good, Isen,* his watchful voice said to himself. *What kind of half-baked question is that? You're stalling.*

"Uhmm." Tilden paused and pressed his thumb and

forefinger into his eyes, as if considering whether or not to dignify the question with an answer. "I guess they're going for the propaganda value of capturing the South Korean capital. You know, something that'll play in the world press."

"They're ignoring the military objective," Isen went on, the picture making more sense to him now, "that is, the South Korean and American field forces, for the political objective of capturing the enemy capital."

Dan Pelham, the battalion S2, or intelligence officer, caught on to Isen's train of thought.

"It may be tied to the power struggle in their government, you mean."

"I hope so," Isen went on. "If the North Korean government were stable, they'd go for the military objective."

"What makes you think so, Mark?" Tilden was obviously tired, but he appeared willing to indulge his bright young company commander.

Isen tried to think of an example. One of the staff officers, obviously out of patience, got to his feet and zipped his rain jacket noisily.

"When Grant took over the Union forces, he told Lincoln that he was going after Lee's army instead of after Richmond, as all his predecessors had done. The enemy army was the objective."

"But with the problems in the North Korean government," Pelham continued without missing a beat, "they need to come up with a flashy victory—and quickly—so that the military can stay in control."

"So they may be going for the capital, instead of the enemy, for the propaganda value. If the rest of the world sees North Korean tanks rolling through Seoul, the public-opinion war might be over before anything is decided on the battlefield," Isen finished.

"At least," Tilden gave them, "that's one sensible explanation." He looked at Isen, but stayed lost in thought. Then he caught the younger man's eyes and a small smile broke through the grime and exhaustion.

"Good thinking, men. Dan, why don't you talk to the Brigade S2 and see if we can't pass this idea up the chain?

Maybe if we know what we're looking for, we can ask some pointed questions of the prisoners we have, like: were you told the war would be over once you took Seoul? Can you guys think of anything else?"

No one had anything to add, and Isen suspected that the already tired men had been further exhausted trying to follow his question.

Bock approached Isen. "Good thinking, Mark. Maybe if we stop the bad guys outside Seoul, the whole shebang will fall apart."

Isen was embarrassed at being singled out.

"Of course, I could be wrong about all this."

"Yeah, Mark, you could be"—Bock put his hand on Isen's shoulder as the other staff officers got ready to speak—"but you're thinking."

The staff explained how the move was supposed to work. ROK trucks were to pick up the companies near a small village about a kilometer south of Charlie Company's position. The move would take two to three hours altogether, depending on the traffic and the condition of the bombed roads. During that time the battalion would be broken apart and travel as companies. If anything happened, the units would be on their own. As the S4, an overworked first lieutenant named Terry, talked about the ROK trucks, Isen remembered that Bock had said that the maps at brigade headquarters showed armored units at the point of the North Korean spearhead. He made a mental note to ask the S4 again about explosives, which would be essential in preparing tank barriers and traps in a built-up area.

Isen watched Tilden as the older man got his gear together for the recon. Tilden swung his equipment onto one shoulder, paused, then pulled his rolled map from the cargo pocket of his trousers. He didn't look at it, but held it in his hand and beat a slow tattoo against his leg as he stared at the ground.

Isen wondered if the colonel had more on his mind than he was letting on. When the S4 finished, Isen approached Tilden.

"Sir, what do you expect to find up there?" Isen thought it was a stupid question even before it left his mouth, but he couldn't very well accuse the old man of holding back vital information.

"I don't know, Mark," he said without looking up as he buckled his pistol belt around his middle. "I'll meet you guys as you come in with the companies, though, and fill you in."

Isen could see that the colonel was trying to be positive, to portray optimism. It was the acting that bothered Isen. Tilden was normally an optimistic, positive commander. The fact that he had to force it unsettled his subordinate.

The S3 followed Tilden to the commander's vehicle, and once they were seated, Tilden looked at Isen again and paused, but said simply, "Good luck, Mark."

Isen snapped his hand from the edge of his helmet in salute as Tilden drove off.

Isen had his company down at the pickup point fifteen minutes before the trucks were to depart. No sign of the trucks. When they still hadn't shown up at the time they were supposed to be driving off, Isen sent Barrow off in the company vehicle to look for them.

The men had been lifted somewhat by the prospect of moving. Though they had handled themselves well enough in their first contact, they had no sense of satisfaction over what had happened on the ridge. The first afternoon's success against the tanks had given way to a paranoia that the tanks would return and bowl them over. The loss of almost all of Padilla's patrol, coupled with the fact that they hadn't engaged an enemy force, but only haphazard attacks, gave them the collective feeling of having been hit without seeing who had hit them.

They stood in good order by vehicle load as they waited, dispersed, alert and off the road. After the first hour, fatigue set in and the NCOs adjusted the formations so that the men could get some rest, half a platoon at a time.

Barrow returned an hour later. He hadn't been able to find any ROK units that knew anything about moving Americans. Three hours after the scheduled pick-up time, just as dusk was falling, Isen was visited by the battalion S4, who told him they were aware of the problem, but were at the mercy of the ROKs and the battle developing to the west of them, between Seoul and Uijongbu. Isen moved his company about seven hundred meters farther south to a small knoll that was at least defensible, then allowed the men to get some rest after they had set up the crew-served weapons and prepared hasty defensive positions.

Around midnight Isen got a call from Haveck, whose platoon was watching the pick-up point. An ROK officer had shown up and said transportation was on its way and that the Americans must hurry, please hurry. Isen had Voavosa move the company down to the road again, only to find that there were no trucks in sight. After another thirty minutes the ROK lieutenant reappeared with four civilian buses and their shanghaied South Korean drivers.

Voavosa was having none of it.

"Sir, I've seen some weird shit in my time, but this about takes it. We're going to ride seventy-five miles through a combat zone in *these* things?"

The ROK officer apparently didn't speak much English, but there was no mistaking the first sergeant's message. He started nodding his head furiously, pointing to the soldiers and then to the buses. "We go now. We go now."

"Sure, you ass, you'll be riding in that thing," Voavosa said as he pointed his thick arm at the lieutenant's jeep, which had an M-60 machine gun mounted on a pedestal in the center. A skinny ROK soldier stood by the gun, watching them. "What if we get hit on the road?"

Isen pictured his company, packed into the buses, caught in an ambush.

"Well, Top, we need to get moving, 'cause we're way behind schedule. But there's nothing says we can't . . . er . . . reconfigure these buses."

Voavosa smiled. "I got you, sir."

As Isen sent Murray off to get the platoon leaders, he heard the first sounds of breaking glass. Voavosa had the soldiers knock out the windows and all the external lights.

One bus driver tried to stop the soldiers as they began smashing the windows, but the ROK lieutenant came up behind the man and shoved him to the ground near Isen's feet. The young Korean officer was frantic, shaken far beyond what the situation called for. Isen wondered how much the man knew about the situation to the west of them. He pulled the lieutenant aside.

"What's going on west of us?"

The Korean looked at him blankly.

"Over there." Isen pointed west, then shrugged his shoulders. Even if the man didn't understand a word he was saying, Isen thought he'd get the sign language. Unless he didn't want to get it.

The ROK started to turn away, but Isen pulled him by the shoulder.

"Uijongbu," Isen said emphatically. Even as he said it, he saw something in the man's eyes. The lieutenant knew something he wasn't telling, and he knew Isen was on to him. He stared back at Isen in silence, his wide face a mask.

David and Murray, Isen's RTOs, helped the bus driver to his feet, and the man made his way to the front of the bus without raising his head or looking at the ROK officer.

Isen noticed several of his soldiers watching the scene, but Voavosa started shooing them on the buses. "All right, let's go, we ain't got all night."

The men responded, as they always did, to the first sergeant's order. Isen climbed into the company vehicle with Barrow and they pulled out behind the ROK jeep, with the four civilian buses grinding gears on the road behind them.

14

Near Cheongpyeong, Republic of Korea

27 April · Wednesday · 0110 hrs

The first hour of the road movement was uneventful, and Isen found himself nodding off occasionally, lulled by the rocking of the vehicle. Barrow was asleep in the back, and Isen, whenever he turned around to check the buses behind them, could see the lieutenant's dark form swaying with the bumps in the road.

As they got closer to the main battle area, more and more traffic appeared on the road. They pulled off the track to let a column of four ambulances, headed southwest, pass them. Isen and his driver watched in heavy quiet as the little box-like vehicles bounced along in the darkness. They had to stop again while a wrecker dragged the remains of a two-and-a-half-ton truck off the narrow roadway. Isen used the break to walk back along his line of buses, which, he was glad to see, had managed to keep their spacing at the halt.

As he came to the first one, he could clearly see the muzzles of weapons bristling from where the bus windows used to be. Marist stepped off the bus as Isen approached.

"Hey, sir, what's up? We close yet?"

Isen could just make out the lieutenant's outline; his dark features were hidden in the gloom.

"We have to wait for a wrecker to clear something off the road up ahead. And we still have forty miles or so, maybe fifty or sixty when you figure in all these winding country roads. How're your guys doing?"

"Well"—Marist took a step back toward the bus—"if you look closely, you won't see much movement."

Sure enough, Isen could see one soldier whose head was resting on his chest, his weapon pointing at the sky.

"It's going to be a long night, Paco. Why don't you switch off conning this thing and see if you can get some sleep? How's the driver doing?"

"Oh, he's holding up, I guess. He's pretty nervous about what we're driving to, so he ain't gonna fall asleep on us."

Isen found the same situation on each of the other buses. The platoon leaders were awake, watching the road, making sure the drivers kept the right distance between the vehicles. Too far apart and they risked breaking up the convoy; too close, and they might all be caught in the same ambush. The lieutenants would be the last men in the platoons to get any sleep, and the busiest men once the company stopped.

After another hour of stop-and-go driving, Isen saw a village up ahead as the convoy headed into a small valley. A surprising quiet washed over them when they dropped beneath the rim of the surrounding hills. Isen caught the scent of hogs and cattle as they wound along the little dirt road. But even with the familiar smells, there was still something that nagged him. There were only the smells of the animals, there were no animal noises.

The jeep carrying their guide, the ROK lieutenant, came to an abrupt halt in the village, and Isen got out to investigate. He told his driver to back up a few yards and pull the vehicle off to the side of the little path, out of view in one of the corrals. He walked forward slowly, his rifle resting in the crook of his left arm. There were no sounds at all in the village, and Isen stared hard into the darkness of the abandoned houses. He couldn't see what was in them, but he could see personal belongings and clothes and household items scattered in the dooryards of the simple farmers' houses, artifacts of daily life spread in the mud.

The ROK jeep had stopped at a small bend, and Isen could see the lieutenant about ten meters up the road. He called to him, quietly, so as not to startle him, then walked up.

The entire street here was intact, right up to where the lieutenant was standing at the edge of a crater. The artillery shell had been dropped neatly in the main crossroads intersection. A few meters ahead there were more craters. The contrast caught Isen by surprise. One side of the little street was in perfect order, as if at any moment the shop owners would come out and push back the wooden doors that covered their homes at night. But the opposite side of the street had been destroyed. At his feet, Isen saw a child's coat in the mud.

The artillery fires had been the same type of harassment and interdiction fires the Americans and the South Koreans used, indiscriminately shelling behind enemy lines, hitting road intersections and key terrain such as hilltops and bridges. The North Koreans, sure that the ROKs were trying to mass forces north of Seoul for the battle for that city, had every reason to suspect that they would hit a worthwhile target, just as did the Americans and their allies. Isen had never before seen the cost of such an assumption.

As he turned around to walk back to the buses, Isen saw one of the small tractors, not much bigger than an American rider lawn mower, that the more affluent Korean farmers used to work their fields. The frame of the little tractor was mangled and lay across the legs of a young farmer. Isen, wondering if the man might still be alive, went over and crouched a few feet away, switching on the flashlight he had strapped to the suspenders of his load-bearing equipment. The young man's eyes were open. His hands were at his sides, elbows tucked in, his supplicant's palms open and up. Isen swept the flashlight over the corpse, which was not pinned under the tractor. The body had been severed just below the waist.

As the ROK lieutenant looked through the village for a way around, Isen went back to the buses. Barrow was awake and standing by the side of the vehicle.

"What's up, sir?"

"We have to go around the main road up ahead. The North Koreans dropped some H and I in and tore up the road."

"Sure is creepy-quiet," Barrow said, "a ghost town."

It took them another hour to get moving, and Isen watched the sky nervously. He checked his watch again— 0445. He figured they were not going to be even close to their destination by the time the sun came up. That brought in a whole new set of considerations. It was one thing to be riding in these stupid buses at night, quite another to be parading around in the daylight. He had just about decided that they would off-load a half hour before dawn, no matter where they were, when the ROK jeep ahead of them stopped, flagged down by a man who was now walking toward them on the road.

Isen figured the man for a GI; he was at least six feet tall and had, around his middle, the thick belt of equipment that the American Army felt compelled to make its soldiers carry. Isen got out of his vehicle and walked up to find Bock, who was having little luck communicating with the ROK lieutenant. The S3 was clearly agitated; his rain jacket and uniform shirt were ripped, as if he had been caught in concertina wire. Bock's map, unprotected and folded sloppily, stuck out of the cargo pocket of his trousers.

"Mark, this road movement has gone to shit."

Isen didn't say anything because he already knew that, and because Bock was so out of sorts that Isen figured the best thing he could do was listen.

"Alpha and Bravo are even more behind schedule than you guys, and the roads they were using have been completely cut by artillery and refugee traffic."

Isen thought about the ghost village. *Where had all those people gone? Maybe the other companies had also been swallowed by the night, by this spooky countryside.*

Isen blinked. *Get a grip,* he told himself.

Bock went on. "They're not going to be able to close up for hours yet, maybe not even before dark tonight."

Tilden and Tilden's radio operator, a big husky Iowa kid named Melden, came out of the darkness and approached the jeep. Isen straightened up a bit, pushing himself off the ROK vehicle.

"Morning, sir."

"Hey, Mark. Jan tell you what's going on?"

Bock answered, "I've only been able to tell him about the other companies, sir."

"Go on, then, go on." Tilden dropped his rucksack off his shoulders. Melden backed off the road a few feet and dropped to the ground in what the troops called a rucksack flop, leaning back against the ready-made rest of his overburdened pack. Isen could see the few others who made up the command group shuffling around in the shadows a few meters behind the colonel. They had all come here to tell *him* something, and he suddenly had the sense that he was about to get some bad news. Bock went on. "Worse yet, Mark . . ."

Here it comes, Isen thought.

"Worse yet, we got a group from the friggin' division command element pinned down in a village about four klicks ahead of us. Don't ask me what the hell they were doing snoopin' around up here, but the word is the division chief of staff is up there."

Bock paused to let this sink in. The division chief of staff was a full colonel whose job was to coordinate all the many activities that went on across the whole division staff. He was a crucial player in the division's planning, running the daily operations of the unit so that the general could concentrate on the battle. Isen couldn't imagine what the chief was doing up ahead of the rifle companies.

"I'll tell you what happened," Tilden interrupted, as if reading Isen's thoughts. "Colonel White got a wild hair and decided he was going to go see some action, like this was some sort of freakin' game we're playing up here. He thinks he has to put his two cents in before the show's over so he can get a fucking medal or something."

The outburst seemed to have drained Tilden, who was angered that he was going to have to take time out from gathering his battalion to get involved in this sideshow. It also smacked of his experience as an NCO in Vietnam, when his platoon leader and company commander had to listen to layer upon layer of helicopter-borne commanders circling above and calling down conflicting instructions.

Bock, sensing that Tilden was finished, went on. "So we get to pull the chief's chestnuts from the fire."

Isen looked down in the darkness at where his boots would be, and shook his head.

"Here's what we got," Bock went on. He squatted by the side of the jeep with a ration case, the cardboard box that held twelve individual meals, and flicked on his red-filtered flashlight. Isen knelt next to him.

The S3 made a quick sketch with a ball-point pen, drawing an L-shaped box, its long axis running east and west and an arrow with an "N" for north. The lines were barely visible in the red glow.

"There's some North Koreans, maybe a platoon, maybe even two, holed up in this school," he said, indicating the L-shape. "The chief and some GIs are pinned down by one of these small buildings." He added a few more smaller shapes just in front of the open angle of the "L," on the south side of the school.

"For some reason, the North Koreans haven't moved against the chief and his group, but that doesn't mean they won't soon. Right now, they have automatic weapons up on the roof, and our guys will get creamed if they try to move. The school is on a little hill, and the slope falls away pretty sharp just behind this fence." Bock added a fence that ran behind the school and along the right, or east, side. In front of the school, on the south side, he drew a street parallel to the long axis of the building. Several more streets ran into this at right angles from the south.

"How do you know all this?" Isen asked, wondering about the accuracy of the sketch and of the information.

"One of the drivers of these vehicles"—Bock quickly added three rectangles to the sketch, on the same side of the school as the outbuilding—"went over to the side of the street, south of the school to take a leak, and he was there when the shooting started. He got out and managed to find"—Bock looked at Tilden—"us."

"What I want you to do, Mark," Tilden added, "is conduct a movement to contact from the south side of the town, and an attack on the school. See if you can't root those North Koreans out of there, or at least tie them up enough so that we can extract the division staff guys. If you do that, we can pull back and blast them with the battalion mortars." He paused and looked back down the road beyond where the Charlie Company buses were parked. "Whenever the hell they show up."

"When do I move, sir?"

Tilden looked down at Isen. "Now."

"Okay, sir. We got any artillery or other kind of support? Any ROK units in the area?"

"Nobody here but us, Mark. Even if somebody were around, they'd be blowing through hell-bent-for-leather either toward or away from Uijongbu. I'm afraid it's just us."

"Right." Isen was off on his own now, kneeling right next to the S3, but war-gaming what his attack would look like. This was a little closer to the type of fighting he had expected. He was going to a particular place to fight the enemy, going after him in a way that his company had rehearsed. But still there was no artillery support, no hard knowledge of how many bad guys there were, or exactly how they were arrayed.

"One question, sir," Isen said. "What's a North Korean platoon or company or whatever-the-hell doing off by themselves like this?"

Bock had an answer. As tired and as frazzled as he was, he was still on top of things, still thinking two steps ahead of good guys and bad.

"Up until yesterday, or the day before maybe, the North Koreans were still trying to find a place to break through. They were using infantry, not their best infantry, but their second-string guys, to make limited attacks all along this corridor between Chunch'on and Uijongbu. It looks like, once they found a place they thought they could get through, they left a lot of these small units, the ones that were doing the probing, out here to fend for themselves."

Isen said, "So these guys should be pretty worn out. Maybe we could talk them into giving up."

"It might be worth a try," Bock said.

"Mark," Tilden said, "I'm going to stay with your company for a while. I'll drop off when you get there—it's your show—but I have to look after the chief. I'd like to let Jan here use your vehicle to go back to find Alpha and Bravo. Our vehicle went into a ditch this morning, and the frame got bent," Tilden explained.

Isen nodded. It wasn't as if he had a choice about giving up the vehicle. "Okay, sir. Can I have one of the KATUSAs go with me, in case we get a chance to talk to these North Koreans?"

"Sure, if you think it's worth a try," Tilden said. "Unless you've got something else, I guess that's it."

Bock stood up. "Your vehicle back here?"

"Yeah. Send Barrow and Voavosa up, will you?"

Isen figured he had around fifty minutes to an hour before the sky started to lighten. Thirty minutes after that and the sun would be coming up. He wanted to cover as much ground as he could in the darkness. Within ten minutes Isen had briefed his platoon leaders, giving them enough information to get the platoons off the buses and moving. He told the lieutenants to come back and walk the first leg with him so they could work out the final details of the plan. As the lieutenants trotted off in the darkness, Isen hoped again that Bock's sketch was close to being right.

Lake hurried back to his bus, the second in line, trying to lift his boots and leaden legs out of the mud on the road.

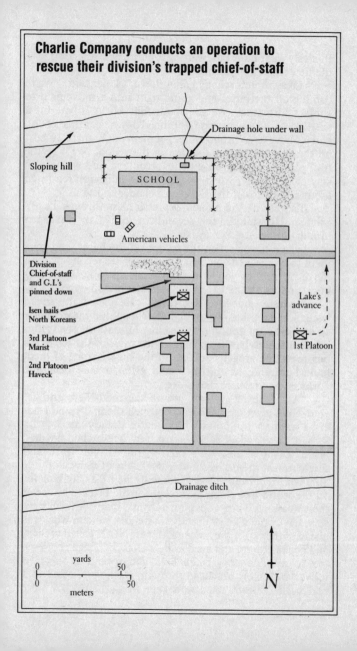

Charlie Company conducts an operation to rescue their division's trapped chief-of-staff

Drainage hole under wall

Sloping hill

SCHOOL

American vehicles

Division Chief-of-staff and G.I.'s pinned down

Isen hails North Koreans

3rd Platoon Marist

2nd Platoon Haveck

Lake's advance

1st Platoon

Drainage ditch

yards
0   50
0   50
meters

N

Bladesly was off the bus, waiting for him, but said nothing as the lieutenant approached.

"Okay, here's what's going down," Lake said. "We're coming off the buses and going right into a movement to contact formation. We got about four klicks 'til we hit a small town. There's some GIs pinned down near this school, and we have to go in and either get them out of there, or bust up the North Koreans that are in the school. We'll be the trail platoon in the movement to contact, and we have to stay close enough when we get to the built-up area to go around the flank if the CO sees a chance to use us."

Bladesly had remained expressionless through Lake's briefing. He waited a few seconds to see if Lake could tell him anything else. "Okay, sir."

Lake went on. "Get the troops off the buses, and start them moving when you hear from me or see second platoon move in front of you. I'm going back up to walk the first klick or so with the CO to talk about this some more."

Bladesly nodded. "Right, sir." He called the squad leaders, telling them to unload their men and move off the side of the road and into a traveling formation. The troops dragged themselves from the tangled mess of the too-small bus seats and groggily spilled off the buses. Some of them looked around, as if they could glean a clue from the darkness as to where they were.

"All right, let's move, get off the road there and get yourselves together," Bladesly coached them. "Squad leaders, I want an 'up' pronto, like, you're already late."

As Lake walked back toward Isen, he watched the men begin to move, urinating on the side of the track and scratching at themselves under the layers of filthy clothing. Some of them rubbed their eyes with their fists, looking for all the world like children, except for the black outlines of their weapons. They were punch-drunk, many of them were sick; few of them knew exactly where they were or what was ahead of them. Yet they moved as their NCOs called to them and coaxed them, and even as he walked by, Lake could see the sense of urgency catch hold and spread as the men moved into their practiced formations. In spite of all that had been done to them and kept from them, they were ready, once again, to do what they were told. All they asked, Lake realized, was a fair chance and competent leadership. And in that instant he saw how a man could devote his life to the service. There would always be these young men who needed someone to lead them, and lead them well. Shuffling along in the dark, moving among the soldiers as they got off the road and away from the buses, Lake felt an immense satisfaction in his association with them, not for what he could offer them, but for what they gave to him.

Lake found Isen, Haveck, Marist, and Staff Sergeant Richards, the mortar section leader, up near the head of the forming column. Barrow came and stood beside them, and Isen started talking as soon as his leaders were closed in.

"We're going to get away from the road, in case anybody's watching it. We'll move in traveling overwatch: third, second, mortars, then first platoon," Isen started off. "I want to maintain freedom of maneuver with first platoon. I see second platoon as helping provide a base of fire for third, since you guys are so understrength, Pete."

Haveck nodded quietly. Barrow wondered if the company would get replacements anytime soon.

"I want to get to the town as quickly as we can and go right into a hasty attack. I don't want the bad guys to have any time to react once we get on the scene. We'll pause only long enough to give the mortars a chance to set up, and me a chance to look around.

"Mike," Isen was looking at Lake now, "I don't intend to pause long. If the S3's information was right, there's a couple of parallel streets running toward the school. Third platoon will lead up one of the streets in a more or less direct approach. Plan on taking your platoon up another to try to get around behind this school. Be ready to move up even with third platoon."

Lake started to visualize the attack now as Isen unfolded it for them with a crude sketch and minimal instructions. The training—all the hard work together as a team—was paying off right here in this group of men who understood one another.

Isen continued. "I'll be with second platoon in the

move; I'll probably move up with the lead platoon when we get closer. The XO will be with the trail platoon and will come up if something happens to me. What did I forget?"

"The KATUSA, sir," Barrow said.

"Oh, yeah." Isen added. "I have one trick up my sleeve. Depending on what things look like up there, I may try to let Yu here talk the NKPA out of the building. They must know they've been abandoned. Maybe they'll give up."

No one said a thing, but Lake was once again amazed at the range of responses Isen always explored.

"What else?" Isen asked.

Voavosa spoke to the platoon leaders. "Tell your men not to ignore any buildings that we pass on our way into this burg. There may be bad guys in any one of them, waiting for us to pass so they can hit us from behind."

"Roger that," Isen agreed.

David tapped Isen with the radio handset. "Juliet five five is ready, sir." Somewhere nearby, Tilden was getting ready to follow Charlie Company into action. He had stayed away while Isen was doing his planning and briefing, and Isen was grateful to the old man for that courtesy.

Isen looked around at his platoon leaders. "We're going to get a chance here to do something we trained for. That doesn't mean that it will be what you expect, so keep your heads up, and you'll do fine." He paused for a few seconds. "Okay, Paco, take 'er away."

Lake stepped back onto the road as Marist moved off in the darkness. Lake planned to let the company move by, then rejoin his platoon when they came abreast of him. In the dim light of predawn, he could see the platoons pick up the easy gait of their movement formation. The fire teams of four and five formed small wedges, and the small wedges nestled into one another, so that each platoon was a series of these V-shapes, the men facing forward and out, providing the company security to the flanks and the front.

As the mortar section passed him, Lake stepped off the road and into the mud of the adjacent paddy to wait for his platoon. He could see the outlines of the small mortars the soldiers in front of him carried, skeletal against the lightening sky. He found his platoon and his place in the platoon.

One by one, each of the squad leaders came and walked with him so that he could pass the word about the upcoming operation. There was so much he couldn't tell them, so much he himself didn't know.

Isen walked with Haveck in the thin ranks of second platoon. They did not talk. Isen thought about what might happen ahead, trying to plan for all the possible contingencies. As the light grew, the countryside slowly revealed itself to them. They had not spent much time walking since their arrival in Korea, and this was the first tactical foot movement the company had made. Isen began to see the outlines of the soldiers around him, felt connected to them as the formation adjusted to the steady, practiced pace, the men maintaining the distance between themselves, between the formations and within the formations as they glided over the paddy walls and irrigation channels and the gentle undulations of the ground. The scene was familiar; Isen had walked like this with his men many times. He drew comfort from their nearness and their quiet—and he allowed himself, for just a moment, to think that they were back on peacetime maneuvers. But the temptation to escape through daydreaming, sweet as it was, was dangerous. Isen dragged himself back to reality and concentrated on what was being revealed as the darkness melted away.

The land was quiet, and the few farmhouses they passed remained dark, even at this hour when farmers start their day. The paddies had been readied for planting, and the earth was turned and pungent. Their detour was taking them north, and as the light grew to their right, Isen saw the expected Korean vistas, the small treeless valleys with their toy-like houses. But the infantryman in him couldn't afford to sightsee, and he scanned the hills and buildings for likely ambush sites, for the unexpected machine gun that would split the damp darkness. He knew that the formation could be spotted from a good distance if there were anyone around interested in what was going on. He wished he had some artillery on call in case they started to get fire from one of the hilltops.

David broke into Isen's reverie. "The Lima element

just called in checkpoint seven, sir." The Lima element was Marist's platoon, and checkpoint seven was three and a half kilometers from their start point, and about eight hundred meters short of where Bock thought the schoolhouse was located. Isen took the handset from David.

"This is November five five; let's move a bit until we get the November element under cover, over." Isen didn't want Marist's third platoon stopping while the rest of the company was still strung out in the open behind them.

"Roger, over," Marist came back. In Charlie Company, platoon leaders didn't end transmissions with the company commander; Isen had taught them that.

The radio, though nearly indispensable in fast-moving operations, could be a source of great frustration. All the speaker had in his hand, after all, was a disembodied voice, and just at the moment when he wanted to exert the most control, the voice could disappear behind static, or in a failed transmission, or the operator at the other end might just be ignoring the boss. Commanders handled this differently. Some cursed the terrain. ("Why is it we can put a man on the moon and I can't talk to somebody on the other side of this friggin' hill?") Others refused to talk to their platoon leaders' RTOs; still others expected an instant response to a call; hesitation was insubordination. Isen insisted that his platoon leaders wait to see what he had to say before they ended a transmission.

But he didn't want to take a chance at broadcasting their position just to get the last word in, so he let Marist's voice hang.

Isen was already up with the lead element by the time Marist held up a clenched fist, signaling the platoon to stop. It was now light enough to use hand and arm signals.

"What do you see, Paco?" Isen asked him. A good-sized drainage ditch, maybe fifteen feet wide, ran across the northerly azimuth they had been following. On the far side was a dirt track that ran beside the ditch. At least two small streets joined this track at right angles, stretching off up the hill to the north, where they could see the edge of the village. They would have to go through the ditch to make their way up one or two of the streets.

"Looks pretty much like the S3's sketch, sir. Don't you think?"

"Yeah, I guess it does." Isen and Marist were on a small earthen dike built to contain the water in the ditch before them. A good deal of the paddy field behind them was sheltered by the dike.

"I'm going to have the mortars set up here." Isen was thinking out loud. "David."

"I got it, sir." David was already making the radio call to Richards, the mortar platoon leader.

Within minutes Lake and Haveck had moved up as well, and Isen decided to take the three rifle platoon leaders on a recon of the other side of the ditch. If Bock's information was right, the school was too far off for anyone to spot them yet.

"Pete, I want you to give us four guys to go along as security, one of them with a SAW."

Isen could see that Haveck thought he was taking a lot of people on the recon, but Isen had anticipated that. The commander particularly wanted the SAW along. "We can't afford to get stuck up there. I may leave your guys in place as guides if I find a good spot."

Isen had read once about a company commander who, in the short fight for Grenada, had gone out on a recon just like this one, but had not provided for his security. He got himself and an NCO killed.

While Haveck walked back to get his men, Isen and the others looked at the village through binoculars. It was a little more affluent than most of the villages they had been in, and this one also looked deserted. Most of the houses and shops they could see were made of concrete block instead of the wood-frame and mud-brick construction they were used to seeing in the countryside. The village was on a small hill that climbed to the north as it moved away from the ditch they were beside.

"One of the things you'll have to tell your men," Isen said as he scanned the buildings, "is that their rifle fire, and probably even the SAWs, won't go through these types of walls. We'll have to use more hand-grenades than anything else."

Haveck returned in a few minutes with four of his soldiers. Isen could see that Haveck was unhappy that his platoon had been reduced to being split up for missions like this. But Isen planned on using the full-strength platoons to their full advantage.

They crossed the ditch, wading through cold water that swirled in filthy eddies around their thighs. This village, even with its upscale construction, still used open sewers.

Isen moved to the foot of each of the two main streets. He could not see to the top, could not see anything that looked like a school building. He suspected that it was just beyond his vision, near the crest of the hill. He left two soldiers at the foot of each of the streets, then he and his officers moved back to bring up the rest of the company.

The platoon sergeants were sitting in a small circle, waiting for the leaders to get back. No one had told them to collect there, but they knew Isen would come back with instructions for them.

"Great," Isen said. "I want first platoon to go up the street on the right. You'll have to keep your eyes open so that you don't get ahead of third platoon on this street on the left." He was using a stick to draw a quick sketch in the dirt. "I'll be with third and second platoons on the left, 'cause I think this one leads right to the school. I plan to use third as the main assault force, depending on what we find."

He turned to Lake. "Mike, first platoon should be able to stop near the top of the hill to lay down some supporting fires from the right side. If the school isn't at the top of this street that I'm going up with third, we'll adjust from there."

His subordinates were hanging on his every word, and though he felt confident in his plan, Isen wished he weren't making it up as he went along.

"If I can get a solid fix on our guys and the bad guys, I may try to use some mortar fire to loosen things up a bit. It's going to be tight up there, with no room for error with the indirect fire, so we'll start off with a single round for a marker, okay, Sergeant Richards?"

"Got you, sir."

The plan had an appealing simplicity, Lake had to admit. It would put Charlie Company's strength up close enough to make a difference, but still maintained freedom of movement with one platoon off to the side and one smaller platoon, Haveck's, in reserve.

Isen moved with Haveck's platoon over the small dike and through the drainage ditch. His trousers and boots were already soaked through from his first crossing that morning. He heard some muffled curses as one of the men in the squad behind him lost his footing on the steep bank and slipped into the water. When they climbed out on the other side, he glanced back and saw the mortar platoon already setting up their tubes and the red and white aiming stakes that gave them their bearings. He crossed the road that paralleled the ditch, then looked back again and saw Lake just emerging from the drainage ditch. He motioned to the foot of the street on the right. Lake nodded and his lead fire team adjusted their direction of movement.

The first two squads in Marist's third platoon each took a side of the narrow street they were on, the small groups of men leapfrogging their way slowly, cautiously, up the road. They watched everything, the buildings, the windows on their side and across the street. The street was quiet, and Isen could plainly hear the crunch of broken glass on the sidewalk as his men shuttled from doorway to doorway.

Isen moved up closer to Marist, staying right behind the last squad in the lead platoon. He caught a glimpse of Lake's platoon moving on the parallel street.

He radioed Lake and told him to slow it down, and he could see the platoon, through the narrow yards and alleys on the right side of the street, respond to his call. After five years in the infantry, it still amazed him that he could control these men, this company, spread over two blocks, as if by the sound of his voice. He called, they responded. The men were conducting a textbook advance, responding to the silent hand and arm signals of their NCOs, staying low as they moved, spread out and watchful as misers. Isen thought to himself, *This is the easy part.*

The first rounds hit the wall of a house just inches above the head of a soldier in Marist's lead squad. He and the men around him on the left side of the street dove for cover wherever they could find it, and the men in the squad behind them immediately returned fire. Marist was on the opposite side of the street, and he figured he was out of the line of fire, so he moved up a few more meters before he stopped. He couldn't see the school or anything that looked like it might be a school. He yelled to his lead team leader, Corporal Parrish, the soldier who had handled the Dragons so well in the ambush.

"What can you see?" Marist hollered.

"Nothing. I think they can't see us down low here; the first rounds were high."

Marist had to admire Parrish's grasp of the situation. The North Korean gunner, wherever he was, had stopped firing, probably because he had no targets and, Marist hoped, limited ammunition. The Americans had probably disappeared from his sight when they went to ground.

"Move up and see if you can't give us a call for fire." Marist told him.

"Negative," Isen shouted from behind Marist. "We have to get a fix on the GIs first."

"Okay, sir." Marist was conscious of his mistake. "Lead squad, continue to move up, slowly. Let's get some smoke up the street there."

The grenadiers in the trail squad on the left side of the street responded by dropping three forty-millimeter grenades onto the cracked asphalt of the road, about a hundred and fifty meters ahead of the point man. One of the grenades sputtered, its fuse wet from the stream crossing. The other two fizzled and put out a short-lived smoke screen. Marist's men continued to advance.

Isen called Lake. "Delta six one, this is November five five. What do you see from your side? Over."

"Nothing over here, five five," Lake called back. "I can continue to work this side, over."

"Roger, delta six one, but slow it down a bit so you don't get out of synch, out."

Isen was having a hard time watching the men advance. He wanted to be everywhere at once, to see everything and control everything. He had to restrain himself from taking over the direction of the lead fire team, reminding himself that he was the company commander, and to do so would undercut the whole chain of command that included a platoon leader, a competent one at that, a squad leader and finally, at the very lead of the unit, a good fire team leader. He had to content himself with moving slowly behind the platoon and watching.

"Murray, give second platoon a sitrep so they know what's going on." Isen filled a few seconds this way.

The machine gun up the street opened up again, but the shots were not aimed any better, and the rounds sent plaster splattering into the roadway. The men hesitated, but Parrish was up and moving again in seconds, rushing from one covered position to the next. He lunged into the recessed gateway of a large house and called back to Marist.

"I see the school, I see the school! They're shooting from the roof. Get the M-60s up here. We can get some fire on them."

Marist signaled to the two M-60 gunners, who were behind him on the right side of the street. One team of gunner and assistant gunner jumped up and ran across the road toward Parrish. The heavy gun carried by one man and the metal boxes of ammunition carried by the other made the movement awkward. The men moved quickly, but Isen imagined that the street seemed as wide as the Mississippi. Some half-hearted shots came from the top of the street, but Isen couldn't see where the rounds hit.

The gunner set up quickly, and Isen saw the second team begin to move.

"*No!* Wait 'til we get some fire up there," Marist shouted.

The soldiers, caught by the order in the first few steps of their run, hesitated, and the North Korean machine gunner, alerted by the earlier movement, found the target. The rounds walked up the roadway in small dusty geysers until they found the legs of the assistant gunner, who spun around and hit the ground without uttering a sound. The gunner took a juke step back to grab his partner's shirt, to try to drag the man out of the street, but the North Korean machine gunner corrected quickly. The second man went down just as Marist's other gun got off his first shots.

"*Medic, medic!*"

The call was repeated all along both sides of the street, but was quickly drowned out as Marist's men, shocked and

219

angry, fired at the building, which for most of them was just over the top of the road and invisible. The squad leaders tried to regain control of the fire, yelling at the men to hold their fire if they couldn't see anything.

"Second squad, move up the left side," Marist shouted as he stripped his gear off, dropping his weapon and his rucksack against the curb where he lay, only a few meters away from his two men. Isen couldn't see any movement from the gunner or assistant.

Marist's second squad moved up the left side of the street quickly, and the M-60 gunner kept up a rapid rate of fire, trying to make up for the missing gun. The men gained targets quickly as they climbed the rise, and they began to open fire with rifles and grenade launchers.

Isen saw that Marist intended to dash into the road and pull his men out. As soon as the lieutenant moved out of the shelter of the curb, Isen saw another soldier sprint from the left side of the road. The two men reached the wounded and began tugging on them. As the North Koreans opened fire again, Marist dropped one man and grabbed the other arm of the assistant gunner. Along with the soldier who had come from the left side of the street, the lieutenant pulled the wounded man and the machine gun to safety. The dead gunner lay only yards from the rest of the platoon, alone in the middle of the street.

Isen moved up to Marist, reaching the lieutenant just as he was buckling his equipment back on. The platoon's medic was applying a battle dressing to the wounded man's leg, but the whole lower part of his body was soaked in blood, and the medic was shaking badly. David, Isen's radio operator, dropped to his knees and tore his own battle dressing off his suspender. He immediately began talking to the wounded man, who was conscious, though his eyes were fluttering.

"Good job, Paco," Isen said.

"I don't know who the hell that was that ran out in that street, sir," Marist said, "but it sure didn't feel like me."

He turned on his knees and took off in a crouch to reach the farthest point of his platoon's advance.

Isen turned and saw that David was now cradling the

wounded man's head. The medic, calmed by David's actions, was fixing a tourniquet to the man's thigh. He had his other hand deep in the gore on the man's other leg, pinching, Isen supposed, the artery at the top of the thigh. Isen saw in a flash that the soldier wasn't going to make it.

David spoke softly to the man, a soldier by the name of Potter, who had joined the company just before Christmas.

"It's okay, man," David crooned. "It's gonna be okay, you'll see, I got you, man, it's gonna be all right, hang on, man, hang on."

Potter was intensely calm, holding on to one of David's hands with his own bloody one. He looked as if he wanted to speak, but couldn't muster the strength. He stared hard at David's young face.

"He's gone, man." It was the medic. He reached past David and closed the soldier's eyelids. David pulled the man closer to him, then lay him gently down on the street.

Isen had no idea what to say to him, but David spoke first, his voice an uncertain whisper.

"Ready, sir?" And the act went on.

Isen took the handset from Murray, who was standing nearby, and called Marist.

"Lima six one, this is November five five, over." It took Marist a long minute to come up on the net.

"This is lima six one, over."

"Get me a fix on the school and the GIs as soon as you can, so we can drop some mortar fire on them, over."

"Wilco, over."

"Five five, out."

Isen handed the radio handset to Murray, who looked more tired than Isen had ever seen him. David was staring down at the medic, who had covered the dead man with a poncho.

Isen spoke to David as quietly as he could with all the shooting going on. "We got to move now."

"I'm with you, sir," he said, his voice grim, older. He hunched his shoulders, adjusting the heavy radio and rucksack, and brought his rifle up across his middle. "Let's do it."

Isen moved up the right side of the street. Most of the

shooting was going on from the left side. He still couldn't see the school from where he was. He got a call from an excited Marist.

"November five five, this is lima six one. I've got a fix on the friendlies and the enemy, over."

Isen thought that this might go their way. "Can we call for fire? Over."

"Roger, five five, gimme a minute."

"Take a couple, over," Isen said. In these tight quarters, with only a short distance between the mortars and target, and with friendly troops all around, they had to be extra careful.

While Marist worked up the grid for the mortars, Isen hurried forward. He reached a point in the street where he could see the school building, just as Marist called back to the mortars.

The school lay on a flattened place at the top of the small hill they had just climbed. There was a small playground on the south side of the building, the front as Isen looked at it, with three American vehicles parked in the yard. One of them, a HMMWV, was burning. Off to the far left, Isen could see a small building in a lot adjacent to the school yard, and he suspected that the division guys were behind that. There was enough room here to drop a few mortar rounds in. As the first marker round landed, Isen worked up the correction but let Marist call it in. Isen called Lake.

"Delta six one, where are you? Over."

"This is delta six one. I'm one block east of you, over," Lake came back. Isen crawled back a few feet to look down a nearby alley and saw one of Lake's soldiers. The soldier gave him a cheery wave, as if they were on an outing.

"Stand by, out." Isen wanted to see if he could do the work with the mortars. The taxpayer spent all that money on ammunition so that Isen wouldn't have to use up-the-middle tactics, and he planned on using it.

He was disappointed when the first three rounds came in. The school, like many of the houses in the village, was made of brick, and the small sixty-millimeter rounds did little damage. There was only a small chance that they could drop a round right on the narrow roof, and Isen didn't have much ammunition to start with, and no prospect for a resupply anytime soon. He called Lake.

"Delta six one, this is November five five. Did you see those rounds? Over."

"Affirmative. They didn't do much, over."

"Give us a few minutes to set up a base of fire here, then you move to see what you can do on your side. A red star from you will shift our fires left, over."

"Understand red star will shift your fires left, over," Lake responded.

"Roger, out."

Isen planned to bring Haveck's machine guns up along-side of Marist's, and use the four of them to place fire on the south wall of the school building, where it faced the street. Even with the brick walls, the enemy inside would be forced to keep low. Lake would work around the right side of the school. If he found an opening on the right or behind the building, he would pursue it and try to get inside. If his troops were about to come into the line of fire from the machine guns in front, Lake would fire a red star cluster, a hand-held pyrotechnic, as a signal for the gunners to shift their fire left, away from where it might hit friendly troops.

It took the two platoon sergeants four or five minutes to get the M-60 machine guns, one of them with a new crew, set up across the street from the school yard. The gunners had to work to find covered positions from which their fires wouldn't be masked by the vehicles in the school yard. Isen watched the school through his binoculars. There was nothing moving that he could see. His soldiers had been pecking away at the building with rifle fire, placing their shots carefully in the darkened windows. Isen wondered how many North Koreans were trapped in there, wondered if they knew the noose was tightening. He sent a runner back to where he had seen Tilden following the company, telling the runner to ask for the battalion's translator.

Isen was still waiting for a call from Lake when the M-60s opened up, firing a choreographed, rippling fire. Charlie Company's gunners used a timing device that Voavosa had taught them, pulling the trigger and saying to themselves, *Fire a burst of six,* then releasing the trigger. As soon as each gun finished firing, the next gunner picked it up. The effect was like a giant and insistent hammer, knocking away at the school building and daring anything to move there. Marist had positioned riflemen to watch the sides of the school so that no one could get out of the building without being seen.

Isen's radio handset squawked. "November five five, this is delta six one, over." It was Lake.

"This is November five five, over."

"I can see the back of the objective. I can get up close and try to get through the wall, over."

Isen turned and looked behind him. He could just see his runner and the KATUSA translator picking their way carefully up the hill.

"Stand by, delta six one. I'm going to try something else from here, out."

When the KATUSA got closer, Isen motioned him over. Yu was clearly frightened and fascinated. Once he realized there was no return fire from the school, he relaxed visibly. He and Isen were completely prone, sheltered behind a small retaining wall alongside a driveway. Off to their left, the machine guns roared away, but Isen could still hear, above the din, the strangely musical sound of the expended brass casings falling on the concrete.

"I'm going to call a cease-fire in a few seconds," Isen told the young Korean. "There are some North Koreans holed up in there. We don't know how many. I want you to ask them to surrender; we have them cold."

Yu looked confused, and Isen realized he might not understand the slang. "We have them surrounded, there's no chance for them to get away," he shouted.

Yu shook his head violently. "They never give up, never surrender."

Isen wasn't used to being refused by privates. "First of all, we have nothing to lose in trying this; second, I don't think we're dealing with Special Purpose Forces. I think these guys might be reservists. They're not all out to be martyrs. They may give up, and that would save us from having to go in and shoot it out with them."

Isen paused, then thought to himself, *What in the hell am I explaining this to you for?*

He pointed at the school, and Yu nodded. Even American officers, tolerant as they were, had a limit. Yu had no desire to get sent back to his own army as a rifleman. He had a better chance of surviving as a translator for the Americans.

Isen called to the guns to cease fire. A few seconds later there was a tremendous, ringing silence as the noise abated.

Yu let go a rapid-fire string of Hangul, then paused, listening. There was no answer. He looked at Isen, who thought he could detect an I-told-you-so light on the soldier's face. Isen pointed, and Yu went into his speech again, louder this time. Still no response.

Yu turned to face Isen. "North Koreans will not surrender. They are sure they will all be killed anyway."

Just as Isen was about to tell the machine guns to open up again, someone called from the building.

"What'd he say? What'd he say?" Isen pressed Yu.

"Something about wounded. I do not make it out." Yu wasn't through with his remark when they heard a pistol shot from inside the school. Almost immediately, the machine gun on the roof opened up again, sending dust and dirt flying over the low wall and onto Isen and Yu.

I wonder what that was all about? Isen thought to himself. He nodded to the machine-gun crews. "Open fire."

"Get Lake on the horn," he told David.

When Lake came on, Isen told him, "Go ahead. Watch the friendly fire, out."

Lake gave his handset back to Janeson, raised his arm, and pointed toward the school, giving Staff Sergeant Hall, his lead squad leader, the go-ahead sign. Hall was a block east of Marist's lead squad, and almost a full block east of the school, which lay across the street, diagonally off to his left. Hall turned and nodded to Lamson, who was only a few feet in front of him.

"Let's go."

Sergeant Keith Lamson raised himself up off the ground. He had been lying flat, peering around the corner of the last building that separated them from the school yard. Ahead of him and to the left, or west across thirty or forty meters of ground littered with construction equipment and garden tools and rickety fences, he could see a concrete block wall that guarded the back of the school yard. The wall sat at the northernmost edge of the hilltop. Beyond it, the ground fell away to the north, and Lamson could just see the tops of some houses that sat in the low ground.

Lamson looked over his shoulder to see if the men in his fire team—Cipriotti, Boste, and an Arkansas native named Mitchell—were ready. Satisfied that they were, he sprinted for a fence that was about ten meters away. He held his breath as he ran, waiting, expecting to hear fire from the school. There was nothing. Cipriotti followed, then Lamson made for a thick clump of bushes. His men followed in short rushes, working their way steadily across the yards that separated them from the school. Lamson headed for the slope behind the school that would hide him from the North Koreans. He hugged the lip of the hill as he made his way along, keeping his eyes on the top of the school, trusting that his men were following him.

Cipriotti turned his ankle as he followed Lamson over the edge of the hill, twisting it viciously in the soft dirt of the slope. He lay on his back for a few seconds to let the shards of pain subside. Boste caught up with him.

"What's the matter?" Boste was breathing heavily, more than he should have been from just the short run.

"I twisted my ankle, man."

"Is it broken?"

"I don't think so," Cipriotti forced out between clenched teeth.

Lamson, who was becoming more and more agitated as they neared the school, called to them in a harsh whisper, "Let's go, let's go, let's go."

Cipriotti forced himself up. "Guess I'll just have to miss sick call today."

Lamson followed the edge of the hill to the northeast corner of the wall, where he paused to take stock of the situation. The wall stretched to the right in an unbroken line all the way along the back side of the school, and to the left toward the street. There didn't seem to be any way in. He looked for Lake, but couldn't see the lieutenant, who must now be hidden in the yard where Lamson had started. He had been so preoccupied with getting across the space in one piece that it hadn't occurred to him that he might not know what to do when he got to the wall.

Cipriotti went a few feet past him along the north wall. "Hey, Sarge," he called.

"What?"

"I think I see a hole in this wall, or under it, at least."

Lamson came up beside him. "Good job, Sip."

Cipriotti had found a space under the wall where some sort of drainage had worn away enough of the soil to let a man get underneath.

Lamson looked up at the top of the wall, wondering if he would be able to fire over the top if Cipriotti got in trouble. "Let's wait until we get the other fire team up here, in case you get into trouble as you go through."

Cipriotti looked at Lamson. *When I go through?*

He thought about mentioning his ankle, which was already starting to swell against the inside of his boot, pressing the laces. But he thought better of it. The alternative was for Lamson to go through, in which case he, Cipriotti, might be left in charge. And he wanted no part of that.

Boste and Mitchell were up with them now, and Cipriotti could see the lead man from the second fire team, which was moving up to support them. He felt the little build-up of men press against him. They couldn't very well stay there forever, and the only way out was through the wall. He stuck his hand in the water that was running out under the wall. It was cold. Worse yet, it smelled bad. Just as it occurred to him that it might be one of the open sewers, maybe a drain from some child's latrine, Lamson prodded him, "Okay, ready?"

"What the hell." Cipriotti dropped to his stomach in the slime and pushed with his good leg in the slippery mess beneath him. He poked the muzzle of his rifle through the hole. All he could see was a whitewashed patch of concrete a few feet away from the wall. He moved ahead, bumped his helmet on the wall, then realized he would have to go under on his back, just as they had been taught in basic training.

He backed up, flipped over, and moved forward. He couldn't have felt more exposed had he been naked in Philadelphia's Independence Square.

He crawled through, looking for the top of the wall. He was halfway through when he realized he was looking at some sort of outbuilding that shielded him from the school. Cipriotti pulled himself completely through. He was thoroughly soaked now, covered back and front in a sticky green slime that smelled of stagnant water and chilled him through. He leaned back down to the hole and called Lamson.

"Come on."

Lamson pushed under the wall, then Boste started working his way in. Cipriotti was peering around the wall of what turned out to be an outhouse. The back door of the school building was only ten meters away at this point. There were windows all over the back side of the school, most of them broken out. They could hear the machine guns chattering away at the front of the building.

Lamson moved from the outhouse to the back of the school and crouched there as Cipriotti and Boste moved up. Lamson said, "We'll wait until our squad is through, or maybe even two squads, before we go in." He sat against the back wall of the school and watched as Mitchell made it through the wall. The next head to appear was Sergeant Hall's, the squad leader. He looked in at Lamson, who signaled him to come on through.

Suddenly there were excited voices above Lamson. He looked up in time to see the muzzle of an AK-47, the standard assault rifle of the NKPA, stuck through the window only two feet above his head. He ducked as the rifle fired, hitting the wall of the outhouse where Mitchell's head had just appeared. Lamson saw a quick flash as Cipriotti opened up, pointing his M-16 rather generally in the direction of the window. He held the weapon above his head, and could not see what he was shooting at, but the fire stopped and Mitchell was able to dash up to the building wall.

"Looks like they know we're here, Sarge," Cipriotti said, more calmly than Lamson could have imagined.

Lamson could see the hole in the wall where they had come through. There was no one visible there now; they were the only ones inside. He would have to do it with just his team.

Hall shouted at him. "Lamson, we can't get in."

"I know," Lamson yelled back as Cipriotti and Boste took turns firing into the window, "I'm going in the building."

Lamson pulled a fragmentation grenade from the strap of his equipment, yanked out the pin, snapped the clip, then let the grenade "cook off" for a few seconds in his hand before tossing it in. In these close quarters, the idea was to let some of the grenade's five-second fuse burn, so that the people inside couldn't toss the grenade back out. The men crouched against the outside of the wall and waited for the explosion.

Cipriotti watched a blade of grass, and he thought how odd it was that he would notice something so small just before the rush.

Lamson followed the blast of the grenade, rolling over the shattered frame of the window, keeping his body low to the silhouette of the wall.

Cipriotti, hearing Lamson firing inside, followed him in. The room was dark compared to the outside, even for all the uncovered window space. Cipriotti couldn't see in the gloom, and he was afraid of hitting Lamson, so he held his fire. As his eyes adjusted, Cipriotti could see a North Korean soldier sprawled backward over a pile of smashed desks. Lamson was a few feet away, on his stomach, peering out the door of the classroom into the hallway. Cipriotti skidded along the floor and came up behind him.

Lamson held up his hand, palm flat, signaling for quiet. Cipriotti stopped breathing, and noticed that the school was deadly quiet. They could hear the machine-gun rounds spattering against the front of the building.

Lamson turned and motioned for Boste to come in, and Cipriotti turned just for a second, just long enough to see Boste start over the sill. When he turned back, he saw the quick flash of a hand, and a North Korean grenade hit him square in the chest and dropped to the floor. Cipriotti stared at the sputtering grenade on the floor for what seemed like hours, but must have been only seconds, before Lamson batted the grenade back into the hallway. Cipriotti dropped to the floor, pressing his face into Lamson's side as the grenade went off.

Cipriotti hadn't recovered from the shock—*It hit me in the chest*—when Lamson was up on his feet and in the hall. Cipriotti stepped behind him into the hallway, hugging the right wall and pulling his rifle up to his shoulder. Down the hall to the right, he spotted the North Korean who had thrown the grenade. He pumped several shots at the man, but the rounds hit the walls around him. The North Korean disappeared into the shadows at the bottom of a staircase that probably led to the roof of the one-story building.

Lamson and Cipriotti stepped back to check on Boste and Mitchell. Lamson's team was now inside the building, and the North Koreans knew they were there. They had secured only one room, and there was at least one more to their left that they had to clear before they could start working their way to the right, down the long axis of the building, to systematically clear all the rooms on the floor. The stairs were at the far end of the hall. Fighting up them to the roof would be even tougher. Lamson paused to get his breath, looked each of his soldiers in the eye, and briefed them as to how they would go about their task.

"We'll split into two-man teams, Sip and Boste, me and Mitchell. We'll go first, to the left. Once we clear that room, we'll cover you guys as you start down the hall to the right. You take a room, then we'll pass you and take the next one. Remember the drill, but don't throw a grenade unless you hear or see something in the room; we don't have enough. First man in flattens against the wall—stay low—and fires. Second man comes in at the floor and flattens on the opposite side. How many grenades you got now?"

"Two," Cipriotti said.

"I got three," Mitchell said.

Boste had two and Lamson had two.

"Okay," the young NCO continued, "room to room, slowly and carefully. We'll isolate the bottom of the staircase 'cause I think they have some people up on the roof. Ready?"

The men didn't answer him, but he could read their wide-open eyes, could almost hear their pulses racing over the sound of his own. "Let's go," he said as he took the first step out into the hall.

Outside the school-yard back wall, Lake heard the grenades exploding and knew he would have to back up the four troops he had inside.

"Pull your guys back, Sergeant Hall," he said as he moved away from the hole in the wall. He saw what he wanted on a soldier who was crouched on the lip of the hill. "Come here," he said, motioning to the man.

When Hall had the men clear, Lake took an LAW from the man he had called, extended the launcher, checked the back-blast area, and fired at the block wall. The round hit just above the opening the water had made, drilling neatly through the block, but not doing much to extend the hole for the men to crawl through.

Hall shouted at him, "Doesn't look like that's gonna work, el-tee."

"I know," Lake came back. He dropped the launcher and crawled back to the hole, then placed a grenade inside the loosened block. He let the spoon fly once he had the grenade wedged in, then hurried out of the way. The men who were watching him had their heads down even before Lake got out of the way. *That should do it,* he thought to himself.

The grenade expanded the hole by several feet, blowing bits of block and concrete and plaster over the men on the hillside. Lake tossed a red star cluster to Hall.

"When I get inside, I want you to wait until you hear me call for this, or for four minutes, whichever comes first, and pop this thing."

Hall realized that Lake meant to lead the rest of the men through the hole. "We'll be right behind you, sir."

"I hope so," Lake said, managing a grin.

Lake's stomach barely touched the ground beneath the widened hole, he was moving so quickly. He heard rifle shots as he pumped his legs in the mud and raised his upper body on the other side of the wall, like a sprinter coming out of the blocks. *I should have tossed smoke in here.* He felt chips of the wall hit the backs of his legs, but he was out of sight in a second, and the North Korean, probably firing from the roof, didn't have a chance to adjust. Lake crouched behind the wall of the children's outhouse and surveyed the school yard.

All he could see from this vantage point was the top of the one-story building that stretched away to his right, in the direction of the trapped division-headquarters GIs, who were on the opposite side of the building. He figured that Lamson and his men had gone around this outhouse unseen, because he wouldn't be able to get past this spot without getting hit from the roof.

He pulled a grenade from the straps on the side of his ammo pouch, popped the clip and pulled the pin, holding the spoon tightly. There was a chance that he might hit Lamson and his own men if they were working their way up on the roof; there was also a chance that he might overshoot the roof itself and send the grenade into the school yard in the front.

"Lamson!"

His call was met by several rounds of rifle fire pattering against the front of the outhouse. The rifleman was still on the roof. No answer from inside. He didn't know where his men were. Could he throw the grenade? He stood slowly, behind the wall. He was completely out of sight from the roof.

Then he heard someone in the building shout *"In here."* Satisfied that there were no friendly troops on the roof, Lake acted. He kicked some loose dirt out to his right, from behind the shack, then jumped to the left as the rifleman on the roof shot at the dusty ruse. Lake tossed the grenade lightly up onto the roof, then jumped back behind the outhouse. He heard it hit the wooden roof as he crouched and covered his ears with his hands.

Inside the building, Lamson and Mitchell had just checked the first room, the one to their left, when the grenade went off on the roof above them. Cipriotti and Boste were crouched by the door of the first room they had cleared. The explosion rocked the small building, sending pieces of the ceiling down on them, the sound crashing and echoing through the small room.

"Did you guys throw that?" Lamson yelled.

Cipriotti leaned out past the doorjamb and shook his head. Lamson pointed up the hallway, and Cipriotti tapped Boste and moved out into the dusty darkness. He tripped over a small desk that had been tossed into the hall. He flattened himself against the wall at the entrance to the next room on the right, checked Boste's position, and turned to go into the room. Just as he did, a North Korean soldier stepped into the hall a few doors down and fired a long burst from his rifle. Cipriotti dropped to his stomach as the rounds chewed up the wooden doorframe he had been leaning on. Boste returned fire immediately, dropping the North Korean in the middle of the hall. Cipriotti stayed flat, trying to control the waves of shock washing over him. Boste stepped neatly over his unwounded buddy, and checked the room they were supposed to be clearing.

"Nothing in here," he said, as calmly as if they had been looking for the missing schoolchildren.

Cipriotti hauled himself up. "Sonofa*bitch.*" He looked back down the hall and motioned for Lamson to come forward.

Mitchell led this time, and he and Lamson cleared the next room on the opposite side of the hall. Cipriotti and Boste watched from their side, and they could see Mitchell give them the "all-clear" sign as he leaned against the wall inside the other room. He lifted his hand, then was thrown forward as machine-gun rounds pumped through the wall he'd been leaning on. The North Koreans were one room farther down, firing through the wall.

Cipriotti rushed into the hall, Boste a step behind him, and raced up to the doorway of the next room. He saw two North Koreans, a machine-gun crew, bent over their weapon, which had been trained out the window before they heard Mitchell. They were frantically trying to move the tripod and swing the gun all the way around to the hallway. Cipriotti shot the gunner, who seemed to leap backward toward the open window as the rounds caught him across the top of his chest. The assistant gunner went for his rifle, which lay only a foot or two away from him. Cipriotti, who was standing not more than four feet away, took aim, bringing his rifle up to his shoulder as the man exposed the whole length of his body. He pulled the trigger. Nothing. No jolt, no report, no sound except that of the North Korean rolling on the floor and scrambling to bring his own rifle to bear. Cipriotti, thinking he was completely outside the room, stepped to the side, but bumped into the doorjamb. He had moved inside the room and now, for an agonizing second, it looked as if he wouldn't be leaving in one piece. He cringed, as might a child who expects to be struck, but the next sounds came from behind him as Boste opened fire, his SAW tearing the scene apart. Cipriotti saw sparks fly as the bullets hit the North Korean's rifle, then walked across his torso, sending dust and blood flying up from the filthy clothing.

Boste had saved him twice within the space of a couple of minutes, and all Cipriotti could do was look at the man he had suspected, a few nights before, was a coward.

"Thanks, man."

Lamson was in the hall now. "Mitchell's gone. We gotta get this last room."

Boste gently pulled Cipriotti away from the wall nearest the room at the end of the hall, the last they had to clear. He checked his weapon, and fired through the wall that separated the rooms. When he stopped firing, the building seemed suddenly quiet, and Lamson wondered if it was a trick their hammered ears were playing on them. He took his last grenade from his belt and got ready to toss it up the hallway. They heard a single rifle shot, then something clattered in the hall. They pulled back, thinking it was a grenade. When there was no explosion, they looked out to see a single AK-47 rifle tossed among the wreckage of desks and papers on the floor.

Lamson cautiously peered around the doorjamb, leading with his rifle. There were two wounded North Koreans crouching by the foot of the stairs, which were at the very end of the hall, across from the door to the last room. One of the men was near collapse, his head and face a mass of fresh and dried blood.

"Come down here," Lamson shouted, sure that they would understand what he meant.

The two men moved slowly, obviously terrified. Lamson and Boste moved out to the hall. The less seriously wounded prisoner began talking, pointing back to the room at the end of the hall.

Lamson held his weapon on the prisoners while Boste walked slowly down the hall.

"Holy shit," he said, jumping back from the door of the last room.

Lamson thought he'd had about as many surprises as he could stand. "What is it?"

"There's a whole mess of 'em in here."

Boste pulled a grenade off his belt and, without removing the pin or exposing himself, flourished it with one hand in front of the door so that the North Koreans inside could see it. A chorus of excited, terrified voices shouted at him.

"Then come on out, one at a time, with your friggin' hands in the air."

Cipriotti crouched in the hallway behind Boste and watched in amazement as one, two, three, four, five, six, seven, eight, nine prisoners came out of the room. Some of them were wounded. Some of the wounds were obviously a few days old and had not been dressed recently. All of them, even the unwounded ones, were drained, as if the life had already been bled from them.

Boste lined them up facing the wall, their hands and feet spread as in a police roundup. While he searched them, Lamson hollered over his shoulder toward the back of the building.

"YO! Anybody out there?"

Lake called back, "Yeah, we're right here. Wha'cha got?"

"We got some prisoners downstairs. I haven't been able to check the roof."

"Stay still," Lake said.

Lamson heard the sound of running feet, and his stomach rolled over as he thought he might have missed some North Koreans. But it was only the next fire team.

"We're coming in. Hey, Sergeant Lamson, we're coming in!"

The team from Hall's squad moved past Lamson and up the stairs. "Two dead ones up here," one soldier shouted down seconds later.

Cipriotti stood in the doorway of the next to last room

in the hall. His head had started to swim as soon as the shooting stopped. He looked back in the room as he tried to see what was going on out front, and as he did he noticed the crushed tables and small desks that littered the classroom. There was a globe over in one corner, knocked completely off its stand, resting on the floor like a ball waiting for some odd game.

"Sip, you okay?" It was Lamson.

"Yeah, I guess so. Thanks to Brian."

"I want you to take these two out back of the school. I don't think they're in any shape to try anything, but watch yourself."

Cipriotti motioned, with the muzzle of his weapon, for the North Koreans to move down the hall toward the door at the opposite end. They paused for two men from the squad who were lifting Mitchell's body into a poncho they had spread on the floor. Cipriotti noticed that the North Korean soldiers did not look up as the Americans shuffled along with their burden.

Once Isen saw his soldiers waving from inside the building, he had David call all the platoons to make sure they all got the "cease-fire" order. Then he stood and waited as Tilden walked up from a house just behind Charlie Company's line. Isen and the battalion commander then walked together over to where the division chief of staff had been pinned down behind a small building on a lot just to the west of the school yard.

Tilden saluted Colonel White as he approached, and the incongruity of saluting on literally, the battlefield, was lost on the colonel. Isen said nothing.

"Splendid work there," White said to Tilden, "simply splendid. I'll be sure to tell the old man about this."

Isen noticed a major and a captain, along with two soldiers he assumed were the drivers of the vehicles in the school yard, standing sheepishly behind White.

"Tell me, sir," Tilden said, "what were you and your men doing up this far?"

If White knew he was being confronted, he didn't acknowledge it.

"Trying to keep up with what's going on at the front. We

thought we saw those North Koreans go into this building. We were on an adjacent street. So we came up here to root them out. I thought it would be good to let these junior officers"—he motioned at the major and captain, who cringed—"get a taste of the old powder smoke."

Tilden was obviously fighting an explosion.

"Well, sir," he said, his voice flattened by the effort to control it, "next time you want to go grandstanding, you can get your own ass out of a sling."

Tilden didn't wait for White to reply, but turned smartly and walked away. Isen looked at the major and captain. He felt sorry for them; they were being dragged around by this officer who didn't know the difference between audacity and foolhardiness.

Isen turned and caught up to Tilden.

"If it wasn't for those soldiers standing there, Mark," he said, "I swear I'd have hit the sonofabitch." Tilden removed his helmet, then punched at the webbing that made up the insides. "I can guaran-damn-tee he wouldn't have told the old man. If the general finds out White's been out here joyriding, he'll can him for sure."

That explained Tilden's language, Isen thought. *He probably could have told White to fuck off and die and it wouldn't have gone any further.*

Isen left Tilden and walked around behind the school. The company had done well, going into action at a dead run after a night of driving, with almost no planning time and certainly no time to prepare. They had put together a workable plan that had accomplished a hastily contrived and fairly difficult mission. When he saw the first of Lake's soldiers through the windows of the now-quiet school building, his greeting was enthusiastic. He allowed himself to feel good about what they had accomplished.

"Hey, sir, we got something interesting in here." It was Lake, talking to him from inside the west end of the school building. Isen went over to the first-floor window, through which he could clearly see the room Lake was in. There was a welter of equipment on the floor: belts of ammunition and pieces of web gear and bloody bandages and even a boot. There were two bodies on the floor, lined up neatly beside each other.

"What do you make of that?" Isen asked his platoon leader.

"Both of these guys were shot in the back of the head, sir. And it doesn't look like it happened in the fight. One of them is an officer, a lieutenant, I think."

Isen crawled in through the window for a closer look. The body Lake was referring to had a leather belt with a pistol holster attached. The other man wore a web belt with rifle ammunition.

"He may be an officer, Mike. So what?"

"Well, if you look here, sir." Lake pointed to the back of the soldier's head. There was a small hole just above the base of the skull.

"This man has been shot with a pistol, at close range. The officer had a pistol at some point. But the officer, if he is that, was shot with a rifle, and the placement of the shot is not as exact, as if he were shot from the other side of the room."

Lake seemed to be on to something, but didn't quite know what it was. He was too tired to make all the threads come together. But Isen knew one of the missing parts.

"Somebody yelled at us when we offered them a chance to surrender, somebody who may have wanted to come out. Could be," Isen went on, "our officer here didn't take kindly to the suggestion that they surrender, and offered a bit of battlefield justice. But by the time Lamson and his guys were blowing things up in the next room, the officer wasn't in control."

"You saying he was shot by his own men?" Lake asked.

"Looks like it," Isen said.

"Well, that's a hell of a different picture of the NKPA supermen, if that's the case."

Their conversation was interrupted by a runner, who said that Voavosa was out back with ammunition.

Isen made his way through the dark hallway of the school, nearly tripping over a jumbled pile of North Korean weapons. He found the back entrance to the school, and found Voavosa directing some soldiers who were stacking ammunition in piles, one for each platoon. Isen grinned when Voavosa looked up.

Isen was pleased with the company's performance, and

he planned on telling them so. As he stepped down from the threshold of the door, Isen noticed the three poncho-covered forms that lay close to the back wall of the building. He stopped short, then looked up to see some of the men watching him. He walked over to Voavosa.

"Hey, sir," Voavosa said, "the company did a damn fine job today."

"So why are these guys here?" Isen said, mostly to himself.

Voavosa took Isen's arm. "Sir, the bottom line is we did a good job; it could have been a lot worse."

"Yeah, I guess." Isen knew that Voavosa was right, though there was more to it. "Our job now is to look for a better way to do things."

"That's true, sir. But you know what?"

Isen hoped Voavosa wasn't going to start his string of rhetorical questions.

"It'll never get better, or be any easier to take."

Isen looked at Voavosa, wanting the older man to finish his thought.

"In most places," Voavosa went on, "there are good days and there are bad days. Here, there's just bad days. Even today, when we did everything that was asked of us, on a half-assed mission like this one, we did the best we could, and we still lost good men."

Voavosa had a point, Isen knew. He could not change the nature of what they were about; there was nothing he could do but try to keep disaster at bay.

Even if there were such a thing as a good day, he thought as he turned to see some men getting ready to move the bodies, *even if we had one good day, I'd always have with me this picture, the sight of these three ponchos.*

15

South of Yeoju, Republic of Korea

27 April · Wednesday · 1930 hrs

The helicopter sat in the paddy, leaning drunkenly forward where the right front skid support had collapsed on impact. None of the three men aboard, a pilot and two passengers, had been hurt. After the engine lost power unexpectedly, the pilot brought the bird down on auto-rotate, using the lift that remained in the rotating blades to lower the craft in what was, in fact, a controlled crash. The pilot tried for half an hour to raise someone on the radio, but without success. Armed with only a nine-millimeter pistol, he had elected to stay behind and guard his helicopter while the two passengers, also lightly armed, set out on foot to get help.

One of the two passengers was the operations officer, or G3, for the First Cavalry Division. Lieutenant Colonel Ray Collom had set out to do a reconnaissance of the routes his division might use to move north from the port of Pusan, in southeast Korea, to the battles north of Seoul. He had spent the whole day checking routes suggested by the officers from his staff whom he had sent to Korea as soon as the "First Team" was alerted. Collom was accompanied by a captain from the division intelligence, or G2, section. Both men were distracted; Collom by what he had seen from the air, and the younger officer, a Californian named Steve King, by the realization that he was on foot in a war zone, armed with a pistol and some serious doubts about his choice of a military profession.

"Those goddamn roads are a mess," Collom snapped. "The sonsabitches in Eighth Army shoulda told us the ROKs were gonna use all the paved roads to move their stuff. They left us *shit*."

He punctuated his sentences by swinging a folded map through the air in front of him. King, who was taller than Collom, had to struggle to keep up. The colonel always walked fast when he was agitated, King had heard. *And he's pissed now,* the captain thought.

"It's bad enough we're not getting good information from the people over here," Collom continued unabated, "but the fuckers give us a broke-dick helicopter too."

King stole a quick glance back to where the crashed aircraft was quickly receding in the distance and the failing light of dusk. He, too, had been surprised at the lack of intelligence that was made available to them by Eighth Army, the headquarters that controlled American ground forces stationed in Korea. The few Eighth Army staff officers that had met them when they arrived, by aircraft, in Pusan tried to help the First Cav staff put together an accurate picture of the situation in Korea. But the information was changing too quickly, and the existing communications systems, adequate for peacetime traffic, were being overwhelmed. And it didn't help that every headquarters staff in Korea imagined a North Korean paratrooper behind every bush. The mere possibility of attacks on command centers had done a great deal to limit the effectiveness of American and ROK command and control.

"My damn watch broke when that bird hit. What time is it, King?"

"It's seven . . . I mean, it's nineteen thirty-five, sir."

"Great. We were supposed to be done this recon and back in the rear to brief the old man by twenty thirty. Not that I have much to tell him."

King looked at one of the maps he was carrying for Collom. The G3 had marked three major road systems that led north from Pusan. He had made extensive notes in the margins about road conditions, bridge classifications, drainage, bottlenecks, even possible locations for supply dumps along the way. King knew it would take a lot of highway space to move the whole division, with all its support elements, the length of the peninsula. And some of the roads they had identified as "possibles" had been filled, when they flew over them, with refugees heading south, and ROK Army supply convoys heading north. The blue lines Collom had drawn ended near Yeoju, a small city that sat in a river valley fifty miles southeast of Seoul, and about seventy miles from their best guess as to the location of the 25th Division units with which they were supposed to link up. Collom had intended to fly as far north as he could go without getting shot down, so that he could choose the best route for the tanks of the First Cav to ride to the rescue of the grunts up north.

Now it looked, to King, as if the mechanical failure of a single helicopter engine, from among the thousands of such engines in the army, was going to defeat that mission. All the massive combat power of the division, brought across the ocean in dozens of ships and aircraft, was due to arrive in Pusan in the next thirty-six hours. But that terrible might could not be applied, at least not quickly, without the information that he and Collom held, somewhere on the edge of a rice paddy in the middle of Korea.

"Here's what we're gonna do," Collom told King. "We're going to head north on this road until we hit Yeoju. I'm going to grab somebody who can give me a ride farther north, so that I can get a look at what's going on. You're going to head south until you get in touch with *our* division staff. Give them the info we have so far, so the old man can get the tanks rolling. Then you're going to get me a helicopter, a goddamned *First Cav* helicopter that'll go as far as I want it to, and you're going to come back and get me."

King couldn't imagine trying to brief the division commander on everything he had seen that day. Collom had talked almost nonstop since they took off that morning, and King didn't think he could recreate a third of the information Collom had to report. Nor could he see himself commandeering a helicopter. Technically, he outranked the warrant officers who flew most of the aircraft. But he did not have the self-confidence that he knew marked most army officers, and he had always avoided confrontations, especially with crusty old NCOs and warrants. He was afraid to go south, and he was afraid to head north.

"Maybe you should go to the rear, sir, and let me keep heading north," King said, surprising himself.

Collom turned his head and looked at the captain, who

lagged a few steps behind. *Maybe he's not as big a pansy as I thought he was,* Collom thought.

"No." Collom walked a few more meters, then stopped abruptly. King caught up to the colonel and stood next to him.

"Look, King, I'm going to fill you in on a few things. If you know what we're looking for out here, you'll be better able to answer the boss's questions."

Collom took him by the arm and led him to the side of the road, where they sat down with their legs hanging off into the small roadside drainage ditch. It was almost completely dark, but King could still see the G3's face. The older man stared into King's eyes for a moment, as if he thought King might refuse to hear whatever secrets he was about to offer.

"Things have gone to shit over here in the last twenty-four hours. The Eighth Army commander told our boss that he's not even sure what's going on north of Seoul. The ROKs keep sending units in, and they keep getting chewed up. It's like a friggin' black hole up there: we're not even getting accurate reports out. The LIDs that have been over here are under ROK control, and Eighth Army staff is afraid that they're going to be sent in piecemeal. If that happens, they'll get wasted. It's gonna take our division three days, maybe four, to get our logistics set up and get our units up there. We can't just race north in half-assed formations, 'cause we might just run into the North Koreans headed the other way."

Collom paused, took off his helmet, and wiped his face with his sleeve.

"The old man sees it this way: what happens near Uijongbu is gonna decide this thing. The ROKs, understandably, are concerned only with stopping the NKPA. The CG of the 25th is complaining that they're piecemealing his division, using parts of unit while they keep most of the infantry off to the southeast of the fight. But the Supreme Commander, the American in charge over here, put them under the South Koreans. To pull them out now would look like an abandonment of the ROKs. Now, the ROKs probably don't care much if an American division or two gets used up—their army is being bled white. If the ROKs stop them, the North Koreans are gonna turn and run for the thirty-eighth parallel, hoping that we won't chase them over the line. The South Koreans will try anything to stop them from making it to safety, otherwise the bad guys live to fight another day. Our CG is concerned that the ROKs might get desperate enough to throw our LIDs in the way of the NKPA retreat—in front of North Korean tanks. The old man wants to be there before that happens, or those GIs are out of luck."

Collom stopped and shook his head. "But, in the meantime, we're not sure exactly where we should be going, what roads we're going to take to get there, or even if we'll make it in time. The only thing we do know is that we've got to hurry, or the only light fighters we see will be in body bags."

King was not surprised at Collom's assessment of the situation. It had been clear enough to him, from the demeanor of the Eighth Army staff officers, that things in Korea weren't going well. What surprised the younger man was the doubt in Collom's voice. King had always assumed, perhaps subconsciously, that someone, somewhere up the chain of command, knew what was going on, had a plan, was in control of things. But here he was, sitting across from the officer who, with the commanding general, made the plans that would commit the division—*the whole division*—to combat, and Collom was almost as clueless as were the privates who were unloading the ships in Pusan.

"I'll make sure this stuff gets to the CG, sir," King said.

"Good. Now we'd better get moving. Our pilot friend back there is probably wondering what the hell happened to us."

It was now completely dark. Collom put his helmet back on, and the two men stood up. The sudden movement of shadow startled two sixteen-year-old South Koreans, nervous militia guards who were walking on the road not twenty meters away, on the lookout for North Korean infiltrators.

One of the youngsters was armed with only an ax handle, but the other carried an antique shotgun. He raised the gun to his shoulder and fired at the movement, forgetting, in his fear, that he was supposed to challenge whomever he met. The shadow seemed to divide, and he realized that there were two men. Both of them went down, and he heard one of them groan in pain for the long seconds it took him to reload. When he looked up again, he could clearly distinguish the two forms against the light sand of the road. Only one was moving. He dropped to one knee and took careful aim. Just before he pulled the trigger, he made a mental note to chastise his partner, who had run away, for not being brave enough to face the enemy.

16

Near Cheongpyeong, Republic of Korea

28 April · Thursday

An anxious Charlie Company spent the night of 27–28 April in a hasty defensive position near the town. Isen moved the troops out of the built-up area near the school because he wanted something more open, a place where they had a better chance of defending themselves if challenged. Technically, they were behind "friendly" lines, but the battle so far had been so fluid—with North Korean armored forces trying end runs—that Isen wanted to be prepared for anything. They set up in a three-hundred-and-sixty-degree perimeter, what Voavosa called "circling the wagons," for the night.

During the night the two other rifle companies of the battalion, Alpha and Bravo, moved in nearby, so that by 0300, the company positions described the points of a loose triangle on the low hills west of the village. All through the night Isen could hear the deep-throated rumble of sleepless artillery off to the west.

Isen was awake an hour before stand-to, and by 0530 he had checked, to his satisfaction, the platoon positions. He and Voavosa shared a breakfast of cold combat rations and lukewarm instant coffee. Isen sat on the ground, his legs splayed in front of him. His trousers were so dirty that they still showed the contours of his thighs, like thick cardboard tubes, even when he relaxed his legs.

David, monitoring the battalion net, warned Isen that the S3 had called and was headed for the company position. Isen passed the word that Bock would be coming in, so that none of his tired, edgy soldiers accidentally shot the battalion's operations officer. Bock found them a half hour later.

"Over here, sir," Isen said, standing up and stretching, swiveling at the waist, hands on hips.

"How are you this morning, Mark? First Sergeant?"

"Could be worse, Major," Voavosa said without getting up.

"What do you have for us today, sir?" Isen asked. He had no energy for banalities.

Bock removed his helmet and rolled his head a bit on his shoulders, stretching his tense neck muscles. "I guess the days of my just visiting for the hell of it are over for a while." Without waiting for a reply, he pulled his map and a few sheets of dirty notebook paper from the pocket on the side of his trousers.

"Looks like the North Koreans are throwing everything into this fight to break the northern defenses of Seoul. A lot of the action is centered in the area around Uijongbu." He paused as he peeled apart the muddied map. The acetate covering was smeared with grease pencil: there were several superimposed layers of symbols vying for attention—red arrows and snaking boundary lines and polka-dotted checkpoints. Bock hadn't erased any of the symbols before applying new ones.

"We been hearing them all night long, sir," Voavosa said, not expecting a comment.

"The ROK corps commander has stripped our division of a lot of our artillery assets, and air assets. I guess they figure this is make it or break it, right now."

"What do you think, sir?" Isen asked.

"I'm not sure how concentrated the NKPA is in this box north of the capital, but I don't see how they can sustain operations, at the pace they've been going, for much longer. They're chewing up units like nobody's business. You could probably walk from here to the Yellow Sea, hopping from one disabled armored vehicle to the next, without your feet ever touching the ground."

"I wonder who's keeping us in the dark?" Isen said, reaching out and unfolding Bock's map, exposing more of the terrain to the immediate south.

"What do you mean?"

"Well, I'm just guessing, of course," Isen went on, "but I've got to wonder where those relief forces are. Somebody must know something. Shouldn't they be getting here soon?"

"Hell, I hope so," Bock said, "I'm tired of being the fire brigade around here. The ROKs are stripping us, taking away combat assets piecemeal and making it even tougher for us to fight. I feel like an old car being stripped for parts."

Bock paused for only a few seconds, looking at the bottom of his map sheet as if, by looking, he could make some American armored unit, part of the relief force, appear there.

"Two of our brigades," he went on, "us and first, are being ordered into a MOUT defense," Bock said. MOUT was the army's term for combat in a built-up or urban area. The acronym meant Mobile Operations in Urban Terrain, but Isen knew that the mobility of light infantry, even though better than that of mounted troops in the tight confines of a city or town, was still pretty limited.

"Alpha and Bravo," Bock went on, "will be together in a fair-sized village here." He pointed to a town named Poechon, about twenty-five miles east-northeast of Uijongbu. "And you guys are going to be off by yourself a little ways, about two klicks northeast, in a smaller village— looks like it's called Kumnu-ri—that sits on a crossroads."

Bock held his finger on the map and looked up, as if expecting Isen to protest.

Isen said nothing.

"This is not a major throughway here; intelligence doesn't expect the North Koreans to come down this way. But there is a major avenue just to the north of your position that runs northeast to southwest."

"For the North Koreans," Voavosa said, "from back to front."

"Right," Bock said. Then, realizing what Voavosa was getting at, he added, "Yeah, you're right, Top. If they decide to throw any reinforcements into the battle, if they have any left, they may very well come down this highway, across your front. But I don't think it will be bad here; I think they're overcommitted already."

Isen studied the map for a few more seconds in silence.

"This is almost the exact situation we were in the other night," he said, thinking to himself, *Was it only three days ago?*

"We were on that hill," Isen went on, "and the North Koreans were supposed to pass across our front. Remember?"

Bock nodded.

"But they got adventurous and headed toward us." He left unspoken the rest of the thought. *And, except for some lucky breaks, we probably would have been overrun by those tanks.*

"Anyway," Bock went on, "you'll need to send an OP out on this hill here, to keep observation on the highway."

Bock indicated a long, low ridge that pointed almost due north from the small village Charlie Company would be occupying. The long axis of the hill was aimed directly at the side of the North Korean avenue of advance that Bock had sketched in red.

"I'm getting the picture," Isen said.

Bock went over some of the details of the defense, how Charlie Company would be tied in to the other companies and what limited support was available. Isen ran over in his own mind the long checklists of setting up a defense. He wondered how much of an armored reserve force the North Koreans might have left to send thundering down that highway toward the teetering battle near Uijongbu.

They moved on foot for the first ten kilometers, heading due north, and keeping good march discipline, Isen thought. This is where all the peacetime conditioning paid off: all the roadmarching on tired feet, all the runs, all the exercise on the warm grass at Schofield, was granting dividends in a tight, alert formation—the familiar inter-

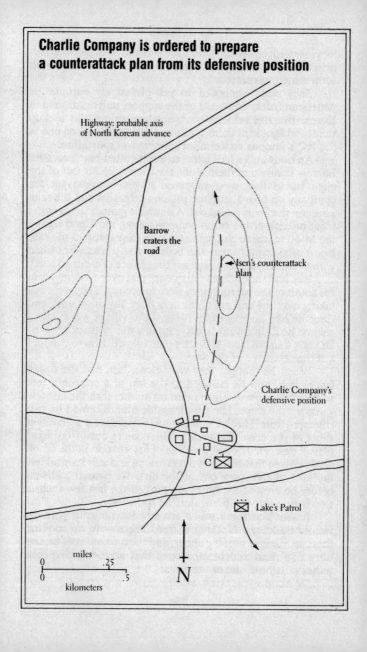

Charlie Company is ordered to prepare a counterattack plan from its defensive position

Highway: probable axis
of North Korean advance

Barrow
craters the
road

Isen's counterattack
plan

Charlie Company's
defensive position

I
C

Lake's Patrol

miles

0   .25

0   .5

kilometers

N

locking wedges—that would keep them from getting surprised and would allow them to react if they ran into something unexpected.

They were supposed to get picked up enroute by American trucks from one of the support units stationed in Korea. But the vehicles were nowhere in sight at pickup time, and Isen kept them walking, sending Barrow on one of the XO's famous chases after missing transportation.

An hour and a half later, an exasperated but successful Barrow finally met them along the road, with six out of the eight trucks they were supposed to get. Voavosa put the company on board, and the platoon sergeants had the men kneel on the floor, facing out. A machine gunner stood in the front of each of the cargo compartments, the bipod legs of the M-60 machine gun resting on the canvas top of the cab. Isen noted happily that the beds of the trucks were lined with two-deep sandbags against the chance of a mined road.

Isen had the company dismount just over a kilometer to the south of the position they were to occupy. They were not taking over the defense of the area from any other unit, and since he had no way of knowing if the village was clear of enemy, he didn't want to drive up in a merry truck convoy. He took a squad from Haveck's platoon with him to conduct a reconnaissance of the area.

When he thought they were close, Isen had the squad leader halt, and he climbed to the top of a steep hill just south of the village. He crawled on his stomach the last few yards up the slope, Haveck alongside him, followed by two riflemen from Haveck's platoon. Isen stopped a few feet short of the crest and took his binoculars out of the hard plastic case. He hooked the sling of his weapon in the crook of his arm so that he could drag it along and still keep all but the butt of the stock out of the dirt. He paused to listen before he crested the hill, then pushed the last few inches, slowly bringing the binoculars up to his face.

Below him there was a crossroads village of perhaps twenty buildings. Nothing stirred. There were no cooking fires, no humans moving about, and the only animals he saw were two dead and bloated cows that were still tied to a tether post near one of the houses.

"What do you think, sir?"

Haveck was next to Isen, looking at the village through his own set of binoculars.

"Looks nice and quiet, doesn't it?" Isen said conversationally. "I think we'll stay put for a few more minutes and see if anything moves. When we go down there, we'll send a squad down first, with a platoon watching from this position. I'd say the range was about three hundred meters, don't you think?"

"Yes, sir. There's that hill the S3 was talking about."

Isen trained his binoculars higher and saw the near, southern end of the ridge that would lead them to the highway the North Koreans might use. The highway itself was out of sight. The whole area was absolutely quiet, and the only sound they could hear was the crunching artillery duel to the west, which by this time had become background noise to everything they were doing.

"Maybe we'll get a few hours rest here, sir," Haveck ventured.

"I doubt that'll happen anytime soon, Pete."

Isen's skepticism was borne out over the next six hours. The company moved cautiously into position, wary of being ambushed in the unfamiliar area. The first order of business was to establish security, and the platoon leaders set one third of the men into positions outside of the village to the north, both to provide early warning of any enemy movement, and to give the other soldiers time to organize a defense if the need arose.

The rest of the company fell to the back-breaking work of establishing a defensive position. First, Isen and his lieutenants marked the sectors for the platoons, looking for the most likely approaches the enemy might take into the area. Isen put the three platoons abreast, facing north, with the flank platoons curving around a bit—"refusing the flanks," in military parlance. The line was bowed slightly forward, and it embraced the village on its concave, southern side.

The platoon positions had to be mutually supporting: that is, the fires had to be interlocking across the front. Then the squad leaders and platoon leaders placed their key weapons—the machine guns, the SAWs, and the grenade launchers—where they would do the most good. Isen conferred with Richards, who set up his small mortars just to the south of the buildings. The leaders decided where and how they would engage targets in the area, and who would be responsible for what sectors. The soldiers laid communications wire to the platoons. Murray and the platoon medics set up a small company aid station, where they could treat wounded in relative safety. The men picked lanes for movement: covered routes they could use to move laterally through the company position to reinforce a threatened sector, distribute ammunition, evacuate a wounded soldier, and even to withdraw. They rehearsed signals for each contingency: audible signals and visual signals (different visuals for day and night) so that the men would not miss the important cues in the din of the fight. And they practiced one of the infantryman's basic arts: they dug in. Every man hacked away at the earth, tearing up wooden floors and even flagstones to get at the ground—the only reliable shelter. Every man, even Isen, busy as he was, dug. They had already seen that such work was the only coin that could purchase protection.

They were bone tired, but they dug. And they practiced the drills, and they rehearsed the signals as they had never done on peacetime maneuvers, even when well rested, because now they knew the cost of being unprepared. They had seen North Korean armor and infantry up close, and they had a better appreciation for what they needed to do to survive. And on top of it all, there was the question as to when the enemy would come—for the attacker gets to choose the time for the battle—and that unknown leaned, with a tremendous weight, on everything they did.

Barrow drove up to the command post, which was set up in the yard of a village house forty meters off the line, just before fifteen hundred. Isen heard the HMMWV and came down to the road to see what his wide-ranging XO had found. He was surprised to see four ROK jeeps behind Barrow, two of them with TOW missile launchers on board.

"What's with these guys, Dale?" Isen asked.

"We were supposed to get three sections out here, sir, but we only got two. The ROKs are short-changing us. They took our battalion's TOWs and left us with these older models." He nodded at the South Korean soldiers. "And I'm not too sure about our comrades-in-arms here, to tell you the truth."

Barrow had a pronounced—and unfounded, as far as Isen could see—mistrust of the ROK Army. *The sin of pride,* Isen thought.

Isen eyed the ROKs. They were driving American-made quarter-ton trucks, the legendary jeeps that the U.S. Army had traded in for the larger HMMWV. The anti-tank weapons were the older version of the ones the Americans now used. The sections were short-handed: the gun jeeps had a driver and gunner, the ammo jeeps carried the section sergeant and another driver, who doubled as an assistant gunner. Each jeep had its camouflage net, large enough to hide vehicle and trailer, stored neatly across the hood. Extra missiles were stowed in the racks. The jeeps were filthy and mud-splattered, as Isen expected, but the weapons themselves, even the rifles he could see in the vehicles, were clean.

Before he could ask Barrow what the problem might be, Isen was approached by an ROK staff sergeant. Even if the South Korean hadn't been wearing the insignia, there was no mistaking that he was in charge. He was older than the other soldiers, thirty or so, Isen judged. He walked up to Isen with a stiff, parade ground gait, stood rigidly in front of him, and snapped a salute. His uniform shirt, though dirty, was tucked in, his trousers neatly bloused into his boots. He was clean shaven, and Isen, returning the man's salute, had to resist rubbing his own stubbled jaw.

"Sir, I am Sergeant Han Won-Taek. I am the commander of these two sections of anti-armor weapons. We are at your disposal for the defense of this village."

The man's English was almost without accent, and Isen wondered where he had learned to speak so well, and wondered, too, if the man had rehearsed all this.

"Glad to have you aboard, Sergeant," Isen said, putting out his hand. Han, though slightly taken aback by this familiar gesture from an officer, shook Isen's hand firmly.

"Would you like to inspect the weapons, sir?" Han asked.

Barrow, standing next to Isen, rolled his eyes visibly. "I'm going to start unloading this ammo, sir. I'll be back in about fifteen minutes to pick you up; we got an orders brief at battalion."

"Okay, Dale, I'll be here," Isen answered. He turned back to Han, who was waiting patiently, almost at attention.

"Okay, Sergeant, lead the way."

Isen, who had a profound mistrust of anything spit-shined, reminded himself that this man was an ally.

"Of course you are familiar with the weapon system, sir," Han said, stopping by the first jeep. The driver did not look at Isen or Han, but sat primly with his hands on the wheel.

The South Koreans had the TOW system (the unwieldy acronym stands for tube-launched, optically tracked, wire-guided) that was one generation behind what the Americans were using. This first one was in pristine condition, obviously well-maintained, but that could mean, Isen thought, that they never took it out to field training. Almost certainly, these soldiers had never fired a live missile before last week.

There is no conventional barrel to the TOW, as there is with a gun. Instead, a kind of fiberglass cradle holds the missile, which comes in its own package. The most compli-cated and most obvious mechanism is the tracker, a large optical sight and control assembly that sticks out from the left side of the launch tube. The gunner sits with the tube over his right shoulder, sighting through the optics and controlling the whole assembly with a combination of elevation and deflection knobs. As with the Dragon, the smaller, man-portable anti-tank missile, all the gunner need do is keep the cross-hairs on the target. The missile corrects its own flight path according to the information sent from the tracker over the thin wire that trails from the tube. Although the missile has good accuracy and can defeat almost any armor in the world, it has a slow flight time. Alert tankers can fire in the general direction of the substan-tial smoke signature left by the rocket motors, throw off the gunner's aim, and cause him to lose the target. Even a minor flinch can send the missile plowing into the ground.

Still, this crew seemed to Isen to be eager and alert. The other gun jeep, as well as the two jeeps that carried the extra rounds, was also in good order. Isen wondered why Barrow had a chip on his shoulder. He turned to Han.

"I plan to keep your two sections together and under my control, Sergeant, rather than splitting them up among the platoons. Since I have a meeting to attend, I'm going to let First Sergeant Voavosa work with you to figure out the best place to use the weapons."

Han nodded smartly at the end of each of Isen's sentences. The effect was that of an eager schoolboy, except that his eyes were dark with seriousness.

"Do you need anything from us?" Isen asked.

"No, sir. We filled our fuel tanks before we left the last position. We are ready to go at your first sergeant's convenience."

"Good," Isen said, looking over his shoulder for David. "Get Top down here, David."

As David walked to the platoon positions to find Voavosa, Isen watched Han brief his soldiers. They seemed to hang on their sergeant's every word. So far, it looked to Isen as if they were taking it all very seriously.

Voavosa joined them within a few minutes.

"Here I am, sir."

"Top, we have two TOW sections here to use in our defense. I have to go to a brief at battalion, so I want you to figure out where to use them. We'll keep them under company control rather than farm them out to the platoons."

Han joined them.

"First Sergeant, this is Sergeant Han. He's in charge of these sections. I've already briefed him on what we're going to do. You can take it from here."

Voavosa stepped forward and shook Han's hand. "Let's take a look at the front of the company sector. You can leave your men here until we get back."

Han nodded, turned, and said something to his driver, then fell into step beside Voavosa, and the two men moved to the company's front. They walked through each of the platoon sectors, then agreed that they would use both of the TOW jeeps on the far right, eastern side of the company. This would allow them the best chance of getting a flank shot at any vehicles that approached. Since the front surfaces of tanks are the most heavily armored, the TOW warheads were better used in flank shots. Additionally, the tank crew, their visibility already severely cut when they buttoned up, would be less likely to spot the smoke signature of a weapon fired from the side.

Voavosa left Han, then returned in thirty minutes to find that all four of the vehicles were in position, concealed among the buildings, virtually invisible from the front. The gunners were working on their range cards, and both drivers were checking under the hoods of their respective jeeps, making sure that the vehicles would be ready to roll when the time came. Voavosa thought about how hard it was to get American soldiers, so used to plentiful support, to do preventive maintenance on their vehicles. Han stood off to one side, studying his map as his soldiers worked.

"You guys don't waste any time."

"We are ready to fight, First Sergeant."

Voavosa eyed Han's uniform. Dirty as the South Koreans were, they were not nearly as filthy as the Americans.

"Where have they been using you the last couple of days?" Voavosa asked, slightly suspicious.

"We were in an engagement to the west of here, up at the DMZ," Han said in a clipped, matter-of-fact tone, "on the day the North Koreans invaded. Our battalion was almost completely destroyed, so the remaining TOW sections were distributed among other units. We were told yesterday that we would be supporting an American rifle company." He missed only half a beat before he asked, "What has your company been doing?"

"A lot of chasing around the countryside, for one thing," Voavosa answered, looking down the narrow valley toward the highway that he couldn't see.

"It is not as you expected?" Han said.

Voavosa looked at him. The South Korean soldier was watching him closely, sizing up the American to see if his lot had been cast with a good unit. For the first time, Voavosa thought of this man as something other than an interchangeable part in the fire-support element. Voavosa shook his head.

"On that first day, nothing went as we expected either," Han said. "Nothing went as we had been told to expect."

He folded his map and tucked it under his arm, pulling a pack of cigarettes from his shirt pocket with the other hand. In contrast to his uniform, the cigarette package was clean, unwrinkled. He lit a cigarette deftly, striking the paper match with one hand. Voavosa remembered watching a drill sergeant performing that same trick when he was in basic training, thinking at the time that it was something very soldierly, something he wanted to emulate.

Han inhaled slowly, luxuriously, his eyes half closed. Voavosa knew the cigarettes, which he had tried on his first tour in Korea, tasted like rope.

"We went into a prepared position just south of the Zone," Han continued. "You know those?"

Voavosa nodded. "You mean the ones with the range cards all worked out and set in the concrete?"

Han smiled. "Yes. We have been preparing for this war for so long, we thought we knew exactly how it would go. But of course, nothing turned out as expected. The North Koreans did not oblige us by coming as we thought they would. They flanked us, because a unit to our right had withdrawn without orders. One of my sections tried also to withdraw without orders, without even firing their weapon." He paused for another drag, and Voavosa wondered if it was true that the ROKs shot deserters.

"Still, we managed to hold our position long enough to fire two volleys," Han said. "By that time there was absolute chaos in our defense. My men could not fire because they were masked by withdrawing South Korean vehicles. The tanks were on us—have you been close to one? I was terrified."

Han stopped again, searching Voavosa's face for some reaction to this admission. Satisfied that the American was not going to judge him, Han went on. "But I remember the point at which I gained control of my fears. I saw two North Korean tanks collide; one was trying to move forward, the other trying to move to the rear. The one pushing forward was trying to force the other back into the fight."

He stubbed his cigarette on the sole of his boot, then stripped the remaining paper and allowed the tobacco to fall to the ground. He put the rolled up paper in his pocket. Voavosa still had said nothing.

"That was when I knew that they were as afraid as we were. After that it was easier, and now I work only to hold my fears in check longer than does the enemy."

The two men fell quiet. Voavosa could hear, in the middle distance, the clang of shovels on hard earth.

"You want some chow?" Voavosa asked Han. "I ain't got much, but I have some leftover beans and wienies if you want them."

"Enough for my men?" Han asked.

Voavosa thought of the meager stockpile he had been guarding against the day the company was shorted rations. *What the hell,* he thought. "Yeah, we're all playing ball for the same team, right?"

The two men walked back to the house where Isen and Voavosa had established the company command post.

"This is the CP," Voavosa said. "Captain Isen is going to a briefing at battalion. They're supposed to tell us what's up with the fighting to the west." Then, without understanding why he felt compelled to share the thought, he added, "Captain Isen is a good guy, one of the best."

"He shook my hand when I met him." Han offered no other comment, so Voavosa didn't know if the Korean was impressed or just thought it odd.

"Anyway, here's a case, well, half a case, anyway, of MREs." Voavosa lifted an open box from under a poncho. He reached inside to count, making sure he had as many as he said he had.

"I appreciate this," Han said.

I appreciate this? Voavosa's curiosity was aroused.

"Where did you learn to speak English so well?"

Han smiled. "I was a translator for the American Army when I was younger. I worked in a headquarters in Seoul for three years."

Something didn't click with Voavosa.

"Didn't that take care of your military obligation?"

"Yes, technically it did." Han seemed eager to talk to someone besides his subordinates, someone with whom he didn't have to play the role of leader.

"When I went to work in the headquarters, my family had a party for me. They were glad that I was not going to be a field soldier with the other conscripts. When I decided to stay in the army after working in Seoul, they could not believe it. I was surprised myself."

"So why did you do it?" Voavosa asked.

"Part of it was youthful rebellion, I guess. There are a lot of professional people in my family, and some of them think they are too good to do hard work to serve their country, yet they are certainly happy with capitalism."

"What else?" Voavosa pressed, sensing that there was more to it.

"This will sound like corn to you."

Voavosa wrinkled his eyebrows. "You mean it will sound corny?"

"Yes," Han said, "but I believed this conflict was inevitable."

"How's that?" Voavosa asked, intrigued.

"We are a small nation, First Sergeant, an island, really, isolated on this peninsula with a hostile neighbor whose sole aim is the violent takeover of our country." Han paused, and Voavosa had the distinct impression that he was not searching for words, but for dramatic timing.

"We are not without our problems, to be sure; and we know many Americans think our government repressive. But we enjoy the benefits of freedom—no people has worked harder to build a good life. We contend even with the Japanese."

"But as the economic gap between North and South Korea widened, the northerners realized that the odds against them grew worse every year. South Koreans, enamored of their new standard of living, would never accept communism, and the Communists, enamored of their own rhetoric, would never accept capitalism. The North Koreans had to strike—or renounce one of the basic tenets of their own existence."

Voavosa narrowed his eyes, trying to follow Han's thoughts in spite of his tiredness.

"Imagine," Han continued, the patient teacher, "if all the groups who are fighting for a Palestinian homeland suddenly admitted that they would never reach the goal. Those groups would cease to exist. So it is with North Korea. If they renounced the Great Reunification, their tottering government just might fall in upon itself."

The South Korean soldier leaned forward seriously.

"With American help, we can stop them. Without American help, the North Koreans would wash the country in blood."

Han took a canteen off his belt and took a long drink, wiping the back of his sleeve across his mouth. Voavosa watched him intently in the weighty silence.

"That is my speech. I must sound like a propagandist, making speeches about Korean-American unity," Han said, smiling at his joke.

"No, though I don't think you could have said it better," Voavosa said. "You should be on TV, American TV. You're wasting your time down here; we're just a bunch of grunts."

"But you people are the most important audience, First Sergeant; there are no politicians out here doing what your men are doing to keep my country free."

Han, perhaps embarrassed by his emotion, but sure nonetheless that it had not been lost on Voavosa, tucked the cardboard ration case under his arm and walked back toward his troops. Voavosa did not know what to say.

"Hey, Sergeant Han," Voavosa called. Han turned to the American. "Thanks."

"Thank you, First Sergeant," Han said, tapping the case of food.

Isen and Barrow found the battalion CP in the village, about two kilometers to the southwest, that was guarded by Alpha and Bravo companies. Bock had the briefing set up in the small courtyard of one of the L-shaped farmhouses. In these country dwellings the animals were frequently kept inside the yard formed by the two wings of the house and the outside wall. One of the soldiers in the headquarters had taken pity on the commanders and thrown some fresh straw on the manure that lay thick on the ground. Isen and Barrow, as well as the other commanders and their XOs, stood.

Bock had his map tacked up on the long wall of the house. Next to the map he had drawn, in chalk on the dun-colored wall, a sketch of the village they were in. He invited the company commanders to come up and give brief descriptions of their defensive positions, so that everyone understood what the other units were doing.

When Isen, who went last, finished, Bock asked if there were any questions. Isen was surprised that there wasn't more substance to the meeting.

"Any word on reinforcements?" he asked.

Bock looked at Tilden, who rubbed his eye sockets with dirty fingers.

"All we have are rumors," Tilden said. "Nothing solid to go on."

"So what do the rumors say, sir?"

"We hear that there are American mechanized and armored units on the peninsula," Tilden said, "but we don't know where."

Several of the group hooted loudly at the news, though it was hardly specific. They were all anxious for some sign that they hadn't been abandoned by the rest of the U.S. Army.

Barrow nudged Isen and said under his breath, "I wonder why we can't get any hard facts?"

Isen thought the question fair, so when the noise subsided a bit, he asked, "Colonel, how is it we're so much in the dark?"

"Commo with brigade is good; commo with division is just okay. Commo between division and Eighth Army is unreliable, and the ROKs are too busy to worry about what we want to know."

"I find it hard to believe the ROKs don't know something," Isen whispered to Barrow. "This is their country, and the lower half isn't overrun or anything."

Tilden went on. "The brigade commander thinks that if we have this rumor, the North Koreans have it too, so they're going to be even more desperate to get to Seoul before help gets here from the States."

"Maybe the South Koreans are deliberately keeping the whole thing a secret." Isen knew he was out on a limb, and just might piss off the colonel if he went too far. "I mean, if their aim is to catch the NKPA south of the thirty-eighth parallel, cut them off and destroy their combat power, then they might not want the North Koreans to get wind of the reinforcements and withdraw before the American units get here."

"Only problem with that, Mark," Bock said, "is that there's probably a bunch of reporters with our guys, and they're not likely to keep a secret like that—*U.S. Forces Land in Korea*—no matter what's going on."

"How is keeping the damned NKPA down here with us an advantage?" Chris Michael, the Bravo Company commander, wanted to know.

"Because we have to whip 'em on our turf. We ain't going over the thirty-eighth parallel," Tilden said with some finality. "That's what got the Chinese into the war in 1950. Besides, the American people aren't going to go for a war *in* North Korea. That makes us the aggressor."

"How do you figure, sir?" Ray Woodriff, the Alpha Company commander, chimed in. "They started it, we should finish it."

"That may be so, Ray, but the reality is that the public back home isn't going to go for an invasion. Can you imagine the demonstrations? 'No more Vietnams,' and all that happy horseshit."

Woodriff chafed at Tilden's comment, and Isen suspected that the other captain had something to say but was smart enough not to venture it with the colonel. Isen decided to oblige Woodriff.

"Like it or not, Ray, that's the political ball game," Isen said.

"That's the whole goddamned trouble," Woodriff said immediately. "There's too many people in the military who are concerned with all the political bullshit. The warrior instinct is to go after the enemy, go for the jugular, and not let up until he's destroyed."

Isen heard Barrow shuffle next to him. Whenever Woodriff started talking about his "warrior" ethic, many of the other officers turned him off. The lieutenants in the battalion, Isen knew, called Woodriff "The Warrior King." Isen remembered Woodriff holding forth at the Officers Club bar one afternoon about how a soldier was someone who put on the uniform every day, whereas a warrior lived and breathed the profession. The implication was that Woodriff was a warrior, while Isen and many of the others were pretenders. Barrow had been sitting on the other side of Isen's table at the time, and Isen overheard him tell another lieutenant that he thought it was stretching the definition of *warrior* a bit to include people, like Woodriff, who had never been shot at.

No one commented on Woodriff's observation, but Barrow blew a long breath between pursed lips. Woodriff's eyes snapped to the lieutenant, but Barrow just gave him a blank look.

"At any rate," Bock said by way of closing, "if we hear anything substantial, we'll let you guys know right off."

Woodriff had wanted an argument, but the other officers got up and abandoned him. Isen felt sorry for Woodriff's XO, who had to listen to the pontificating all the time. Woodriff, Isen was sure, would be truly insufferable after this first combat experience.

Barrow was quiet on the drive back to Charlie Company. The countryside here was scarred from the fighting over the past week, and many of the little crossroads had been all but obliterated by artillery. Isen noticed what looked like a bundle on the side of the road, but as they got closer and Isen's driver slowed, he saw that it was the body of a North Korean soldier. He lay facedown in the drainage ditch, his legs stiff and pointing at the sky.

The three Americans became quiet as they approached, as if the body were surrounded by an invisible circle that demanded silence.

"Their soldiers have no more say in what they're doing here than do ours, or the South Koreans," Isen offered. "All the little guys seem the same, in a way. You know what I mean?" He wasn't sure if he was making any sense, and Barrow seemed lost in some reverie of his own.

"They *are* the same, sir. We're all in the same boat. We're all getting the royal shaft."

Barrow didn't look at Isen. He was afraid he'd lose the sharp edge of what he was feeling now. The smoldering that had been inside him since the day at the river, burning him like an ulcer, was uncovering itself. He was surprised by the sudden emotion.

"I mean, here we are in this goddamn country, and I've been putting guys I know in body bags—for what? For South Korea? For democracy?"

Barrow felt Isen's eyes on him, felt as if he were

betraying Isen somehow by talking this way. He had serious doubts about the rightness of what they were doing, but he respected Isen so much that he passionately wanted to believe they were right—just because Isen thought so. He felt himself losing his grip on what was cause, what was effect. The questions, all too big for him, mocked his attempts to find an answer, and he began to suspect that no such answer existed.

Without looking at Isen, he tucked his chin down onto his chest, folded his arms, closed his eyes, and retreated.

When they got back to the company, Voavosa approached Barrow.

"Got a letter here, sir."

"We got *mail?*" Barrow asked, extending his hand.

"Yes, sir," Voavosa said. "This one's dated the day we left Oahu. The bag was pretty small, but maybe this means that they'll be getting some more through. Sure helps morale."

Barrow stared at the letter the first sergeant had handed him. He recognized the soft curls of his wife's handwriting, and suddenly, unexpectedly, he didn't trust himself to speak without his voice breaking.

Voavosa went on, repeating himself in the awkward moment. "There's a lot of stuff that has to come over on those planes, but I guess they figured out how important mail is to the troops."

Barrow nodded in mute agreement. He walked away from the first sergeant, away from the CP. When he was off by himself, he slung his rifle over his shoulder, wiped one hand on his shirt, then stuck a dirty finger into the small space under the flap. He tore it open and, after checking to see who might be watching, pressed the envelope to his face to breathe in her scent. The paper smelled of musty mailbags and two weeks in the back of some truck, but it was still clean where he hadn't touched it, and he drank in the whiteness of the page.

Dear Dale,
*   Just a note to say we're all right and thinking of you*
all the time.

He wondered how it could be only two weeks since he'd seen her. He—they, he corrected himself—had been wrenched into another life in that short time.

I went to church this morning, the chaplain had a special service for the families still here at Schofield. A lot of the women have gone back to the mainland to stay with family, but I've decided to stick it out here. (Daddy offered to fly me home.)

I'm trying to be strong, 'cause I know that would make you proud of me. It's hard, but I know it's harder where you are.

As Barrow read he saw another message between the lines, one he had written to himself. He had urged her to be strong, but not for the right reasons. He could have told her to persevere for the sake of the children, or as an example for the families of other men in the unit, or for their aging parents, or even for her own peace of mind as she struggled to cope, out in the middle of the Pacific, away from her family and for the most part without news of her husband, while all around her the chaplains and the notification officers made their deadly house calls. When he told her to bear up, it was for appearance, and he only now learned to appreciate that what had so concerned him in every facet of his military experience so far, was facade.

I have to close now. I'm writing this standing in front of the mailroom in the quad, and they say they have to get it out of here so they can get it on the plane. I hope this finds you so you'll know we love you.

> *All my love, always,*
> *Connie*

He held the letter, tasting the flap where she must have sealed it, forcing everything in his consciousness to focus on the reality-to-be of his homecoming, and the opportunity he might yet have to set things straight, to grow up with his wife.

17

29 April · Friday

David hated stand-to. From a half hour before sunrise until a half hour after, the company was on one-hundred-percent security, every man awake, with his sleeping gear packed, alert and manning his weapon. They repeated the ritual at sunset. He once asked Isen why they tortured themselves like that. Isen quoted from something called *Standing Orders for Roger's Rangers,* which said, in part, *Don't sleep beyond dawn. Dawn's when the French and Indians attack.* David remained unconvinced, though he was not surprised that the army was relying on two-hundred-and-fifty-year-old rules.

The next morning, after enduring the hour he had to remain still behind his weapon before he could relieve himself, David headed down to the small creek that ran just south of the village. Making his way upstream, a few yards east along the grassy bank and away from the houses, he passed several spots where soldiers had muddied the bank and water while filling canteens. He moved past these to find a fresher place, stepping into the water where the bottom was sandy, and immersing his canteen with the mouth facing downstream. He pushed down slowly, so as not to stir up sediment. Straightening, he reached into the small Velcro-closed pocket, on the side of the quilted canteen holder, where he kept his water purification tablets. He pulled the tiny bottle free, twisted off the cap, and tilted it into his hand. It was empty.

Just then he heard a sound upstream. In a single motion, he crouched and brought his rifle up from his side.

There were two or three ROK soldiers about seventy-five yards from him, washing themselves in the stream. He dumped his canteen.

Ten minutes later, David was standing in front of Sergeant Geist, the supply sergeant.

"We got any more water tablets, Sergeant Geist?"

"I just gave out my last bottle two days ago. See if you can borrow some."

David asked five men in two different platoons for tablets. No one had any. Finally, Isen gave him two, and he went and refilled his canteen, after moving farther upstream from where the South Koreans had been washing.

War, to a large extent, is a collision of circumstances, accidental and only sometimes avoidable. And so it was with Charlie Company's water supply.

These were the facts: the breakdown—from overuse—of the hand pump at the village well coincided with the depletion of the company's water purification tablets. Add to that the fact that some ROK soldiers and South Korean refugees were using the stream to bathe, wash laundry, and scrub cooking utensils. The result was that the eighty-some Americans who were using the same stream for a water supply were courting disaster. Without the tablets, which made the water smell like cleaning fluid, but neutralized the disease carriers, the soldiers were ingesting all sorts of filth.

As of the afternoon preceding David's excursion, twenty-five soldiers in the company had the "GI trots," so called because the men trotted off to the makeshift latrines several times an hour. By the time David used the tablets Isen had given him, all but a few of the troops were reduced to squatting too close to their positions, because they couldn't make it any farther. The afternoons grew warmer at the end of April, and soon the whole company position reeked with the smell of human waste. Even the soldiers who weren't afflicted risked dehydration, since they refused to drink water from the stream.

Isen, who believed in preparing for any conceivable eventuality, but had not predicted that diarrhea would lay his company low, was at a loss. By the third day, with more than half his men reduced to exhaustion, he made a personal trip to the brigade medical supply point, looking for tablets and treatment for diarrhea. He came away disappointed.

Thousands of miles away, in an obscure and, until a few weeks earlier, little-used warehouse at Travis Air Force Base in California, the tablets that Charlie Company so desperately needed sat crated and on a skid. The boxes had been missed in inventory because the labels faced the wall, in direct violation of standard operating procedures at the facility. They had been turned that way by a forklift operator, an airman who had been working eighteen-hour shifts for the past three weeks, loading the never-ending line of aircraft headed west.

As the weather in Korea warmed, word came back through the intricate, multiservice supply chain, that cold weather sleeping bags and overboots would no longer be needed. Warehouse Number Ten, with the water tablets buried deeply in the shadows, suddenly had to make room for another fifty pallets of cold weather issue. The skids were lined up two deep along the walls, and the tablets were as good as lost at sea.

As Charlie Company experienced its second day of runaway diarrhea, the 25th Division supply officer, a forty-one-year-old lieutenant colonel by the name of Evan Sinnot, prepared to enter the division's tactical operations center. He stood before the entrance to the tent, having passed through three security checks on the way into a well-hidden depression where the TOC rested beneath its vast array of camouflage nets. Inside, he knew, he would meet the division commander, Major General Don Stalling.

Stalling was normally a happy man. Even over the past weeks, with the tremendous pressure of command, he had managed to retain, if not his humor, most of his human qualities. But the combination of events: his unit being stripped of assets, his being kept in the dark—perhaps deliberately—by his allies, all on top of the "normal" stresses of combat, had lately combined to push him near some dark and unfamiliar edge. And now, an alarming number of his men were becoming combat ineffective, laid low by an affliction that had swept through armies for thousands of years. But Major General Stalling, understanding as he was for a general officer, simply could not see that his men should suffer the same indignities and afflictions, in this modern day, as had Washington's and Napoleon's troops.

Sinnot pushed aside the canvas blackout curtain, spotted the commander, and walked purposefully into the room. He stopped two paces from Stalling, and stood at a fair approximation of the position of attention he had learned as a plebe at West Point.

"What in the hell is going on with these goddamn water tablets, Evan? You want to let me in on the problem?"

"We haven't been able to get our hands on any, sir. They haven't come in over the last week, in spite of repeated messages I've been sending through the service support channels."

Sinnot felt a tremendous urge to look down at a notecard he held in his hand. The card was blank, but he wanted nothing more than to escape the withering gaze of his boss. He had felt, for days, that he was letting the division's soldiers down. Now the disappointment had a face.

"I've contacted the ROKs, and I've even made a trip south myself to see if I couldn't scare up some tablets from one of the American bases here." Sinnot had the unnerving sensation that everything he said was merely fulfilling what Stalling already knew, what Stalling already thought of him.

"Do you know that we have at least four thousand soldiers out there," Stalling said, his voice rising, "who are shitting their brains out all over the fucking countryside"—he was almost shouting now—"because the world's most sophisticated air force, and the most technologically complex army in the free fucking world, can't deliver a bunch of little bottles that are no bigger than so many spools of thread?"

Sinnot had no answer. And he knew that the general knew that there was no answer. War, finally even modern war, meant moving the right men and the right equipment and the right supplies to the exact points on the battlefield where they could affect the outcome of the struggle. And the tiny bottles that were conspicuous only in their absence had somehow slipped through the cracks. *My kingdom for a horse,* Sinnot thought.

"Work on it, Evan. We're not going to have the Tropic Lightning Division known as the Diarrhea Divison," Stalling said. And then, more seriously, "Those troops are suffering out there. I want *you* to do something about it."

"Yes, sir," Sinnot said.

"Go away now," Stalling said. "I have to figure out what the next thing is that's going to jump up and bite us on the ass."

18

Schofield Barracks, Hawaii

29 April · Friday

Adrienne Isen drove north up the hill from Honolulu to Schofield Barracks, watching the long light of evening draw down the western sky behind the Waianae mountains. She had accomplished only part of what she wanted by going back to work. She had tried to stay away during the limbo period before Mark deployed, but after the scene at Hickam Air Force Base, she thought it best to restore at least the appearance of normalcy to her life. And that was all that she had done. She drove to work at the same time, saw the same people at the parking garage, and bought the morning paper from the same vending machine, though now she looked first and hardest at the news from Korea. She ate lunch in the same places, with the same people. Even the projects that had disappeared from her concerns for a few weeks were still there, unchanged by the events that had shaken her life.

The sameness of the world outside Schofield Barracks

angered her. She couldn't believe that everything could go on while she tossed and turned at night, at once cold and sweating on the sheets, listening to the insects and the chirping of the gekko lizards on the white cinder-block walls.

She resisted admitting to herself, after one sleepless night, that she had helped create her dilemma. Mark had never been anything but deadly serious about his profession, and she knew with a rock-solid certainty that he had thought it all through: the fact that he could, at any time, be sent away to some godforsaken trouble spot where, for the sake of "national security," whatever the hell that was, he might get himself killed. Mark had made his peace with that knowledge. He had forced himself to think of his training as the "real thing." He never thought of the exercises as "war games," a term he despised. He tried to steel himself for the awful possibilities.

But Adrienne had avoided the philosophical acceptance of what military life might entail. Adrienne thought of what her husband and his men did as "playing army," pretending to be little boys who were pretending to be men. That was how she lived with it all. Belittling Mark's work made her feel less a hypocrite for staying so near something she despised.

She knew that in the peacetime army, a lot of spouses, a lot of soldiers even, could forget what it was all about. There was always the next inspection, or the next field problem, or the next school selection board or promotion board to worry about. It was easy to become lost in the minutiae of daily life. To be constantly aware of what the real mission was required imagination and thinking, and while Adrienne had met quite a few imaginative people in uniform, she knew that a soldier who spent time thinking—just *thinking* —was probably considered an idler.

Adrienne, who was something of an intellectual snob, believed that most people lived their lives on a superficial plane. Most people thought of their lives, if at all, as a series of almost disconnected events, like a tale told by a child: this happened, then this, then this. Mark, she knew, was forever examining his own motives: weighing what had happened to him and what he had done, looking at his experiences and trying to make sense of them, mining reasons and causes, beginnings and endings.

Adrienne, too, was most happy when she led an examined life. Yet because she loved Mark, but could not love his profession, Adrienne struggled to stay away from examination, because she saw the contradiction in her life, and away from imagination, for the scenes she imagined were too terrible.

As she drove home this afternoon at the end of April, she finally had to admit that while the denial was possible amid the boredom of peacetime army life, it was no longer so. There would be no distraction for her, no escaping the constant reminder provided by the hole in her heart.

The phone was ringing as she got out of the car. She ran to the door, unlocked it, and pulled the phone off the receiver, spilling her briefcase and newspaper and lunch bag on the floor.

"Adrienne Isen," she said, using her business voice.

"Adrienne, this is Bette Tilden."

"Oh, hello, Bette," Adrienne said. It seemed as if there was more she should say, some nicety, but she couldn't for the life of her figure out what it might be.

"How are you holding up?" Bette asked.

"Well, I have my work and everything, and that helps a lot," Adrienne answered half-truthfully.

"Thank God for small favors," Bette said. "Listen, Adrienne, I'm calling to ask your help on something. I've been spending a lot of time visiting with the women whose husbands have been . . . whose husbands have become casualties."

The reconstructed sentence didn't escape Adrienne. *Whose husbands have been killed,* Adrienne filled in maliciously.

"It's unpleasant duty, to be sure, but it helps tremendously those who need it most. Even if we just keep the women company until some family is able to make it from the mainland; you know, watching the kids and cooking and doing a lot of the everyday things that would get passed up. I was wondering if you'd consider helping out."

Adrienne couldn't conceive of voluntarily moving closer to such suffering. A million reasons to turn Bette down lurked just beyond articulation. The one she thought of first would be the most controversial in the small community: participating would condone what the army had done to her husband, and she wanted no part in that.

"I don't think so, Bette. I'm pretty busy with work and all," Adrienne said.

"I understand," Bette shot back as if she'd expected to be turned down. She was ready with a persuasive argument, and she forged ahead. "This is part of our 'chain of concern,' which parallels the chain of command. This is how army families take care of one another. We need the women whose husbands are the real leaders—the company commanders and first sergeants—to make this thing work. Some of us who have been around for a while try to help the younger wives cope with what's going on. Everyone needs a support system."

Bette paused, but Adrienne didn't answer. The woman pressed on, apparently undaunted.

"Of course, the most serious thing I ever had to deal with before was when one of Rand's troops was out in the field while his wife was delivering their first baby. I wound up being a delivery room coach for a woman I had laid eyes on only once." She paused, as if she couldn't decide whether or not to chuckle at the anecdote. Adrienne enjoyed making the woman uncomfortable.

"Then, we were at Campbell in 1985 when a planeload of one-oh-first soldiers went down in Newfoundland, on the way back from the Sinai peacekeeping mission. I remember seeing, on the television news, the wife of the battalion commander who was killed along with most of his troops. She came to the airfield when some other planes arrived, days later, with the rest of the unit. A reporter asked why she felt the need to be there, and she said that her responsibility to those soldiers had not ended with her husband's death, and that she was exactly where he would have wanted her to be."

Bette paused, self-conscious after what must have sounded like a sermon.

"Anyway," she continued, "I was hoping you'd come along and give us a hand."

Adrienne took the cowardly way out. "I'll think about it, okay, Bette?"

What she wanted to say was that she couldn't be more opposed to the whole show; she wanted to lash out at any figure or group that shared complicity in this accident of history, or had contributed to it by sins of omission or commission. She wanted to tell Bette Tilden that what she *was* thinking about was the idea of joining one of the antiwar demonstrations she had seen downtown by the state capitol. She knew that Mark, in all his prim, habitual compliance, would be horrified; secretly she knew that part of the attraction of flirting with such outrageous—for the wife of an army officer at war—behavior was the effect it would have on her husband.

Deep down inside her, in parts of her makeup that even she resisted confronting, Adrienne held Mark responsible for what had happened to their life together.

Adrienne had always been something of a rebel in the staid circles of the army community, and any action on her part, especially if it involved an anti-war demonstration, would never be construed as being political. The military didn't work that way. It was all well and good for civilians to protest; that was their right, after all. But in the service family, even for Adrienne, who was technically a civilian, the unwritten law was: you're either with us, or against us. No one would ascribe her actions to political motives. No one would assume that she was merely concerned about America's involvement. There was too much emotion at stake. She had only to look as far as the first GI pickup truck with the popular bumper sticker: *Boycott Jane Fonda, American Traitor Bitch,* to know what they would think of her.

Bette Tilden must have expected a more abrupt answer; she was almost happy that Adrienne had given her even a shred of hope. "Okay, Adrienne, that's great. You think about it, and please let me know . . . or, better yet, I'll call you, you know, to see how you're doing, even if you decide not to come along. Great. Okay, good-bye now. You take care, hear?"

* * *

Adrienne decided to work on Saturday, the day after she spoke to Bette, and entertained her first thoughts about the anti-war demonstrations. She got an unexpected and close-up look at a small protest rally in Honolulu.

Unable to get a permit to picket the State House, the protestors chose instead the old government building on King Street. There must have been no more than twenty-five or thirty pickets, marching in a solemn circle around the huge statue of Kamehameha, the warrior king who unified and became the first true ruler of the islands. Kamehameha stood above the marchers, solemnly glaring into the distance. From his great outstretched arm, from which children would hang ten-foot-long leis on the holiday named for the warrior, one of the protestors had strung a placard with badly spaced lettering that read: *No More Vietnams.*

Adrienne walked down there on her lunch hour, standing among the curious onlookers just behind a bank of newspaper and television reporters, all of whom seemed colossally bored with the scene. A small group of counter-demonstrators shouted at the pickets.

Adrienne moved closer to the protestors, surprised that they weren't the rabid, long-haired anarchists that she remembered from films of the sixties: angry youths and veterans and Gold Star mothers besieging the Capitol, or the White House, or burning cars in the Chicago streets in the fiery summer of 1968. She stood on the sidewalk, watching thoughtfully and trying to muster the courage to move forward and talk to one of the protestors.

She picked out one: a local man in his forties with a pronounced beer belly and the wispy beard of a Polynesian. He wore a camouflage hat, the kind Mark called a bush hat, and she could see that there were medals pinned to it, two rows of faded, dingy ribbons with large metal pendants. He carried no sign, and did not participate in the shouting match that seemed to be confined to the younger protestors and most of the counter-demonstrators. But he was the one Adrienne watched. She remembered such men—wearing parts of uniforms and immensely sad looks—from her visit to the Wall, the Vietnam Memorial, in Washington.

Certainly the veterans are the ones who know best, she thought, *about how wrong all of this is.*

She wanted to approach the man, tell him she was a soulmate, that she understood, that they shared a bitter bond. But there was a gulf, its edge marked by some weird sense of propriety. Finally, she turned away and walked back the way she had come.

More frustrated than ever, Adrienne drove the familiar road back to Schofield, up the center of the island, oblivious to the stunning beauty of the highway's steady rise above the Pacific. At the gate to the post she saw a few more protestors, standing in a small knot across the highway. They were watched closely by the Military Policemen manning the gate, National Guardsmen who had replaced the 25th Division MPs.

The Guard, she thought, won't be going off to Korea, at least not anytime soon. All the dirty work is done by the regulars. As she waited in the left-hand-turn lane for the homebound traffic in front of her to move, Adrienne allowed herself to become more disturbed. The fact that the Guard wouldn't be going anywhere was further evidence, to her, of the country's lack of commitment. It was too easy, she believed, to send off the professionals—men like her husband—and not arouse too much real public furor. But start pulling Joe Citizen out of the workplace and America would sit up and take notice. The whole picture disgusted her, and seemed further evidence that her husband and his fellow soldiers were mere board pieces in some cosmic power game.

She turned onto the post, and the MP rendered a lackadaisical salute, recognizing the officer's registration sticker on the car. She turned right at the Division Museum, the only building on post that still bore the scars of the Japanese attack in 1941. There were fewer than a half-dozen old bullet holes on the side, small marks on the volcanic stone, circled in red paint. But there was no identifying sign, nothing to tip off the curious, to remind people. Planned forgetfulness, accidental forgetfulness—the results were the same.

As she turned right onto the beautiful Waianae Avenue, lined with towering royal palms that soared fifty and sixty feet straight up, Adrienne noticed a car pull out of the quadrangle that housed Mark's company. It caught her attention only because cars were not allowed in the barracks areas, but as she got closer she noticed that the plain blue sedan had government license plates. In the back of the car she could see an officer, a major, in the short-sleeved green shirt of the class "B" uniform. It was unusual, she thought, for a major to be chauffeured in a sedan. As she sped up to pass on the two-lane, one-way street, she saw that the man in the front passenger seat wore black clerical clothes. Startled, Adrienne realized that she was looking at a notification team, going off to some home with news of a husband, or a father, wounded or killed.

She decelerated, easing up on the gas, but the other car seemed to slow also, and the sedan turned left where she had to. The two cars moved slowly down the street at the same speed, locked together. Adrienne, mesmerized, stared at the back of the officer's head, as if by concentration she could drive him off. She willed them to turn at the intersection by the Post Exchange, but they went straight ahead into the officers' housing area. She fought panic and nausea as the car took a slight dip in the intersection. A hundred yards later, and the sedan turned onto Porter Loop, her street. Adrienne began to shake, and she could feel the butterfly trembling of her lower lip against her teeth. The two cars came closer and closer to her driveway, and her heart pounded against the confines of her ribs, her breath coming in spikes.

Then the sedan passed her house.

As it rounded the corner a little way ahead, Adrienne's foot slipped off the accelerator, her hands off the wheel, and she was taken by grief and fear and regret as her own car slowed, gliding gently into the curb, rocking her softly.

Around the bend in the street, the blue car stopped.

19

Near Kumnu-ri, Republic of Korea

29 April · Friday

Isen was glad to have the first twenty-four hours in the defensive position without interruption. The men made good progress solidifying the position and making it tenable. Isen thought they might even have a chance against armored vehicles if his luck held.

Just after 0900 on Charlie Company's first full day in the MOUT site, Bock sent Isen an encoded message on the battalion net. Isen stood and looked over David's shoulder as the young soldier decoded the nonsensical word groups. The message called Isen to a briefing at the battalion TOC, for a platoon-sized patrol. Isen immediately decided to take a lieutenant with him, since one of the junior officers would lead the patrol, but he wasn't sure which one.

Haveck was out. His platoon was at just about sixty percent strength, not an effective force for what Isen was sure would be a combat patrol. If the S3 was looking to send out a reconnaissance patrol, somebody to look around, he would have asked for a squad.

Marist was the most experienced platoon leader, and perhaps the best man in the battalion for the job. But Isen felt that sending Marist would strip the largest part of the company of its best combat strength. Lake, on the other hand, was relatively inexperienced, but had shown good potential.

If only I had had more time to train these men! he thought.

Lake also had Bladesly, who was the best platoon sergeant in the company. Isen pictured the two lieutenants in his mind as he mulled the decision over for a few seconds.

Just before he made his choice, he had a mental image of Sergeant Padilla, the young NCO who was killed, with most of his squad, on the company's first night in action. Even as he told David to call Lake to the CP, he wondered what he could have told Padilla that might have changed things, and he wondered what he would say to Lake to prevent another such disaster.

In peacetime maneuvers such decisions frequently had to do with which platoon was the most rested. Now Isen felt, as he looked down the small street where he expected Lake to appear, that he was playing some dangerous roulette, trying to guess the mostly untried ability of junior leaders, and then betting the lives of several dozen men on his decision.

Lake appeared around the corner of a small outbuilding near the CP, and Isen studied him as he walked. He carried his rifle in one hand, balancing it near the magazine well, and he had his map case slung over his shoulder. He walked gingerly, his footsteps spread farther apart than normal, an odd result of the rampant diarrhea.

A year ago, Isen thought, Lake had been a senior at West Point, probably worrying about which date to invite to the Graduation Dance. Tonight, a captain he had met only two months earlier was about to send him out to combat.

"Over here, Mike," Isen called.

"Intelligence thinks they've pinned down the location of some of the North Korean irregulars that have been tearing up our supply lines," Bock said.

The three had met at the makeshift battalion TOC, which was little more than a few HMMWVs huddled together under some trees. Bock was kneeling on the ground, spreading before him a map he had drawn from a plastic case in his vehicle. As Isen and Lake watched, the S3 placed a piece of tracing paper, which had just a few control symbols on it, over the map.

"What do you mean by 'irregular forces'? This is the first we've heard that term," Isen asked.

"Well, they're not sure if we're dealing with guerrillas or Special Purpose Forces. All the information we have says they're dressed in civilian clothing."

"But what would a bunch of guerrillas be doing back here?" Isen asked, pointing at the place on the map where someone in the brigade intelligence section had marked the objective area. The egg-shaped objective was due south of Charlie Company's position, at least seven klicks, Isen guessed.

Bock shook his head.

"Sounds to me like the intell guys don't know what's going on," Isen finished, not sure what he wanted to make of the point.

"So I'm running an ambush patrol to catch these guys, right, sir?" Lake had been studying Bock's map and making marks on the acetate covering of his own.

"They've been moving out of this particular patrol base for two nights. The sightings by South Korean civilians indicate that they haven't left the area," Bock said.

"But isn't that contrary to how their Special Purpose Forces operate? Wouldn't they shift around every night?"

Lake grew visibly uncomfortable as Isen quizzed the S3. But Isen felt something was fishy about the information they were getting, and it sounded to him as if Bock, who had received the briefing from the brigade S2, hadn't been suspicious enough.

"That's right, Mark," Bock said. There were a few awkward seconds as the captain and the major, both of them exhausted, both of them nervous about what might come spilling down the excellent highway that crossed in front of the battalion position from the northeast, just stared at each other, locked in an impasse. Lake spoke up.

"Well, sir," he said, not sure which man he should be addressing, "it could mean that we are, in fact, dealing with irregulars and not the first string. Or it could mean that they're worn out, exhausted, especially if they crossed the DMZ last week and have been going continuously since then. Everybody lets slip some when they're tired," he finished, proud of his assessment.

"Or it could mean the information is screwed," Isen said. Bock let him have the last word.

"Is that all, sir?" Lake asked the S3.

"Yeah. Good luck, Lake," Bock said.

* * *

As soon as he got back to his platoon position, Lake called his squad leaders together for a warning order, letting them know right away what was going on, so they could begin their preparations. Bladesly stood in the back of the little group, and he nudged with his boot one of the squad leaders who, he'd noticed, wasn't taking notes. The man pulled out his memo book without having to be told.

Bladesly watched as Lake went through the checklist provided in a little book the lieutenant carried, *The Ranger Handbook*. The book, the size of a pack of index cards, held planning guides for operations, from a simple coordination meeting to resupply by air. In Bladesly's experience, there were three kinds of lieutenant when it came to such checklists. There were those who thought themselves too accomplished to carry such a crutch. This attitude, coupled with a lack of experience, led to missed movements, forgotten plans, and screwed-up operations. At the other end of the scale were those lieutenants who relied too heavily on such books and cards and checklists. The army loved printing such things, and some junior officers loved reading them, in all their mind-numbing detail, instead of giving an order, as if the checklists freed the officer from final responsibility.

In between the two extremes there was a narrow sampling of young men who knew instinctively when and how to use such tools. Lake was one of those. As he briefed the squad leaders, he held the book open in his hand. He glanced at it periodically, but maintained eye contact with the sergeants. The book removed the fear that he might be forgetting something, and without that worry Lake was confident. And confidence, Bladesly knew, had a way of spreading.

Later, as the platoon sergeant watched, Lake checked and rechecked the squad leader's understanding of the briefing he had given. Not a single one of the men tripped up on a question. *Not bad,* Bladesly thought, *for a guy who, just a few days ago, had to be reminded to sleep inside his fighting position.*

In spite of the intricate patterns, in paragraphs and subparagraphs, suggested by the *Ranger Handbook,* Lake stuck to a simple plan, because he believed it most important that his soldiers understood what was going on.

The busywork of planning had calmed him a bit, but after he briefed the platoon, he was left with some time to himself as the squad leaders prepared their men for final inspection by Bladesly. Lake knew that this kind of mission was what the light infantry was best suited for—close combat in restrictive terrain, under limited visibility. Yet he also knew, from the low-threat environment of training, that all of these things made control and execution of a mission that much harder. Even though he had done well in the infantry Officer's Basic Course and in the pressure-cooker training of Ranger School, he had never gotten over the feeling that he was holding on to order by the slimmest margin, in the face of impending chaos.

As he stood aside, letting the NCOs do their work without interference, he tried to visualize the mission. As a boxer at West Point, he had frequently used the same mental wargaming to work out his success beforehand, to "visualize" in the athletic vernacular, and he believed in the technique. But this afternoon was different, and Lake could only conjure disparate images of control and disaster.

"Good plan, Lieutenant."

Bladesly appeared next to him, as if he had materialized out of the tension.

"Thanks, Sergeant Bladesly. Did I leave anything out?" Lake asked.

"Not that I could see. I think we'll do all right."

Lake drew confidence from Bladesly's assessment. He had a great deal of respect for the older man's experience and intelligence. Lake felt like a child who had just been given a pat on the back by a teacher.

Sergeant First Class Martin Bladesly, who had spent all but two of his thirteen years of service in rifle companies, wasn't conscious of playing a role to soothe his lieutenant's fears. For all his service, his combat experience was only as extensive as was Lake's—a few days. And if anyone had asked him, he would have guessed that he was just as nervous as the newest private.

Bladesly and Lake conducted the final inspection in the failing light of dusk, checking the equipment and weapons and ammunition and water of each of the men. Finally, the preparation was over. Lake turned and saw Isen watching them.

"All set, Mike?" Isen asked.

"All set, sir," Lake answered, wondering if he was telling the truth.

He turned to Bladesly and nodded, and the big platoon sergeant moved to the rear of the twenty-nine-man formation, where he would make sure the patrol did not leave any soldiers behind in the darkness.

Lake took his place near the head of the formation, much closer to the point than he normally traveled. He was anxious to exercise as much control as possible in this new venture. He checked his compass, and reminded the soldier behind him to keep a pace count, in case they had to figure out where they were by dead reckoning: distance traveled and direction. Finally, he could think of nothing else that needed to be done.

He checked his watch, and at exactly 2145, start time, he nodded to the darkening figure in front of him.

"Let's go," he said.

There would be a moon up shortly, and that would give them enough light to communicate with hand and arm signals. Lake had been on many of these patrols in peacetime training, and all of this night's surface elements appeared the same. He followed the luminous tape on the man in front of him, watching carefully for the branches that could materialize in front of your face to scratch the eyes. Suddenly they seemed to be making a tremendous amount of noise. He heard sticks and brush snapping as the men walked; he was sure he heard the jangle of loose equipment, though Bladesly had checked the men thoroughly at inspection, making each of them jump up and down to see what came loose. In the darkness, all the sounds were magnified to the point where Lake felt an enemy could hear even his breathing. Once they left the protection of the company position, the darkness took on a sinister character, for it hid men who wanted to kill him.

He checked the luminous face of his compass again. Steady at one-seven-zero degrees. They had six kilometers to go before they would stop to set up the objective rally point, the position from which he would look over the objective area before he placed his men in the ambush site.

Lake checked his watch again—2155.

He tried to absorb everything that was going on, watching the men around him, the ones he could see; passing on the head counts that came up periodically from the rear of the formation; checking the terrain around him against the sector of the map he had committed to memory through the afternoon. But his thoughts kept drifting.

What fate, he wondered, draws one patrol into the kill zone while another misses, turning away at the last moment? What makes a leader choose one path over another, and in that choice decide the fate of the whole patrol? What is it that makes a running soldier move from one position to another a few seconds before the first is smashed by a mortar round? Training and skill did not seem an adequate explanation. Some of his soldiers, Lake knew, believed strongly in luck: good luck charms and small rituals of preparing their weapons and equipment. Lake also enjoyed the comfort of ritual, carrying in each breast pocket a government issue New Testament that he had gotten from a chaplain. He had read somewhere about a soldier whose life was saved by a bullet-stopping Bible, but every once in a while he wondered if he needed the Old and the New Testament together, or if just the New would do. He wanted to believe he could affect things, but finally, he did not, and he was sure only of stalking chaos, of randomness.

Two kilometers south of the objective area that Lake had marked on his map, Lieutenant Kang Min-Chul, of the North Korean Special Purpose Forces, checked his men as they slept. He had finished briefing them at dusk, and had told them to get some rest before they left, after midnight, for the night's mission.

Kang had only six men, besides himself, left of the original nine who had ambushed the American convoy three weeks earlier. Two of his men had been killed outright when a South Korean convoy they ambushed counterattacked viciously. Kang's men had performed well, but they were forced out of their positions and had to leave the two dead men behind, which upset Kang and his men deeply.

Another of Kang's soldiers had been wounded in the exchange, and the group had carried the man for many miles through the night and the next day. Without medical attention, the soldier deteriorated quickly. Kang finally had to shoot him in the back of the head to put him out of his misery and to relieve the remaining patrol members of their physical and psychological burdens.

Most of the remaining men had some sort of wound which hampered movement. They were all sick, a few with advanced cases of dehydration and exhaustion. They had existed on roots and leaves for the past two days, and they hoped tonight to get their hands on some rations in the raid Kang had planned. They had located, almost by accident, a signal relay site manned by fewer than a half dozen ROK troops, south of Kumnu-ri. Kang planned to strike before the site moved or could be reinforced.

His men slept fitfully, and Kang stood guard for them. Support troops such as the ones Kang expected to encounter tonight would not normally present much of a problem for Kang's soldiers. But Kang's men were tired, ill, and hungry, and nowhere near peak fighting form. As he watched them sleep, he wondered when their luck would run out, and he wondered how many of them would see the morning.

For all of his doubts, Lake's navigation was dead on, and he easily found the area he had selected, from his map study, for the first halt near the objective. He stopped the platoon, and Bladesly set up a perimeter. The moon was up now, and Lake saw the terrain in surprising detail. He told Bladesly that he would take a look at the objective area, where he would leave several soldiers once he knew the place was clear of enemy. Then he would return for the rest of the platoon.

He approached the objective area cautiously, made a sweep of the area, selected his kill zone and the locations for his squads. Then he positioned as guides some of the soldiers he had brought with him, so that they could, as quietly as possible, lead the rest of the platoon into place.

He headed back to the platoon, worried all the while about approaching even his own men in the darkness. Lake had a flash of one of his military history classes at West

Point, where he had learned that Stonewall Jackson had been shot out of the saddle by one of his own men, a nervous sentry, while returning from just such a reconnaissance.

But his navigation was right on again, and his confidence grew. Now, if the enemy would just show up in the right place.

Lake briefed Bladesly and the squad leaders on the lay of the land in the objective area.

"According to the map, there are two east-west trails that pinch this hill," Lake said, rustling his map in the close air under the poncho they had spread over them to hide the light. "But the one on the south is just a footpath, while this trail, on the north side, is practically a road."

Lake had already drawn a line alongside the large trail on the map, indicating that he would set up the ambush to hit elements traveling there. But as he looked at it, it struck him as wrong. Isen had taught him to look at the terrain as an enemy might, to put himself in the enemy's position.

"Scratch that," Lake said as he licked his thumb and wiped the line off the map. "I don't think they'll use that big trail after all."

Just before he woke his men, Kang looked at his map again. His map did not show the trail network in the detail that Lake's map did. Kang's philosophy was to stick to the low ground as they moved, staying off hills and moving through the shadows cast by their bulk, especially when the moon was as bright as it was this night.

It took his soldiers longer than usual to prepare to move, and Kang had to prolong his inspection while he waited for a soldier who went off behind some bushes to vomit. The sharp sounds reminded Kang how sick they all were.

Still, they moved in good order as they set out from the hide location, and Kang was pleased at their alertness after all they had been through. Nevertheless, he was suspicious of the night and even of the comforting light of the moon they walked beneath.

Kang raised his hand, halting the patrol. He moved to the point, where he squatted in the thin undergrowth and listened. There was no sound out there, and Kang wondered if he was starting to imagine sounds. He turned abruptly to the point man and motioned him forward again. The soldier wondered if he had done something wrong; his lieutenant seemed remarkably and suddenly disturbed.

Kang was frustrated by the lack of evidence to support his feeling that something was wrong. He had learned, during these past weeks of combat, to trust his instincts, like an athlete, or a dancer. But he had lately become worried that his pained body would interfere with the signals he trusted.

Every footstep was painful; every time he crouched or stretched his stride to step over a root, his body screamed in silent protest, and the incredible static threatened to cloud his judgment. He trusted that his head would clear in an encounter with the enemy, as everything became focused on the fighting. But after that, he knew, would come the drained exhaustion and the letdown. And there would be no rest as long as the battle heaved above Seoul.

As hard as he was on himself, Kang was superb in the darkness—cat-like, and noiseless as smoke as he glided through the woods.

Kang's point man raised his hand, palm flat—the signal to halt.

Kang inched forward until he and the lead man were practically occupying the same space. The soldier lifted his arm and pointed, but Kang saw nothing.

Then he heard the sound, a tiny clicking, no more than twenty meters away. Kang felt the exhaustion wash off him like rain as he focused his attention on the sound, and knew once again the almost nauseating exhilaration of impending combat.

A short distance away from where Kang crouched in the bushes, two of Lake's men, manning the platoon's rightmost security post, watched the handset of their wire telephone as they tested the link with the platoon CP. There was a small, luminous disc which signaled an incoming call. The disc was meant to replace the audible signal at times when noise discipline was a prime concern. The soldiers hardly noticed that the spinning disc itself made a tiny noise.

Kang moved forward less than five meters, to where he could make out the two figures. One of the soldiers stood, and Kang could see the distinctive shape of the man's helmet against the moonlit sky.

They were Americans.

The position was just off the low part of a hill that lay along Kang's route. Behind the Americans, to the north, the dark bulk of the hill was quiet. But Kang knew these two were not alone. They were not part of a defensive position this far from the fighting, and he doubted that they were guarding a rear area. He correctly surmised that they were a security element for an ambush. He remembered the large trail that ran on the north side of this hill, and he assumed that these Americans were rear security for an ambush along that trail. He knew that the enemy would have, at the minimum, three security positions: one on either flank and this one, in the rear. The fourth side, the large trail in this case, would be the kill zone.

Kang moved slowly back to the main body of his patrol, and then led the little group even farther to the southwest, away from the Americans, so that he could brief his men without risking being discovered.

He was amazed that the Americans would set up an ambush on the large, well-used trail. But he had been told for years of the laziness of Americans, and he suspected that if the Americans were moving at night, they would use just such an easy trail instead of forcing their way through the tangled undergrowth in the low ground. They would expect the North Koreans to use the same trail. Instead of questioning why his enemy might do something so completely and obviously wrong, Kang, encouraged by his mind-numbing fatigue, accepted the easiest explanation. As he prepared to brief his men, he pushed out of his mind the insistent worry that his physical condition was interfering with his decision-making ability. Instead, he rested on a mindless and self-assuring notion of American sloth.

* * *

He gathered the men, seven desperate but still very deadly soldiers, huddled together in the night.

"The Americans have set up an ambush on the north slope of a small hill, about six hundred meters from here. I have discovered one of their security positions," he said, realizing that it sounded self-congratulating.

"Wu and I will take out the security position," he said, nodding toward the healthiest of his soldiers. "We will then move up the south slope of the hill, over the crest, and hit them from behind. We will not sweep through the area, because they no doubt have mines and explosives on the trail. We attack them in their ambush position, and then withdraw to the north, our original direction of travel."

Kang looked around at the circle of faces, dimly visible in the washed-out light of the moon. The men were alert, and he thought to himself that these must certainly be among the best soldiers in the world, not because of what the propagandists told the recruits, but because of what he had found these men capable of over the past weeks.

Lake was down in his right flank security position.

"We thought we heard something, so we checked out the area. We didn't see anything out there, sir, but Barrone is convinced he heard something, so we thought we'd call you."

Kent Norrick had been a team leader in the platoon before Lake's arrival, but had been busted because he had gotten into a fight at the Enlisted Soldiers' Club. Norrick's only problem was his size. He stood just a shade over six two, and had the triangular torso of a diver. Lake believed Bladesly's version of the story: that Norrick had stepped into a fight to protect a buddy, and that the brawlers naturally went for the big guy. But the battalion commander had busted him anyway, because the incident was the third such in the battalion in as many weeks.

During their recent field training, and especially on the Team Spirit exercise, Lake had come to respect Norrick's soldier sense. So when Norrick called with a report about noise, Lake went down to the position himself instead of sending a squad leader.

"What did it sound like, Barrone?" Lake asked the younger soldier.

"It just sounded like someone was moving around out there, sir. I didn't imagine it, Lieutenant. I mean, I'm not making this up or anything."

"I know you're not, Barrone. You're out here to listen and give us warning." Lake was satisfied with that much, but wasn't sure what else to tell these men, isolated as they were on the platoon's flank, thirty meters from the main body. He wanted to send two more men down, but the platoon was already spread thin along the edge of the kill zone. Lake would have to leave them out here alone again.

"Keep your eyes and ears open," he said. And then, to himself, *Well, that sounded pretty stupid.*

Only much later would he think that he should have told the men to move to another position.

At first Kang couldn't find the two soldiers again. He was sure he was in the same spot, but he did not see the silhouettes. He watched carefully, moving his eyes continuously around the edges of where they should be framed, because that was the best way to enhance night vision. Still nothing.

The pain behind the bridge of his nose mounted with the increased effort of concentration. What if the Americans had moved? What if they were looking for him, or if the two men had been a security element for a patrol base, and even now a platoon or a company was stalking him? In steadier times he was sure that his men would not panic, would not open fire on a larger group of enemy if they had no chance of winning. But all of them were exhausted, and in those few seconds of vacillation, he began to ride another emotional roller coaster, and he felt the slipping of self-assurance, the beginning of doubt.

When he looked up again, he saw movement.

Kang reached out with his right hand and gently tapped Wu on the side. They began to inch closer in a low crouch. Kang would have liked to crawl, so that his silhouette would be invisible, but there was a tradeoff: crawling made a lot more noise.

When they were within a few meters, Kang lay on the

ground and reached into the front of his shirt, where he had hidden a small rock. He hefted it in his hand, leaning over on his left side to free his throwing arm. Just before he let fly over the Americans, he thought about how the simplest approach was often the best.

Norrick heard the sound off to the left, and he first thought it was Lake coming toward them again from the platoon CP. But Lake wouldn't have chanced an approach without calling them first. There was something about the noise that didn't register. It was too abrupt; it was not the slow, even sound of a man pushing through brush, but a thud, such as when something is thrown.

He reacted even before his mind articulated the thought, turning completely around and leveling his weapon waist high. Something large and dark caught the muzzle of the rifle and pulled it down. He followed the dark form as he fumbled with the selector switch on his weapon; he heard Barrone, who had not even had a chance to stand, let out a sharp breath as the man who had jumped them raised and lowered his arm quickly, in almost comic quickness, again and again and again.

Norrick was looking down, and so never saw the second North Korean approach. Kang had to stretch to his full height to plunge the seven-inch blade of his fighting knife into the American's throat.

Twenty meters away, the rest of the men in Kang's patrol heard nothing, and wondered if their lieutenant had been able to find the Americans again.

Farther up the hill, Lake took the night-vision device away from his eyes to allow them to readjust to the darkness. As he watched the southern slope, he thought about the men who might come along the trail, wondering if they had any inkling of what was waiting for them. Small unit actions such as this were shaped by the leader's decisions: where to put the platoon, where to place the weapons, which trail to follow, what night to change hide positions. He was sparring in the dark, with someone he knew nothing about, whose actions he could only anticipate. The showdown would be between two men who had never seen one another, who would never speak to each other or understand each other—and in that regard it was the quintessential experience of war. The only immediate reason to kill was to avoid being killed.

Kang was once again confident after his success against the sentries. Although he would never be called an overly sensitive man, he was somewhat ashamed of the bloodlust that had overtaken him. Lock gazes with a dying man, Kang thought, and you draw from him some terrible power; you look through him, in that embrace, as if through a window that will close in an instant, and into the abyss which all men fear. Kang became more eager for such a glimpse, for such knowledge, with each death.

He felt the excitement in his rush to get the rest of the patrol in position to attack, and he hurried, with Wu close behind, because he did not want to lose the feeling before they encountered the rest of the enemy element.

He took his position at the head of the file. He planned on heading east until they were along the southern base of the hill. Then they would execute a simple left face and move north up the slope. In the darkness and silvery moonlight he could see the hill to his left, and he made an effort to slow his racing thoughts, so that he would not set up too hastily. With only six men left he had to disperse his troops so that they could inflict as much damage as possible.

He looked for the spot where he and Wu had killed the two soldiers, using it as a landmark to guide him. When he thought they were centered on the hill, he halted. The men turned to their left, automatically correcting their spacing so they wouldn't be bunched up. He moved one more time down the few meters his meager formation spanned, reminding them to use their remaining hand grenades first, in order to confuse the Americans as to the orientation of the attack. As he moved, he noticed for the first time that they were standing parallel to a small path that ran on the south side of the hill. This trail was not marked on Kang's map.

Lake was startled by the first noise he heard in front of him. He had not received a report from his right flank security, Norrick and Barrone, that any targets had entered the kill zone. He was just about to pick up the phone and signal them when he saw the dark shape moving below him on the southern slope. He saw only one, but heard at least several more. Incredibly, they were moving directly uphill. Somehow, they had missed the trail and so had gotten in between Lake's platoon and the claymores at the bottom of the hill.

The figures moved closer, and from his vantage point Lake could now see two and hear at least two more just outside his field of vision. They were only a few meters away now. The GIs waited.

Lake picked up one of the grenades he had in front of him and yanked the pin. He let the spoon fly, counted *one thousand, two thousand,* and tossed it lightly down the slope.

Kang, on the right end of the approaching line, was knocked over by the explosion. He lost his hearing and sense of direction, and he felt a wetness across the outside of his right arm and on the side of his face. But the shock of the pain was nothing compared to the crushing realization that he had guessed wrong about the American position. They had walked right into the teeth of the ambush.

A machine gun opened fire only a few feet up the slope, and when a flare popped behind Kang, lighting him up as a perfect target, he had only enough time to hope that the gunner's aim was true, and that he would not suffer being wounded.

Lake's men fired furiously for only a few seconds. There was no return fire from the enemy.

"CEASE FIRE, CEASE FIRE," Lake called, the last of his words trailing off in the ringing quiet that followed.

"SITREP," he called out, and the squad leaders began checking for casualties, preparing to give their situation reports.

"Search team," Lake said, his voice in control now as his hearing began to return to normal. "Send somebody down to check on the right flank security," he called back to Bladesly.

One fire team from each of the two squads he had on the assault line moved cautiously down the slope, the eight men peering forward where the enemy had gone down. Lake caught up with them and walked down the hill, at once exhilarated and nervous, unconvinced that the action could be over so quickly.

"Over here, Lieutenant," one of his soldiers called.

The man was standing over several bodies.

"Looks like some of them are alive," the soldier told Lake.

In fact, three of the North Korean soldiers were still alive. Lake called for the platoon medic, a specialist named Thacker, and in just a few minutes he was treating the enemy soldiers.

"We're going to lose one, sir," Thacker said. "The other two can make it if we take our time moving them."

This was something Lake hadn't anticipated. In the rough terrain, in the darkness, it might take as many as four of his men to carry each of the wounded North Koreans. That would mean nearly half of his platoon, and although he was reasonably sure they would not run into another enemy patrol, he was not anxious to take any chances by tying up half his combat power as stretcher bearers. But there was no way around it.

"Get them ready to be moved," he told Thacker. Then, turning to Janeson, his RTO, he said, "Tell Sergeant Bladesly that we'll need a detail of stretcher bearers."

Lake saw Thacker bend down again, and then jump up.

"Holy *shit!* He's rigged to blow up."

The few men Lake could see in the immediate area scattered, but Thacker stood still. In spite of his fear, something was keeping the medic next to the wounded man, who was suddenly somewhere between patient and still-dangerous enemy.

Lake could see, under Thacker's flashlight, that the man had three long tubes of explosives under his shirt. There was a pull ring taped to the front of the tubes, and the soldier's hand rested loosely there. One of his eyes had swollen shut, and he followed his captor's movements through one glassy eye.

Lake stepped forward and, using his survival knife, cut the thick bandages that bound the explosives. Even in the moonlight Lake could see the surprise on Thacker's face.

"Check the others."

Lake's men worked quickly, following the example of their platoon leader. Before Thacker could get the makeshift litters rigged from ponchos, a figure crashed through the underbrush from the direction of Norrick's position. Lake could not hear what was said, but the soldier was talking when he should be working, and Lake wanted to clear out of the area as quickly as possible. He turned to the noisy group.

"What the hell's going on?" Lake asked.

Thacker was standing now, his flashlight resting on the ground beside one of the wounded men, casting a strange pattern of shadow and light on two or three men who stood near him.

Lake came up to the little group and saw one of his men, a corporal named Dreschler, holding the muzzle of his weapon against the head of one of the enemy wounded that littered the slope.

"What the fuck do you think you're doing?" Lake demanded. He could feel his self-control drift away in anger, even as he recognized that the situation called for calm handling.

"Norrick and Barrone had their throats cut." Dreschler was almost shouting, and the loud noises, sudden in the darkness, riveted the men around them. "These fuckers did it. Barrone's head is almost off; he looks like they took fucking turns on him."

Lake couldn't see Dreschler's face clearly, but he knew that the thin control the corporal had held up to this point was shattered. There was a noticeable stiffening in the atmosphere as the few soldiers nearby realized what was going on.

"What do you think you're going to do about it, Dreschler?" Lake asked, surprised at his even tone.

Dreschler drew back his foot in a quick arc and delivered a vicious kick·to the wounded man. There was a sickening thump of flesh giving way, and Lake felt his stomach drop. The North Korean did not make a sound; he was probably unconscious.

"I say we kill them all. They're no better than fucking terrorists; they don't even have any uniforms on."

Lake wasn't sure if Dreschler was smart enough to do

what he was doing on purpose: try to change the issue, to make the prisoners responsible for everything.

"Besides," Dreschler said, "if we carry these guys back, it will take most of us, and if there's any more of them after us, we'll get waxed. I don't want to wind up like Barrone."

"We don't execute prisoners," Lake said, trying to sound final.

Dreschler didn't move. Lake could not gauge the reaction of the rest of the men around him. In the dark they were inscrutable; silent, they may have been threatening him.

Another voice came out of the dark, from behind Lake. He couldn't identify the speaker.

"I say they're terrorists sneaking around in civilian clothes. If we'd caught them in the daytime, they probably would have pretended to be farmers or something. And besides, I'm sick and tired of fucking terrorists."

The voice wanted revenge, Lake realized, out here, in the deep dark of the Asian night, far away from the trappings of law, where no senior officer might ever find out what went on.

"We came out here to kill them, Lieutenant," Dreschler said at last, with some assurance that he was winning his point.

Lake was supremely isolated. Nothing in any of his training had addressed anything even remotely like this; this leader's problem went far beyond any textbook. Whatever happened in the next few seconds, Lake knew, would stay with him the rest of his life.

He walked quietly up to Dreschler, and paused, his face only inches away. He could feel the man's stale breath on his own face, could hear his shallow breathing.

"If you shoot him," Lake said, his voice low, "I'm going to shoot you. So if you've got the balls, you'd better do me first."

Lake hefted his weapon, and turned away from Dreschler, wondering if he had done the right thing, wondering if he was drawing his last breath.

One step.

Two steps.

He addressed the small circle of men as he walked.

"Let's get these litters rigged. What the hell are you waiting for?"

As he walked back up the slope, Lake heard Thacker's voice.

"Get the hell out of the way, Dreschler," the medic said. "I got work to do here."

20

30 April · Saturday · 0730 hrs

Lake left out the details of what happened after the ambush when he made his report to Major Bock at battalion. Bock sent the lieutenant back with a message for Isen that Tilden and the brigade commander, Colonel Hastings, would be visiting the Charlie Company position sometime in the next few hours. They would escort a South Korean colonel from the staff of the ROK Corps to which the 25th Division was attached.

Voavosa was standing next to Isen when Lake told him.

"You want us to do anything special, sir?" Voavosa asked.

Isen shook his head. "Charlie Mike, First Sergeant."

Voavosa grinned. "Roger that, sir."

Charlie Mike, the first sergeant thought to himself, *continue the mission.* Voavosa walked toward the platoon positions, where he had been headed before he stopped to talk to Isen.

Voavosa had worked for a lot of officers who, in peacetime, would have had a blowout at the news of so much brass approaching on such short notice. Even in combat, Voavosa suspected that some officers—he thought of Alpha Company's Captain Woodriff—who would have dropped everything to prepare some sort of dog-and-pony show for the old man. He liked Isen because the young captain knew when something was important enough to get excited about. That had proven true over the last year, and had stayed true over the last weeks.

"Charlie Company," Voavosa said out loud, though no one was around, "you're some lucky sonsabitches. Me and Captain Isen in the *same* company."

The senior officers drove up to a dismount point just south of the company CP. All vehicles had to be left there, hidden behind a small knoll, so that unloading supply vehicles did not signal the exact positions of the platoons within the town. Isen met them and they moved up on foot.

The South Korean colonel was much younger than Isen expected, about thirty-five. Even from a distance, before the vehicle was close, Isen noticed something unusual about the man. He found himself staring as the vehicle pulled to a stop, and it didn't occur to him what it was until all three colonels were out of the HMMWV. The South Korean officer was remarkably, obscenely clean.

Tilden had tremendous purple lines under each eye from lack of sleep; he had washed his face fairly recently, but Isen could see the telltale ring just under the collar of his green T-shirt that told him that the colonel, like so many of the men in his battalion, hadn't seen a clean change of clothes in some time. Hastings, who wasn't as dirty as Tilden, was sporting a torn and blood-spattered trouser leg. Isen tugged at the bottom of his uniform blouse, straightening the front.

The South Korean colonel had on a clean uniform. His face was scrubbed and closely shaved. His boots had a light, almost imperceptible coating of dust, and as Isen watched, the man wiped each boot on the back of the opposite trouser leg. He couldn't have looked more foreign if he had stepped down from a spaceship.

The ROK officer said nothing as Isen took the group with him on a quick walk through the sector. Instead, he looked imperially down his nose at the GIs, none of whom acknowledged his presence with so much as a nod. The contrast between their appearance and the visitor's, and what that contrast said of comfort, was not lost on them.

When they returned to the vehicle, the ROK officer finally spoke up.

"You have a fine defensive position here, Captain. You and your soldiers have done good work." He bowed his head toward Tilden several times as he spoke, as if to make sure that Isen's boss knew he was serious.

"I will tell my general that this sector is in good hands."

With that, the interview seemed concluded. Isen wondered if the Korean expected a salute. Tilden thought such grandstanding foolish and even dangerous so near the enemy, so Isen decided to skip the formalities. The visitor looked at him long and hard.

As he got back into the vehicle, the ROK officer said, almost as an afterthought, "This area would make a good avenue for a counterattack."

Hastings, who was in the back, didn't appear to hear the comment. Before Tilden, who was going to stay and was standing next to Isen, could respond with a question, the South Korean waved his hand and snapped his finger forward, and the driver pulled away.

"What do you think he meant, sir?" Isen asked.

"I'm almost afraid to ask, Mark," Tilden said as he watched the vehicle drive away along the stream.

Less than two hours later, while Tilden was still visiting Charlie Company, they had an answer.

Bock called them up and told them that they had just received a written order that each company in the battalion was to prepare a counterattack plan. Alpha and Bravo had limited objectives, close enough to each other that the units could provide mutual support. Charlie Company's objective was the highway that ran northeast-southwest, less than two kilometers north of the company front.

"I can't believe this," Isen said as he looked at the message David had received over the wire. "I thought he was talking about passing a *mechanized* unit through here, or an armored unit, maybe, to hit the North Koreans on the flank. What the hell does he expect us to be able to do against an armored force?"

Tilden exploded. "I can't believe the son of a bitch was right here with us and didn't have the balls to tell us what was going to be coming down. He tried to slip it in as he was leaving, the bastard."

Isen was surprised, even shocked at the news, but what he saw register on the battalion commander's face was more than that. Tilden was absolutely furious, to the point, Isen thought, of striking someone. He had dozens of questions for Tilden, but he had to wait for the storm to blow over. In the meantime, the battalion commander continued to vent, as if some sort of safety valve had given way.

"I knew they'd do this, the stupid fuckers; I knew they'd throw us into this thing once it got desperate."

His diatribe fell one noise level at the last remark, as if he had thought of a new angle.

"I should've expected that it couldn't be helped. They're on their last legs up there." Tilden paused, as if he had to catch his breath and get his bearings again after his reaction.

"Of course they know what will happen if they send a light infantry unit crashing into the side of an armored thrust," Isen said.

"Yeah, they know, Mark, but I don't think they have a choice. I think the ROKs must be expecting something to come down this highway, and they're not sure that they can stop it. Anything they do to wear it down a little will help them, maybe even save the capital. They don't have the resources to be choosy about which forces to use."

Isen could see what was coming. Tilden had, finally, to accept the fact that they had been ordered to prepare the mission, and at last, there was no way around it. For all he knew, the ROK units fighting around Seoul were up against the same problems.

"We're back," Tilden continued, "to the same problem as before: we have a unit that is tailor made for certain types of missions, but the situations don't always fit those missions. And if we're the only people available, then we get stuck with the job, and all the niceties of the plans they make back at the infantry school for using light divisions in low-intensity conflicts and all that bullshit go right out the window."

"Well," Isen said after they had stood in silence for a moment, "preparing a plan is a long way from having to execute it. Maybe we'll still get off the hook."

Tilden had no response.

Isen returned to his CP, where he met Barrow. He had David send the platoon leaders a warning about the counterattack mission. Isen planned to brief them late that evening or the next morning. He and Barrow then sat down to share a meal.

Barrow had somehow come up with three carrots. They weren't fresh, but they were the first things that either of the men had had to eat in days that didn't come out of a package of dehydrated food. Isen's gut still burned with diarrhea, but he decided to chance eating.

Barrow nibbled slowly at his carrot, trying to savor every morsel, as Isen told him about the order for the counterattack.

"Sounds like CMH time, sir."

It was a morbid joke, but at least it was a joke. CMH was the abbreviation for Congressional Medal of Honor; it was also an acronym for "Coffin with Metal Handles." The two things seemed, to the troops, like interchangeable awards for a dangerous mission.

Isen was aware of his responsibility as commander to present a positive image, though he almost choked on the attempt.

"The ROKs are getting desperate, Dale. I really don't think they'd send us in if they weren't at the end of their rope," Isen said, trying to sound convincing.

Barrow gave him a deadpan look. Isen could almost hear the lieutenant's mental wheels turning. *Right, Captain.*

Barrow didn't say anything, but continued to stir his instant coffee over the slight blue flame from a heat tab. The chemical fuel gave off an odor that always reminded Isen of burning plastic. Still, he was grateful to have it; even slightly warmed food was a great luxury. The two men stared at the flame, mesmerized by the steady color and the wispy, dancing light.

Isen looked at Barrow's dirty face, lined with exhaustion. He felt a remarkable kinship with the young man.

Though he didn't necessarily share Barrow's cynicism, he felt responsible for him, closer to him than perhaps any other man in the company.

"Any way you look at it, sir," Barrow said, breaking the spell, "the next few days are going to be biggies."

"How's that?"

"Doesn't sound like the ROKs can sustain this effort, not if they're at the point of wasting light infantry in counterattacks against tanks, for Christ's sake. If they don't stop the NKPA soon, the North Koreans are gonna be looting Seoul."

He looked up at Isen as he licked the spoon clean before putting it back in the pen pocket in his shirt.

"And whether or not we get out of this shithole," Barrow continued, "will also probably be decided in the next few days. All the cards are on the table."

Isen felt an incredible, gnawing emptiness, as if he were trying to piece together a puzzle without having all the parts. He was desperate for some solid news of American reinforcements, for some word that they only had to hang on for a day, or two, but not indefinitely.

Later in the afternoon, Isen and a three-man security element walked the route he had selected for the counterattack, based on his look at the map. He walked out of the small village and headed north, climbing the slight slope of the ridge that lay before the company position. As he made his way along, staying several meters below the top on what is called the military crest, he saw the southwest-running, flat valley that the North Koreans, if they chose to come this way at all, would undoubtedly use. His advance would run him into the southern flank of such an attack.

"What a great route for tanks," he said.

"What's that, sir?" one of the soldiers with him asked.

"Nothing. Just thinking out loud, I guess."

He walked to the end of the ridge closest to the highway. This was as far as his men would be able to advance; to go farther down onto the low ground was an invitation to the tanks to drive over them. But from this point, his Dragons would not be able to reach all the way across the valley floor, and the tanks, with their longer-range guns, could shoot at his men with little risk to themselves. He envisioned the attacking North Koreans, surprised and annoyed by the nuisance from the flank, turning suddenly and enveloping the ridge, cutting off their retreat. His men would never be able to move fast enough to get back to the relative safety of the company positions, a klick and a half to the south.

Isen stood on the low northern end of the hill and envisioned the whole thing played out before the unwilling audience of his imagination. His men, unable to get close enough to the tanks to do any damage, wind up doing little more than exposing themselves to long-range enemy fires. The tanks speed around the steep sides of the hill, their long-range cannon and machine guns eating away at the tenable ground so that Charlie Company is finally isolated on the ridge, as far away from help as was Custer on the lonely hilltop above the Little Bighorn River. The picture sickened him.

"All right, let's go," he said to the two soldiers with him.

"Seen enough, sir?" one of the soldiers said, without any intention of irony.

"Yeah, I've seen plenty."

Isen headed back to his command post to draw up his plan. Voavosa was not there. David and Murray had set themselves a place in the front room from which they could watch the north side of the house. Isen withdrew to what used to be one of the bedrooms. More than half the floor was peeling and curling up where rainwater leaked on it from a hole in the wall. He crouched against one wall, pulling his map case to him across the wooden floor. He was more alone than he had ever been.

Strictly speaking, an order passed down from the ROK Corps commander through Isen's own chain of command was a legal order. He was duty bound to obey. On the other hand, he knew that the order to counterattack against an armored force was suicide for Charlie Company.

He sketched on his map the only real possibilities for the approach to the highway. *Not much room for variation there,* he thought to himself. He put the map down on his lap and leaned his head back against the wall. He had already accepted his role in what was going on around him, accepted that he might die. He had also accepted that the role of a leader was to make hard decisions that might send other men to their deaths. As long as he had the leeway to make intelligent, informed choices, he thought he might even be able to adjust to that terrible responsibility. But now he had been given a mission that made little or no sense, at least not from the perspective he occupied. For all his preparation, he had never anticipated such a dilemma.

Finally, there was something missing. He didn't know enough about the larger picture to make sense of this senseless small part of it. It might be necessary, he knew from his study of military history, to sacrifice a small force in order that a larger effort might succeed. But none of those historical accounts asked how the members of the "small force" felt.

During the Battle of Midway, he remembered, one American torpedo bomber squadron pressed its suicidal attack against the Japanese aircraft carriers, only to be chewed up by the fighter cover. The Japanese fighters were then refueling and rearming on the decks when American dive bombers jumped the carriers. The Japanese were unable to defend themselves, and the resulting loss of ships marked the beginning of the end for the Rising Sun. Isen doubted that the pilots of the torpedo squadron knew how their mission and their sacrifice would fit into the neatly reconstructed historical picture of the battle. Like Isen's men, they probably knew that they were afraid, and that they might die. In that situation, Isen knew, there was little clear beyond the immediate concerns; there was no big picture. The men who had to do the dying were never around to appreciate the world they created.

Isen took out his memo book and made a list of the reasons he should comply, trying to work out, in an orderly fashion, something that resisted ordering. But all of the courses of action he devised required that he take his company into a battle in which they stood a very good chance of being destroyed. He was left, finally, with his duty versus his desire to stay alive. He drew a line down the center of the page. On one side, he wrote "Midway," on the other, he wrote "The Charge of the Light Brigade." He passed a long night alone with these thoughts.

21

Isen woke up to the sound of a noise just outside the hole in the wall to his front. His flashlight was still on his lap, the light fading. He realized he must have been asleep for some time. He switched off the feeble red light and paused to listen.

He heard the sound again just as he was beginning to think that he had dreamed it. There was someone shuffling through the debris outside the house.

In the darkness, Isen reached slowly for his rifle, picking it up by the pistol grip, wrapping his hand around it and sliding it off safe. He checked the magazine well with his other hand, trying to remember, in his sleep-muddled brain, how many rounds were in the magazine he had left in the weapon. There was no sound from the front of the house, where David was pulling watch with Murray and the company medic.

Isen brought the rifle up to his shoulder, to the fire position, then he stood up. His legs were wobbly from being still so long, and for a scary second he thought he would lose his balance. But he stayed upright.

As he took his first step forward, he had a nightmare vision that while he was asleep, something had happened to his company; the North Koreans had penetrated the position, the company had been caught off guard, things had fallen apart while he slept.

He stepped lightly toward the man-sized hole in the wall, which was marked by the just slightly lighter morning sky framed against its jagged edges. He did not hear another

305

sound, but a figure showed itself through the hole. Isen swung the muzzle around, placing the dark stud over the man's face, but just as he started to pull the trigger, he realized that he was looking at a middle-aged civilian.

"God*damn*," Isen breathed as he lowered his rifle. He leaned over, and the sudden rush of blood to his head made him dizzy. He placed one hand on his knee, holding the rifle loosely in the other. The man framed in the dim light attempted a smile, as if apologizing for almost getting his head blown off.

"American soldier," he said in heavily accented English. He raised his voice as he spoke, as Isen had noticed Americans did when they spoke to Koreans, as if volume could overcome the language barrier.

"Yeah," Isen managed to force out.

"This is my house," the man went on, touching the jagged edge of wall as if it were a wound.

"Oh," Isen said. He felt as if he had been discovered in a petty theft. He put out his hand to help the owner up into the room.

The man who scrambled up the few feet off the ground, entering his house through what used to be a solid wall, looked to be about forty-five years old. He was very thin, and, like the rest of the men Isen had been around in the past weeks, very dirty. Isen half expected him to be angry about the condition of his home, but the owner looked around with a fairly happy look.

"It is not so bad as it looks from the hill," he told Isen. He took a few steps into the gloom, then reached to pick up a small piece of the flooring that was working its way loose in the rain leaking in.

"May I come in?" he asked.

Isen did not know what to say, since it was the man's own house. He nodded dumbly.

The man turned over his shoulder and called quietly out into the predawn shadows. Within a few seconds, a woman appeared at the same hole in the wall. She did not contain her feelings about the condition of the house, but immediately started talking. Isen, who did not understand a single word of what she said, judged by her tone that she wasn't talking to either of the two men; she was talking to console herself about the condition of her home.

She got down on her knees and ran her hand along the floor, as if she could smooth out the cracking wood. She never stopped talking, but moved toward the front of the room, finally directing something of what she said to her husband.

Isen did not follow them through the small rooms, but sat back down with his thoughts. He watched the light grow in the patch of sky he could see through the wall. He turned his notebook over to where he had been writing in it the previous night, unhappy at the prospect of wrestling with the same question again.

A half hour later, the man and woman came back into the room where Isen sat with his back to the wall. The woman carried a dented aluminum basin, and Isen could see steam rising from it as she set it down beside him. The man stood behind her and handed her a bar of rough soap and a torn but clean piece of towel, which she passed to Isen.

"You wash?" the man asked.

Isen smiled thinly at the couple, and he felt their eyes on him as he knelt before the bowl as before some small altar. He took his blouse off, but not his T-shirt. He felt his smell might drive the couple away. The warm water pulled at the grime on his face, and the water in the basin muddied as quickly as if he had been washing his boots. He scrubbed at his face with soapy hands, running the lather up around his neck and his ears, where he could feel the sandy grit accumulated. He washed for four or five minutes, but still soiled the towel when he wiped his face.

He couldn't imagine anything more luxurious than that bowl of warm water.

Isen sat back on his heels and looked at the couple. He noticed for the first time that the man was carrying a pistol, an old revolver that looked as if it might be as dangerous to the shooter as to the target.

The man said solemnly, "I will stay and fight the North Koreans here with you."

Isen wasn't sure he heard correctly. "Pardon?"

"This is my home. I will fight," the man said more

simply, as if Isen might have trouble understanding English. "You will let me stay here with your men?"

At first it seemed almost laughable, and Isen caught himself wondering if his troops looked so haggard that this man thought he could help. But there was more to it than that, and the man, small and tired-looking in the dim light of morning spilling through the broken walls and windows of his home, was emblematic of a great resolve, and Isen believed he spoke for more people than just himself.

"Thank you for the water," Isen said to the woman. And then, to both of them, "Thank you, but you must go back to where you were hiding before. We will do our best to see that your home is not completely destroyed."

He saw immediately that he had spoken too quickly for the man to translate, but he believed that the couple understood what he was trying to say. He showed them out again, as if he were in his own house.

Afterward, he dressed again in his dirty blouse and LBE, and he walked out of the house to see how stand-to was going, and to tell his platoon leaders that he would brief the counterattack order within the hour.

By noon the sounds of the battle to the west had intensified above what the men were starting to think of as normal. A few hours later, Isen was sure he could distinguish the sounds of individual volleys of artillery and, every once in a while, the sharp smack of tank cannon. He called his platoon leaders to have them make sure the men were in their positions.

Isen was holding the wire telephone in his hand, standing just inside the doorframe of the house, when the first rounds of artillery fire landed.

There was no conscious thought involved with the movement, but Isen was on the floor and crawling madly for the corner of the room, where David and Murray had dug holes for them, in a split second. He could feel splintered wood and pieces of wall falling lightly on his back as he moved, and he wondered if the roof beams would hold. There was an alternate position outside the house, but he wanted to get under cover as quickly as possible.

David was huddled against one side of the hole, the

phone pressed to his ear. He shouted into it, then handed it to Isen. It was Lake, calling from his platoon position forty meters to the front.

"We got a report of movement from the OP on the ridge." Lake was screaming, Isen could tell, but his voice sounded incredibly far away. "I'm trying to get more info now," the lieutenant said.

Good, Isen thought. Lake knew that such a vague report was of little use, and he would press his soldiers for a more detailed picture of what was going on in the valley in front of them.

As suddenly as it began, the firing stopped, and the quiet reverberated through the few buildings in the town.

"Get a report from each platoon," Isen shouted at David before he remembered to lower his voice. "See if they've taken any casualties."

"Line's out," David said with some disgust. Without having to be told, he turned to his radio and began trying to raise the platoons.

Isen stood stock still just outside the house, his mind racing.

The artillery did not seem to have been directed by an observer; there wasn't enough fire for that. It was much more likely that it was harassment and interdiction fire, shot at the village solely because it was near a crossroads. But the fact that the area was targeted at all meant someone was thinking about it.

There were only a couple of hours of daylight left. The North Koreans favored night attacks, and even though the fires were too early to be used as preparation for a deliberate attack, it could be that the gunners were getting their range. He needed to talk to Lake's OP, to find out what was going on in the valley in front of them.

"Have you reached first platoon yet?" he called to David.

"No, sir, I'm still trying."

An awful lot of the business of being in charge, it occurred to Isen, was looking for information on which to make decisions.

"Let's go down there, David. Murray, you stay here."

David shouldered the radio and jogged over to Isen.

The two men took off in a low crouch, headed for first platoon. As they moved, David started to let the other platoons know where the commander was headed. By the time he got through to the mortar platoon, he was winded and his message went out in gasps.

Isen found Bladesly first. He was bent over at the waist, his hands resting on his knees, and as Isen came up he saw that Bladesly was looking down at something.

It was a soldier.

The boy was on his back, his arms spread evenly out from his sides. There were no marks on him, and for some strange reason Isen thought of the game they used to play as kids, making angels in the snow by lying just this way and waving their arms.

"I think the concussion got him," Bladesly said. "Not a mark on him." He lowered his head farther still at the last remark, and Isen thought he heard him curse under his breath.

"I can't figure out why he left his position," Bladesly said, trying to explain to himself as much as to Isen. "I just checked him a few minutes earlier." He paused, as if wondering what he had to do to keep his men alive. "Jesus," he said at last.

"Any others?" Isen asked tonelessly. Bladesly shook his head.

"Where's Lake?"

"Over there, in the CP."

"Check your wire commo," Isen told Bladesly. "I think we lost a good deal of it in the shooting."

He and David walked slowly to the first platoon command post, where they found Lake trying to radio his OP.

"What have you got, Mike?" Isen asked, crouching by the hole in which Lake stood.

"I've lost contact with my OP, sir. The line is cut and they're not responding to the radio calls."

Isen desperately needed to know what was going on up front. At the moment he was a blind man, listening for the footsteps of an attacker.

"Send a squad up there to look for them. We've got to know what's happening out there," Isen said. Then to

David, "Call the rest of the platoons. Tell them to stand by for an attack."

"Sir," Lake said, "I'd like to take the squad out myself."

"You need to be here in case the shit hits the fan," Isen told him, fully expecting Lake to respond.

"But if there is an attack in progress, I can't send a squad out there to run into it while I sit here," he said quickly.

Isen's mind framed a response. *You can if I tell you the platoon needs you here.*

"Okay, Mike," Isen said. "Make sure you stay in direct contact with me the whole time you're out there, and you have to be back by nightfall."

"Wilco, sir."

Lake would have liked an hour or two to plan and brief the patrol, but he recognized the need for urgency. For all any of them knew, the North Koreans might already be approaching their positions. The company desperately needed advance warning, and Lake wanted to know what had happened to his men.

Minutes after getting the instructions from Isen, Lake briefed Bladesly and Staff Sergeant Hall, whose first squad would go out with the platoon leader. He gave a quick run-through to the assembled squad of what they would do, and they set out with an hour of daylight left, hurrying across the flat paddies in front of the company position to the southern end of the hill. The high ground of the west slope offered no more protection, but at least gave them the advantage of being able to see what was around them.

Lake decided to follow the commo wire that linked the observation post to the platoon. But as they neared the far, northern end of the hill, the wire simply ran out. It had not, after all, been broken by artillery fire. Instead, the end of the wire clearly showed the marks where the cover had been stripped away so that it could be inserted into the phone jack. The telephone had been removed. There was no sign of the two soldiers who were supposed to be manning the position, not even a scrap of litter from a ration bag.

All the while they had been walking, Lake had been

preparing himself to find his men killed by artillery, or to run into an advancing North Korean element. He was not prepared for this. He examined the end of the wire where the point man had found it. He turned to see Sergeant Hall watching him, waiting for instructions. The man didn't want to wait, exposed on this hillside with the possibility of enemy around, for Lake to come up with a plan.

"Let's make a sweep of the area," Lake said. "Leave a fire team here, and I'll take a team with me. We'll come back here to meet you. If anything happens, make for the company position and we'll meet you there."

Better to be moving, Lake thought, than doing nothing. His team made a search of the immediate area, moving in a circle a bit off from the stationary element.

Nothing.

Lake looked up at the eastern sky, already darkening as the sun chased down the west.

Isen's voice crackled on the radio.

"Romeo nine one, this is bravo two two, over."

Lake knew his sitrep wasn't going to be very impressive.

"This is nine one, over," he said to the mouthpiece.

"What do you have, nine one? Over."

Lake figured he should have called Isen first; he should know what to make of the missing telephone; he should be able to tell his boss, who was sitting in the company CP on pins and needles, waiting for word of what was going on to the front, some information he could use, he could act on.

"Negative report, two two, over."

"You haven't found anything? Over," Isen said.

Lake looked up. North of the ridge, the valley was quiet and, as far as he could see, empty.

"This is nine one, the wires were not, I say again, not cut. The phone was removed, the team is gone. There is nothing going on out front, over," Lake said.

There was a pause, and Lake pictured Isen in the CP, holding the handset pressed to his face, wondering what the hell to do with a lieutenant who couldn't execute a simple mission. Isen would never chew him out over the radio, and Lake really wasn't too concerned about that at all; he just didn't want to let Isen and the rest of the company down.

"You have fifteen minutes, nine one, then head back in, over," Isen said.

"Roger, over." Lake couldn't think of anything else to say. The situation was suddenly very clear cut. Find your men in the next fifteen minutes. Period.

Lake hurried along the hillside now, describing a wider circle in his search, covering both the east and west slopes. He kept looking down into the valley below as it appeared and disappeared through the sparse vegetation, half expecting to see a North Korean armored column down there. The valley was as empty as the hill.

He checked his watch again.

When he had only four minutes left on the deadline Isen had imposed, he found his men. They were crouched in a small depression on the northeast side of the hill.

"What are you two doing over here?" he asked, barely controlling the anger in his voice.

"It got too hot over there when the artillery started coming in, Lieutenant," one of the men, a specialist named Steen, told him. "So we decided to move over here." Then, as if he were trying to figure out why his platoon leader was so angry, he offered, "We brought our phone with us; we didn't lose it."

Lake experienced the simultaneous feelings of wanting to choke him and hug him. But there was no time.

"Let's get out of here."

After linking up with the other team, he called Isen and reported that he had found his men and was heading back in. He tried to control the elation in his voice, tried to keep the radio call crisp and professional. But he felt a profound sense of relief, as if he had just passed a difficult and unexpected test.

The ambush patrol had been hard, but this mission had been somehow harder. He had made it up as he went along, reacting, without very much of a plan. And although they had not run into any real difficulty, hadn't even seen an enemy soldier, Lake had felt very much exposed on the hillside.

Most important, he had found two of his men that he had feared were dead. He had kept his unit together for another day. Lake was pleased with himself. He had handled it. He might make a good infantry officer after all.

They made their way quickly toward the company, hurrying against the dying light. Later, none of the men would recall hearing the *crump* of the artillery piece. They did hear the short hiss of the incoming round, and several of them had time to dive to the ground. The single round landed off to one side of the formation, throwing hundreds of pieces of hot shrapnel in a thirty-meter circle. Only one of all those pieces found its mark, killing Lake instantly.

22

Schofield Barracks, Hawaii

1 May · Sunday

For the whole sleepless night following the incident with the notification team, Adrienne thought about her role in what was going on in the community at Schofield Barracks. Riding behind that team, convinced that it was going to her quarters, she had glimpsed an abyss of pain dark enough to consume her soul. Other women had entered that abyss.

She had to do something besides stew in her own vile unhappiness and isolation. When she could think of nothing else, she called Bette Tilden. Delighted to have a volunteer, the older woman invited Adrienne to lunch on Sunday.

Adrienne was surprised when the door to the Tildens' quarters was opened by a lanky teenage boy who looked shyly down at Adrienne.

"I'm Adrienne Isen," she said, extending her hand.

The boy was clearly embarrassed, but took her hand. His adolescent awkwardness gave him away as a tall fifteen.

"C'mon in," he said at last, as if he had expected she would go away before he invited her in.

"Hello, Adrienne. I'm so glad you could come."

Bette Tilden glided into the foyer, wearing what Adrienne thought of as her battalion-commander's-wife smile.

"Darling, why don't you go out back and call your brother. He's working on his car." Then, to Adrienne, "The boys will be joining us for lunch."

"That'll be nice," Adrienne said as she flashed her gaze around the room. She wondered if Bette had made her sons stay home on a Sunday afternoon just to impress the visitor. Adrienne followed Bette to the lanai in the back of the house.

"I'll just be a minute," she said.

Another teenage boy—Adrienne judged this one to be about seventeen—joined her. The older one was much more at ease.

"Hi, I'm Jonathan," he said, offering a hand he had just dried off on some paper towels. "You must be Mrs. Isen."

"Please just call me Adrienne."

"Yes, ma'am."

Adrienne had encountered this oddity before. In the army, you were much more likely to be called "ma'am" than by your first name. Even the NCOs in Mark's company who were older than she was called her that. When she complained that it made her feel old, Mark told her she might as well enjoy it, it was the only executive benefit that went with the job.

"Did you meet my little brother?" Jonathan Tilden asked.

"Yes, but I didn't catch his name."

"That's Tom. He usually has better manners; he's been pretty upset by all this," Jonathan said. He looked at Adrienne intently, as if to see if he should be telling her this. "Not that we all aren't."

"I understand perfectly," Adrienne answered honestly. She decided she liked this kid.

Bette came out of the house, carrying a bamboo tray with four enormous salad dishes. Tom was close behind her, carrying a pitcher set that sweated condensation.

"I hope you like this," Bette said. "It's a variation on a green papaya salad." She placed the trays, which were garnished with banana leaves, on the table, and Tom poured them each a tall glass of iced tea. The light fare, so appropriate for the tropics, matched the light conversation. They tiptoed around the subject of the war.

Bette encouraged her sons to talk about school and sports and the upcoming prom. Many of the teenagers who lived at Schofield had decided that it wouldn't be appropriate to go, with so many fathers in Korea. Jonathan thought that the whole student body would decide not to have the dance at all, as a show of support for the children of military families.

"I don't think they care," Tom said, speaking for the first time.

"Of course they do," Jonathan said, looking at his mother with an exasperated look. *Here we go again,* he seemed to want to say.

Tom lapsed into a morose quiet, and Adrienne felt uncomfortable, as if she were intruding on a family fight.

"You know what we talked about, Tom," Bette said, in something different from her glib hostess tone. "As long as we support your dad, that's all that matters. We have our own community here."

The line sounded to Adrienne as if it had been used before, though it was not without sincerity. Adrienne was watching a woman try to hold her family together singlehandedly, in the face of terrible uncertainties.

"May I be excused?" Tom said without raising his head.

"Thank you for joining us," Bette said formally.

Tom stood up and pushed his chair back under the table. He turned to walk away, then twisted back again.

"It was nice meeting you, Mrs. Isen," he said. He looked right at Adrienne when he spoke, but she didn't think he saw her.

Jonathan was shoveling food into his mouth.

"Wait, Tom, let's head up to Haleiwa." He bolted from the table, then remembered his manners and pushed his chair in as he chewed furiously. He got a "nicemeetingyou," past cheeks swollen with food, kissed his mother, then chased out into the driveway.

Adrienne watched the two boys as they loaded boogie boards—short surfboards that kids rode on their stomachs —into the family station wagon. They were handsome young men, Adrienne thought, tanned, healthy, and singularly undeserving of what was happening to them.

When she looked back at Bette, the older woman was crying softly.

"I'm sorry," Bette stammered, "I must look like a fool."

"It's okay," Adrienne said, putting out her hand to touch Bette on the shoulder, settling it finally on her arm.

Adrienne thought she knew what was coming next, some sort of soul-defining revelation about how Bette was trying to cope.

"I hope I didn't ruin your lunch," Bette said, trying to smile through her tears. The woman's vulnerability was a surprise to Adrienne.

A phone rang in the house.

"I'll be right back," Bette said as she got up, seemingly relieved to be able to break the awkwardness.

Adrienne stood and walked along the back side of the patio. The Tildens' quarters backed up to some similar sets, also occupied by field grade officers, majors and colonels. The house immediately behind the Tildens' was closed up tight, which was unusual in this weather. The windows and doors were shut, and Adrienne could see where a dog's dish was overturned in the backyard in the uncut grass. She wondered where the family was. It hadn't occurred to her that there were newly emptied quarters over here.

"That was Barbara Michael," Bette said, emerging from the house. "She was calling from some quarters over past the elementary school." She looked down at a piece of paper she had in her hand, folding and unfolding it. "She's been with the woman since the middle of the night, and was calling to see if we could spell her a bit so that she can go home and feed her own kids."

Adrienne dreaded what she knew was coming next, feeling as if she had been tricked into being here for this very reason.

"Will you come over with me, Adrienne?"

It was too hard to back out at this point, so Adrienne tried another tack. "I'm not very good at people skills, you know. I'd probably get in the way."

"You can be a help just by coming along. And besides,

some of the women have practical, immediate questions about how to get back to the mainland and all that. Most of the survivor assistance officers are men, strangers to boot. Maybe you could help that way."

Adrienne was cornered. "I'll get my purse."

They took Bette's car; Adrienne had walked over from her quarters. As they drove down the one-way street that ran along one of the athletic fields, one that she had driven hundreds of times before, Bette made a wrong turn.

"I'm sorry. God, how stupid of me. I can't believe I did that. I don't know where my head is, honestly I don't."

Adrienne thought to herself, *I know exactly where your head is, lady. You're worried about your husband, and about your boys, one of whom isn't handling this at all; you're worried about what you're going to say to this young woman when we get there; you're worried about what you're going to say to your sons if you get one of these visits. And on top of all that, you're probably worried about what snotty little bitches like me are thinking about you as you try to hold it all together.*

Bette was clearly nervous, and that made her much more human for Adrienne, who saw, with a sudden clarity, how her aloofness must have hurt Bette. All along, she had been treating the woman as a symbol of something, rather than as a person in her own right. She had accepted the invitation, she now had to admit, because she thought she would find in Bette-Tilden-as-symbol some target that could handle all of her anger. What she found was a woman and two boys. Adrienne thought she felt a slight tugging at the glacial facade she felt compelled to project—always in charge, always cool and logical and detached, always above it all.

Adrienne and Bette found Barbara Michael and the new widow, a woman whose husband was a buck sergeant in Bravo Company, sitting on the lanai in front of the quarters. As they drove up, Adrienne saw the two women sitting quietly on plastic garden chairs. Adrienne had somehow expected the physical makeup of a person to change after such a shock, as if the old way of walking erect, or of speaking, or of meeting people, would no longer be enough in the changed world.

Barbara asked Bette if she would accompany them on a walk around the block; the woman was coming off some medication that the doctor had given her to calm her down. Barbara asked Adrienne if she would stay at the house. There was a two-year-old napping in the front bedroom, and so someone must stay close in case he woke.

Adrienne watched the three women walk slowly down the sunburned sidewalk. When they were gone, she turned and went into the living area. The quarters had exactly the same floor plan as her own, although this young couple had very little furniture. Everything was the same—the paint, the hideous dining room lamp that looked like an artist's version of a UFO, the gray floor. The similarities overpowered the individual attempts to carve a home out of the standard-issue quarters.

Adrienne sat on a wicker love seat that had been painted too many times. The creaking startled her in the quiet house. The sensation of being in the same type of house was unnerving, as if the tragedy could be easily transferred to her house, her own life.

She jumped at the sound of a turning doorknob. At first she thought the other women were back, but the door to the front bedroom came open slowly, and a small child padded out of the room to confront her where she sat on the love seat. He was dressed for his nap in a diaper and a too long T-shirt. Blond, tanned, and plump, he was the epitome of what the Hawaiians called a "poi baby," after the chubby appearance local children got from eating the starchy island vegetable.

He rubbed his eyes with his hands, and looked at Adrienne again, as if she might have disappeared.

"Mommy?" he asked.

"She's right outside, honey," Adrienne answered, confident that she could make up something to keep the child from panicking. "She's taking a walk. She'll be back in a few minutes, okay?"

"Daddy?"

Adrienne felt as if she had been struck. She had no answer.

The child turned and walked into the master bedroom, and Adrienne, trapped on the couch, could only listen to the child's bare feet on the linoleum floor.

Finding nothing in the bedroom, the baby went to the closed bathroom door and, perhaps believing that his dad was in that room, or maybe only hoping, he began to knock gently with the flat of his hand.

"Daddy?"

Adrienne felt as if she had been skewered, and she found herself fighting tears. In the sound of that soft knocking, she heard the resounding crash of all her defenses, all her walls. She saw how much patience and concern and time it would take to reconstruct so many shattered lives, and she knew that she could no longer be so guarded.

23

North of Ichon, Republic of Korea

1 May · Sunday

Even after two days of stop-and-go driving, Staff Sergeant Jeb Stuart Bartow of the First Cavalry Division was so happy to be back in the commander's hatch of his tank that he almost forgot about the ocean voyage. He had looked gleefully back over his shoulder as his tank rolled off the pier at Pusan, on the extreme southeast corner of the peninsula, catching a final glimpse of the ship that had been his prison for three weeks.

Bartow had been anxious to get off the ship, which was crowded beyond belief with various elements of the relief force. But he found the port just as crowded as the ship.

He had been lead tank in the platoon, and had tried to

follow the Military Police vehicle that was supposed to lead him through the winding streets and out to the countryside, where his unit could reconstitute, but he lost the jeep in a maze of civilian trucks. He stood on the commander's seat and tried to make visual contact with the other tanks in his platoon, but all he could see was a mass of Korean and American vehicles that moved with such a remarkable lack of pattern that the whole affair seemed to *writhe*.

He had seen, over the past days, some of the elements of the vast logistical array that the armored units needed just to keep moving. He had often heard the support system called a "tail," and after what he saw at the docks, he thought he knew what it looked like. Hundreds of trucks were spread out across the Korean countryside, shuttling back and forth with fuel, spare parts, maintenance teams, and electronics repair teams, all just to keep the tanks moving. And when the shooting started, as Bartow knew it would soon, the division would have to move thousands of tons of ammunition across the same choked roads and panicked countryside. He didn't envy the logisticians their task.

Since that first afternoon's link-up with his unit, they had been on a hard march, moving steadily north.

The tank in front of his had stopped some hundred and fifty meters ahead of him. Bartow took out his map and checked their location. He guessed that the platoon leader, in the lead tank, was somewhere near the crossroads that appeared half a kilometer to the north. He had his driver pull off to the side of the track, in the shadow of a small crossroads store. Two Korean children peered at him from the door, which they held open only a few inches. When he waved at them, the children pulled back into the house, although he thought he heard them giggle.

Within a few minutes, Bartow's platoon leader, a new second lieutenant named Reddle, walked up to Bartow's tank.

"What's going on, sir?" Bartow asked.

"I'm not exactly sure. The word I got from the CO is a little confusing. Why don't you jump down here?"

Bartow removed his tanker's helmet after telling his

driver that he was dismounting. Reddle was flipping through the pages of a notebook he had pulled from his map case.

"We're supposed to hold up for the night in a village just west of here," Reddle said. "That puts us about thirty miles southeast of Seoul, and, I'd say, about fifty miles or so almost due south of Uijongbu." Reddle dragged out the last syllable of that city's name, so that in his Tennessee drawl, it ended with a heavily weighted *booo*.

"That doesn't make much sense, sir. I mean, we been going hell-bent-for-leather since we rolled off the ship, and now we're going to hold up?"

In the back of his mind Bartow knew he was hearing only half the story. They had been hurrying since the roll-out at Fort Hood. Even the long ocean voyage was filled with map exercises, commo exercises, and as many drills as they could possibly do without actually moving the tanks, which were chained down in the dank holds.

They had been told, over and over again, that the GIs already fighting in Korea needed their help as soon as possible; that it was only a matter of days before the ROKs and the American light units were out of action. Now they were supposed to hold up.

"The old man," Reddle went on, "says it's a communications problem. We're getting conflicting information about where the enemy main effort is, and where they want us to hit the North Koreans."

Reddle knew more than he was letting on. His company commander had implied that some of the American units, which were out on a limb, might be left out there if it looked like the battle for Seoul might go to the NKPA. The newly arrived armored and mechanized units first had to defeat the North Korean drive for the capital. The commander of the relief forces had decided that this was not something to debate throughout the command, though the troops would soon figure it out.

But Bartow had picked up on Reddle's use of the words *main effort*. Up until this point, he hadn't entertained the idea that their main objective was anything other than the rescue of American units. He had been comfortable with that—it made perfect sense to him. The idea of rescuing

South Korea had been an abstraction, a pleasant side benefit of their dash north.

Suddenly it seemed that the larger, political objective might supplant the human one he had imagined every day since leaving Fort Hood. He had clearly pictured the beleaguered infantrymen hailing the tanks, and he conjured up the picture whenever he began to worry about what might happen to him personally. But now those imagined faces were being replaced with something intangible. In his rational mind, he knew that they would do what was necessary; they had to first win the war.

But he also knew he would not be able to stop thinking about those Americans holding out somewhere to the north, waiting for his tank.

24

Near Kumnu-ri, Republic of Korea

1 May · Sunday

Lake's men did not call in a casualty report. Instead, they entered the company position carrying the lieutenant's body wrapped in a poncho. They carried it directly to the company CP, where Sergeant Hall told Isen what had happened.

"Tell Sergeant Bladesly to see me when he gets a chance, sometime in the next hour. Have somebody bring Lieutenant Lake's gear up here to the CP. Make sure you get out all the signal stuff, flares and lights, and any platoon equipment he might have had."

"Yes, sir." Hall was surprised at the commander's reaction, or lack of one. He wondered if he and his squad had done something wrong, something that led directly to this result. Like Lake, he had felt pretty good about completing the mission, finding the men. Now he was not as sure.

"That's all," Isen said.

All at once and unexpectedly, he thought of Adrienne. He wanted to be near her, wanted to know that she was thinking of him, as if that could prove that not all the world was falling apart on him. He wanted to know that somewhere, normalcy still reigned, that some things were predictable and constant.

The next time he was alone, he promised himself, before someone else came up to him and asked him to do something, or decide something, or come look at something, he would mourn Lake. But it could not be now. He could not allow himself the luxury while so much depended on him.

The intermittent shelling resumed, so that Isen was no longer sure if it was harassment or a precursor to something else.

In the last light of the day, the soldiers of Charlie Company were able to see, just over the horizon to the north, the acrobatics of at least a pair of A-10s, the air force's stubby-winged, deadly tank-killers. Isen heard some of his men cheer as they watched the planes pivot and wheel against the darkening sky. After several days of sitting still, tormented by rumors and weakened by diarrhea, the men were glad of some sign that there was a friendly force still out there, fighting on their side.

But Isen saw something else in the aerial show. The planes were a dark sign, like buzzards circling over some prey. Their targets, Isen knew, were the lead elements of the expected North Korean reinforcements. The armored spearhead of the North Korean push was not far off.

Isen saw Voavosa's large shadow approach him quietly.

"They're headed our way, Captain," was all he said.

"Looks like it, Top."

"What are we going to do if we get the order to do that counterattack, and we know it's an armored force?"

Isen was surprised at the first sergeant's question. He had already briefed the company on the desperate plan; now he wondered how many other soldiers in the company thought they would get some reprieve, even if the orders came through. Isen looked at Lake's poncho-wrapped form, where it awaited transport to the rear, and he had a mental image of his whole company lined up just so.

"I guess we'll do the best we can," Isen answered.

Thirty minutes after twilight, Dale Barrow was still sitting at a crossroads a dozen miles to the south of the company position, a dozen miles from where he was supposed to be at the time. He checked his watch: 2005. Isen had told him to be back at 2000. As he rehearsed what he would tell his commander, he heard a truck approaching from the west. He got out of his HMMWV, and motioned for one of the two soldiers in the back, an engineer buck sergeant who had been attached to Charlie Company just that day, to follow him. He walked to the center of the road, and signaled the driver of the truck to stop, using a small red chemical light, no bigger than a candlestick, that he shielded with his hand. He figured he had at least a fifty percent chance of getting run over by a driver who was too tired to watch the road, or who was suspicious of anything moving after dark.

The truck pulled up, and Barrow jumped on the running board.

"How you guys doing tonight?" he said into the open window on the driver's side. If they noticed that he didn't use a password, they didn't show it.

"You guys headed into the ASP?"

A few meters down the road, east of where Barrow had stopped the truck, was the entrance to an ammunition supply point, an outdoor warehouse for all kinds of ordnance. Two hours earlier Barrow had stood outside the ASP as the engineer sergeant went in to try to procure some explosives. They had been turned down because they didn't have their paperwork in order. Barrow had then tried blustering his way in. But he abandoned the theatrics at the last minute, backing out with an ingratiating smile and a better plan forming in his head.

"Yes, sir," one of the dark outlines in the cab of the truck answered. "We got to pick up some explosives for cratering work we're doing in our area." The voice was gravelly with exhaustion.

"It's a bitch, ain't it?" Barrow said. "Have you guys been working steady for two weeks, like us?"

"Longer than that. I bet we've set cratering work in a hundred places in the last three weeks. We was at it before the North Koreans came across the Z, and we're still at it."

"Well," Barrow said, leaning in the window, "I hate to be the one with more bad news, but we had to move some of the stuff out of the ASP. The old man thought it might get too hot here, so we took a bunch of stuff to a spot farther back, away from the fighting."

The driver groaned, his head sinking onto the wheel of the truck.

"Let me see your paperwork," Barrow said helpfully, "and I'll tell you if you can draw your stuff here or if you have to go back."

"Well, I'll be a sonofabitch," the voice on the passenger side said, handing Barrow some folded papers. Barrow reached for the red filtered flashlight on his web gear.

"Better not turn that on here, el-tee," the driver said.

"Yeah, you're right." Barrow gave them an embarrassed laugh, then stepped off the running board and crouched close to the vehicle's body, where the truck's bulk would hide the light. The paperwork had the approving signature and job number noted in the right boxes.

In the cab, the driver gave his NCO a knowing look in the dark. *Fuckin' stupid lieutenants.*

Barrow reappeared in the door of the truck.

"I'm afraid you have to head to the new site," he said, passing some folded papers back into the dark cab. "Let me give you the new grid."

There was a shuffling of paper in the truck as the NCO tried to find something to write with. He dropped the papers that Barrow had just handed him onto the cab floorboard.

"Just write it on your hand, or something," Barrow offered.

"Shoot."

Barrow gave the man the new location of the ammunition point. He had selected the location himself; it was far enough away that he would be able to do what he had to do and be long gone before the truck could get back to this spot.

"Thanks for your help, Lieutenant," the NCO said

sarcastically. Barrow stepped off the running board and waited until the truck was out of sight. He signaled his driver, who brought the vehicle up.

"Bingo," he said as he got into the front seat and pulled the sergeant's approved ammunition requests out of his shirt.

"Let's go shopping," he said gleefully to the two engineer soldiers in the backseat. The buck sergeant shook his head in amazement as Barrow's driver turned into the ammunition supply point, which had not, after all, been moved.

By the time Barrow drove up to the dismount point, Isen had about decided that something had happened to the XO and the other men. Barrow started talking first.

"Sir, I know I'm late, but I have a good reason."

Isen nodded.

"I got a bunch of demolitions for us to crater this little road that runs from the highway south, right into our position. Up near the north end of this ridge out in front of us, the valley is squeezed by the hills on either side. I figure if we blow up the road in what's already a natural bottleneck, we'll make it harder for the bad guys to drive right up to our doorstep."

Isen showed no reaction to the news. The battalion S4, Barrow knew, had been trying to get explosives for days, but with no luck. He wondered if Isen suspected how he had gotten the explosives.

Maybe the old man already got a call from some supply peckerwood, wondering where the hell all the stuff went. Naw, I'm sure I got away clean, he reassured himself.

Barrow decided not to tell Isen about how he got the material. That could wait until another day, maybe over a cold beer.

"Sorry, Dale," Isen said. "We lost two guys this afternoon; a kid from third platoon named McKelvey, and Mike Lake."

Barrow suddenly thought of Lake at a company party they had back in the quad to celebrate the end of Team Spirit. The mental picture was of him laughing, obviously relieved to have done well enough to be accepted into the company as a real member. Barrow pushed the thought from his mind.

"I'm sorry, sir." It was time to move on. Barrow also could hear the approaching battle, like huge, growling dogs wrestling over the hills to the north.

"I think we can protect ourselves by blowing some craters in that choke point up there, sir."

"Where do you propose we do it?"

Barrow reached down the side of his leg to the cargo pocket and produced his map. He flipped it over to where it was folded to show where the axis of the expected North Korean advance crossed Charlie Company's front.

"The valley is pretty narrow right up here where the road turns off the highway and heads toward us."

Charlie Company sat at the southern end of a narrow valley, about fifteen hundred meters long, that was formed by low north-and-south-running ridges. At the northern end, the little road that ran on the valley floor formed a "T" with the highway that North Korean reinforcements might use to move southwest to Uijongbu. Such a move would take the North Koreans across the company front, but Isen wasn't willing to bet that the enemy wouldn't notice his company, sitting so close to their flank.

"We're supposed to cover obstacles like craters with direct fire, Dale, so we can shoot the bad guys when they slow down. If we don't have anybody out there, the North Koreans will be able to drive through after a couple of tries. If we do put somebody out there, they'd be all by themselves."

Barrow recognized Isen's tone. He was thinking out loud, playing the devil's advocate.

"But if we make it just hard enough to discourage the North Koreans, I think they'll stick to the main highway instead of branching off. They're going to be looking for the fastest route. The idea is to make sure this road that leads right up to us isn't the fastest way."

Suddenly Isen saw some hope for his company. Clearly the ROK Corps commander was hoping that the North Koreans wouldn't try this sector: if they found out it was protected only by light infantry, they'd come barreling through. But he couldn't very well leave it completely unguarded. That was why Charlie Company wound up with this peculiar mission. Just as he decided he liked Barrow's idea, the XO hit him with another suggestion.

"I'd like to go forward and do the cratering myself."

So that's what this is all about, Isen thought.

"That isn't your job, Dale," Isen said unconvincingly.

"Yessir, but the company is already short a platoon leader, and we have another platoon that's understrength; and there's no doubt that the first sergeant can do anything I can do—better, and besides, you did send me up front once before."

Isen thought about that first day, and how he had dreaded sending Barrow, or any of his men, out of the protection of the company position for fear of losing someone. But he had, and the gamble had certainly paid off. It was time again.

"Okay, Dale, you win. Brief me in a half hour on your plan."

Barrow hurried to his vehicle to fill in his driver and the two engineers. As he jogged along, he formulated a rough plan in his head. It occurred to him that he had been dreading being turned down by Isen. There was no reason he should be so happy about having the chance to go forward of friendly positions at night, with a good chance of getting himself and several other men killed—except for a deep conviction that this was a good plan, and that he could do it better than anybody else.

25

2 May · Monday

Isen approved Barrow's idea, and just after midnight the lieutenant was driving north, forward of the company position, the HMMWV loaded down with four hundred pounds of explosives.

They drove slowly up the small valley, hugging the bottom of the ridge on the right, until they reached a point about five hundred meters short of the spot Barrow had chosen for the crater. He signaled his driver to stop.

"I want you three to stay here; Sergeant Luden, you're in charge," he said, pointing to the engineer NCO and indicating the other engineer and the driver. "Me and Merritt and Lincoln are going to go forward on foot to scout this place out." Barrow had brought five men: two soldiers from Haveck's platoon, his driver, and the two engineers.

Merritt and Lincoln, the two soldiers he had brought to help with security, climbed out of the vehicle. Their nervousness was almost palpable. Barrow felt he should do something to calm them down.

"Look, all we're going to do is go up to the head of this little valley and establish an overwatch position. I'm going to set you guys up so you can give us some warning if anything goes wrong."

He thought he saw Lincoln flinch, but it was tough to tell in the moonlight. *Wrong thing to say, slick,* he told himself.

The three men climbed the slope of the ridge they were following, where Barrow thought they'd be less visible in the thin undergrowth. He led the way almost to the northernmost point of the ridge, where he set the two men in where he thought they could see most of the low ground on three sides, and where he thought they could defend themselves if need be. They had a radio with them.

"You got the callsigns I gave you, right?" Barrow asked.

Lincoln held up a piece of paper Barrow had given him.

"And what's your job up here?" he quizzed them.

"To let you know what's going on; not to get into a shooting match," Lincoln answered, sounding even less confident than he looked. Merritt, a slight kid who was eighteen but looked sixteen, stayed quiet.

"Once we get the explosives rigged, I'll be back for you. We'll blow the charges once we're all back at the vehicle. It should take us an hour, okay?"

The two soldiers nodded. As he moved away to link up with the others, Barrow felt as if he were leaving children who weren't old enough to stay without a baby-sitter.

Barrow had Onofrio, his driver, move the vehicle up closer to the spot he'd selected for the craters, so they wouldn't have to carry the charges so far. The engineers had loaded the vehicle so that the explosives would come off in the order they were needed. First came the fifteen-pound shaped charges: small, wastepaper-basket-sized canisters that stood on spindly wooden legs three feet over the surface of the road. These would blow holes, like large post holes, into the surface of the road. After that they would manhandle the forty-pound canisters that would do the work of laying open the roadway, tamping these down into the holes made by the shaped charges.

Barrow became absorbed in the heavy work, and he suddenly felt more energy than he had since they had arrived in-country. The steady movement and the single attainable goal of denying the use of this road to the enemy all made sense to him, much more so than most of what he had been doing lately. When they finished, he walked to the sheltered position Sergeant Luden had picked out for the detonator.

"All set?" he asked.

Luden was kneeling on the ground, and Barrow was looking down at him. There was just enough moonlight to show the man's features as he looked up and opened his mouth to speak. The sound of gunfire drowned out whatever he was trying to say.

"Get these holes blown after I clear the area," Barrow said immediately, already heading for the security position. "Then set the cratering charges and signal me with this when you're ready." He tossed Luden a red star cluster from his pocket. "If you see enemy in the roadway, blow it, no matter what."

He turned even as he gave this last instruction, and bounded off for where he had left Lincoln and Merritt, one hundred meters north and east. He ran fully upright until a burst of tracers sailed above his head like malicious shooting stars. He crouched, then crawled as he got closer, finally calling to his men.

"Lincoln, Merritt!"

He thought he heard an answer in between bursts of rifle fire, but couldn't make it out. He paused, listening for the familiar sound of the M-16 in between the much heavier volume of fire from the AK-47s the North Koreans carried.

"Over here."

He crawled to the sound he heard last, thinking that at any minute a burst of rifle fire would tear into him. He kept his head low, but the grasses all around him blocked his view, limiting whatever night vision he had, so that he couldn't tell what was going on.

He found Merritt and Lincoln exactly where he had left them. Merritt had a field dressing tied sloppily around one leg. Lincoln was on his back, his legs twisted sideways, as if he couldn't decide how he wanted to lie down.

Merritt, who had appeared terrified when Barrow had left the two of them, seemed calmer now.

"There was a patrol, maybe six of 'em, sir. We wanted to call, but they would have heard us. Then we was going to lay low, but they walked right up on us." He looked up from where he was fussing with the bandage.

"I got at least two of the fuckers." He nodded toward his inert buddy. "Lincoln went down right away."

"They must be scouting out this valley for the reinforcements," Barrow said.

He got up on one knee, but was knocked flat again by the burst of a hand grenade a few meters down the slope. He was stunned, and could see nothing but the imprint the flash made on his vision. He finally heard Merritt talking to him.

"What?" Barrow asked.

"I said, I don't think they know exactly where we are."

Merritt was on his hands and knees, one foot still touching Lincoln's corpse, peering over the top of the grass to his right front. He thought the enemy had approached from the eastern slope of the ridge, where the GIs had the least visibility. Barrow couldn't believe this was the same kid he had left out here an hour before. The lieutenant continued to shake his head, hoping to clear the ringing.

"I bet we can let them go past us a bit, and get them from behind," Merritt said.

Barrow picked up Lincoln's SAW and checked the drum. It was almost full. He swung his own rifle over his shoulder.

"We'll wait a few minutes, then lead with grenades before we move."

The night lit up with a great flash as Luden exploded the first charges, opening the holes in which he would bury the other explosives.

Merritt fell back to a sitting position. "I think I'm losing a lot of blood, sir," the boy said.

Barrow touched Merritt's boot. It was soaked. "Can you move?"

"I think so," Merritt ventured, "but not too fast."

Barrow listened for movement, but heard nothing. He wasn't sure if the North Koreans had moved back, or if his hammered eardrums simply weren't registering.

"I'm gonna give you a head start," Barrow said, worried about getting cut off. "I'll throw these." He started loosening the grenades on his belt. "You head back to the point I showed you where we were gonna blow the road. Tell Sergeant Luden to get everybody loaded on the vehicle."

Merritt nodded, not at all convinced he could make it.

"Go," Barrow said as he lobbed the first two grenades over the crest of the hill onto the east slope. Merritt was gone by the time the first exploded. Barrow remembered to close his eyes for the blast, and when he opened them he saw a figure moving below him, still to the north of him. *Haven't been cut off yet,* he thought.

He fired at the shadow, then heard voices off to his left, in the direction of the engineers. They were trying to work around him, get between him and where the rest of the charges were being set.

He pulled his last grenade from his belt and threw it far down the slope, due north. He started to move backward toward Luden and the others immediately after the explosion, wondering how long he had given Merritt to get ahead of him. All time seemed to have compressed and expanded. As he moved, he caught a glimpse of Lincoln's body, and he wondered what would happen to it if the North Koreans came rolling down the valley at daybreak, or before.

He grabbed the body by the boots and started tugging it after him. He heard the hiss of a star cluster behind him, and turned to see the red rocket streaking into the air almost overhead.

When he turned back around to reach for the body, he looked directly into the face of a North Korean soldier who'd stopped no more than fifteen meters away. Barrow's weapon was at his side, so he rolled to his left, down the hill. The North Korean soldier pursued him, thinking that Barrow had run away. When the soldier stopped to examine Lincoln's body, Barrow shot him at point-blank range.

He checked the path for other enemy, but didn't see any. He picked Lincoln up in a fireman's carry and stumbled in a half run back toward the vehicle. The two weapons and the incredibly heavy dead man beat against his every step, so that Barrow felt as if he were running in quicksand.

He reached the spot on the near, east side of the road, where Sergeant Luden was to have set up the detonator. There was no one there. Just as he felt the bottom drop out of his stomach, he heard the HMMWV start up, close by, where they had hidden it. But there was no detonator.

Barrow heard voices, Korean voices, behind him, near the base of the ridge he'd just left. He tore at the last pyrotechnic, a parachute flare he had taped to his suspender. He fired the flare, then got down on his stomach in a perfect, rifle-range-prone position behind the SAW. When the flare popped, he caught two North Korean soldiers in the open at the base of the hill, about seventy-five meters away. He fired at them and saw one toss his arms and rifle up as if surprised. The other simply disappeared from sight in the flash from the muzzle.

As he looked about before the flare went out, Barrow spotted a body halfway across the clearing of the road. Something told him it was Luden, and he convinced himself, unwilling to accept failure, that Luden was carrying the detonator.

Now all I have to do is get out there, he thought.

He waited until his flare died out, then he made a short rush toward Luden. No one shot at him.

He made another rush, longer this time, desperate to close the space. He never heard the shot, but he did hear the round cut the air by his ear. He hit the ground flat out from a dead run, tearing his hands and knees on the hard surface of the roadway, dragging and scraping his chin on the rocks. He felt as if someone had touched his face with hot metal.

Luden was dead, but still clutched the detonator.

He must have had a problem with the circuit and come out here to fix it, Barrow thought. *I hope the sonofabitch works.*

Barrow cut the wires where they ran under Luden's body, trying to maintain enough presence of mind to strip them and tie them into the detonator's terminal posts. It occurred to him that perhaps he could make it back to cover, but the thought of standing again was beyond him. He cowered behind the corpse, trying to control his shaking hands. He stuck one wire into a post, then he heard shouting across the clearing at the foot of the ridge. They didn't seem to be sure where he was, but were getting ready to make a run for him. He cut the second wire through, slicing his palm neatly on the edge of his survival knife. He shredded the plastic cover, working by feel as the wire was covered in blood.

Another burst of automatic weapons fire passed over-head. *Unaimed,* he thought to himself. *I can do this, I can do this.*

He got the second wire into the other metal post and looked up. He could see at least two shadows working clear of the larger bulk of the hill behind them. One of the figures fired again, and Barrow thought the man was at least as scared as he was, and was firing just to reduce his own fear.

Barrow was scant yards from the hole, and he realized now—too late—that he would probably go up with the roadway. He decided to wait for the advancing soldiers to take them with him.

As the North Koreans rushed past the narrow holes where the explosives were tucked beneath the road surface, Barrow shoved the plunger.

The ground swelled beneath him, pushing him away. He landed with the plunger beside his face, the sharp handle tearing at his jaw and ear. His first thought was that he had ripped his ear off. His second thought was that dead men don't feel pain. He had made it. He stumbled to his feet, turning as he lifted Luden's body.

He found the HMMWV where Luden had told the men to wait. The soldiers were crouched on the side of the road, watching to see if they saw Americans or North Koreans materialize from the darkness first. Barrow couldn't remember the password; the best he could do was call out a muffled "It's me, it's me!"

Onofrio, terrified because he couldn't tell what was going on down the road, and certain that they were about to be overrun by the whole NKPA, drew a bead on the lieutenant's chest.

"I think it's your lieutenant," Zendoff, the other engineer, said.

Onofrio lowered the muzzle of his weapon, unconvinced until Barrow was within a few meters. He got up and rushed out to meet the XO, surprised when he got close enough to see that Barrow's face was covered in blood.

"Where you hit?"

Barrow couldn't imagine what Onofrio was talking about. He put his hand up to his face, where he felt the raw skin of his chin and jaw, and a wet stickiness down his throat and into his shirt.

"I'm all right," Barrow said.

He let Onofrio help put Luden's body in the HMMWV. Then the two of them went back to recover Lincoln's body.

They laid the two dead soldiers side by side, and Barrow felt as if he should somehow apologize to them.

"Let's get out of here," Barrow said, throwing himself into the front seat.

In the back of the vehicle, Zendoff was tending to Merritt. "Sergeant Luden had trouble with the firing circuit. He sent us back to the vehicle and said he was going to fix it himself."

Barrow turned in his seat. He could hear, but not see, Zendoff tear open another battle dressing for Merritt's leg.

"Onofrio, you know how to get back, right?" Barrow said.

"Yes, sir."

Barrow didn't answer, but raised his hand where he thought Onofrio could see it, giving him the go-ahead sign. Then he passed out.

26

Schofield Barracks, Hawaii

1 May (local)

Adrienne sat on a stool in the galley kitchen of her quarters. She opened one of the drawers below the counter workspace and shoved into it some of the papers, unopened mail, napkins, pencils, and other junk that had collected on every horizontal surface in her house in the days since she'd last cleaned. She put a yellow legal pad in the center of the cleared space and wrote on the top line, "Dear Mark."

She wondered what he was doing at this very moment, as she sat, with the long light of morning reaching in the jalousie windows. She drew a line with her pen along the red margin on the left side of the sheet.

I've just figured out why I was so angry, she thought to

herself, listening for how her words would sound to Mark. But even as she said it, she wondered if it was true. All she had done, finally, was to find more questions.

I have been fighting a losing battle for control, the small, honest voice told her. *What I've found is that there is no control to be had. I even wanted to blame you, as if you had conspired in this thing, bringing us here even though you knew what might happen.*

But now I think of you and wonder what you're doing. I know you'll do the best you can. I also know that you'll be too hard on yourself, and that you'll expect more out of yourself than is reasonable.

The mental picture she had of Mark was suddenly strong, though she could only picture him in the surroundings she knew. She had once come into his office while he was concentrating and so didn't notice her. His back was to her as she stood in the doorway, and he was staring at a huge piece of paper he had taped to the wall—something he called a horseblanket—as he tried to puzzle out how to best organize all the training his company had to do.

Even then she had been angry at him for his reputation in the battalion. The other officers always talked about how much field time Mark Isen could squeeze out of a crowded schedule and tight budget, like water from a rock. When she once complained that he was gone more than he needed to be, he had told her he owed it to his men to take them to the field. They couldn't learn their craft playing intramural sports in garrison, he'd told her.

She'd watched him that day as he stared hard at the little symbols and different color notations he had made on the horseblanket. He was stone still for several minutes, and from where she stood, his strong back was framed by the chaotic mess on the chart. And that was the way she thought of him now, standing still and thinking amid some swirl of chaos. And it occurred to her only now, when he was thousands of miles away and doing God only knew what, that the fundamental difference between them lay in just that. She saw order as the natural state of things, and so was forever disappointed in people. Mark assumed that chaos was the natural state of human endeavor, and so could forgive others their shortcomings, as he doggedly tried to force order on things that needed ordering.

Finally, there isn't much we can do, is there? her composing voice continued.

"I wanted to let you know that I love you," she wrote under "Dear Mark," filling the top line. Below that, the blank paper stretched away empty.

27

2 May · Monday · 0130 hrs

During the time that Barrow was struggling to get away from the North Korean infantry, Isen was glued to the radio set, waiting for some word from his lieutenant. He listened so intently that when the first blast reached them, he jumped. Then there was a long wait of nearly twenty-five minutes—with no word from Barrow.

The sound of the second explosion rolled down the valley, a thick, stately presence. The flash lit the doorway of the house, and Isen knew Barrow's mission was a success. But he was still desperate for some word.

When the field phone rang next to him, he forgot that it couldn't be Barrow, and he grabbed it and used his radio callsign.

"This is X ray one seven, over."

"Mark, this is Bock," the voice on the other end said. "What's with the radio stuff?"

Technically, everyone was supposed to use radio callsigns, even on the more secure wire net. But it was an unwritten rule that it was more macho to bend the rules on the wire a bit, just as it was considered cool to stretch them some on the radio.

"I'm waiting to hear from my five," Isen said, using a shorthand designation for the second in command of any unit.

"I have a message here for you; it's cacked up, so you might want to put your RTO on."

"Cacked up" meant the message was encoded; it would come in groups of letters that David could decipher. Isen handed the telephone to David. "Prepare to copy," he said.

David had the message turned over in just four minutes. It seemed to Isen that the more bedraggled everyone else became, the more efficient David was. Or maybe the youngster was maintaining and everyone else was in a downhill slide.

David had written the message on short lines all the way down the page, just as it came to him.

WARNING ORDER
CHARLIE COMPANY EXECUTE AIRMOBILE 020530 MAY
DEPART CURRENT POSITIONS NOT LATER THAN 0500
ORDERS BRIEF IMMEDIATELY
S3

Well, Isen thought, *now we're really going to be in the thick of it.* Just for a moment he let himself forget about the men he had forward of his position as he worried over the new part they'd be playing, and where the hell they'd be going on an airmobile.

He heard what he thought should be Barrow's vehicle, and he waited for the XO to find him with a report. Instead, Voavosa came in some minutes after the vehicle noises had stopped.

"The XO's cut up a bit, sir. He's down getting patched. I thought I'd come and give you some word while you're waiting."

"Let's walk down to see him," Isen said.

"He got the road blown, but we lost two KIA, one the engineer noncom, the other was Lincoln."

Lincoln. *Another one,* Isen thought. *Another kid who'd been alive when the sun went down.* Isen pictured the serious young kid from Haveck's platoon. On a sunny Hawaiian evening not too long ago, Isen had been leaving the company area around seven when he had run across the soldier lovingly polishing his used-but-new-to-him car. The young man had been so proud of the work he had done that he invited Isen to go for a ride. Isen had obliged him, adding fifteen minutes to an already long day. Lincoln had never forgotten that gesture, and had always done his best work after that. Now he was dead.

Isen and Voavosa walked to where the company medic had set up in some brush fifty meters behind Isen's CP. They got a look at Barrow, whose face was pretty torn up, but who would be fine. Isen told him to rest for an hour or two, and left it at that.

"I have to go to battalion for an orders brief, Top," Isen said to Voavosa. "I want you to give the company the warning order. We have a PZ time of five-thirty, but they told us to be ready to move at zero five, so the pickup zone can't be far. Make sure the squad leaders refresh their people on airmobile techniques, especially the pickup."

"We're un-assing this place pretty fast, eh, sir?"

"Everything's happening fast now. I just hope somebody has a handle on it," Isen finished.

By the time Isen reached the battalion TOC, the meager setup had already been disassembled. Unlike operations centers in heavy battalions of mechanized infantry, with their dozens of vehicles to haul tents and radios and tables and chairs and generators and coffee pots, the light infantry division was positively Spartan.

Lieutenant Colonel Tilden favored a bare-bones operation. Isen, who had spent his first tour with a mechanized unit in Germany, was always pleasantly surprised to walk up on the battalion's nerve center and find that it consisted of a couple of vehicles parked near one another, with plastic-covered maps affixed to the camouflaged sides.

Isen was the only company commander present.

"Over here, Mark." It was Bock. The S3 was poring over a map sheet spread over the high top of one of the HMMWVs. He held a canteen cup of coffee in his hand, and he was stirring it slowly with a felt-tip pen.

"Where's everybody else?"

"Chris won't be here," Bock said, explaining the absence of the Bravo Company commander. "His company is already moving."

"Damn, we are in a hurry," Isen said as he tried to figure out what map sheet the S3 was studying. The only light was from a weakened chem light.

"I was going to wait for Woodriff. You and he are going into the same objective, and I wanted to brief you together, so you both got the same poop, but he says he'll be at least another forty-five minutes getting here." Bock looked into the cup. "I told him to let his first sergeant and XO get things ready, you know, brief the warning order. I think he thinks his company can't do anything without him."

Isen didn't offer any comment about his peer.

"Well," Bock went on, "let's you and I get started anyway."

He pulled the map off the vehicle and placed it on the ground directly under the winch on the wide front bumper. The two men got down on the ground, and Bock switched on a red penlight. He read from his issue memo book, and Isen prepared to take notes in his identical book.

"The ROKs are getting ready to launch a big counterattack from the area just south of Uijongbu, between there and the capital. They'll come around to hit the enemy advance on its left. The old man, and the ROKs, think the NKPA has shot its wad." Bock might have grinned at the obscenity; Isen wasn't sure.

"The bad guys don't have much, if anything, left to throw into this fight. Now's the time to hit them back. Our brigade is responsible for three air assaults. Our battalion is doing one, with you and Alpha. Bravo is going into the brigade reserve."

Bock had traced circles on the map as he talked, though he didn't indicate which units in the brigade were going where. The oversight was uncharacteristic, and it reminded Isen how little real sleep any of them had had over the past weeks.

"You guys are going into this little town here," he said, leaning closer to the map and tapping it with the point of his pencil. Isen hoped the pickup zone was close to where his company was now located, so they wouldn't start the operation with a forced march.

He leaned forward. Bock was indicating a village that was twenty or so miles due east of where they were located now. But it was north of Uijongbu.

That meant that it was behind where the North Koreans had been located on nearly every map Isen had seen in the last five days.

Holy shit, Isen thought. *These people have really lost it now.* He showed Bock nothing.

Bock drew a sketch of yet another village on a blank page of his notebook. Isen wondered why none of the Americans ever used the place names to designate these little towns; they treated them as if they were generic.

"There's only one good landing zone near the objective, here on the south side, right next to the village. Alpha Company will go in first and occupy a blocking position on the northeast. You guys will go in second and block to the west and southwest." Bock paused as Isen copied the sketch. Bock had never seen the town himself; the information he was passing on was third-hand—at best—from some South Korean civilians in the area, put together by the ROK intelligence section at the corps level. As he watched Isen draw, copying carefully, Bock thought of the children's game that they called Telephone, where a kid at one end of the line told a secret, which, as it was passed down was inevitably distorted so that it came out, at the other end of the line, virtually unrecognizable.

"Okay," Isen said, indicating that he was ready to go on.

"The commander's intent is to use the brigade to cut this road network"—Bock swept the point of his pen over an area of several square kilometers—"and deny its use to the enemy. The other two brigades have similar missions, one brigade on either side of us. I think we have the toughest job. The other brigades are part of a safety net, so to speak, to keep the NKPA from maneuvering. Our brigade is actually closing the door behind them, blocking the north-east-southwest corridor they used to advance. We expect them to try to back through us once they get hit in the nose."

The idea was simple enough, Isen had to admit. They would use helicopters to get behind the North Koreans, blocking their escape, then the ROKs would hit them from the front. He remembered the term "hammer and anvil" from somewhere, but the only steel in the equation would be in the retreating North Korean tanks.

Bock saw a pair of legs approach, walk once around the vehicle as if looking for something, then stop next to them. Then the owner of the legs sat down.

Tilden looked worse than any of the men in Charlie Company, Isen decided. Where he could make sure that his men got some rest, at least, no one was likely to do the same for the boss, and it showed.

"What's the word, Jan?" Tilden asked as he stretched his legs flat out on the ground in front of him, reaching in vain for the toes of his combat boots.

"I just went over the commander's intent, sir."

Tilden chuckled. He seemed, to Isen, to be genuinely amused.

"That's a good one," he said. "The ROKs are telling us that their counterattack is successful in the early stages. They've moved some fresh—relatively speaking—units up to lead this attack."

"What's the problem, sir?" Bock asked.

"We've been out of contact with division for a few hours, and, frankly, Colonel Hastings doesn't have a lot of confidence in the liaison officer the ROKs sent to brigade. But they're banking on two things. The ROKs now believe that their estimate of enemy strength was wrong. There aren't, and maybe never were, any significant NKPA reinforcements left to the north. That's why they feel they can take us out of this sector. And they're telling us that the American reinforcements are in-country, that it's not too early to commit our forces to this airmobile."

"That they're not hanging us out on a limb, you mean," Bock finished the sentence.

"Yeah, I guess that's what I do mean. If those boys don't get here soon, no telling what'll happen once we're spread out from hell to breakfast."

Isen remained quiet. He didn't exactly blame the ROKs for the lack of information; they were trying to keep a bad situation from getting worse. Apparently, they didn't have time to explain everything carefully to their allies. Tilden felt differently. The battalion commander was suspicious.

"I'll be going in with Alpha Company, Mark," Tilden said.

Then, suddenly very serious, he went on. "Listen, we can't put a lot of stock in rumors. We can't fight looking over our shoulders. We have to play this like it was our game, all the way. In spite of all the rumors, this may not be the last battle we have to fight before help arrives."

Isen looked at his sketch, where he had drawn a bold arrow, representing the retreating North Korean armor, pointing to his blocking position. *But there are other ways this may be our last battle,* he thought.

Isen and his leaders worked through the remaining few hours of the night, preparing their plan for the airmobile assault. Isen looked around at the circle of tired faces as he gave his order. They would not become completely nocturnal, he decided, because they didn't get much rest after dawn. But they had reached a point where they were no more tired in the middle of the night than they were in the daytime.

As Isen spoke, all of them could plainly hear the artillery duel to the west intensify as the South Koreans pressed their all-important counterattack. All during the previous day, the sounds had moved farther to the southwest, so that Isen imagined he could hear the battle front in its fiery slide across the landscape toward the capital city.

An hour before first light, Charlie Company was ready to move to the pickup zone, the PZ. Isen stood with Voavosa near the approximate center of the company mass. As with any operation, there was always a lull just before jump off. Though it varied greatly in duration, from minutes to hours, there was always time for the imagination's morbid work.

In those few minutes, Isen was surprised to find that he wasn't experiencing the same jitters he had up to this point. Some part of his brain wanted to panic, as if calmness meant he had missed some critical aspect of planning. But he found it easy to rest quietly next to Voavosa. Some soldiers stirred nearby, trading predictable banter.

"I can't decide what I want to have first, soon as I get the chance," the first voice from the darkness said, "a piece of poontang or a hot bath."

"I can solve that," a lower whisper came back. "I'm gonna have both together. I might get me *two* mamasans in the tub with me, and lots of hot water, and some good-smelling soap."

"Your tired ass can't handle no two women, hear? You send 'em my way, and I'll take care of 'em."

They expect to live, Isen thought, drawing strength from the simple optimism as if it were a comment on the trust they had in all their leaders.

The battalion operation was not a complicated one as far as these things went. Still, Isen was concerned because of the short fuse on this operation.

Alpha Company was to be picked up first, from another PZ. Then Alpha's two TOW sections would go in, slung on nylon straps under the bellies of the powerful Blackhawk helicopters. Charlie Company would go in next, once the helicopters had made the round trip, followed by Isen's attached TOWs, under Sergeant Han.

Isen had been relieved to hear that there would be two Cobra gunships running interference for the assault. These helicopters were slowly being replaced by the newer Apache, but were still quite formidable weapons systems. Isen supposed they'd come armed with their oil-drum size rocket pods filled, and plenty of ammunition for the nose-mounted gatling gun. If the LZ, or landing zone, needed a little softening up, these were the guys to do it.

It took Charlie Company only fifteen minutes to move south from the village and the defensive positions they were abandoning, to the pickup zone. They settled into the undergrowth on either side of their PZ to wait. In the dim light of predawn, Isen could see Marist crouched near a wall out in the dry paddy that would serve as a PZ. Marist waited to signal the helicopter pilots as they came in. The men, crouched in the undergrowth and drainage ditches along the sides of the field, would wait for Marist's signal to move to the aircraft.

Isen had David and Murray sit next to him, and he used David's radio, set on the battalion command net, to monitor Alpha Company. Woodriff wasted no time getting on the horn; his voice came up just as Isen picked out the sounds of the approaching aircraft.

"Papa one seven, this is Juliet one seven, I have no contact with escorts, over."

Woodriff was calling Tilden, reporting something that Tilden, who would control the Cobras with his own radio, already knew. Tilden didn't answer.

Woodriff repeated the call, and even over the static background of the radio transmission, Isen thought he could detect some out-of-place emotional note—exasperation, or the encroaching shadow of panic.

The division's artillery assets, Isen knew, had been one of the first things stripped from the American units and committed in support of the battle nearer Seoul. The division commander had protested loudly, but finally he was powerless, and had to settle for the promised support of South Korean artillery units. But the priority of missions for those units were, of course, calls from ROK units. The Americans expected to have to fend for themselves.

Now Woodriff faced the possibility of going into a landing zone without fire-support assets, and with an unclear picture of what might already be on the ground in the spot where he was supposed to land his troops. The battalion's four eighty-one-millimeter mortars were back behind the position that Alpha had just left, and so were too far away to support. Woodriff's own mortars, the two pop-gun sixties, would go in with him and so wouldn't be set up to help immediately. Isen didn't like the picture, and it was becoming obvious that Woodriff didn't either.

"Papa one seven, this is Juliet one seven, over," Woodriff called.

Tilden answered him. "This is papa one seven. I am aware of the problem. Continue the mission."

Isen heard Woodriff key the handset. The captain wanted to say something, and Isen could only imagine the effort it took for him to refrain from screaming into the radio about the injustice of it all. Woodriff was being sent—as was Charlie Company, within the hour—to do a job, without the basic tools he needed to insure the safety of his command. Isen thought about the earlier plan, the counterattack against the NKPA flank, and the reprieve the airmobile had offered. Now he wasn't so sure that things had improved.

In the hanging seconds of static, Isen could hear the helicopters approaching Woodriff's PZ. The show was going on.

Isen kept his ear pressed to the handset as he watched his officers and NCOs making some final checks, talking to the soldiers, reminding them to fan out from the birds, spread out, get down, look for the chain of command. There were a million details, and they couldn't go over all of them if they had hours and hours, and they had only minutes.

As the helicopters moved away, the strength of the transmissions faded. Isen could hear only scraps of what was being said.

But the tenor of the unidentifiable voices took a sudden turn, and then there were other voices on the command net—pilots, Isen figured, though they were without their usual panache, their cool tones.

Then a voice that might have belonged to Woodriff's younger brother screeched above the electronic din.

"I HAVE ONE SHIP DOWN ON THE LZ; WHERE ARE THE FUCKING GUNSHIPS?"

"One ship down, I say again, one ship down, Indian leader," a calmer voice repeated. The unauthorized radio callsigns were the hallmarks of army aviators, and meant there were more aircraft on the way. Isen hoped it was the Cobras.

Then Isen heard Tilden's voice, sounding, thanks to the accelerating blades of his ship, as if he were underwater. "We have to go around again; the gunslingers are coming in."

The LZ was "hot," Isen now knew, meaning that there were enemy there, waiting for the exposed Americans. Woodriff's company had lost at least one helicopter. Isen had just enough time to wonder if it went down with its cargo of ten or eleven soldiers on board.

"GET OUT OF THE WAY," Woodriff yelled.

Isen guessed that the lift helicopters were making another pass at the LZ, swinging in a wide circle so that the Cobras, late onto the scene, could punish the LZ.

"I HAVE TWO VEHICLES ON THE LZ." It was unmistakably Woodriff, screaming into the radio at the Cobra pilots. "GET THEM GET THEM GET THEM."

"This is Indian leader," a voice said out of some cool, removed distance. "I have the targets in sight. Engaging two light armored vehicles now."

Isen was a frustrated eavesdropper, trying to put together a picture from fragments of hectic conversation that fell to him from the ether.

More voices.

"Scratch one," the voice of Indian leader came back. Isen could hear, through the radio, the thrumming of the gatling guns mounted on the Cobras, reaching out to tear up the LZ and whatever had been out there to hit Alpha Company.

The airwaves went silent, probably because the choppers had dipped below the level of the hills surrounding the objective. Isen checked his watch, calculating the minutes left to his own PZ time.

"Pass the word that we got a hot LZ," he told David.

As the seconds ticked by and he held the silent radio handset to his face, Isen thought about the men fighting out there, struggling to gain control of a piece of land that he didn't even know the name of.

Woodriff came back on the battalion net.

"Papa one seven, this is Juliet one seven, over."

"Papa one seven, over," Tilden came back.

"Have destroyed the second vehicle," Woodriff said, panting for breath, drained. "Am moving into position, over."

"Watch your back, Juliet one seven. We'll reconstitute when the X-ray element arrives; out."

Tilden's voice disappeared into the frustrating nothingness. *Reconstitute?* Isen thought. *How many men did they lose?*

He gave the handset back to David, and, wanting

something to do, he walked out to Marist. The lieutenant was near the center of the PZ, still waiting to signal the helicopters as they came in.

"We got a hot LZ, Paco," Isen told him. "Sounds like Alpha Company was in some shit, but they have control now."

Marist simply nodded, keeping to himself whatever he was thinking.

Isen heard the big Blackhawks a good thirty seconds before he saw them. They swept around a hill at the south end of the PZ all at once, or so it seemed, filling the sky with their black, monstrous shapes, like huge prehistoric birds looking for a place to light. There were only six now, instead of seven.

The sound shook Isen. He could feel the vibrations through the soles of his boots as the helicopters, with a lumbering grace that seemed paradoxical in war machines, settled onto the dry paddy.

As soon as the ships were on the ground, the Charlie Company soldiers started to move from their covered positions to begin loading. But Isen saw some of the crew chiefs scamper from the ships and wave the soldiers back. His first thought was that the pilots weren't going back into the hot LZ. He hurried to the lead ship, ready to force the pilots, somehow, although they certainly held all the cards.

As he approached the first bird, he saw several of his soldiers sling their weapons and begin helping the crew chief unload bundles from the aircraft. One of the bundles trailed an arm in the mud as two men struggled to get it off the ship without dropping it. He counted the bodies he could see— at least a dozen. He watched as one young rifleman fell backward with his burden, pushing at the dead man, struggling to free himself from the corpse. The boy's mouth was open, though no one could hear his scream over the thunder of the great blades that cut the air scant feet above their heads. The spinning black arms bent the men over, as if their burdens weren't enough.

The off-loading set them even further behind schedule, but the leaders got the men on board. Isen put on a headset which he could use to talk to the pilot. He gave the aviator the thumbs-up sign, and the ship tilted forward, the windshield suddenly full of the earth as the ground slid away beneath them. Isen looked out the open door to see the battalion medics hurrying around the PZ, separating the dead and the dying from those who had a chance of surviving. In less than twenty minutes Alpha Company had lost, by Isen's count, almost one-fourth of its strength.

Isen brought his eyes back into the ship. He watched the crew chief leave bloody footprints where he walked through the aircraft.

First Sergeant Voavosa was in the trail aircraft. He had moved quickly down the line in the last few minutes on the ground, telling the platoons to adjust the formation for one less aircraft. They had responded well, sliding men into the groups with a minimum of confusion.

Just a year ago he had seen one such drill nearly ruin a company mission on a field problem on the island of Hawaii, where the division had its largest training areas. One helicopter was diverted from that airmobile exercise, and the sudden shift in the number had completely destroyed the plan. He had watched as soldiers rushed from one group to another on the PZ. The result had been a complete screw-up, with soldiers of different platoons mixed together at the landing zone, NCOs separated from their men, platoon leaders without their RTOs, without their platoons.

Voavosa had made fixing the company's airmobile capability his special project. First, he had drilled the NCOs, keeping them out on an open field on Schofield where they practiced various techniques for instantly reconfiguring the aircraft loads. It was more than a matter of squeezing men on board. Small units had to maintain integrity: the bosses had to know where the troops were before they could lead them. Voavosa had become the scourge of the pickup zone. He was sure that the NCOs thought he had lost his mind, but he had never regretted the work. Now he hoped that some of them would remember what he had done, so they, in their turn, wouldn't be afraid to be sons-of-bitches when the time came.

Voavosa gritted his teeth as the helicopter swerved viciously in the narrow valleys, the treetops only meters

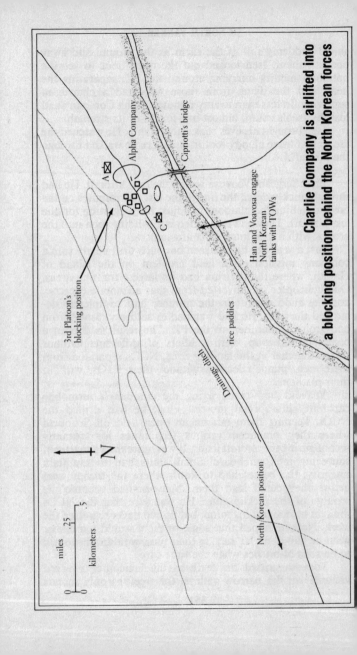

Charlie Company is airlifted into a blocking position behind the North Korean forces

miles
0   .25   .5

kilometers
0

N

Alpha Company

Cipriotti's bridge

3rd Platoon's blocking position

Han and Voavosa engage
North Korean tanks with TOWs

rice paddies

Drainage ditch

North Korean position

away from where he watched the toes of his boots in the open doorway. He had his map out on his knee, holding it pressed down against the suction from the prop with one large hand. But the birds were going too fast for him to keep up with where they were. He knew they were heading west, because the sun was at the chopper's tail, and that much was right. Anyone on the LZ, looking for the aircraft, would be looking into the sun. But Voavosa recognized only one landmark, and so would have to trust the pilot to put them down in the right spot.

As they neared the objective, he felt the ship pull back, slowing its forward motion. Below he could see a small bridge. No buildings were visible from his side of the aircraft, but he did notice a burning vehicle, on the south bank, that looked to be some sort of reconnaissance car. There was a dark path of churned earth that led up to the vehicle and then stretched on beyond the smoke and flames. *Cobras must have juiced him,* he thought.

Suddenly the bird was down, and Voavosa leapt from the edge of the deck. He took two steps and hit the ground, his heavy rucksack frame coming up to smack him on the back of the head. Voavosa turned his head to the side, pressing his face into the dirt, and watched the men in other ships leap and fan out. Some of them fell to the ground gracelessly, others struggled to save themselves from the impact, especially the ones carrying radios, machine guns, mortar ammunition, and all the other heavy items that they had to bring in on their backs—or do without.

In seconds the lead helicopter lifted off again, and Voavosa watched, fascinated, as one by one they jumped into the air, eager to get away. The wind from the ship he'd come in on pushed him down, driving dirt and bits of grass and sand into his eyes and nostrils. Voavosa watched, and just as the ship cleared the trees at the western end of the LZ, it exploded in a white-hot burst. Voavosa was stunned by the light, then the sound. The helicopter was gone, though the huge blades remained in place for a few long seconds, spinning eerily above the vanished ship, twisting and dark against the pearl sky.

There were more North Korean soldiers out to the west, Voavosa figured, armed with shoulder-fired ground-to-air missiles. If the enemy had been startled by Alpha's arrival, caught unprepared, they were ready now. The other pilots took immediate action, dropping even lower than the mere dozens of feet they were already flying. But another aircraft buckled with an explosion. Its tail snapped off completely, and without the tail rotor to hold it in place, the thick body of the ship spun with the torque of its engine, careening into the ground.

Voavosa had been watching, riveted by the macabre show, so when he heard a buck sergeant screaming at his men to move, the first sergeant jumped up as if he were a private who'd been caught napping in the motor pool. He ran toward the western end of the LZ, where he thought he would find Isen. He passed the men of the mortar platoon, who were collecting the sixty-millimeter ammunition, two rounds from each rifleman in the company. He saw the rifle platoons moving north through the edge of the village, which turned out to be a collection of even fewer buildings than the area they had left that morning, to the paddy walls on the west side.

Voavosa heard firing on his left, toward the river, and the men on either side went to ground as they searched for the firer. Voavosa stopped and got down on one knee when he reached the small east-west road that split the village and the company sector. He was not a foolhardy man, but he had learned how personal combat was, how much a matter of confidence, steadiness, and for him, as a leader, how much a matter of example. Whenever the men around him were prone, he would kneel; if they were kneeling, he would stand.

Voavosa could hear Bladesly, whose platoon had the southern part of the sector, near the bridge Voavosa had seen from the air, yelling to his machine gunner. Seconds later he heard the steady, reassuring bark of two M-60 machine guns as they scattered some barely visible North Korean stragglers in the low ground by the river.

The first sergeant surveyed the area. To the east, there were the several small buildings of the crossroads village. Alpha Company would be on the other side of those, blocking the northeastern approaches. The main road here, the northeast to southwest avenue that Charlie and Alpha were to block, ran straight through the center of the village. Parallel to the road and two hundred meters to the south was a fair-size stream—Voavosa supposed one could call it a river. There was a small bridge over the river, and the road across it intersected the main road in a "T" in the village. On the north side, some bald hills reached to the edge of the village, and lined the road where it went off in either direction. As he looked west, toward the pillars of smoke from the burning wrecks of the helicopters, Voavosa was looking across a good two or three kilometers of fairly flat, mostly open ground. All of it had been prepared for planting, and all of it lay empty. There was some vegetation —high grass and small trees—down by the edge of the river, and patches of undergrowth along the highway that led southwest. The western approaches to the village were tailor-made for tanks.

Voavosa heard the sound of jeep engines, and he turned to see Sergeant Han waving to him as he barreled down the main road from Alpha Company's side of the position. Han's jeep was followed by the other three TOW jeeps.

"Well, it's about time you showed up," Voavosa said above the racing engine of the vehicle when Han stopped. "I thought maybe you were going to miss the party."

"Actually, First Sergeant," Han said with a smile, "we were here first, and I was just coming to welcome you."

"Why don't you stash these buckets in some cover and you and me will go find the old man to see if he has anything useful for a couple of old shitheads like us to do."

"A splendid idea."

Isen was watching the dike on the near edge of the fields, near the southern end of his company's sector. Bladesly's platoon was trying to dislodge some enemy soldiers who appeared to be holed up there. The steady, light thumping of grenade launchers marked Bladesly's progress.

As Isen watched, he saw several dark forms spring up from behind the wall and try to race away from Bladesly's advance, running for the riverbed. They looked ridiculously small and vulnerable, Isen thought. It occurred to him that he had not seen any of the enemy alive, in the daytime, before. As he watched, several of first platoon's riflemen opened fire over the dike, knocking the running men down into the paddy.

David's radio crackled to life.

"Go ahead, Yankee three one," Isen told Bladesly.

"We got three, maybe four enemy KIA, but some of 'em got away. You want me to pursue? Over."

The thought of enemy soldiers running back with a report of the American stranglehold of the roadway bothered Isen, but his first priority had to be establishing the defensive position.

"Negative, Yankee three one," he told Bladesly. "Let's get set up here, out."

Isen walked his company position as his men worked frantically to get ready for the inevitable North Korean assault, from the southwest or the northeast. Word of the escaping NKPA soldiers got around the company even before Isen did, and the men put two and two together. Soon, the North Korean units responsible for the rear security of the attacking formations would know the retreat was blocked, and they would try to roll over Charlie Company.

Isen put Marist's platoon on the company's right, where he thought the North Koreans might try to use the hills to the north of the village as a way of getting into the position. He put Bladesly's platoon on the left, the southern flank, nearest the river. He had not anticipated the undergrowth there being so thick, and that side was suddenly more significant for all the cover it might offer an approaching attacker. He had Bladesly send a team out to recon the bank and set up an OP along that side.

He put Haveck's understrength platoon in the center. They were backed up against some of the flimsy houses, and they dug in behind the low earthen walls that bordered the paddies. Haveck's men seemed to have recovered from the shock of losing such a large part of the platoon on the first night. With fewer men to command, the lieutenant lavished more attention on each individual, not coddling attention, but exacting attention. He demanded, and got, hard work and results, and his platoon had a solidity that they had not had before the loss of the squad, as if that blow had driven them together in an effort to stay alive. Isen had no worries that Haveck and his platoon would not perform well.

"X ray one seven, this is papa one seven, over."

Isen recognized the voice of Tilden's radio operator. David answered, then gave the handset to Isen.

"X ray one seven," the battalion commander said, "meet me in the center, over."

Isen found Tilden waiting for him, leaning against one of the small houses at the center of the village. Tilden's two radio operators lay sprawled against their rucksacks at the foot of the wall.

"All set, Mark?" Tilden asked immediately.

"Yessir. Some enemy infantry got away from us. I imagine they've sounded the alarm, and we can probably expect company."

Tilden nodded, as if he knew, or was immune to, the bad news piling up.

"Alpha's in bad shape, Mark. They lost a bunch of guys coming in here. They don't have a good head count yet, but it might be the equivalent of a platoon." Tilden paused, and for a long moment Isen thought he might say something about how he could have done something differently to prevent the loss.

"There were at least two recon vehicles on the LZ. They got the chopper coming in with a heavy machine gun, and one of them managed to avoid the Cobras. Woodriff's men had to root it out of the buildings with LAWs, and they took a few more casualties.

"I've called for help," Tilden went on, "but they're not releasing the aircraft. They lost some on your side?" he asked.

"Yes, sir. Two of them went down just after takeoff. I don't think they were expecting missiles."

"I'm trying to get the Cobras to come back on station, too. But we're not having any luck there, either."

So it's just us, Isen thought.

"So it's just us," Tilden said.

The battalion that had deployed from Hawaii with nearly five hundred men, hundreds of thousands of dollars worth of sophisticated weapons, and the best training of any army in the world, was now going to meet the enemy with two battered and understrength rifle companies. Reinforced by a handful of anti-tank missiles, and the smallest mortars made, they now sat astride one of the major escape routes for a seasoned and desperate North Korean People's Army.

As he thought about their situation, Isen noticed that the firing behind him, down by the river, had stopped.

Nine miles to the southwest, the division operations officer was cursing the bank of radios mounted in his vehicle.

"God*dammit,*" he swore. The radio operator cringed in the back of the cramped HMMWV, even though he knew the communications problems weren't his fault.

Lieutenant Colonel Pat McMenamin was, at thirty-seven, the youngest G3 in the United States Army. He was a classic type "A" personality, and the only thing that kept the men who worked for him from hating his guts was the fact that he drove himself harder than he drove them.

"Try Second Brigade again," he hollered, directing his rage at the radio more than at the operator. The machines sat dumb and unaffected.

"Where's the goddamn CESO?"

The operations NCO, a master sergeant named Hadley, had already sent a runner to look for the communications electronics signal officer, the CESO, who would have the unpleasant duty of trying to explain why the G3 couldn't reach the brigade operations sections. The young captain would have to be a seer, Hadley thought, to be able to figure out what was going on in the jam-packed electromagnetic spectrum, but the G3 wanted him present.

"Send a runner for him," McMenamin thundered, and Hadley motioned to another soldier, who went off to look for the hapless young officer.

"Well?" McMenamin demanded as he leaned into the open door of the vehicle. His face was fiery red, the veins on his neck standing out in dark cords as he worked himself into a towering rage.

"Still nothing from Second Brigade, sir," the operator said.

"Try calling the battalions directly."

He pivoted on one heel and turned away from the

vehicle as the operator searched for the right callsigns. A few moments later McMenamin heard the operator calling one of the battalions that had been airlifted into the enemy rear. He turned back to the vehicle, determined to hear an answer, as if he could will the machines to speak. The amplifier attached to the radio was silent.

McMenamin threw back the door of the vehicle, slamming it so hard that the window cracked.

"We send those guys out on a limb and now we can't even fucking *talk* to them?" he demanded of the sky. He paused for a moment, as if to see if he would get an answer, then he walked around behind the vehicle to where a map board was posted under the cover of a tent fly.

There were so many symbols crammed into the area between Seoul and the DMZ that he could barely distinguish the units, but he did see that red markers, for the NKPA, outnumbered the blue.

McMenamin grabbed the side of the board to steady himself as a wave of nausea passed over him. He forced his body to hold itself upright. In less than forty-eight hours he would be dead of a massive, stress-induced heart attack. But even if someone could have told him what was coming, he would have stayed with his job—fighting, by sheer force of will, to force an order on events as the battle churned around him, and his unit (he thought of it as *his* division, though he had never said that out loud) was piecemealed out for the fight.

As he watched, a noncommissioned officer whom he recognized as being from the G2, the intelligence section, posted several battalion-size blue markers off in the less crowded space behind the North Korean advance. These were the units that had been airlifted to block the expected NKPA retreat.

"How come there's no North Korean markers back there?" McMenamin asked in an even tone. He rarely yelled at an individual, preferring instead to save his rage for whole crowds. Beleaguered though they were, few people in the headquarters felt as if they had been singled out for persecution.

"We're not sure what's back there, sir," the man replied. "We do know that one of the operations"—he turned back to the map and found the village occupied by Isen's and Woodriff's companies—"I think this one," he said, tapping the map lightly with a clean finger, "hit some scout vehicles going in. They lost three choppers and took an as yet undetermined number of casualties."

McMenamin hated when the headquarters types slipped into their formal staff language, as if they could sterilize what was going on in the field by talking like some damn field manual.

"You tell the G2 I need to know what the bad guys have out there. If I ever get commo with those battalions, I want to be able to tell them what to expect."

McMenamin and the division intelligence officer were peers, both lieutenant colonels. But McMenamin knew that his staff position carried the most clout, and he had the ear of the division commander. McMenamin wasn't a small-minded man, but he didn't hesitate to use his status to bully other staff sections, *if* he thought they should be working harder—which happened to be most of the time.

"But, sir," the NCO started. A little light went off in McMenamin's head: *Got a whiner here.*

"We've lost most of our intelligence-gathering assets, especially things that can range that far. We just can't see out there."

"I *said* I want to know what the fuck is going on out there," McMenamin spat, suddenly furious. "Now you tell your section that I don't care if every last swinging dick in the whole G2 shop has to walk out there on a mother-fucking patrol to see with your own two eyes—*I want to know what's going on!*"

"Yessir," the noncom said, turning back to his work.

McMenamin wasn't one to feel bad about rattling someone's cage, but he knew that a large measure of his edginess was due to the fact that the division was stretched dangerously thin over thirty square miles.

The ROK counterattack was to have begun at midnight. The plan called for a South Korean armored column to move north from Seoul and strike the left flank of the NKPA advance. American and ROK air force bombers were to attack the North Koreans as they tried to reorient toward the new threat, making the maneuver, and the retreat if there was to be one, difficult, even impossible. Forced into a corner, the North Koreans would be desperate, trying to win before American reinforcements arrived to bolster the ROK counterattack. The 25th Division was in just as hairy a position. If the NKPA turned northeast to try to escape over the thirty-eighth parallel, they would roll over the small blocking forces like so many traffic cones.

McMenamin shook his head; it felt clearer now, and he walked back over to the vehicle where the radio operator was still trying to contact the battalion S3s.

After he was sure that McMenamin was gone, the intelligence section NCO squatted before the map. He hadn't wanted to explain the half-baked information he had been told to post. On the lower right-hand corner of the map, well to the southeast of the main battle area, he drew a blue rectangle with the single slash that denoted an American cavalry unit. At the top of the rectangle, where the size marker belonged, he drew a blue question mark.

28

May 2 · Monday · 0820 hrs

Tony Cipriotti looked south, where the vegetation that lined the riverbed marched nearly up to first platoon's position on the company's left flank.

"Not very good fields of fire," he said to Boste, his partner.

"We're going to have to go out there and cut some of that stuff down. I wonder if it will burn?"

Cipriotti didn't think so; it looked too green. He was worried about North Korean infantrymen creeping up under the cover the grass provided until they were within hand-grenade range. Cipriotti didn't like the exposed position his squad leader had assigned him, but he could see where they didn't have much choice. Charlie Company's line, on the western end of the village, was too large an arc for the depleted company to cover adequately. Scuttlebutt said that Alpha Company had lost a bunch of guys on the airmobile, and so Charlie Company had to take up the slack and cover more than their share.

"We got an OP out there, right?" Boste asked.

He was looking for something hopeful, Cipriotti knew. "Yeah, they're out there." *We had LPs out the night the North Koreans got into the platoon position,* he thought, remembering how close he had come to losing the knife fight.

"Cipriotti," someone called from behind him. It was Staff Sergeant Hall, his squad leader.

"Sergeant Bladesly wants you up at his hole. He's got something for you to do," Hall said.

Cipriotti didn't like the sound of that message, but he pulled himself up and made for the center of the platoon position. There was a soldier Cipriotti didn't recognize standing near Bladesly's position. His rucksack was misshapen and appeared to be loaded with something other than personal gear.

"Cipriotti, this is Zendoff," Bladesly said, indicating the young soldier. "He's an engineer, and I want you to take him out to that bridge"—he raised his arm, pointing back the way Cipriotti had come—"so he can wire it for demolition."

Great, Cipriotti thought, *I think I liked it better when everybody thought I was a worthless shitbird. At least nobody trusted me to do anything.*

"Sergeant Hall will let you know how he wants you to leave and come back into the position," Bladesly went on. "Shouldn't be too hard. I think he can see the bridge from the platoon sector. He'll be able to keep an eye on you."

Bladesly paused, and Cipriotti wondered what kind of questions he should ask.

"Okay, Sarge."

"Don't call me Sarge, Cipriotti," Bladesly said.

Cipriotti and Zendoff walked back to where Boste was digging behind one of the numerous paddy walls. Hall and

Sergeant Lamson, Cipriotti's team leader, were standing over Boste.

"How'd I get volunteered for this little detail?" Cipriotti asked.

Hall looked at him oddly, but apparently Lamson thought he deserved an answer.

"Because you can handle it. It isn't a very tough mission."

"Compared to *what?*" Cipriotti asked.

"Quit bellyaching," Hall said. "Sergeant Lamson is moving over to second squad since they lost Jacobsen. You're the new team leader. Take Boste here with you. We'll keep an eye on you from here. We don't have an extra radio to send with you."

Cipriotti thought that since he was in charge, he might as well act like it. *What do I do first?*

"All right, guys, check your shit. Make sure you got everything you need," he directed Zendoff. "We ain't coming back to pick up anything you forget."

Boste and Zendoff looked into their ammo pouches, then Zendoff bent over his rucksack and checked the load of explosives he carried. Cipriotti looked over the boy's shoulder to see the paper-wrapped blocks of C4 plastic explosive.

"You got grenades?" he asked Boste. As Boste went to switch some grenades from his rucksack, which he wouldn't be carrying, to his web gear, it occurred to Cipriotti that Boste was actually senior to him, and so should be in charge. But Boste seemed better off being a follower. Cipriotti had learned in the school building that Boste was cool when it counted, but he had no business making decisions.

They left the perimeter less than fifteen minutes after Bladesly's briefing, making their way along the drainage ditch that followed the road leading south to the bridge. Cipriotti led the way, followed by Zendoff, who struggled to keep his footing in the muddy ditch under the heavy load of his rucksack.

"Why don't we just walk on the road, Sergeant?"

Cipriotti didn't answer Zendoff at first. It took him a moment to realize that the young engineer was addressing him. *He called me sergeant.*

"Because the ditch puts us at least three feet lower, and

the area here is open enough without us waltzing down the road," Cipriotti said with new authority.

They were within a hundred and fifty meters of the bridge when Cipriotti raised his hand, halting the little group.

"I'm going to go take a look," he said over his shoulder.

The early clouds had burned off, and the morning had turned brilliant. Cipriotti felt that the bright sunlight was a spotlight on him as he crawled forward through the muddy water. When he reached the bridge, he looked over the sights of his rifle at the other side. He could hardly believe that there was no one around. It was as if the bridge, maybe the whole village, had been forgotten. *Wouldn't that be good news?*

He turned to wave at Boste and Zendoff, who moved to join him. He posted Boste on the near side and sent Zendoff to work under the bridge while he crawled across to the other side. The stream flowed southwest, from Cipriotti's left to his right. As he crawled, he watched the greasy water slide under him through the spaces between the deck boards. The span couldn't have been more than fifteen meters long, but it seemed like miles as Cipriotti slid on his stomach along the dusty track.

Zendoff worked quickly, though Cipriotti checked his watch three times in the first five minutes.

"Yo, Sarge," Zendoff called from somewhere under Cipriotti on the south bank. *So that's what I sound like,* Cipriotti thought.

"Yeah?" Cipriotti leaned over the right side of the bridge. Zendoff was only a few feet away, standing with his feet in the water's edge.

"I got it done," the engineer said. "We just have to . . ."

Cipriotti didn't remember hearing the shots. The first thing he noticed was the splintering wood on the beam closest to Zendoff, and Zendoff dropping into the water. Cipriotti felt as if he were reacting in slow motion. He pushed at the edge of the bridge and rolled backward, toward the other side of the roadway. He had unhooked his web gear, so the belt and suspenders tangled up beneath him as he rolled, slowing his movement. Just before he dropped off the left side of the bridge on the side away from the

shooting, he caught a glimpse of a North Korean infantryman on the other side of the bridge, kneeling in some grass
just downstream and on the Charlie Company bank.

There was a small dirt embankment where the bridge
met the roadway, and Cipriotti sat with his back against it as
he fought for his voice.

"*Zendoff,*" he called under the bridge.

"I'm okay," the engineer called back.

"What can you see?"

"I don't see anything," Zendoff said. "You okay?"

"Yeah." *Just fucking great,* Cipriotti thought. *How the
hell did I get into this fucking mess?*

"I think I got a fix on them," Boste called from the
other, north side of the bridge.

"Okay," Cipriotti answered, a plan taking shape in his
mind. "I'm gonna toss a grenade, and we'll come across the
river," Cipriotti called to Boste. "You hammer them with
some covering fire when we move. Got it?"

He didn't know where the plan came from, but it
seemed workable to him. He pulled two grenades from his
belt, straightening out the pins for a quick pull as he
convinced himself it would work.

"Zendoff, you ready?" Cipriotti yelled under the
bridge.

"Uh, not exactly, Sarge."

"What's the matter? You hit?"

"No." He paused. "I can't swim."

Cipriotti fell back to a sitting position. *Isn't that just
great?*

He turned his attention to the North Koreans, wondering why they were being so timid about advancing if they
were concerned about the bridge. Then it occurred to him
that they would have had to pass the OPs to get where they
were, and that didn't seem likely.

*Unless these are some of the ones we thought we chased
away,* he thought, *some other nonswimmers.*

The platoon's machine guns had the range, Cipriotti
knew, and the fields of fire to hit anybody who tried to cross
the bridge, which would explain why the enemy stragglers
hadn't tried it. But the gunners wouldn't be able to see down
into the riverbed itself, and so weren't much help right now.

Still, with this rudimentary intelligence work, he felt more in control of the situation. These North Koreans weren't phantoms after all, but scared, trapped men. *Just like me.*

Cipriotti leaned under the bridge. "Boste."

"I'm right here."

"I'm going to toss the grenades, and me and Zendoff will start shooting. I want you to move upstream a little ways, then try to make it back to the platoon. They probably heard the shots, but I don't want them to walk right into those guys in the bushes. Tell Hall he can probably get them with mortar fire, okay?"

"Okay," Boste answered.

Cipriotti looked down at Zendoff, who had joined him near the roadway, and mouthed, "Ready?"

The engineer shouldered his rifle, and Cipriotti hurled the grenades as hard as he could toward where he had seen the North Korean. The throw was a long one, but if he at least kept their heads down while Boste moved, it would be enough.

The two men fired over the top of the roadway, though neither one of them identified any targets. Cipriotti was concerned about their running out of ammunition.

"Hold your fire, hold your fire."

He dropped near the water's edge and peered under the bridge, looking for some movement. He could see the small, smoking craters from the grenade explosions. He waited a long minute, then moved his legs farther down to the water's edge, where he thought he might be able to see something.

The water jumped across the surface in short geysers, which worked their way toward Cipriotti's legs. He scrambled back up the slippery bank in time to take cover behind the abutment. He leaned against Zendoff in the cramped cover, fighting panic. Though he had moved less than three meters, his breath came in hard bursts. *No getting used to the idea of someone shooting at you.*

"Looks like we're stuck here," he said to Zendoff.

"You're not," the boy said. "We could move upstream on this side, maybe, and you could swim back. No sense in both of us getting caught here."

Cipriotti looked into the soldier's eyes. Hope was sliding away.

"Hey, man, we got all the cards here," he said, half believing it himself. "Those are the guys we pushed off the paddies a little while ago. They're stuck on that side of the water. And we got more guys around than they do. Sergeant Bladesly will take care of 'em."

Zendoff looked unconvinced. "What if they make a move before help gets here?"

Cipriotti didn't have an answer for that. He looked off in the direction where Boste had disappeared, wondering how long it would all take. "Fuck 'em," he said, "we're staying."

Back in the company position, Isen told Bladesly that mortar ammunition was too short to use unobserved fire against suspected target locations. That made sense to Bladesly.

"We'll move closer," he told the two squad leaders he had decided to take with him. "Then we'll call for mortar fire, or we'll just root them out ourselves."

Bladesly studied the area from Cipriotti's empty fighting position. The only approaches were the frontal one, right across the open ground south of the company's sector, or east along the river itself. In order to take advantage of the cover offered by the river, he would have to go out the north side of the company's sector, move west a good distance, then double back. It would take a while, but the North Koreans probably wouldn't be expecting an attack from their rear. He explained his plan to the squad leaders and gave them five minutes to be ready to move.

Bladesly left one of his squads to hold the platoon's part of the company position, and he took two squads with him north, to where Marist's third platoon was holding.

"Tired of this place already, Sergeant Bladesly?" Marist asked playfully.

"Yessir. Haven't you noticed a pattern developing with all these podunk towns? I don't think they want us here."

Bladesly worked his two squads along the base of the hill that marked the northern flank of the company position. He noticed, as they passed, that Marist already had at least a fire team up on the high ground, where the east-west ridge was so narrow that a team could easily keep enemy infantry from running along it to get behind the company's flank. Marist wasn't going to give anything to the North Koreans.

Bladesly worked his squads several hundred meters west, then turned south to get into the low area around the river. They moved cautiously in the tall grass, still conscious that they did not have all the time in the world.

Cipriotti checked his watch. Boste had been gone for nearly an hour. He wondered if Boste had even made it back. He hadn't heard any more shooting, but the worst case scenario kept forcing itself into the fore of his consciousness. He began to wonder whether he could swim the river, somewhere upstream, pulling Zendoff along with him.

"You know how to make a poncho raft?" he asked the engineer.

Sergeant Lamson, Cipriotti's former team leader, had taken point because he was the healthiest man in his new squad. He placed his steps carefully in the grass, but still didn't see the rifle until he stepped on it. His first thought was *booby trap!*

Bladesly was close enough to see Lamson go stiff, and he moved up without hesitation. Lamson's right foot was on the stock of a North Korean assault rifle that lay discarded in the underbrush along the bank. Lamson was staring down at it.

Bladesly looked off to the side, looking for more evidence. He found some.

"It's okay," he said, coming close enough to Lamson to whisper right into his ear. "It's the stuff those guys dumped before they jumped into the water—the guys we got earlier."

Lamson turned his head slowly toward the bank. A few feet away he saw a bedroll and some web gear that a North Korean soldier had discarded just before leaping into the water. *This stuff must belong to the men we saw trying to get away,* Lamson thought.

He hadn't moved another three meters when a North Korean opened up at point-blank range.

Lamson heard the rounds sing by the side of his head as

he yanked back on the trigger of his own weapon, sending unaimed rounds in the general direction of the threat. He dropped to the ground, but the thick grass buoyed him, holding him off the mud. He squirmed to get lower as the other man fired again. These rounds went nowhere near Lamson, and he saw a flash of dark and realized the man had turned and was running away. He heard some shouting and suddenly found himself getting up again, stumbling heavily through the grass in pursuit. Two conflicting thoughts snapped through his head. *The fucker almost got me,* and *What am I doing running after him?*

Lamson tripped in the grass, then gained his footing again as he heard Hall behind him, calling to the rest of the squad, "Let's go, let's go, let's go."

They must think I know what I'm doing.

Something caught his foot, and he thrust his rifle forward as he went down, pulling the trigger when he saw the shape of a man through the grass. The silhouette disappeared from his view as he fell, but Lamson wasn't sure if he had hit anything. He tried crawling, but the saw blades of grass were too thick. He moved forward in a low crouch.

By the time Lamson found the first body, Hall had the squad moving up on the left, on the paddy side of the brush. Lamson could hear several of the other men as they broke into the open and raced upstream toward the bridge, easily outdistancing the North Koreans who were struggling to get away through the brush.

He knelt beside the body. The man was very small, not much more than five feet, with tiny, child-like hands and feet. Lamson's last shots had caught him across the lower back, and the American noted the small entry holes the rounds made. He knew that the wounds on the opposite side, where the tumbling rounds exited, would be large.

The Korean moved one hand. He was alive.

Lamson moved the man's rifle away from his side, then grasped the shoulder and rolled the soldier over. There was an incredible stench, and Lamson saw that the man's entrails had been torn open. The dark mass across his middle included whatever had been in his stomach, in his bowels. Suddenly Lamson was pushing back the bile in his throat. The North Korean's eyes fluttered, closing for the last time against the bright sunshine.

Lamson leaned off to the side, his stomach heaving. Somewhere ahead of him, his squadmates fired into the brush, shouting with the excitement of the kill.

Bladesly counted four enemy dead along the river's edge. He still thought they had been left behind because they couldn't swim. The river here was only ten or twelve meters wide, but with steep banks and a fair current. Unable to use the bridge because the Americans had it covered with direct fire, these men had been trapped, and had died less than forty feet from safety. He called his report in to the company CP, then he had his men toss the North Korean weapons into the water, where they dropped quickly below the muddy surface.

When he stepped clear of the growth onto the edge of a paddy, he glanced to the west, where a low rise in the ground marked the limit of what the company could see to its front, where he saw a dozen or so tiny figures hurrying into the open, heading toward Charlie Company.

"Get down, get down."

His soldiers dropped to the ground behind the paddy wall, or ducked back into the grass. Bladesly could hear the squad leaders issuing instructions to get the men under cover and spread out, even as he was thinking the same thing. He loosed his binoculars from their case and focused on the distant figures. Janeson, the radio operator, was at his side in an instant.

"X ray one seven, this is Yankee three one tango, over," Janeson said into the mouthpiece, using the suffix that identified him as Bladesly's radio operator.

"This is X ray nine five, go ahead with your transmission, over."

Nine five was Barrow. Bladesly didn't know where Isen was, but he assumed that the XO was in charge, at least momentarily.

"This is Yankee three one. I have enemy infantry in the open, moving across the ridge at"—he paused as he snapped his map open to read the grid coordinates, remembering to release the push-to-talk button so that the transmission couldn't be fixed—"at one seven one, three zero two."

He dropped the map and looked back up at the North Koreans. "Request fire, over."

The mortar section must have been monitoring the net, waiting for a call. The response would have been fast for a peacetime mission on the range at Schofield. Bladesly barely had time to get his compass out before the first rounds landed behind the enemy, to the left as Bladesly looked at them.

"Direction two eight zero," he said into the mouthpiece, "right one hundred, over."

The mortar platoon section sergeant plotted the correction on his board. He now had a location of the target and a line that passed through Bladesly as well as the target. He marked the correction—right one hundred meters—and computed the new firing data.

The tubes were set and the rounds sliding down the tubes in less than sixty seconds.

Bladesly heard the second set of *thumps* as he found the enemy infantrymen with his binoculars. Some of them had taken to the ground right where they were. In the open area of the paddies there was little cover. Bladesly was sure now that he wasn't looking at well-trained infantry, but at some reserve or support unit sent to dislodge the roadblock.

Satisfied that the formation had been broken up, or at least slowed, Bladesly decided to pick out some hide positions for Dragons along the riverbed. He sent one squad back to the company and kept one with him for security as he moved west in the grass. He was soon joined by Voavosa, who had come down to the low ground for the same reason.

"We set some Dragons up in here, we can really mess with anything that comes over that hill," Bladesly said, referring to the rise that was due west of Charlie Company's sector.

"I was thinking more along the lines of setting TOWs up out here," Voavosa said.

Bladesly could see the advantage. The riverbed, to the south of the company, and the ridge to the north, both ran east and west, and defined a kind of gallery in front of

Charlie Company. The mostly flat series of paddies and dry fields stretched for almost two thousand meters to the west. There, where Bladesly had just mortared the enemy infantry, a fold in the ground prevented them from seeing farther. The TOW's range would allow them to reach out almost as far as they could see.

"Those trees might be a problem," Bladesly said, pointing to the intermittent growth along the road that ran west from the center of the company positions, "if the wires are dragging."

"I'm gonna tell the CO that I think we should use the TOWs out here and send you guys back to the company position. We don't have enough riflemen to hold what we have, much less sending some out to an ambush site."

Voavosa called Isen and requested Sergeant Han's TOW jeeps. Once he had approval, he sent Bladesly and the riflemen back, and settled down to wait by what the troops were already calling "Cipriotti's bridge."

The sound of the approaching jeeps covered the noise made by the heavy diesel engines of two North Korean tanks that struggled to find a hull-down position behind the ridge to the west.

Sergeant Han found several good firing positions in the brush along the riverbed, and he briefed his drivers on the shoot-and-move sequence he wanted to use. They would engage from one spot, then move quickly to another position as soon as the missile reached its target, in order to avoid the counterfire that was sure to follow. When Han looked across the valley floor, he saw the top of one turret peeking just over the grassless ridge.

He spoke calmly in Hangul, and his crew immediately went into action. Voavosa, who was twenty or so meters away, saw the commotion and came running.

"What do you see?"

"I have one target identified. He's in a hull-down position just beyond where you can see those bodies out there," Han said.

"Well, it didn't take them long to get serious about opening this road, did it?"

Han went on in his own reverie of planning. "I think we should wait until he makes a move from there. I'm curious to see if there are any others. We need to get them out in the open so we can reach them."

"I wish we had some friggin' artillery," Voavosa said as he reached for his radio handset, "to hit them behind that hill." He crouched in front of one of the gun jeeps and called in the report to Isen. Above his head he could hear the smooth sound of machinery as the gunner, his eye pressed to the sight, swept his aiming point along the ridge, searching for a target.

Isen was in the center of the two company positions with Tilden, Bock, and Woodriff when he got the call about the tanks.

"We still need those gunships, sir," Woodriff said to Tilden. The battalion commander was agitated enough without Woodriff reminding him of the obvious, as if Tilden didn't know that they needed support.

"When was the last time we heard from them?" Woodriff continued. He was fighting to keep control of his voice, and Isen thought he could read on the man's face the picture of that helicopter going down with so many of his men, and the one-sided fight against the armored vehicle before they gained control of the LZ.

"How many tanks are there?" Woodriff asked Isen. "Did they say how many tanks are out there?" He took two steps, as if he were going to start pacing, then turned back to Isen. *"Damn,"* he said.

Bock was on his radio, trying to raise his assistant S3, who was out looking for the Cobra support.

There was plenty of reason to panic, Isen thought as he watched Woodriff. The fields to the west of the village didn't have adequate cover to hide a tank's approach, but with imaginative use of artillery and smoke, the armor could be on them before they could do much about it.

Isen thought about how he might get his company out of the village if they were overrun. He got on his net and called Barrow.

"X ray nine five," Isen said, "alert the platoons, make sure we have a good distribution of the anti-tank stuff. I'll be there in a few, out."

Isen was walking back to Charlie Company's trace when Bock came through on the battalion net.

"X ray one seven, this is papa six five, over."

"X ray one seven, over," Isen answered as he walked. David stepped in front of the commander so Isen could easily use the handset as they walked.

"I have two alpha one zeroes coming on station in three minutes. I'm going to turn them over to you, over."

Isen couldn't believe the luck of his timing. Bock was turning over control of two air force A-10s, which would be in position to support them in three minutes. Isen figured that Bock, who usually controlled such assets, must be busy with Alpha Company. It would be up to Isen to direct the pilots of the aircraft against the tank or tanks he suspected were hiding just out of sight.

"Understand three minutes, over," Isen checked.

"Affirmative. I'll call you with any changes, over."

"X ray one seven, out."

Isen broke into a slow run, conscious of David having to carry the heavier load. He did a quick analysis of the problem. Unlike his first encounter with North Korean armor, these guys seemed to hold all the cards: there was no approaching darkness, no close quarters of woods, and very little promise of surprise. The air force was a godsend.

They reached a point near Marist's CP on the company's northern flank from which he thought he would be able to see what was going on. There were no tanks visible, but the platoon had gone into a sudden frenzy of activity when they got the report. Marist knew that if the tanks couldn't be stopped with missiles, the infantrymen would have to withdraw completely into the village. Staying in the clear by the paddy wall, which was separated from the nearest village buildings and trees by thirty meters in some places, would be suicide.

Isen called Voavosa on a land line that had just been put in.

"Where are the targets?"

"We haven't seen them for a few minutes," Voavosa said. "I've been watching the spot where Han said he saw one, but nothing's moving out there. What do you have?"

"I have two A-10s coming in"—Isen looked at his watch—"in less than a minute. I'm looking for targets."

Voavosa lowered the telephone and addressed Han. "Anybody see anything?"

Han checked with his gunners. They had no targets.

"Nothing out here, Captain," Voavosa said. "Why don't you have the mortars drop a marker round at Bladesly's last correction to give the pilots a look at the area we're talking about?"

Isen sent the message to Richards, the mortar section sergeant.

The aviators came up on his net before the mortars could respond.

"X ray one seven, this is brewery flight leader. Do you have targets for me?" *What a strange handle,* Isen thought. The voice sounded close by, but Isen did not yet hear the aircraft.

"I have marker rounds coming in . . ."

"Negative, negative, X ray one seven," the pilot said frantically. "We're too close. No indirect fire. I say again, no indirect fire."

Isen called a cease-fire to the mortars. There was a slim chance—very slim—that a mortar round might cross paths with one of the low-flying aircraft. The aviators, understandably, weren't interested in testing their luck.

Isen talked the planes in, identifying the terrain features for them. Marist offered to pop a smoke grenade to mark the friendly position, but Isen wasn't sure that the North Koreans knew exactly where the Americans were located. He didn't want to help them.

His initial elation about having the aircraft was dimming; he wasn't sure how well the pilots would be able to find targets, flying as fast as they were.

The planes came in from the south, turning sharply west above the village that Charlie Company occupied. The aircraft demonstrated their tight turning radius, passing directly over the low hill to the west behind which, Voavosa was sure, the North Koreans were hiding.

"You've got to see them now," Voavosa said to the distant pilots. He waited for the streak of rockets and the steady ripping sounds of the planes' thirty-millimeter tank-busting guns. He was sure the aircraft would be able to find other targets west of the hill, hitting them before they came down to make trouble for Charlie Company. The aircraft made two passes over the ridge and withdrew.

"Understand, flight leader," Isen said. He dropped the handset. "The A-10s couldn't find any targets," he told Marist, who was kneeling nearby, watching the efforts through binoculars. "They're out of gas."

"Where the hell are they going?" Voavosa said as he lowered his glasses to search the wide sky for the planes he thought would save them. "I can't believe they couldn't see any targets. What the hell do I have to do, stand on the tanks and fucking wave? What were they looking at?"

Han was still watching the ridge through his own glasses, thinking that the North Korean tankers were smarter than the infantry they had just engaged. The tankers had been smart enough to hide.

Two thousand meters to the west, Lieutenant Kim Chi'o peered out the open hatch of his tank at the circle of blue sky above his head. The American planes were gone.

Two days earlier, similar planes—they looked like crosses when they dove at you—had jumped the remnants of the armor battalion to which Kim belonged. In a matter of minutes they had reduced to charred wreckage one of the few North Korean armored units that had any semblance of its original strength left. Since that time, Kim's tank and the other tank that remained from his company had been shuffled about the battlefield. No one bothered to form the remaining tanks into a new unit, and no one seemed to know what to do with the survivors. Only hours earlier he had been ordered to proceed to this crossroads, take charge of the troops already there, and force a breakthrough of an American blocking position. Without being told he knew that this road would be used to sustain a retreat of whatever forces were left behind him, to the west.

Kim didn't have a lofty, general's view of what was

going on around Uijongbu, and he knew the battle extended far beyond what he could see. But he was no fool either.

The NKPA and the South Korean Army were in a death struggle. All of the plans he had learned in his training, the plans that called for stinging dashes into the fine South Korean road system, had been discarded. The two armies were locked in the northwestern corner of South Korea, determined to settle everything there. And Kim saw that his army wasn't faring well. The South Koreans merely had to hold on until American help arrived. The North Koreans, working with much longer supply routes, had to break the ROKs, take Seoul, *and* consolidate their gains enough to withstand an American attack. And they had to be politically deft enough to use America's distaste for war against her, so that the American people clamored for a return of their forces from the peninsula before the U.S. Army could bring its considerable weight to bear on the NKPA.

But during the past thirty-six hours, Kim had heard frightening rumors about a South Korean counterattack that had broken the spearhead of the NKPA advance. Just that morning, several hours before dawn, he had come across two fuel trucks headed *east,* away from the battle. The sergeant in charge of the vehicles had all but refused the order to stop and give him fuel. Kim had even seen a combat command center, its vehicles laden with radios and map boards, moving to the rear in the darkness. Everyone he met seemed more concerned with what was behind the army than with what was to the front.

The high command was trying to create a rear guard that could keep the road clear behind the reeling North Korean formations. Kim knew that much from his latest orders. But the support area, the area behind the main battle, was a tangle of units. Supply columns tried to move stores forward to feed the insatiable need for fuel and ammunition; medical units scoured the battlefield to treat and evacuate the wounded; maintenance units tried to fix broken and combat-damaged vehicles as close to the front as possible, so that the weapons could be turned around and sent back into the fight; and everywhere, it seemed to Kim, there were dazed men and fragmented units wandering aimlessly in the wake of the violence. Turning around, the army found the escape routes blocked by its own tail.

Kim, quite frankly, thought the jig was up. And he was not at all eager to die in what he was already thinking of as a lost battle.

Kim also had no illusions about his abilities as an officer. He knew that his men thought he didn't even look like a tanker. He was slight, even for a Korean, and fair enough to be a woman. More than that, he was terrified of the machines he commanded, even in peacetime. On maneuvers, he almost always let another lieutenant take the front position for the company. Even in his platoon he encouraged the other tank commanders, NCOs with more experience, to lead. He was content to hang back, to follow.

When his tank had been hit by shrapnel from exploding artillery, tearing away the communications equipment, he had been so afraid that he had lost control of his bowels. He was sure his crewmen knew it, even with the overpowering stench of burned powder in the tank. But they hadn't let on if they did.

Kim didn't think of himself as a coward, exactly, but he knew he was no hero. But his best chance of survival—his overriding concern at this point—was to carry out his orders to break this roadblock and be one of the first headed back across the thirty-eighth parallel. He feared the Americans, with their remarkable weapons and their far-reaching air power. He wanted terribly to be anywhere else in the universe but here, but he had no choice. He would gladly have let another officer, even one junior to him, take charge of the situation at the roadblock, but there were no other officers present. It was up to him.

His goal lay just on the other side of this small crossroads.

As he looked around at the confused scene behind the cover of the ridge, Kim thought that even he looked like a soldier in comparison to the reserve company of engineers that had occupied the crossroads. The unit had lost most of its equipment even before the American helicopters landed almost on their heads. Whatever had been left after weeks of fighting they had abandoned last night in their haste to get out of the village. Kim met a sergeant who told him that they had shot down three of the enemy helicopters, but Kim had seen the wrecks of only two.

He had driven up just in time to see several squads try to cross the open ground between the ridge and the village. The Americans simply dropped mortar rounds on the formation, stopping the attack cold. Even the unwounded lay still in the fields, as if waiting for the American fire to find them. Kim watched them from the hatch of his tank, peering just over the steel lip.

Someone banged on the side of the tank. Kim turned to see an NCO, probably from the engineers. The man's arm was wrapped in a bloody sling. He pointed, with his good arm, to the fields between them and the village the Americans occupied.

"We must use the tanks," was all he said. It was not a request, and Kim knew the man wasn't showing the proper deference to his rank. But he suspected that the sergeant knew the tanks had sat still instead of joining the attack. He was afraid to confront the man, afraid this truth would come out.

"Are there any other soldiers available?" Kim asked.

The sergeant simply stared at him as if he didn't understand.

"I need some foot soldiers to watch for anti-armor missiles. We cannot see the smoke when we are inside these things." He patted the side of the turret, as if the NCO might have missed the tank.

"You are looking at my men," the sergeant answered, twisting his head toward the field where the bodies lay in the bright sunlight.

Kim squirmed on the metal seat of the commander's hatch, his filthy tanker's coveralls reminding him of his shortcomings. *What an unlikely hero I am,* he thought.

He gave the other tank's commander the arm signal for *follow me.* "Driver," he called down into the vehicle, "move forward—slowly."

Isen was on the right flank of the company position, in Marist's platoon sector, when he heard the soldiers shout.

"I see something moving. Something's moving out there," one soldier called. Then, in a louder but still calm voice, "It's a tank."

All around him Isen heard and felt the rustle of activity as the men strained for a glimpse of the monster approaching from the west. He looked through his binoculars and saw what might have been the top of a turret pass by a break in the brush.

"Call the first sergeant," he said to David. "Tell him we've got a tank at—" He paused as he oriented his map to the terrain, then pointed at the location. David read the grid.

When he raised his glasses again, Isen saw the tank more clearly. Portions of its turret were exposed as it nosed through the low ground, trying to find a route to the American position. Behind it, he could just make out the hurrying figures of a dozen or so foot soldiers, and a shadow in the thin cover of the fields that looked like a second tank. The trail vehicle, which wasn't moving, looked to be several hundred meters behind, and just to the south of the leader. He would have to use mortar fire to separate the soldiers, who were there to spot anti-tank missiles, from the tanks.

"Call for fire," he told Marist, who was watching the same scene.

Marist sent in the request and completed the call just as the first North Korean mortar rounds started to come in several hundred meters short of the Charlie Company line.

Isen and Marist stretched out in the shallow hole Marist had dug at his CP. Behind him, Isen could hear David and Murray scraping away at the soil with their entrenching tools.

"Go for the tanks," he told Marist. "We want to make sure they're buttoned up."

The first rounds from Charlie Company's mortars did the trick of separating the infantry from the tanks. And although he couldn't see very clearly, Isen was sure the tankers were closed up inside their vehicles. The small mortar rounds would do no damage to the hulks, except for shearing off the occasional antenna or box of tools. The real danger for the tankers now was from the unseen missiles.

Three mortar rounds landed behind the platoon trace.

If they have us spotted at all, Isen thought as he pulled his helmet down and unconsciously hunched his shoulders, as if against a driving rain, *the next rounds will be on target.*

Voavosa didn't spot the lead tank for almost a full minute after David's call. Han's men were up and ready to fire before he saw the target.

"I see them," Voavosa said. Han gave a string of orders in Hangul at the same time, and Voavosa lowered his binoculars in time to see the nearest missile launcher turn slowly as it tracked the lead tank.

Han turned to him.

"We do not have a clear shot. The tank is driving well, using the cover. But he will make a mistake soon."

Just to the north, Voavosa could hear the crunching impact of mortar rounds in the company area.

"I don't know how long we can wait."

Kim was having trouble keeping radio contact with the mortar unit firing for him, and he could barely see the target area. His tank had a makeshift antenna, and the transmission kept fading in and out. Kim alternated between yelling into the handset and yelling down at his own driver.

"Driver, right turn, *right turn,"* he screamed as the tank inched too close to a clear spot.

The driver obliged by throwing the tank into a sharp turn, banging Kim's head against the thin rubber padding inside the commander's hatch. His head ached terrifically from the noise and the strain and the bruises. Below him, the gunner threw up all over his own lap, sick from the fumes and the jolting.

"Smoke, smoke," Kim screamed into the radio. *"Drop five zero meters. Give me smoke."*

There was no response from the stupid machine, but Kim saw half a dozen smoke rounds burst in and around the target area. The Americans still had not exposed themselves, so he was shooting in the dark. If the mortar unit behind him knew he was wasting precious ammunition on targets whose location he could only guess, they would no doubt stop firing.

Kim could see only haphazard glimpses of the ground

in front of him. It was as if he were inside a giant cement mixer, tumbling about and trying to keep the machine from falling into a pit as it inched forward. He thought about opening the hatch of his vehicle, but the mortar rounds could start again at any moment. He was caught between wanting to know what was going on outside, and the chilling fear of being hit by shrapnel. The smell of vomit below him suddenly overcame the fuel smells, and Kim struggled to control his own stomach.

He wanted to get out of the tank and crawl into a hole and let the whole battle pass by without him.

Outside, he saw several patches of green as the periscopes, fixed in place on the turret, swept up and down over a view of the riverbank to his right. *I should have chosen that route to advance under cover,* he thought. *I wonder what's in there?*

Han watched the tank ride exposed for a full minute. The tank driver either could not find any more cover, or had been made confident by the smoke screen that was breaking between the tank and the village. Han was concerned that the thick brush along the various paddy walls between him and his target might interfere with the missile's flight. But the shot was not going to get any better.

Han picked up the telephone that linked him with the second TOW.

"Gunners, fire when ready."

The commander of the trailing NKPA tank was afraid that Kim, whom he called "The Chickenshit Lieutenant" even in front of his men, had forgotten about the second tank. Unable to raise the lieutenant on the radio, he had stopped in a ditch that was barely large enough to hide his tank. He had the turret turned to one side so that the bulk of the tank was hidden from the front.

He raised the hatch to try to spot the platoon leader, who had uncharacteristically taken the lead. He was looking directly along the tube of the main gun when he saw the flash and the smoke.

"Gunner, fire," he shouted, reacting immediately.

* * *

Voavosa was left of the TOW launchers, and had time only to cover the ear on the side next to the gun jeep when the two missiles took flight, almost simultaneously. He was amazed that he could see both of the slow-flying rounds as they made their erratic way to the targets.

The tank round passed only a dozen feet overhead, the proverbial crack of doom. The gunner in the jeep nearest Voavosa lost sight of the trail tank, and the missile took a sudden turn straight up, then twisted and lunged to the ground only three hundred meters from the launcher.

The second gunner, who was located a hundred and fifty meters farther west along the riverbank, fared a little better. He seemed to maintain control of his missile, but at the last minute, the command link wire that trailed behind caught in some small trees, and the round plowed into the ground fifty meters from the target, sending up an impressive but harmless shower of dirt and flame.

Kim heard the crack of the tank cannon from behind him, and knew that it could mean only that the Americans had exposed themselves. There were no armored vehicles out here—the enemy had helicoptered in—so the enemy must be firing anti-tank missiles.

"Driver, right turn," he shouted, turning the handle on the hatch above his head. There was no way he could fight this battle from inside the tank. As the fresh air rushed in and pushed away the smell of vomit and fear, Kim felt exhilarated with the drama of the chance he was taking.

He spotted the missile launchers in the brush by the river to his right as one of them moved to get a better shot. He pulled his machine gun over and fired a burst at the line of brush, some twelve hundred meters away.

Behind him, he could see the other tank from his platoon dash toward the river. The cannon belched again.

"Forward," he shouted to the bright air, wondering in some part of his mind who had taken over his body.

Voavosa watched the men in Han's section work to reload.

"C'mon, c'mon, c'mon," he cheered them under his breath.

There were two tanks exposed now. One had fired two main gun rounds, neither of them aimed. And the commander of the lead tank had suddenly appeared in the hatch, firing his machine gun like a madman. But Voavosa didn't believe that either tank had a good fix on their location. That would change when they fired the TOWs again.

"We'll not do much with a frontal shot," Han said beside Voavosa.

"Do we have time to move?"

The South Korean looked at the two tanks, charging aggressively, trying to use the limited cover they had, and even making use of the small trees they knew would disrupt the flight of the wire-guided missiles.

"No."

Kim saw the second volley of missiles leave the line of brush and trees, now only nine hundred meters to their front. He pulled back on the stiff trigger of his machine gun, swinging the heavy muzzle through a wild arc that he hoped would hit the missile, or the gunner, or both.

"Look at Old Chickenshit!" the commander of the second tank hollered to himself. His own machine gun had been damaged by artillery fire, and he had to wait a few seconds for his loader to rearm the main gun. He wasn't watching the line of the river for targets, and it was just as well. He would have seen the missile speeding straight at him, and would have known, for a terrible millisecond, that there was nothing he could do about it.

Kim saw the missile flash past, a streak against the background of the muddy field. He turned to see the turret of the trail tank rock with an explosion as the warhead burned through in a split second, incinerating everything inside. As he watched, the second missile burned by the stricken tank. *The Americans have no fire control,* he thought. *The second one should have been aimed at me.*

Kim saw movement in the dark brush ahead, and he took the time to aim his weapon. He was suddenly and unexpectedly in control, and knew exactly what he must do.

He laid the weapon's sight on the target and rocked back on the handles.

Voavosa heard the rounds strike the metal hood and grill of the jeep. He turned in time to see the gunner and assistant leap clear. But the heavy bullets from the North Korean tank commander's gun tore the missile launcher from its mount, spraying bits of metal and fiberglass.

Voavosa and Han were on the ground.

"He's still coming," Han said.

"Let's get to the other launcher," Voavosa shouted.

The two men moved back into the concealment offered by the band of underbrush—here some fifty meters wide—along the bank. They raced west for the other gun jeep. Voavosa had no idea what they would do if both were wrecked. He wasn't even sure what they were going to do once they got there—other than try to stop the North Korean tank.

They found the second TOW launcher in good shape. The gunner had pulled back into a small depression, where the tank couldn't see him. But he could no longer see the tank.

"I will have them load the weapon," Han said. "I am going to send the rest of my men back, First Sergeant. I will stay here with one driver and engage the second tank from up there." He indicated a track that led up to the edge of the brush.

"I'm staying put," Voavosa said. "I was driving before these guys were born. So you might as well send all of them back."

He didn't wait for an answer, but began to work his way back toward the field to spot the target tank.

Kim had dropped his tank into a ditch alongside a paddy wall. He stood on his toes on the commander's seat and scanned the dark line of undergrowth with his binoculars, looking for targets. The entire tank, he was sure, was hidden.

There was no sign of the enemy.

Behind him, the foot soldiers who had started out with

him had disappeared with the first impact of mortar rounds. His only other tank burned furiously in the middle distance.

"We will have to do this on our own," he shouted into the tank. He felt a new kinship with the crew, something he had suspected existed but he himself had never experienced. He supposed this is what the other lieutenants meant when they spoke of camaraderie. He was intoxicated with the excitement.

"We will move south to the line of those small trees, by the river, and advance on the Americans from there."

"Aren't there other missile launchers in those woods, Lieutenant?" his gunner asked.

I don't know, he thought. "I don't see anything," he said.

Voavosa was in the driver's seat of the jeep, which he had turned broadside to the field, when he saw the tank break from cover less than five hundred meters from them.

"See it?" he asked calmly.

"I have him," Han replied.

Kim felt the left side of his tank lurch ahead of the right side, and he knew immediately that they had thrown a track. He looked behind him and saw the long metal ribbon snaking out in the mud. The tank spun helplessly into a depression, burying most of the steel prow. They were stuck.

He saw the smoke signature of the missile in the woodline, saw the missile itself approach, surprisingly close to the ground, as he manned his gun.

The back left corner of the tank had lifted when the nose dipped, and the missile caught the very corner. There was no jolt—the missile was mostly hollow aluminum—but there was a great sound and flash as most of the shaped charge's energy burned itself out behind the tank after passing through a corner of the engine compartment.

Kim fired into the woodline, cursing his helpless immobility. For all the times he had wished to be anywhere but in a moving tank, on this day he had experienced, though only for a few minutes, an exhilaration and power that he had never imagined. And now it was denied him.

The tank filled with black smoke, and Kim heard the

driver crawl out of his hatch on the front. The loader worked his way out of the hatch next to Kim's.

"Where is Cho?" Kim shouted over the thickening sound of the flames inside the tank.

"Dead."

The two soldiers leapt off the tank without being told, and Kim saw one of them, he wasn't sure which, head back to the doubtful shelter of the ridge, running as fast as he could across the open field. As he ran, he stripped off his helmet and pistol belt.

Kim continued to fire his machine gun, but he was blind with rage now, and his targets had moved back under cover. Some metamorphosis, tantalizingly close, had been denied him, and he was furious.

The flames reached for his legs, and he knew there was a danger of the tank's ammunition exploding. He climbed out of his hatch and stood on the turret, all five foot four inches of him defiantly exposing himself to the unseen enemy in the treeline. Then he walked slowly off the turret of the crippled vehicle and stepped onto the ground where the hull was buried deepest.

Behind the tank, he found Nam, his driver, sitting on the ground, holding his leg. Even through the grime Kim could see that the man was a pale, chalky white. Nam held his leg, and Kim could see the blood seep through his fingers.

Kim did not speak, but simply picked up the larger man, slung him over his shoulder, and started walking back to the western ridge.

"We stopped 'em," Han said.

"For now," Voavosa answered. "Let's find a new spot."

While Kim was learning about armored combat, another North Korean officer assumed responsibility for breaking the impasse. Lieutenant Colonel Hong Myong-jin paced back and forth as he listened to the commander of the newly arrived infantry reinforcements brief his subordinates.

Hong had been given the mission of breaking through the American blocking positions once it became apparent that the enemy was serious about staying put. Hong was known as a ruthless man, crude but effective, a man who could get the job done without a lot of time wasted on niceties. Men like him were in great demand this day.

When he was assigned the mission, he was supremely confident that he would succeed. But his self-assuredness was shaken by what he saw on his ride to the rear early that morning. All along the westbound tracks behind the embattled NKPA, supply and services units were already preparing to withdraw. Even the few uncommitted combat units that made up the tiny reserve were looking rearward. Hong was appalled at what he saw, shocked that commanders—his own peers—would so openly cast their lot with the defeatists and pessimists. It didn't occur to him until he had almost reached his destination that those supply units and signals units and headquarters elements were not moving without orders. Someone high up in the NKPA command was already preparing to withdraw. He fought to ignore the niggling voice in his brain: *The American reinforcements must be close; perhaps the battle is lost.*

When he called his higher headquarters to report that he had arrived at the objective area, he received a coded message over the radio.

Be prepared to pass units through to the east within eight to twelve hours.

His mission took on a new significance. If the worst was true, he could save the NKPA from destruction.

He had been aghast at what he found on the west side of the ridge. There were remnants of an engineer unit that had had all its officers and most of its noncommissioned officers killed resisting the initial air assault. To the east, he could see the burning remains of two tanks. Somewhere, there was a tank lieutenant who had been sent out to get the job done. Obviously, he had done nothing to take control and had merely squandered time and men.

The retreating units were only hours behind Hong. He had to open the road.

Hong had brought with him a company of infantry, a composite company really, made up of the survivors of three rifle companies that had been chewed up in the maelstrom around Uijongbu. The infantrymen, good soldiers all, were understandably demoralized, and Hong was worried about how much ardor they would bring to the task before them. He was concerned that they might just take to the hills and try to escape.

In briefing the infantry captain he had put in charge of the upcoming assault, Hong had tried to convey the seriousness of the situation, shouting about how little time they had and about how the battle was not lost. The man appeared clever enough, and his plan to distract the Americans with a small attack on their southern, river flank, followed by a main effort from the north, was a good one. But he lacked fire.

Hong was wondering just how to kindle that fire when someone led a small, blood-covered lieutenant up to him.

"Colonel," the small man said, straightening, "I am Lieutenant Kim, and I—"

Hong cut him off.

"You were in command of those tanks, and these men?"

"Yes, sir. We arrived only an hour ago," Kim said, guessing at the time. "I have come to report that the Americans have anti-armor weapons in the line of trees by the river. But I think we can make an assault that way."

He was about to add that he wanted to lead the infantry back, but Kim was sure that it was clear from his stature and his even tone that he was the man for the job. He felt six feet tall, felt, for the first time in his life, like a soldier.

Hong saw that the infantry captain and his lieutenants were watching now.

"Where is your tank?" Hong snapped.

"I lost two tanks in an assault here, sir. I—"

Hong cut him off. "You failed in your mission, and you wasted precious time here, Lieutenant. You are a disgrace to the people," Hong said.

The lieutenant's face registered shock, and Hong relished watching it turn to disbelief—or was it terror?—as the colonel pulled his pistol from his holster and shot Kim in the center of his chest.

The lieutenant stumbled backward, his legs collapsing under him. He was dead before he hit the ground.

Hong turned to the infantry officers nearby.

"This road will be opened."

29

2 May · Monday · 1300 hrs

The incoming fire had withered as the two tanks fought it out with Voavosa and Han, but picked up again around thirteen hundred. Isen had no targets identified, and did not have the mortar ammunition to fire blindly at the ridge two klicks away. Nor was there any fire support available from the artillery. On the radio, Isen could hear Tilden, Bock, and Woodriff. The rest of the frequencies were empty—as if the two companies had dropped off the map. He and his men had to simply hunker down and wait out the barrage.

Isen had set up his command post behind Marist's platoon on the right, or northern,' side of the company sector, because that was the most likely place enemy infantry would try to get at them. He thought he heard rifle fire on the ridge above them, just to the north, but could see nothing through the drifting smoke that the North Koreans were still dropping in on them sporadically. He stood straight up to get a better look. David tugged on his trouser leg.

"Better get down here, sir," David said as he offered the field phone. "You don't want to attract attention."

Isen sat. Marist was on the phone.

"We got some visitors up on the ridge. My guys aren't having any problems keeping them away, for now. Can we use some of the mortar ammo?"

"What's the strength of the element trying to get through up there?" Isen asked.

"My guys figure it's less than a squad."

That's not the main thrust, Isen thought.

390

"Have the mortars fire a few rounds to get the right location," Isen told his lieutenant. "You call in the corrections, and keep your eyes open for some action around the base of the hill."

Even as Isen was trying to figure where the main enemy effort would come, the two arms of the North Korean attack were reaching for Charlie Company, one on either flank.

The captain whom Hong had entrusted to lead the North Korean effort, a twenty-five-year-old reservist named Chong Sang-tu, had divided his available men into three platoons. He sent one east along the river to strike the southern side of the American position. When this diversion was in progress, he would launch the main attack against the northern side of the village. He had already sent a reconnaissance patrol along the finger of the ridge above the Americans. As he suspected, they had the area blocked. As he and his men moved cautiously through the sparse vegetation along the base of the ridge that marked the northern side of the small valley, he wondered how close they would get before they were discovered. He wondered, too, if the crazy colonel's promise—to find some tanks and send them into the battle—was valid. Without a radio, he could only wonder how much progress the other wing of his attacking formation was making.

South of Charlie Company, Voavosa and Han waited in the thick grass for the next assault. They sat quietly by the vehicle, one of them always manning the gun, while the other one made periodic visits to the edge of the undergrowth to look for more tanks, or even infantry.

"Nothing still," Han said, returning from one visit to the edge of the shadows.

Voavosa was beginning to wonder what had happened to the North Koreans. He removed his helmet and wiped the back of his neck with a rag soaked in water from his canteen. As he twisted his head to the left, he saw a North Korean soldier step boldly into the clearing.

Voavosa dropped the canteen and turned for his rifle, but it was on the other side of the launcher. He could see the North Korean raise his rifle to fire.

Voavosa thrust his shoulder up under the launcher, flipped the safety cover off the trigger, and mashed down on the red firing button. The missile made an unbelievably large sound in the small clearing, and it hit the ground at the feet of the North Korean. The warhead did not detonate, but it knocked the man over and gave Voavosa time to react. He grabbed his rifle and jumped from the jeep, firing as he fell to the ground. He did not see the bullets hit, but the North Korean didn't move.

Han was off to Voavosa's left, nearer to the river.

"Get down!" Han yelled as he sprayed a long burst of automatic fire into the shadows. Voavosa couldn't see anything, but he didn't think it prudent to wait around. He ducked into the grass and stumbled north, toward the clearing of the paddies, before he realized he no longer knew where Han was.

"Han," he called.

He was answered by a burst of rifle fire, half a dozen shots that pounded the grass beside him, chopping the tall stalks.

He judged that Han was still off to his left, so he tossed a grenade to the front. When it exploded, he pulled back a few meters. He found Han on the eastern edge of the clearing that held their now-abandoned jeep. The North Koreans were somewhere on the western edge.

Han crawled close to him.

"They're trying to get at the company through this grass."

"We can hold them up here for a while," Voavosa said. "This is a natural choke point."

And indeed it was. The vegetation here was thick, but only about thirty meters wide from the edge of the bank to the edge of the field, where it was clear almost all the way up to Charlie Company. The small clearing where the jeep was parked was about five meters wide, right in the center of the swath, so the advancing North Koreans had to split up on either side of that.

Han and Voavosa pulled back a few more meters. As Voavosa expected, the North Koreans led their first attempt with hand grenades, which exploded near the jeep. The infantry followed right behind the explosions, shouting and firing from the hip as they ran. But the North Koreans, audacious as they were, did not have any targets. They hoped to carry the position by shock and firepower.

And they might have succeeded, but Han and Voavosa remained calm, selecting their targets and firing three-round bursts at the charging soldiers. The small pop of the rifle rounds seemed inconsequential after the TOWs, but the targets fell.

Voavosa saw that the North Koreans had fixed their bayonets to their rifles for the close-in fighting. An enemy soldier rushed at him, his rifle level at his waist, his menacing bayonet aimed right at Voavosa. The first sergeant shot him once, and the body pitched forward. The man struggled to reach his target with the blade, an effort that fell short by less than a foot.

The attackers seemed to hesitate, and Voavosa used the pause to throw two more hand grenades into the clearing, trying to buy some time and keep the enemy at bay while he and Han withdrew a few more meters. Now the two allies had to separate themselves a bit in order to be able to see across the whole width of the overgrown bank. Voavosa checked his ammunition. He had less than sixty rounds left.

When they were still again, Voavosa heard splashing in the water. He crawled over Han and down to the bank. There were two North Koreans moving along the edge of the water on the far side, struggling to keep their footing against the current, holding their weapons and ammunition belts above their heads.

Voavosa fired. He thought he hit one, but both of the enemy dropped below the surface before he could see. He fired a few more rounds into the water, then heard Han shout for him.

"You know if we don't get out now, we'll never make it back to the company," Han said when the first sergeant joined him.

A few meters away they could hear the North Koreans gather for another rush. Voavosa looked at the situation. They had almost no fields of fire, and no chance of surprising the North Koreans. They were out of hand grenades and low on ammunition. The only working radio was back with the jeep. There was at least one and probably more enemy making their way along the riverbank to get behind them, and they could not even adequately cover the bank they occupied.

"Give me your ammo," he told Han. "I want you to head back and tell Isen what's going on. If he can get some mortar fire here, he can stop these clowns."

Han started to protest, but Voavosa was right. The most important thing was to stop the North Korean advance on the company's southern flank.

"You will follow me by a few meters?" Han asked.

"Yeah, yeah, I'll follow you," Voavosa said, believing it himself. "Now you get moving, and make sure you get that message to Isen."

Han looked hard at Voavosa, as if trying to memorize his face.

For his part, Voavosa thought he had done a pretty good job out here. They had killed two tanks and screwed up the North Korean timetable, and they had not lost a single man from Han's two sections. Not yet.

He felt, not terror, but a detached and morbid sadness at being left alone. He listened to Han crawl away behind him. *So much waste.*

Voavosa heard the enemy advancing, slowly this time, crawling along near the water's edge on the left, and again off to the right side near the paddy. He had no targets. He thought he should move one way or the other, cutting off at least one advance. He settled on the right, toward the fields where they had destroyed the tanks.

Han judged that he was about fifteen meters from where he had left Voavosa when he stood up to run for it. He heard some rifle fire, and thought that the enemy was closing in on Voavosa. He was surprised when he found himself facedown in the grass, and he wondered who had punched him in the back. He lay perfectly still, believing that the pain would go away. He did not know how long he was there, but the pain did begin to fade at last, running off his back with his blood, staining the spring grass and the thick black soil beneath him.

* * *

Voavosa hit the ground at the sound of the firing. Looking up, he saw two men against the light sky of the open field. He drew a bead on the second one and dropped him with a single shot. The lead soldier, who could not have seen what happened behind him, dropped to one knee. Voavosa placed the sight picture on the side of the man's head and pulled the trigger.

He turned and hurried back across the neck of vegetation, back toward the river. He was sure that Han must be close to the company by now, and he wanted to clear out of the area before the mortar rounds came in. He lifted his knees to make better time in the grass, and had the strange mental image of himself as a small boy, running in the blue and white surf of his native Samoa.

As he rushed, he made more noise than did the slowly advancing enemy. One of the North Koreans saw him, a short, stocky man running almost gleefully through the brush, not more than fifteen meters away. An easy shot.

The attack against the company's northern flank started off with a heavy smoke screen that drifted south over the village. The rounds landed only two dozen meters from the front trace of Marist's platoon, and effectively blinded the men in the fighting positions.

"They're coming. They'll be right behind that smoke," Isen heard Marist tell his platoon.

The platoon's machine guns opened up before Isen could see any targets, but he was confident that Marist wouldn't waste ammunition. The American M-60s were answered by at least two, and maybe three, Korean guns. Isen could see no effect from the incoming fire, but then the North Koreans started dropping grenades, with remarkable precision, on the American position.

Isen was blinded by the smoke, and something told him the North Koreans were about to make an assault. He heard shouts below him.

"Left, left, they're to the left. Fire on my tracers," one squad leader shouted as he sent a light stick of tracers at a target for his squad.

The volume of fire increased dramatically as the smoke began to break up. Marist's blocking position was on a finger that pointed directly south from the ridge that dominated this end of the company area. Some of the North Koreans had worked their way onto the foot of the high ground, in between Marist's tiny outpost and the main body of the platoon.

Isen radioed Marist.

"Your fire team on the hill is cut off. Do you have anybody who can maneuver against those guys at the bottom of the hill?"

"I have the people but I'm not sure what we can do in the open," Marist answered.

Isen couldn't see what was going on.

"Guess what," he said to David and Murray.

"We're going down closer to the fighting," David answered correctly.

Isen reached Marist's CP just before three Koreans tried to rush the center of the platoon position. They might have reached at least one of the positions—Isen couldn't tell, couldn't see in the feathery remains of the smoke screen. Men were hollering for the medic, other men were screaming for ammunition, and everywhere there was the Hollywood *pop* and *zing* of bullets flying about. The platoon was in chaos.

Marist's platoon sergeant called to him.

"El-tee, I can't move. We got to get some ammo down to the sixties on the right. They're about busted."

The machine gun on the right flank of Marist's platoon, which was hammering at the ridge, was running out of ammunition. Marist didn't react to the platoon sergeant's call. He simply looked at Isen.

"Get the ammo out," Isen said. "I'll start at the left side and we'll get this put back together."

Marist was losing it. Isen could see the self-doubt well up in Marist, as if it were something visible, like tears.

Grenades exploded a few meters behind their hole.

"Move," he yelled into the lieutenant's face, sending the man into action.

Isen told David and Murray to stay put. He took one radio out of the RTO's rucksack and strapped it, on its carrying board, to his own back. David did not seem relieved that he and Murray were being left.

"I'll be back," Isen told the youngster.

Isen looked down from Marist's CP to the left side of the platoon line. The first position was about thirty meters away, across a slight, bald rise in the ground. He pulled a smoke grenade from his rucksack and tossed it down to a point just behind where he could see one rifleman firing from his hole.

He followed the small canister down, rolling the last few meters. The radio banged against his head and dug into his back. He dropped into the hole with the soldier, who didn't seem to notice him.

Isen could clearly see the man's targets, and he engaged them with his own rifle, adding only slightly to the already deafening noise. After a minute the soldier noticed that someone else was in the hole and firing. He turned to Isen, nodded a simple acknowledgment of the commander's presence, and went back to his grim work.

Off to the center of Marist's platoon, about twenty meters to his right, Isen could see some figures running above ground. That could only mean that the North Koreans had broken through. He was up and running for the gap as soon as he made radio contact with the mortar platoon, calling for fire just in front of the platoon position, in order to cut off any Korean reinforcements that might try to widen the hole in the American line.

He dodged from side to side as he ran, like a halfback on a broken field. He passed the first hole he found and ran into a thick bank of green smoke from a sputtering canister at his feet. He ran full force into another figure in the smoke, and the two men bounced off each other. Isen, because of his size and because of the momentum he had with the added weight of the radio, was left standing. His first impulse was to reach down and help the other soldier up, but his brain registered another signal, and he landed a hard kick between the fallen man's legs.

The North Korean soldier grunted, a terrible breath of pain. Isen brought his weapon down and pointed it at the man's head. The soldier was on his side, holding his hands between his legs and trying to bury his face in the ground.

Isen kicked the man's weapon away.

The smoke clouds had broken up enough now so that

Isen could see what had happened. At least two of Marist's positions had been overrun; the GIs in them were dead or holed up somewhere else. Off in the brush fifty meters beyond the line and to the north, he thought he could make out the forms of several more North Koreans preparing to rush the gap. There were no signs of any of Marist's men who might hold the threatened line.

Isen crawled forward as fast as he could, skinning his elbows and knees, banging the back of his head with the radio. Just before he dropped into the vacant hole, he saw the North Koreans begin their rush, speeded along by the mortar rounds dropping behind them.

He pulled two grenades from his belt and yelled back to where he hoped there were some more of Marist's men.

"They're coming in, look up, look up!"

Isen threw the two grenades like baseballs, straight and hard at the running North Koreans. Two of the enemy he could see dropped to the ground, and it was only then that Isen heard rifle fire—outgoing—to his right. He glanced in that direction and saw a single soldier come running up to join him on the line, manning the adjacent position. The man stood upright in the shallow hole, exposed from the waist up. The arms of his blouse were ripped, and the tattered sleeves fluttered around his sweating arms. He rocked just a little with each burst of three rounds, but never wavered. Isen doubted that the man was engaging any targets—his firing was fast and furious—but he was getting rounds down range.

The sound of a grenade exploding behind his position drowned out the already overpowering sounds of the battle. Isen felt as if he had been attacked by a swarm of wasps that stung him across the back of his neck and shoulders. The pain was a sharp bite at first, then his skin registered the heat of the shrapnel, and the sudden stabbing brought him to his knees in the hole, where he swayed from side to side against the dirt walls and breathed out his agony. Animal sounds rolled up from his groin, rippling nausea. *Uhhhh . . . uhhhh . . . uhhhh . . .*

He pulled himself to his feet, the pain bringing tears to his eyes. He knew that the shrapnel would cool, though he couldn't convince himself that the pain would lessen. He pressed his face against the loose dirt of the hole's edge. The battle was still going on, demanding his attention.

Isen brought his rifle up. Only one North Korean soldier was still moving, running with his head and shoulders down. Isen tried to draw a bead, but his vision was blurred, and the man dodged from side to side. Isen let fly one round, two rounds, three, but the soldier kept coming, closing the distance rapidly now. When he was less than ten meters away, the bolt of Isen's rifle locked open—the magazine was empty.

The North Korean soldier screamed as he charged over the last few meters, his bayonet-tipped rifle lowered directly at Isen. Isen had nowhere to go, and nothing to fire. The hole had become a trap: he couldn't get out, couldn't move, could do nothing, it seemed, but wait for the bayonet.

Suddenly the charging soldier's head snapped to the side, farther than Isen would have thought possible. His body twisted to follow, and he toppled across the front of the hole, stone dead.

The GI in the next hole was already firing to the front again when Isen looked over.

"There's more of 'em coming, Captain," was all he said.

By the time Isen reloaded his weapon, there were three more third platoon soldiers in the adjacent holes, plugging the gaps in the line.

The North Korean attack washed back out.

Isen limped back to where he had left the helpless North Korean who had broken through the line, discarding his radio, which had been riddled by shrapnel. The man was in the same position: knees up, elbows locked, and arms straight down between his legs. But he was relaxed now. As Isen got closer, he saw a neat hole in the man's temple. The other side of his face, turned toward the ground, was shattered and mixed with the dirt.

30

2 May · Monday · 1500 hrs

The survivors of the failed attack on the northern end of the American position filtered back toward the ridge where Lieutenant Colonel Hong Myong-jin waited, watching through his field glasses.

He had not heard from the smaller element that had advanced along the river, and although he hoped that meant they were having more success, he knew they were just as likely to have stopped in the cover of the brush. He could not fault the efforts of the infantry captain who had led the attack. But he was not saddened when he saw the man carried by, his hip shattered by small-arms fire.

The wounded were piling up in the lee of the ridge, and there were an alarming number of stragglers showing up from the west. Hong shouted and screamed at them, trying to force them into ad hoc formations that he might use.

Around three o'clock three more tanks appeared on the road from the west. These, too, had been sent ahead of their parent unit to smash any remaining blocking positions. The commander of the lead tank was a youngster named Park Chun Han, who didn't look old enough to be trusted with a car. He was surprised to find the way still blocked at this point.

"My orders were to push through to this village east of here," Park said, offering Hong his map, "and wait there for the rest of the column." He hesitated a moment, as if taking measure of Hong's worth, or ruthlessness. "We did not expect to run into this American position," he added cautiously.

Hong knew that the boy had probably been told the

block would be gone, and though the lieutenant had every reason in the world to fear him—he had no doubt heard of Hong's summary execution of the other tanker as soon as he had arrived—there was still a hint of disdain in the lieutenant's eyes. Hong was infuriated.

All around him the evidence of failure mounted: his own, his army's, his party's. The cries of the wounded men, most of whom were simply lying about in the open, without shade or water, seemed harbingers of his own fate. If the Americans or ROKs didn't get him, surely his boss would execute him as ignominiously as he had shot the lieutenant. He had never before considered that he might fail. The comeuppance shook him, and suggested that such unpleasant surprises were universally possible.

Lieutenant Colonel Hong was a desperate man. Like the rest of the leadership of the NKPA on this day, he faced a deteriorating situation. Immediately behind him, to the west, the vast and confused flotsam of battle and the elements of the long logistical tail snarled the roadways. West of this chaotic zone, the combat units that could help him crush this puny blockade were being pummeled by enemy airpower. And those combat units could not even begin disengagement—the most difficult battlefield maneuver—until the artillery was in position to fire on the ROKs, who were now on the offensive.

Every North Korean soldier caught in front of Charlie Company was keenly aware of his distance from the thirty-eighth parallel and the protection it offered.

Hong's actions had taken on an unexpected importance. He suddenly felt supremely unsuited for his role as the fulcrum in such a sway of history. *How could so much depend on one man? How did it happen to be me?*

"You will attack on the north side with your tanks," he told Park. "Use the limited cover at the foot of the ridge as best you can. I will send the foot soldiers along the cover of the riverbed against the enemy."

The lieutenant looked about him at the gaggle of wounded and exhausted men, some without helmets, others without weapons, and some even without boots. He could not imagine their carrying the day.

"The enemy is there," Hong said to the tanker, raising

his hand and pointing to the village. "Go to him, and crush him."

Barrow was supervising the removal of the wounded to one of the houses in the village. The medic had used tape to hold the bandages in place on his face, and as he worked he could feel the tape slipping from his filthy skin. The chinstrap from his helmet hung loose beside his jaw; the gauze on his chin was too thick to button the strap. Just as he was about to make another round through the platoon positions, Isen called him to the CP.

The XO saw, while still several meters away, the blood on Isen's neck. It was smeared and diluted with sweat, and it wrapped around his throat from behind like a colorful scarf. As he got closer, Barrow noticed a slight sway in the commander, as if he were watching a man trying to stand still on a gently rolling deck.

"Sir, you need to have the medics look at that," Barrow began.

Isen waved his hand. "There's guys with a lot worse, still manning their positions. I'll be all right." He stepped sideways as he talked, so that Barrow could not see his back. Isen wasn't sure what it looked like, but he suspected that it was bad.

"Any idea where the first sergeant is, sir?" Barrow asked Isen.

"Last time we heard from him, he was out there," Isen said, nodding toward the river, "shooting at tanks."

Barrow had passed the southern flank of the company position, where Bladesly's men traded desultory fire with some North Koreans who had gotten near the bridge, but didn't seem inclined to come any closer. If Voavosa were still out there, the XO thought, he had been bypassed—or overrun. Barrow didn't mention his speculation to Isen.

"Dale, we're going to have to reconstruct the whole company position. Neither of the two platoons on the flanks have enough men to react to anything that goes wrong. Marist's platoon lost six men in that last skirmish."

Barrow did some quick calculations of the company's strength, but the number he came up with was so low that he questioned his arithmetic. There were fewer than sixty-five men on the line, out of an original strength of one hundred and ten. And many of those left were wounded.

Isen went on. "I want to pull Haveck's platoon back from the center of the line and make them a reaction force, so we can use them if the North Koreans make another breakthrough."

"What about the center sector?" Barrow asked.

"The center is the least likely place they'll hit. There's too much open ground in front of it. We have to make a trade-off, and I think that's the place to do it."

Isen was rightfully concerned about having all of his company's strength up front at once. It left him no room to adjust, to react to threats around the perimeter. If he pulled Haveck's element off the line, in effect taking the center piece out of the arc, he would leave a gap that the other two platoons didn't have the men to fill. On the other hand, it was unlikely that North Korean infantry was going to charge across the open field. As he worried over the condition of the company, Isen heard the brush-fire crackle of small-arms fire suddenly grow on the company's left, near the riverbank.

"Here we go," he said to Barrow as he moved to get a better look at what was going on.

Bladesly's men had correctly guessed where the inevitable enemy assault would come from, and they had prepared for it as best they could, considering they had no mines, no wire, and only limited amounts of ammunition left. Bladesly, now the platoon leader since Lake's death, and the squad leaders, had taken great pains in positioning the men, so that all of the approaches to the platoon area from the thick grass of the riverbed were covered. Bladesly had looked at the terrain as the enemy would, knew exactly where he would place his supporting fires, how he would move his squads across the forbidding open space to get at the Americans. Bladesly had anticipated everything except a massive, suicidal rush from the tall grass.

There was no warning of the move, no opening volley of machine-gun fire, no mortar or artillery fire. Quite simply, at least three dozen men just jumped up at the edge of the brush and started running forward. Bladesly, who happened to be looking at the grass at the instant, thought that some part of the earth had gotten up and was now rushing at him. The North Koreans did not even shout as they ran across the few meters of open ground, and for the seconds before his men opened fire, he could distinctly hear the jangle of loose equipment and their heavy breathing effort as the enemy struggled to close the final gap.

The platoon opened fire, almost as one man. The North Koreans were easy targets, of course, but the sheer number of them and the absolute idiocy of the attack across open ground so stunned Bladesly's men that the GIs managed to hit only a few of the enemy before the bulk of the North Korean assault was on the line and past it.

Bladesly saw one North Korean soldier who was suddenly confused at finding himself behind the American position, not sure of what to do. Bladesly stood and shot him.

"Get down, get down," Bladesly yelled into the melee.

The North Koreans were lobbing smoke grenades all along the line, and the platoon sector was soon engulfed in gray, choking clouds that drifted and swirled lazily. Bladesly could see almost nothing: every once in a while a figure would appear from the haze, half conjured, half complete, and then it would disappear in the next second. The smoke divided the fight into small actions in the clear spaces that opened and closed and opened again across the bloody field.

Bladesly heard the muffled sounds of hand grenades exploding below ground. There was some plan to the North Korean attack after all—someone was dropping grenades into the fighting positions. He wondered if the fight was already over.

"Sappers, sappers!" he shouted at the gray wall.

His platoon had been overrun, but the drill for handling a penetration by just a few enemy might work, might give them control again. He heard his call repeated at least twice amid the cursing, so he knew some of his men heard him. They would get below ground. But there was no accompanying sound of the machine guns' grazing fire slicing evenly across the platoon sector, three feet above the ground.

"Henry . . . Henry!" Bladesly called to his nearest M-60 gunner.

No answer.

He turned to Janeson, his RTO.

"They must have gotten to Henry. I don't hear the gun and I can't get an answer from him."

For a terrible instant Janeson thought that Bladesly was going to order him to get out of the protection of the shallow hole, order him over to the machine gunner's position—something less than fifteen meters away—to find out what was wrong.

"I'm going over there," Bladesly said. "Without those guys we don't have a chance of getting control here."

Janeson was sure now that he was looking at a madman . . . more than that, a madman who was living his last few minutes on earth.

"You can't go out there," Janeson ventured, screaming to be heard above the noise.

Bladesly ignored him.

"Get on the horn and give the CO a SITREP, hear?"

The order didn't seem to register with Janeson. He was staring at the lip of the hole, unmoving. Bladesly grabbed him by the shirtfront.

"Wake up, you fuckhead! The platoon is being overrun. Call Isen and tell him that we need help, *now!"*

When Bladesly let go, Janeson fell back to his sitting position, but he scrambled to find the handset where he had dropped it in a mess of tangled equipment in the bottom of the hole. Everything about him was focused on finding that handset, as if in the bottom of this miserable pit lay his salvation. He found it, tore it free from a tangle of commo wire, and looked up. Bladesly was gone. Janeson did not see him disappear into the smoke that was lit by occasional flashes.

And then it hit him that he was now alone.

The smoke cut him off from all but the sounds of the battle that engulfed the platoon. He couldn't see the men on whom he depended, and Janeson started to come apart.

He keyed the handset, but couldn't remember what to say. He heard the voice of his friend, David.

"Last calling station, this is X ray one seven. Do you read me, over?"

Nothing came out of Janeson's mouth; he felt as if he had been robbed of his breath.

Two figures stumbled out of the blankness five feet from the edge of his hole. He could not see who they were, but through the uncertain light he saw one of the dark men swing his rifle viciously upward at his opponent's chin. The other man fell back, and, horribly, something came loose and bounced at Janeson.

An American helmet dropped at his feet, and Janeson jumped up, scrambling to get out of the hole, treading on the radio and his rucksack. He abandoned his weapon, his platoon sergeant, and his platoon in his mad rush to get away, to get to anywhere other than where he was.

Janeson ran as if in a dream; every step mired him in place. He stumbled on feet that were too big, and he thrashed at the air with useless marionette arms. Suddenly he was out of the smoke, in the amazing clear, and in that instant he knew what he had done. In the still-bright daylight, he was someone who had abandoned his comrades.

Something grabbed his arm. He turned to see Lieutenant Haveck's face almost touching his own. He said the first thing that came to mind.

"Come on, you've got to come back with me," he shouted in a panic, pulling on Haveck's arm.

"Whoa, whoa, slow down, partner. Tell me what's going on."

Janeson could now see that Haveck had ten or so men behind him, spread neatly in a sure line at the edge of a drainage ditch. The other—the chaos—was only a few meters behind him. The contrast was startling.

"They've overrun the position," Janeson said. "Sergeant Bladesly went to try to get the machine guns going, you know, to hit all the bad guys above ground. He told me to . . . to . . ." Janeson stumbled.

"It's okay," Haveck said, "we'll get them out. You ready to lead us back?"

Janeson nodded. "Yes," he answered honestly.

Haveck turned to the group of men who waited patiently, stoically, behind him, calm as statues of warriors.

"Fix bayonets," he said evenly.

Janeson heard the sound of steel settling into place on the rifle muzzles. He wondered, as he turned back toward the drifting wall of smoke and sound, if any of Haveck's men had noticed he didn't have a rifle.

At the same time that Haveck was giving the command to make the fight hand to hand, Lieutenant Colonel Hong reached the edge of the brush, along the riverbank where the North Koreans had jumped off their attack against Charlie Company's southern flank. He had sent thirty or forty men ahead of him into the fight, and he waited in the brush with a reserve of a dozen or so.

He had brought with him the last of the groups he had thrown together from among the shattered remains of units that had stumbled into the battle. He was determined to carry the fight, and he was roused by the sight revealed as the smoke drifted north across the American positions. He saw the line of enemy fighting positions marked out on the ground by the bodies sprawled in horrible poses. But the holes were empty of American soldiers, and his men were still pushing toward the village.

Soon, he thought to himself as he started to run, calling for the reserve to follow, *soon we will be through this roadblock and safe on the other side of the DMZ.*

He drew his pistol as he ran, waving it above his head in what he knew must look like a poster right out of the propaganda ministry. He was caught in the momentum of the fight, and felt as if he could run all day. He congratulated himself on the decision he made earlier.

I was right to shoot that stupid lieutenant, he thought. *Look how it has sparked the soldiers; we will carry the day.*

Hong reached the American line and stepped around an empty fighting position. *I made it,* he thought. Then he saw before him a nightmare sight. Ten American soldiers materialized from the disappearing smoke. They, too, were running, right at Hong, yelling some sort of high-pitched yell and bayoneting the few pitiful forms that attempted to resist.

Hong lowered his pistol and fired, hitting nothing. He turned to give orders to the men he had dragged with him, but found no one behind him. The soldiers had stopped somewhere between the brushline and the American position, and had apparently turned back when they saw the enemy counterattacking. He seethed with hatred at the cowards, and even raised his pistol to punish his own men.

Hong was facing the riverbed when one of Haveck's men rushed up behind him. The GI planted his feet and turned the rifle ninety degrees, just as he had been taught in his training, so that the flat of the blade could enter between the ribs. The hardest part, the GI found, was getting the bayonet out of the corpse.

Isen was watching Haveck's men disappear into the smoke when he decided to go forward himself, to see if he could affect the battle at its critical point. He was brought up short by the sound of Dragons firing.

Off on the northern flank, Marist's platoon had fired two of the missiles, and Isen turned to where their targets should be.

A North Korean tank appeared momentarily along the east-west road that ran toward Charlie Company, but the Dragon rounds both passed high over its turret. One exploded behind the target.

The tank raced its engine and sprinted directly for the company line. Marist's men let fly with one more missile, but this one glanced obliquely off the front of the turret. The tank did not slow down.

Now the men in the platoon were scrambling for LAWs, hoping to disable the beast near the line long enough to defeat it. But the tank kept coming, and in no time it was on the platoon line. Isen waited for the bark of the big cannon, or even of the machine guns, but the tank was silent.

It rode up fairly high over the paddy wall, and several GIs scrambled out from underneath it as the great bow of the tank clawed at the air.

Isen crouched, unable to move, waiting to see what the tank would do next. Everything they had accomplished up to this point, in keeping the armor at bay, had been overcome in the few seconds it took this foolhardy tank crew to rush the American position over open ground.

The vehicle rocked forward, landing with a jolt as its tracks churned the soft earth of the paddy.

Isen saw a soldier trot up to the side of the vehicle, kneel down, and fire an LAW into the tracks. The small rocket had no effect. Then two rockets fired from the other side bounced off the turret and shot up into the air, trailing smoke. The crew inside was probably unharmed, but certainly spooked by what was happening. The tank lurched forward a few feet, firing its coaxial machine gun, but without rotating the turret or seriously threatening any of the American defenders. The driver must have stomped on the accelerator, because the tank shot forward and raced for the village, chased by another flaming but ineffective LAW rocket.

Isen thought the tank was making for the other side of the village. He radioed Woodriff, but no one in Alpha Company had seen the tank.

"I have my hands full already," Woodriff said. "I've had to collapse my perimeter to about half its original size. They've pushed us back into the village."

"Yeah, but I don't think these attacks are coordinated, otherwise they'd be trying to find a seam between our companies. If they don't have any real planning going on"—Isen was grasping at straws to find something to encourage Woodriff—"then maybe their act really is falling apart."

"Mark." Isen could not remember Woodriff ever using one of the other commander's first names, and certainly not on the radio. "I don't think I can hold."

"You've got to hold," Isen told him, "you're watching my back."

Something smacked him in the foot, and Isen let the handset drop, without signing off.

He sat on the ground. His left foot throbbed with a dull, heavy pain as he pulled it up on his right thigh. The boot was cut neatly on the inside of the heel, and as he watched, blood filled the hole and ran out over the muddy sole.

Barrow came up to him, carrying three LAWs.

"I think that tank is holed up in those buildings," Barrow said.

Isen tried to stand, but his left leg was numb and refused to function. He grasped the calf to see if it was still inside the pant leg. Barrow was staring at him.

"That looks pretty fucked up, sir."

"Get me some LAWs from down there," Isen said, indicating the third platoon area, where several men were firing at the point where the tank had disappeared behind them.

Isen was furious at this new wound, and he wanted a minute to figure out how he could beat it. He felt a fluttering in his leg, and knew that his pulse was marking the tempo of the blood loss.

Barrow ran over to where the men were pumping LAWs at the buildings. By this time at least one of the houses was on fire, sending gray clouds, like dirty cotton batting, sifting through the position. He gathered one more LAW and ran back to Isen.

"I'm going in after it," Isen said.

He tried to stand but couldn't get beyond his hands and knees.

"You ain't going anywhere, sir," Barrow told him.

"I have to get that tank in there," Isen came back. Barrow seemed to be shimmering. *I wonder how much blood I've lost?*

Barrow loosened the straps on the LAWs and loaded them, two to a shoulder.

"I'm going into the village, sir."

"Negative, Dale. I need you here to run this," Isen said.

Barrow looked at him. The XO's face was set, his mind made up.

"Do you read me, Lieutenant?" Isen asked.

"I read you, sir," Barrow said, turning away.

"Get back here!" Isen was furious. His own XO was disobeying him. *"Dale, I said . . . Dale, Dale!"*

But Barrow was already too far away to hear him. And the XO was running now. Within seconds he disappeared into the swirling gray smoke.

31

2 May · Monday · 1610 hrs

Barrow made it to the sheltering side of a small outbuilding that sat behind one of the houses. The tank was close by. It opened up with its machine gun, rocking the air with an insistent hammering. Barrow dove to the ground, followed by the loose and rattling LAWs slung on his shoulders.

He couldn't see a thing, couldn't even follow the sound as it bounced off the walls and close-set buildings. He was suddenly afraid that he would not be able to find the tank in the smoke. But when it opened fire again, Barrow saw bits of tile from the roof of one building suddenly shake themselves loose. The tiny bits of evidence were all he needed.

He looked around to see how he might move. He was on the south side of a small building in the backyard of a fairly substantial house. The house sat to the east. Next door, to the north, the next house's roof tiles were shaking loose. Barrow forced open a low door in the outbuilding that must have been an access for animals, and crawled inside. The floor was covered with filthy, matted straw, and the whole place reeked of old manure.

At least there's nothing dead in here.

There was a similar door on the north wall, a warped wooden affair about three feet tall. Barrow pushed it open to where he could just see over the top. He didn't want to attract any attention.

The house he was looking for sat only ten meters away, filling his whole view.

It was much nicer than most of the buildings in the village. Its earthen walls had been whitewashed, and what had probably started out as a thatched roof had been replaced by a light ceramic tile roof of bright red. When the tank fired its heavy machine gun again, causing the whole building to vibrate, more of the small tiles shook loose and slid to the ground under the eaves.

Barrow could see most of the back, or western wall that faced Charlie Company, but the single window and door in the wall were intact. He guessed that the tank was firing from immediately beside the house on the other, north side. He pulled the fiberglass rocket launchers closer to him as he tried to think of a way to get at the tank.

The machine gun opened up again, a longer burst this time. Barrow couldn't see the tank's targets, but knew it was pounding Charlie Company.

As he rushed out into the thin open yard between the buildings, the LAWs swung off his shoulder. He carried them by their flimsy straps as he ran, dangling them like a set of misshapen purses. He ran into the house's southern wall, banging his helmet off with the impact. It rolled at his feet as he tried to gain control of his breathing. He had lost the bandages on his face somewhere, and the gashed flesh was bleeding again. The pain made him nauseous.

The house was rectangular, and he was alongside one of the narrow ends, on the south side. He was within several feet, he was sure, of the enemy, with only a mud-wall house between him and the huge tank cannon.

Barrow peered around the east edge of the building, expecting to see the rear end of the tank parked alongside the north wall of the house.

There was nothing there.

The machine gun opened up again, and Barrow heard still more tiles falling. He flattened out on the ground and looked farther east. Instead of looking at the rear of the tank, he was looking at the front.

The tank was in the remains of a brick building with a collapsed roof, and was farther east than he had guessed. He held perfectly still for several long seconds, then moved slowly backward, hoping that the tankers, busy firing at Charlie Company, hadn't spotted him. There was a row of small bushes to his right that ran past the destroyed building on its south side, and Barrow followed this until he was behind the tank. From this new vantage point, in the shelter of another brick house, he could get a better reading on what had happened. It looked to him as if the tank had driven into the building, taking out a supporting post, bringing the whole roof and large portions of the upper walls down on top of it. The crew was safe inside, of course, but the tank was apparently stuck. It had become a giant metal pillbox. Or a giant target, depending on how one looked at it.

Barrow rolled over on his back and looked up into the faultless blue sky as he extended all four of the launchers. After checking the area again, he kneeled and took aim at the engine covering on the back of the tank, not more than fifteen meters away.

The first rocket found its target, but the explosion seemed to dissipate on the metal grillwork of the vehicle's tail. The tank was not going to explode. Barrow knew that several LAWs might penetrate the back, crippling the tank, but he had no idea what he might do after that.

He could not tell what effect the rocket had. There was no explosion, no visible fire inside the tank. And he did know for certain that the crew, if still alive, would be looking for whoever had fired the rocket.

He dropped the expended launcher and fumbled with the second. His hands refused to obey the commands his brain was sending. He resisted looking up as he heard the whine of the tank's turret, knowing that they would be looking for him.

He saw the turret through the small plastic sight of the LAW. The tank's cannon was still facing west, away from Barrow, and was stuck against one crumbling, but stubborn, brick wall. It wouldn't traverse any farther. The commander of the tank, realizing what was happening, tried to slew the turret in the other direction, but the wall on that side was even closer.

Barrow was safe, for the moment. The fortunate positioning of the brick walls, and the fact that the initiative was his for the next few seconds, meant life for him, and defeat for the four men inside. He had gone up against a tank, and it was beginning to look like he might win.

He pulled the safety release on the LAW and sent the second rocket streaking toward the black mark on the engine compartment made by the first hit. This time, he was rewarded with a thick tongue of black smoke that curled from the monster's tail.

Barrow brought his rifle up when he heard one of the hatches open, but it banged shut immediately. Nothing came out of the tank, so he reached for another rocket launcher.

The rifle fire struck the wall just above his head, sending chips of brick and mortar down the back of his shirt. Instinctively, he rolled for cover, escaping another, better-aimed burst.

He heard someone clambering on the tank, and he kneeled and fired his rifle.

He saw his rounds strike the steel side of the turret, bouncing off in a colorful shower of sparks. His target, a crewman who had gotten out and fired at him, escaped back inside.

He heard the driver shifting gears in a last attempt to break from the trap, but there was no response of power from the engine. Now the thick smoke was pouring from the rear, and it started to find its way out of the poorly fitted troop hatches.

They must be choking in there, Barrow thought.

He prepared to take prisoners, but none came out. He watched, stunned and horrified, as the fire grew. He stared hard at the hatches, and even considered going to one, to tell the men—*these were men, after all*—that he would take them prisoner, that they would not be shot, that they did not have to die in this lost skirmish. But the fire grew too quickly.

The elation he felt in his victory over the tank, and the relief at being the one still alive, were consumed in the flames and the heat that lapped from the tank.

Lieutenant Park, the tank officer Colonel Hong had charged to attack the enemy north flank, had carefully watched the progress of the tank he had sent against the Americans. He had been surprised that the crew made it through the American lines, though they had apparently been killed once they took cover in the village. *Stupid men,* he thought.

He had sacrificed that tank, which was from another unit and whose crew he did not know, in order to get accurate information on the locations of the American weapons. He had carefully observed all the firing positions on the American line. He knew where the Dragons were located—though these weapons had proven virtually useless—as well as most of the crew-served weapons. He had even hoarded the main gun ammunition; when the now-dead tank commander asked if he had any rounds on board, Park had told him no.

He had two tanks, his own and another, with which to attack. Now that he had targets, he was ready to crush the Americans. He stood in his hatch and raised his arm straight into the air, signaling the commander of the only other tank left. *Follow me.*

Charlie Company was a scene of devastation. The defensive line had been punctured and patched several times, and each time there were fewer men to re-form the defense. Isen had crawled north to the third platoon sector, dragging a field phone with him. The numbness that had begun in his foot had moved up, so that now the left side of his body below the waist was almost useless. He had discarded his left boot, substituting a battle dressing, which was now blood-soaked.

Men were sprawled on their backs in their shallow holes, nursing wounds that would go untreated. The group that Haveck had marshaled as a reaction force was huddled near the center of the company area. The mortar section had joined Haveck; there was no more mortar ammunition in the perimeter.

Isen was completely frustrated. He hadn't been able to find David or Murray after the counterattack in the third platoon area. His XO had disappeared into the village, he had no idea where his first sergeant might be, and with his wounds, he needed both men badly. Off to the south, he could hear Staff Sergeant Hall of Bladesly's platoon moving about, redistributing ammunition and trying to encourage the men. Isen looked at his ammunition pouches. The top had been torn from one, and it hung empty on the pistol belt. The other held two empty magazines. He had ten or twelve rounds in his weapon. He reached around to his hip, unsheathed his bayonet, and snapped it into place over the muzzle of his rifle. When he pulled his hand away, he noticed the plastic handle of the bayonet was smeared with blood.

The first main gun round from Park's tank blew through the small earthen berm that sheltered one of third platoon's Dragon gunners, lifting the pile of dirt and the man and his weapon in the explosion.

"Holy shit," Marist said as he hugged the ground. He crawled to a vantage point from which he could see along the base of the ridge that ran east and west near his position. The tank showed itself behind the bright flash of another muzzle blast. The second round was a solid-steel shot meant for tanks. It hit the ground a few meters in front of the platoon trace, tearing at the dirt for a few feet before it skipped over the heads of the men in the positions.

One of Marist's men stood and began to run east toward the questionable shelter of the village a few meters behind the line.

"Get down, get down," Marist screamed. He was astounded that the man was foolish enough to move under such fire—and then it hit him that the soldier was running away. Marist looked at the adjacent positions as the third tank round smashed into his line.

The tank had managed to accomplish, with three rounds, what almost nothing else had up to this point. The men were terrified to the point where they were ready to break and run. A few of them he could see were trying to make their holes deeper, throwing shovelfuls of dirt up into the air, digging frantically in the cramped bottoms of their positions. There was no one ready to return fire.

Marist climbed out of his position and ran to his right, where he knew that one of the Dragon teams had at least two rounds left. He ran bent over at the waist, so that every step nearly sent him headlong into the ground. He was conscious of some of his men watching him, and caught a glimpse of one face, distorted by fear and exhaustion and something else . . . *They know it's over,* he thought.

Marist spotted the well-made position that sheltered

two men and one of the anti-tank weapons. The soldiers were already preparing to fire.

Good men, he thought.

He slid to the hole like a baseball player, anxious to get below the level of the ground again. He reached the small shelter at the same instant that the next tank round tore into the earth just in front of the position. It exploded underground, pushing the front wall of the hole, in an almost solid chunk of earth, against the back, and crushing the three men, like small animals caught on the road.

After his fight with the tank, Barrow had worked his way east, to the rear of Alpha Company's position on the other side of the village. He found the Alpha XO, a colorful friend of his named Zugler, in the remains of what had once been a cellar. There was nothing left of the house above it but charred wood. Barrow, approaching through the village, came up behind the lieutenant and two RTOs.

"Shit," Zugler yelled when Barrow stepped in front of him. "You scared me, man. Good thing I didn't have my hand on the friggin' trigger." With his free hand he motioned Barrow into the hole, then turned his attention to the radio handset he had pressed to his ear.

"What's that? Last calling station, say again last transmission, over."

Barrow climbed down the few feet into the bottom of the cellar. He couldn't hear anything over the radio, but the look on Zugler's face told him there was no response.

"Fuck me," Zugler said. He gave the handset to one of the RTOs. "You keep your ear on that thing. I know I heard somebody calling us"—he turned to Barrow—"and I coulda sworn they said they were *rolling* our way."

"What callsign were they using?" Barrow asked.

"None that I could find in our book," Zugler said, indicating the code book that held radio callsigns only for units in the 25th Division.

"Do you think it could be our armor?" Barrow asked, almost afraid to say it out loud.

"Tilden called us a little while ago and told us that he had a report that there was a relief column headed our way. Didn't you get the word?"

Barrow shook his head.

"I shouldn't be surprised. Commo is fucked up in peacetime, when *nobody's* shooting at us."

Zugler stood and looked out to where his company was trading intermittent rifle and machine-gun fire with unseen antagonists. "If that is armor on the way," he added, "they better hurry the fuck up."

"Have you guys been shooting at tanks over here?" Barrow asked. He stood beside Zugler and looked out at the relatively quiet east side of the village.

"Not since this morning. All we've had to deal with since then are hordes of little motherfuckers who keep crawling right up to the perimeter. If they were smart, they'd wait 'til it got dark," Zugler said, looking worried for the first time. "I'm not sure how we're going to hold after nightfall."

"So how many Dragon rounds you got stashed over here?"

Park's tank dodged from one covered position to another as he followed, generally, the east-west road that led to the center of the American position. Off to his right he could see through his periscope the still-burning hulks of the tanks destroyed earlier in the day.

He halted the tank and the main gun fired again at movement on the left. They were less than one thousand meters from the American line, but Park was determined to move methodically, even slowly. Too many people had underestimated the resourcefulness of these light infantry units in fighting tanks.

He felt the excitement of the sure advance.

This time it will work, he thought. *The Americans do not have any missiles left which will stop our tanks. Who sent them out here like this?*

Park knew that the North Koreans still behind the ridge, by now little more than a collection of wounded and stragglers, were watching him. Since there was no cohesive unit there, the few NCOs left had trouble keeping control over the men. Many of the soldiers had heard the rumors of American forces approaching, and they were in a state of near panic. They wanted only to make sure they were back on the north side of the thirty-eighth parallel when the Americans arrived. Park believed that if he could break the roadblock, the mob of soldiers would be encouraged enough to submit to his orders. He could then move the men, as a group, and clear the road ahead. He refused to think about what would happen if he failed.

He saw movement to the front and gave the fire commands to the gunner. The tank halted slowly—not the jarring stop that he was used to on firing ranges—almost a leisurely stop. Park had no worries about the performance of his own crew, who would do as he told them. *We will succeed here where the others have failed,* he thought.

Isen was furious with himself because he could move no faster than a lame crawl. His blouse was soaked in his own blood from at least a half-dozen puncture wounds, and his left leg dragged behind him, limp, pained, and useless. The steady blood flow had sapped his strength. He had his eyes on one of the nearby Dragon positions, and he doggedly pulled himself north along the ground toward it. Nothing else was moving along the line. His company was powerless, almost beaten before the tank even closed with them. He fought the realization and pushed out of his mind the picture of his men standing about the position, their hands in the air, as North Korean troops rushed up to search them, to kick at the dead and prod the living.

The tank cannon boomed again. The time between shots seemed to be collapsing, and Isen was no longer sure he was getting closer to the Dragon. He had lost his helmet, but couldn't recall where. He still dragged his rifle—the bolt locked open on an empty magazine—with him as he made his tortured way across the few meters of ground.

Behind him, in the center of the company position, Haveck was exhorting his men to get ready to fire the last few LAWs at the tank when it closed on the position and exposed itself. But the attack would be only a futile gesture. There might be, Isen told himself, some hope with the Dragon.

At last he reached the position. One of the soldiers was dead, lying just behind the hole, his midsection torn open. The other soldier was still alive, but he crouched in the bottom of the hole, his arms wrapped around his legs. Like Isen, he had no helmet, and there was a dark crease of blood that started just above his left eye and streaked back into a mass of filth in his scalp. He didn't look up as Isen dropped into the hole, landing on the man's feet.

"Help me get this thing up," Isen said, glad to see the tracker looked undamaged.

The soldier didn't respond, didn't even meet Isen's eyes.

"Nothing to shoot."

"What?" Isen was perched on his good leg. He held his left foot above the ground, like a dog favoring an injured paw.

"There's no rounds left," the soldier said. "We're fucked."

Isen looked over the forward edge of the hole. The tank had opened up with its coax machine gun, swinging the turret slowly from side to side like some great head. As Isen watched, the tank commander's hatch flipped open, and a small figure grabbed the handles of the machine gun mounted just forward of the hatch. Isen could see him plainly, but could do nothing to stop him. Isen hated the man, hated the day, cursed whatever had brought them all to this place. He felt his eyelids flutter, and his eyes wanted to roll back in his head. He held them open with his fingers, determined to witness the final act.

The tank rolled forward, then appeared to jump, as if it stumbled. As he watched, the open hatch belched flame. The on-board ammunition cooked off, flipping the turret to the ground like a discarded bottle top.

Isen could see the northern side of his company, and nothing had come from that end. He turned to the south.

As he watched, there was a balloon of flame behind one of the fighting positions on the southern end of the sector, just below where the road from the west entered the village. Isen recognized it as the firing signature of the Dragon. He turned to the west, where the second North Korean tank that had been approaching the position gunned its engine and raced for cover in a small fold of ground near the road. The Dragon round passed over the tank and fell harmlessly in the field beyond.

The tank turned sharply as it neared the road, and Isen guessed that the driver saw the drainage ditch that ran just beside the track. Had he driven straight ahead, the tank probably would have spanned the ditch. Instead, the driver spun into a hard left turn, so the entire length of the right track tipped over the edge, and the forty tons of hurtling steel jammed the tank onto its side in the ditch. The tank's tread snapped with the strain, firing the thick belt, like a thousand-pound rubber band, into the muddy bottom of the ditch. Isen saw two of the crewmen climb out of the turret. They stayed in the shelter of the ditch as they made their way west, where the sun was just touching the horizon.

Barrow also glanced at the western sky as he ran north, on the edge of the village, to try to locate Isen. He estimated that there was less than a half hour of light left, and he was worried that they wouldn't be able to get the company ready for the infantry assaults that were sure to come with darkness. He heard his feet crunching the gravel as he ran, and he realized that the firing had stopped.

Barrow found Isen sitting on the edge of a fighting position on the northern side of Charlie Company's sector. He was taking advantage of the momentary lull to wrap a piece of cloth around the bandages on his left foot.

"Was that you?" Isen asked.

"Sir?"

"Was that you with the Dragons?"

"Yes, sir. It wasn't me shooting, but I found the rounds. I went over to Alpha Company after that little deal in the village, and they had hardly used any of their Dragons, so I brought a bunch over. One of them even worked."

Isen didn't look good, Barrow thought. The back of his shirt was caked with dried blood, and his foot, under the layers of dirty bandages that he had obviously applied himself, looked to be in pretty bad shape.

"We need to get that foot bandaged correctly, sir," Barrow said.

Isen forced himself to his feet, leaning on his rifle as if on a crutch. His face twisted in pain.

"Not now, Dale. What's going on in Alpha Company?"

Barrow told him about the enemy infantry pressing,

throughout the day, Alpha's position. The XO expected that the same thing would happen to Charlie Company shortly after dusk.

"We'll have to pull back into a tighter position, closer to the village, probably," Barrow said. "Do you know how many men we have who can still fight?"

"Fight? We don't even have enough to carry the wounded," Isen said.

Isen looked tremendously weary, Barrow thought, and he wanted to tell Isen that he would do anything to keep the unit intact. But the prospect of a night in the village—with North Koreans trying to get in among them, with the wounded who would no doubt die before morning, and with the awful feeling that they had been abandoned out here—threatening to drain whatever energy he had left, Barrow could think of nothing. Earlier, when he had left Isen to chase down the tank in the village, he had been afraid he would let his commander down. Now Barrow was afraid Isen was going to tell them that Charlie Company was beaten.

He remembered Tilden's message, but supposed Isen was as tired as he was of promised units that didn't materialize. And the commander still had to ready the company for the long night. Barrow wondered if Isen could handle the news and the disappointment that was sure to follow.

Isen was squinting into the dim fields to the west of them.

"Look, Dale."

Off to the west, Barrow could see North Korean soldiers climbing the ridge that ran along Charlie Company's northern flank. They were heading north, Barrow saw, but there was something odd-looking about them.

"They're not carrying weapons," Isen said, as if in answer to Barrow's thought.

Within minutes word had spread the length of the company sector, so that the surviving Charlie Company soldiers watched through the dying light as the North Koreans abandoned their positions and their equipment and set out on foot—as individuals, rather than as units—

for the safety of the thirty-eighth parallel. To Isen, they looked incredibly small, like children scampering up the hillside.

Finally, there was no fanfare or dramatics attending the arrival of the relief force. Barrow spent the night organizing the walking wounded to carry the worst cases into the shelter of the village. Isen waited two hours before he would allow Barrow to help him off the line.

"Just want to be sure they're gone," Isen told his XO.

A runner from Alpha Company found Isen just before dawn, with a message that they should send a team out to a link-up point south of the town. Isen told Barrow to go to the bridge, but no farther.

"They're riding; let them come to us," he said.

As Isen watched Barrow move south to the bridge below the town, he looked around him at the hard evidence that for many of Charlie Company's soldiers help had come too late.

Barrow saw the M-1 Abrams tank before he heard it, so quiet was its turbine engine. The dark mass moved cautiously toward the bridge, and Barrow had the sensation that he was being watched by other tanks. It reached the far side of the bridge and stopped, so Barrow forced himself to walk closer. One of the hatches lifted open.

"All Cav, sir." A huge staff sergeant stood in the commander's hatch of the tank, which loomed like a battleship compared to the North Korean tanks.

Barrow stood, feeling incredibly small, next to the hull. He spotted the inch-high black letters that marked this as a First Cavalry Division crew.

Barrow had difficulty speaking, so the tank commander went on.

"Is your unit near here, sir?"

"We're in that village"—Barrow used his thumb to point over his shoulder—"have been since yesterday."

"Nobody even told us you were here," the sergeant said, looking sheepish. "Listen, I'm going to call for our XO to come up and bring some medics."

He made a call on his radio, then climbed out of the

turret. He jumped to the ground and held his map for Barrow to see.

"Our other platoon is going to cross this here stream west of us," he said, "and check out this hill." He was pointing to where the Koreans had been hiding the previous day.

"Once we get a foothold down in this here valley"—he looked right and left along the road Charlie Company had been blocking—"we're supposed to head west and tangle with the bad guys." He punctuated the sentence by spitting a long green stream of tobacco juice to the ground.

"By the way, I'm Staff Sergeant Bartow of the First Team," the tanker said, putting out his hand.

Barrow, who had felt a new energy when the tanks showed up, suddenly felt empty.

"Yeah . . . thanks, Sergeant, thanks for making it." *They didn't even know where we were.*

"No problem, el-tee." He signaled the driver, whose helmet and eyes peered above the hull. "Gotta look for someplace to cross. This little ol' bridge wouldn't hold half of one of these babies." The sergeant walked to the front of his tank and climbed aboard.

"Welcome to Korea," Barrow said.

Epilogue

Near Osan Air Force Base, South Korea
125th Evacuation Hospital

5 May · Thursday · 0845 hrs

Dale Barrow sat on the ground next to the stretcher, oblivious to the hospital personnel staring at his haggard appearance and his rifle. The bath he had that morning— his first in weeks—left him feeling skinned, as if some newly familiar epidermis had been removed.

Isen lay on the stretcher, one arm draped over his forehead to shield his eyes from the bright spring sunshine.

"They found First Sergeant Voavosa right near that ROK sergeant who brought us the TOWs . . . what was his name?"

"Han," Isen answered.

"Those two made a mess of the North Korean advance on the river side. Without them, there's no telling how many bad guys would have been on our left flank . . . no telling if we would have been able to hold."

"My guess is that he knew that, and that's why he stayed out there, to give the rest of us a chance," Isen said. "How long did you stay in that village?" Isen went on, suddenly anxious to change the subject.

"About noon that day we turned over the sector to some of the First Cav boys. You know, I didn't realize how bad we looked until we stood near those guys. We were a beat-up-looking crew," Barrow said, smoothing out the fabric on a clean set of BDUs. His hands and fingernails, though obviously scrubbed, were still grimy from the weeks of dirt.

"They went through there in a hurry and hit the North Koreans hard. I heard the bad guys hadn't quite managed to get turned around yet, and they certainly hadn't been able to disengage from the ROKs. Anyway, our cav units got in among the NKPA artillery and their logistical tail, and blew their stuff away. The ones we saw walking over the hill that day may have been some of the only ones to make it back across the thirty-eighth parallel. Driving down here yesterday, I bet I passed thousands of NKPA prisoners being marched south."

"What about our battalion?"

"Colonel Tilden was wounded pretty bad over in the Alpha Company sector," Barrow said, "but it looks like he'll be okay. Major Bock didn't make it." Barrow scraped at some mud on the side of his boot with a pen.

"It's weird," Barrow continued, "but I would have guessed that if anybody was going to be okay, it would be Bock. The man had his shit together."

"But surviving doesn't always have to do with competence," Isen mused, "sometimes it's just dumb luck."

"Speaking of luck," Barrow went on, suddenly more animated, "Woodriff, I mean, Captain Woodriff, not only came out without a scratch, but he's been telling everybody how he pulled our ass out of the fire."

Isen wanted to laugh, but his back hurt when he tried to breathe too deeply. "Tell me about the company," he told Barrow.

Barrow produced his pocket memo book and began to give Isen a rundown of the company status. They had finally received replacements, two days after the fight at the crossroads.

Barrow detailed the newly emplaced chain of command, running through the list of platoon leaders, now all NCOs, and platoon sergeants. Isen watched him carefully, only half listening to what he said. Barrow had come a long way from the exuberant and over-excited young man he had been two months earlier. Instead of a picture of bravado, he was a picture of cool competence—and jaded sadness.

"Bladesly is acting first sergeant," Barrow said, "and Haveck is acting XO."

"He is the XO, Dale."

"Sir?"

Isen smiled at him. "I won't be back anytime soon, if at all. You might as well stop calling yourself the executive officer or acting CO and just accept the fact that you're the commander now."

Barrow closed his notebook and looked up. Several hundred meters away, medical orderlies were loading a burn victim into an ambulance for transport to the flight line. A nurse, a woman of about twenty-seven or so, was supervising. She shot crisp orders at the handlers, warning them to be careful, even as she tenderly held the wounded soldier's hand.

"I used to look forward to taking over a rifle company, sir," Barrow said. He looked down at Isen, whose head was framed against an incredibly clean pillowcase. "But not like this."

The mask of competence seemed to loosen a bit at the edges, and Isen caught a fleeting glimpse of the damage done to this one young man. Barrow had grown up, but he had seen too much loss and waste. Isen had nothing healing to say, so he stuck to the busy problems at hand.

"Look, Dale, of course I'd rather be healthy and with the boys; but since I'm flat on my back, I'm glad I have somebody I trust to turn the company over to."

"Almost time, sir," an orderly said from the foot of Isen's stretcher.

Barrow stood and looked down at Isen as if he wanted to say something. He picked up his gear, something to fill the awkward moment.

"I'll see you back on Oahu, right?" Isen said.

Barrow opened his mouth, then simply nodded. He turned away, then faced Isen again and gave a relaxed, familiar salute. Isen, whose right hand was bandaged, touched his brow with his left.

Barrow had changed a great deal, Isen thought, and it would be a long time before anyone could take the measure of that change.

Two orderlies came and grunted over picking up his stretcher. The little procession joined a longer line of stretchers waiting to be loaded onto ambulances that would carry them to the flightline.

I have learned too, he thought, *and lost, as well.*